Legacy's Promise

A Story of
18th Century Romance, Intrigue and Mystery

by

Lois J. Lambert

Book One of the Legacy's Promise Series

ISBN 978-0-9862268-5-4

Published by
Badgley Publishing Company
Canal Winchester, Ohio
www.BadgleyPublishingCompany.com

i

Dedication

This book is dedicated to my Granddaughter,

Tatiana

With love and gratitude
for her endless enthusiasm and support.

L. J. L.

TABLE OF CONTENTS

Part One
Mary Ann's Deliverance

Part Two
Sarah's Salvation

Part One
Mary Ann's Deliverance

St. Paul's Parish
North Side of Back River
Baltimore County, Maryland, 1717

CHAPTER 1
The Widow's Plight

*T*he entire month of March had been unusually cold, but Mary Ann hardly noticed as it began to snow once again. She sat huddled in the churchyard with her young son on the ground beside the newly covered grave. She felt lost and alone and could not comprehend how her husband had been taken from her.

At first the sickness seemed mild and she assumed, as she always did, that Phillip would soon be robust and cheerful as always. Even when the fever held his sweat drenched body in its unrelenting grip, she assured herself that he could conquer this as he had done with so many challenges they had faced. Now, she realized how foolish she had been.

She was suddenly aware that William was crying quietly and she realized that her son was shivering uncontrollably. His father's strong arms were no longer there to sweep him up and take him to the warmth and safety of their home. But there would be no fire at the hearth for she had failed to cut and bring in the wood. There was no food. She had been so consumed with her grief that she neglected the simplest and most necessary chores for her own survival and that of her child. She had no one to whom she could turn for help.

Slowly, with a sense of foreboding, she came to the realization that this was to be the path of the remainder of her life. She was no longer a child who could rely upon her father for protection and guidance. No longer the young bride who began her married life at age nineteen in a small rented cottage where her husband worked as a shoemaker. Now, she was a widow with a three-year-old son. What would become of them?

She felt paralyzed from the fear, the uncertainty and from the helplessness, which fell like a dark shadow over her and her son. Several seconds passed before she realized that the darkness was not a product of her distraught mind, but rather the presence of a portly figure lifting her to her feet and wrapping her and her son within the warmth of his heavy cloak. She recognized the man as John Hayes, a wealthy neighbor whom she had seen at St. Paul's Parish Church where he was a vestryman. She was aware that he was leading her away from the churchyard and from her cottage. She did not have the strength to object, but was grateful that this man was, she hoped, going to help her.

They passed along a path through a heavily wooded area, and in the distance, she could see a dwelling. As they approached the house she was amazed by its size. It was built of brick and she could see a variety of smaller outbuildings. They climbed a set of stairs, which were quite wide at the bottom but narrowed as they lead up to the entry. The front door opened into a large center hallway that ran from the front to the back of the house. On either side of the hall were several doors, which opened into rooms.

Hayes led her into the nearest room on their right and it, like the hallway, had a high lofty ceiling. She remembered that Phillip had made shoes for this man and his family, and had told her about the extravagant furnishings of the Hayes home located on over four hundred acres of the plantation known as Mount Hayes. It was a well-known fact that Hayes had acquired several large estates over the years through his marriages to two very wealthy wives. Phillip had not exaggerated the opulence of the house. Unlike the cold and drafty cottage with earthen floor she shared with her husband, this home was warm with well-scrubbed wooden floors and heavy draperies at the glass paned windows. She felt comforted and hopeful as he led her and young William to a seat by the fire.

She had seen Hayes before, but had not given him much thought and, in fact, hadn't ever really taken a good look at him. He was older than she, by at least thirty years and was of rather short stature, not much taller than Mary Ann. His face was quite round with a ruddy complexion and was framed by a nicely trimmed beard, and topped by a balding head edged with a fringe of red hair. He had an abrupt manner of movement, which gave the impression of an animal always on the alert for an unsuspecting prey to present itself. It was an impression that was quite unsettling. However, shortly after she and her son had settled themselves near the fire, three young women entered the room and their presence calmed her fears. Hayes introduced them as his daughters.

Elizabeth was an attractive young woman, who appeared to be in her early twenties and she smiled and nodded to Mary Ann by way of greeting. Avarilla had not been graced with her younger sister's good looks and disposition. She seemed very serious, one might say dour, as she entered the room. Avarilla eyed the newcomers with interest, but devoid of any enthusiasm. She moved slowly and with a pronounced limp and took a seat across from the newcomers.

The youngest, Jemima, appeared to be about fifteen or sixteen, and was clearly delighted to learn more about the new visitors. Elizabeth expressed her sympathy to Mary

~ 3 ~

Ann for her recent loss and Avarilla and Jemima nodded their agreement to the sentiment. After that a void of silence hovered over the small group. Aware of the uncomfortable stillness, Elizabeth excused herself and soon reappeared with a tray with cups and a pot of hot cider, a bottle of spirits, which Mary Ann assumed was probably rum, and a small plate of sweets. Elizabeth first handed her father the bottle, which he quickly accepted and from which, he poured himself a generous serving. He took a healthy swallow, settled back in his chair and exhaled with a sigh of relief and satisfaction.

Elizabeth next filled a cup with cider and offered it to Mary Ann, who accepted it with appreciation for she was still chilled to the bone and could not remember the last time she had taken sustenance. She handed cups of the warm cider to her sisters and finally a cup of warm milk along with a small serving of sweets to young William who responded with a shy and appreciative smile.

They enjoyed the refreshments and Elizabeth attempted polite conversation about the weather, William's age, and whatever trivial conversation came to mind. After a short while, perhaps ten or fifteen minutes, Elizabeth excused herself and she along with her sisters left the room.

John Hayes had seemed kindly, almost fatherly in his earlier actions, but after the pleasantries of the refreshments had been enjoyed and the departure of his daughters, his demeanor seemed to change. He sat forward in his chair and looked directly at Mary Ann and his expression became quite solemn as he leaned toward her.

"Now, madam, just exactly what plans have you made regarding your situation?"

Although her situation was an issue that she had only a short time before, acknowledged to herself, she was aghast at the bluntness of the question.

She flushed and stammered an embarrassed reply, "Sir, I...I'm afraid I have not made any plans."

"Ah, hah! Exactly as I suspected. After all, you will have no place to live. I'm sure you have no idea what your husband's financial situation might be. I'm also sure it cannot be good. No doubt he was burdened with enormous debt. And here you are with a young whelp to raise. What a pitiful sight!"

With that, he leaned back in his chair, folded his hands across his portly stomach, shook his head in a disapproving manner and made "tsk, tsk" sounding noises as though things couldn't be much worse for the young widowed mother.

It was too much for Mary Ann. She wanted to flee, but hesitated to rush back out into the cold. She wanted to release her anger and tell this pompous, insensitive old man that she resented the way in which he dismissed her husband's life as though it was inconsequential. She wanted to stand up and make some bold pronouncement about her plans for the future. She wanted to exert her independence, pick up her son, and tell John Hayes what she thought of his arrogance and of the wealth, for which he obviously had never worked a day in his life.

But she didn't. She sat looking forlorn and pitiful and began to cry. The tears were as much from frustration and anger as they were from sadness. His expression softened, and he offered her a handkerchief. She made a mental note of this unexpected gesture of sympathy.

A little voice in her head, warned her against any rash gesture that might make an enemy of this man. He had, in fact, brought her and her son into his home. She concluded that there must be a reason for his actions. He had clearly, throughout his life followed a well planned and executed path to wealth. She, on the other hand, as he so indelicately pointed out, had neither wealth nor position. What then, was his interest in her? She could find no logical answer, but the little voice reminded her that she had her young son to protect. As a matter of practicality and self-preservation she made a decision. She would employ discretion in voice and deed until this man gave her reason to fear harm to herself or to her young son. It was not her proudest moment, nor was it one that she would ever regret. For the first time in her young life, she felt that she might, after all, have some control over her own destiny. Although how that might come about, she had no idea.

Her response to this realization, one would suppose, would have brought a sense of relief that would have calmed her fears. But instead, she surrendered herself to the outpouring of sorrow that shook her small body in the form of unrestrained, nearly convulsive sobs that released the pent up emotion that had been building since the death of her husband. At times, she felt that she must surely suffocate for she found it almost impossible to catch her breath. Slowly, however, after what seemed like hours, her composure gradually returned. It was then that she realized the effect her outburst had on young William who was clinging tearfully to his mother's skirts, his eyes wide with fear and confusion. She drew him to her lap, stroked his hair, kissed him and attempted to console him with her assurances that there was nothing to fear.

When she glanced about the room, she noticed that darkness had fallen and although the fire still blazed warmly, the room was empty save for herself and her young son. She rose and looked out the window watching as the still falling snow obscured the grounds and trees in a misty veil of white. She walked into the hall searching for her hosts and met a middle-aged black woman coming toward her. The woman smiled and took her by the arm and led Mary Ann and her young son into another room where the family members were seated around a table eating their evening meal. Hayes looked up and motioned to Mary Ann to take a seat opposite Elizabeth along the side of the table. She took William's hand with the intent of placing him on her lap at the table. Instead, Hayes shook his head and said to the servant, "Molly, take the boy to the kitchen and see that he eats something."

Mary Ann started to object as William began to whimper, but Molly, with a wide and gentle grin swept him up in her arms and began to cuddle him as she walked out of the room. Once again she had an uneasy feeling about why John Hayes had brought her to his home. The question insinuated itself into her thoughts. How many servants were in this household? Was that the fate that awaited her and her son? She immediately felt anxious, but the little voice in her head reminded her, that for the first time in months both she and her son were warm, dry and about to enjoy a supper prepared and served by another. It was a unique and welcome experience.

Although the table was not heavily laden with food, to Mary Ann the meal was a feast. At home, she and Phillip were fortunate if they had enough corn, cabbage, or other vegetables for a simple stew. It was only on rare occasions that they might have a small piece of pork or chicken to add to the cooking pot. She would serve the stew in a common bowl and they would use trenchers of stale bread to scoop out and eat the meal. But here there was a large piece of venison, sliced and ladled with a strange sauce that she could not identify. There was also a large steaming bowl of vegetables stewed with pork and a variety of herbs that she had never before tasted. Freshly baked biscuits were served with butter on plates of fine china. The preserves made from fresh raspberries that her hosts heaped upon their biscuits particularly intrigued her. It was the most delicious treat that she could remember. Throughout the course of the meal, although fascinated by the bounty, she was fearful that she might commit some clumsy breach of etiquette, and thus watched her hosts carefully so that she might save herself embarrassment. Despite her apprehension, she enjoyed the meal and the companionship of the other women immensely.

When they had finished their meal, Hayes indicated that it was time to leave the table. Molly and a young boy named Henry entered and began to clear away the dishes, while William ran to rejoin his mother. Hayes' daughter, Elizabeth touched Mary Ann's shoulder and motioned to her and William to accompany her up the stairs to the second floor. This was another marvel for Mary Ann had never before been in a home with more than one story. To her, it seemed a palace. Her eyes were wide with amazement with the size of the house and she confided to Elizabeth that she had never been in such a dwelling. Elizabeth promised she would give her a complete tour, including yet another floor below the first, where the household slaves slept and where the family sometimes slept during the heat of summer.

At the top of the stairs, they turned down a hallway to the left and Elizabeth opened a door into a bedroom. The ceiling was high like those on the floor below, and the room itself was larger than Mary Ann's entire cottage. Elizabeth smiled at her saying, "This is my room and you and your son are welcome to share it with me tonight."

Mary Ann gasped in disbelief. She and Phillip had a bed, but it was very old with heavy ropes attached on either side to hold the mattress, which was stuffed with straw. This bed was grand with carved bedposts and heavy curtains hung all around the bed to keep out the cold drafts. And the mattress felt as though it surely was stuffed with feathers. Elizabeth handed her a clean shift and began to prepare a small pallet of several blankets on the floor for William.

Just then a young black woman entered the room with a bucket of hot water. She poured the water into a basin sitting on a small table by the window, and placed a cloth and towel beside the basin, and then left the room. Elizabeth identified the woman as Winny and tactfully suggested that she and William might wish to wash before going to bed. Mary Ann suddenly felt ashamed of her appearance and that of her young son, and she was only too eager to see to some personal hygiene. She first tended to William, who was exhausted and could hardly keep his eyes open as she bathed him. When she had washed herself as best she could, and donned the borrowed shift, she looked longingly at the beautiful bed. It had been a long, stressful day full of events heretofore unknown to the young widow. She climbed into the bed alongside Elizabeth and promptly fell asleep. Once again for the second time that day, she was comforted by the thought that there was a great deal of living yet ahead for her and her son.

At daybreak, early the next morning, she was awakened by the cries of her young son. The room was ablaze with the early morning sun producing a glare as it bounced off the fresh, sparkling snow. The child was confused and frightened to find himself in an unfamiliar place with an unfamiliar person fussing over him. Elizabeth had already dressed and was doing her best to dress the child. Young William was rejecting her attempts with wild tossing of arms and legs and an ever-increasing pitiful wail. Mary Ann practically leaped out of the bed to comfort her son. Elizabeth willingly surrendered the child into his mother's arms, although her face conveyed a wistful expression. Mary Ann smiled and thought to herself that Elizabeth would someday be a wonderful mother to children of her own.

Elizabeth watched the interaction between mother and child for a few moments and then pointed to a chair upon which lay, a pair of stays, a linen petticoat, freshly laundered skirt and bodice, a pair of stockings, and a hair brush.

"These belonged to my half-sister Jane and you appear to be about the same size. I hope everything fits," Elizabeth explained.

Realizing that she had not met her and fearing that Jane might not be as generous with her clothing as Elizabeth, she hesitantly asked: "But I wouldn't want to wear these without her knowledge."

Elizabeth smiled and then laughed and confided that Jane had married well.

"So well, that her new husband insisted upon providing her with attire more appropriate to her station and as she has no further use for her old things, and they are too small for my sisters and I, it would be a pity to not put them to good use."

Mary Ann realized that all three of the Hayes sisters were several inches taller than she and weighed several stones more.

As Elizabeth turned to leave the room, Mary Ann was again overcome by emotion, but this time, not one of sadness, but one of grateful appreciation for the kindness she was receiving. She touched Elizabeth's arm to thank her and the young woman smiled and embraced her. She knew in her heart that she had found a friend, someone of her own age with whom she might be able to share her innermost joys and fears. Her hope was that theirs would be a friendship to treasure.

As she closed the door, Elizabeth reminded Mary Ann to bring young William downstairs to the room in which they had eaten the evening meal and she would wait to eat with them.

She hurried to dress and straightened the bedclothes as best she could. She had never seen so many blankets and wasn't certain just what to do with them. She remembered seeing Elizabeth retrieve blankets from one of several chests in the room, but couldn't remember which one. She folded those used for William and stacked them neatly on one of the chests and hoped that would be adequate.

Downstairs, Elizabeth was already seated at the table with her sisters who were nearly finished eating. Elizabeth called to Molly who brought two bowls of porridge, motioned to William, who this time went to her side without hesitation and she again picked him up and prepared to carry him out of the room with her. Avarilla, with a degree of disapproval in her voice, announced that

Molly would immediately construct a pair of stays for young William.

"It is unforgivable that you have allowed this child to spend the first three years of his life without appropriate attention to his posture," she scolded Mary Ann.

Mary Ann was stunned by the contempt in Avarilla's admonition. It was suddenly clear to her that the Hayes family, at least the eldest daughter, had some very definite rules regarding young children. Once again, her newfound sense of security was replaced by the gnawing fear that she might not be safe after all.

When they were only half finished with their breakfast, Mr. Hayes, as Mary Ann would call him for the remainder of his life, entered the room and instructed her to join him in his room at the front of the house.

Pursing his lips and frowning he announced, "We have important matters to discuss."

She had an uneasy feeling that things were about to become even more unpleasant. Elizabeth saw the concern on her face and attempted to reassure her.

"I'm sure he just wants to discuss with you some legal matters regarding your husband's affairs that need your attention."

Mary Ann had no idea what she meant. She knew absolutely nothing about Phillip's affairs, especially if it involved money. And she was pretty certain they didn't have much, if any, of that. She no longer had an appetite and looked to Elizabeth and with a nod toward the door inquired, "Would it be alright if I go now?

Elizabeth smiled, "Of course. You go ahead and I'll look after William when he finishes his meal."

With a quick "thank you," she turned toward the door, then quickly turned back and gave an embarrassed small curtsy, or bow; she wasn't quite certain which it was, and quickly left the room. She could hear Jemima laughing as she moved toward the front of the house.

There was a fresh fire in the fireplace and Mr. Hayes was standing beside it with his foot propped on one of the large andirons. He was smoking a pipe, looking very serious and watched critically as she entered the room. She stood there, awaiting instructions and was aware that he seemed to be assessing her appearance. She felt self-conscious. *Was it her clothes? Did he recognize them as his daughter's? Did he think she had stolen them?*

She stammered a hesitant explanation, "I'm so sorry, Mr. Hayes. Elizabeth said I might wear the dress but I'll change immediately."

"Nonsense," he interjected, "you look quite presentable, with the exception of your hair of course. That could use some attention. Ask the girls to help you with that. Now sit down for we have much to discuss."

She quickly obeyed and awaited whatever bad news he was about to deliver.

"Now, about your husband's affairs, his estate, if you will. There are court matters to be handled and I fear that you have neither the education nor experience to deal with these. Furthermore, as your neighbor and vestryman of your church, I feel an obligation to assist you in these matters. Someone will have to be selected to inventory the estate. I suggest John Hillen, as he seems best suited to understand the value and purpose of items your husband acquired in his trade."

She thought that sounded like a good idea since Phillip, before their marriage, had been apprenticed to Hillen to learn the skills of a shoemaker.

Hayes continued, "A bond will have to be posted and I'm assuming that you do not have the wherewithal to post such a bond to secure yourself as executrix of his estate."

His next pronouncement caused a panic, which constricted her chest as though an enormous weight had suddenly crushed her chest as she gasped for air. He was talking about her son. She was only vaguely aware that he intended to have himself declared legal guardian of her son. She was becoming more alarmed by the minute. *Was he about to take her son from her?*

The more he talked, the faster he spoke, and the more frightened and confused she became. She had absolutely no idea what he was talking about. She shook her head in dismay and Hayes, upon looking at her, was suddenly fearful that she might erupt into tears again. He sighed deeply, and took a step toward her. She shrank back from him and he realized that she was afraid. In frustration he stomped to the door and called down the hall for help.

"Will one of you girls come in here and explain to this woman that I'm trying to help her?"

All three young women hurried down the hall and saw their father with his shoulders raised and his hands held out to them in supplication as if to say, "What do I do now?"

To his daughters, it was a comical site, for they were accustomed to seeing their father always self-assured and in control of every situation. But here he was, asking for their help. As usual Elizabeth came to the rescue and after giving her father an affectionate hug, guided him to his chair and then went to Mary Ann and sat by her.

"These are matters that must be handled, and father is only looking out for the best interest of you and your son. He feels an obligation to the church and the community to see that you and William will be cared for. Father will be pleased to attend to the details and provide the funds necessary to close the matter with the courts."

"If you would like him to do so?" she was quick to add.

Mary Ann already trusted Elizabeth and, although somewhat relieved by her explanation, was suspicious about the outcome. But, the fact of the matter was that she could see no other alternative. Accordingly, she smiled at Mr. Hayes, nodded her head and replied weakly, "Sir, I would be most grateful for your help."

"Good, good, very good!" And with that Hayes returned to his self-assured, imposing former self.

He hastened to add that there would be some documents that she would need to sign for the courts. "Don't worry if you can't read or write, you can sign your mark when the time comes." He added in an off-handed manner. And with that he left the room.

Just then as if by a signal, Molly returned with William and Mary Ann, for the moment, was distracted from her thoughts and concerns, but the diversion was short-lived and replaced with mounting concerns about her future. She could see no alternative than to accept whatever fate the residents of Mount Hayes had planned for her and her son.

As for the Hayes women, they appeared to consider the matter closed and were prepared to continue with their normal activities, and with that they turned to leave the room.

Mary Ann followed them into the room across the hall, which was the library or morning room where young ladies attended to their daily activities. There were shelves with books, a writing table and chair, in addition to several chairs holding fabrics, threads, needles, frames and items of needlework, which were in various stages of production. Avarilla selected a book from the shelf and opened it to a page marked by a satin ribbon. Noticing Mary Ann's apparent interest in the book, she explained with a certain amount of exasperation that it was a play titled *Hamlet* by William Shakespeare, an Englishman. She added that she was certain Mary Ann had never heard of him. She turned her attention to the book and quickly became absorbed in her reading. She seemed indifferent to the actions of the other women in the room.

Elizabeth smiled and explained that their father had recently purchased several books by William Shakespeare. She acknowledged that they all found them interesting and entertaining, although, a good number of them seemed to be filled with deeds of corruption and jealousy. She confessed that both she and Jemima preferred to occupy their time with sewing.

Jemima was working on a linen sampler, which, as its name implied, illustrated the individual's mastery of a variety of stitches all sewn with an ivory thread. But the most beautiful project was Elizabeth's. She was working on a large piece of linen attached to a very large framework and a beautiful picture of exotic birds and beautiful flowers was emerging in a variety of brilliant shades of yarn. Elizabeth explained that it was called crewel embroidery, and that this, when completed, would be one of four panels to drape a bed. She winked and whispered to Mary Ann that this would adorn her own bed after her marriage. Mary Ann was immediately curious and with a quizzical expression inquired if there was a suitor at hand. Elizabeth shook her head slightly and whispered, "Later."

Young William soon tired of watching the women and constantly climbed onto and off of his mother's lap, demanding her attention. Mary Ann was surprised when Avarilla, with a look of disgust, interrupted her reading, stood up, and announced that Molly would look after the child for a while. With that, Avarilla went to the door and called to Molly. Once again, William readily went to Molly's arms and left the room.

Avarilla, with her perpetual frown, returned to her book without further comment.

Mary Ann felt uncomfortable, insecure, and totally at a loss regarding what might be expected of her. She was unaccustomed to servants and was curious regarding those of the Hayes household. Elizabeth seemed happy to explain that Molly and her husband Isham were slaves who had been brought from Jamaica.

Once she began, Elizabeth seemed delighted to share details of her family. She told how her grandparents had been early colonists of the island after the British seized control from the Spanish in 1656. The Hayes family had arrived there in 1665 and settled in a place called Montego Bay where they became tobacco planters. Her father was only two years old at the time.

Elizabeth proudly shared stories of her grandparents' success with their tobacco plantation and great house they had built. But, tragedy struck in 1678 when both of her grandparents died within a few days of each other from an outbreak of fever that plagued the island. The plantation and house passed into the hands of their eldest child, her uncle Edward Hayes, who was twenty-one at the time, and six years older than her father. His sisters, Helen and Charlotte, age seventeen and nineteen respectively, remained in Edward's care with the expectation that they would soon be married. Their father, who was fifteen, was sent to his uncle William in Maryland. Edward sent his young brother in the company of two young slaves, Isham and his wife, Molly, which he felt to be ample inheritance for his younger brother.

It turned out to be a fortunate situation. William Hayes taught his nephew the skills necessary to run a tobacco plantation, secured for him a position of respect in St. Paul's Parish, and arranged a favorable marriage to Abigail Dixon, widow of Thomas Scudamore. Abigail brought to the marriage a considerable amount of land that she had inherited from her father, John Dixon, as well as that bequeathed to her by Thomas Scudamore in his will. It was a happy, but brief marriage as Abigail died giving birth to a daughter, Jane, whose dress Mary Ann was wearing.

Jemima was eager to join the conversation and told about her father's second marriage to their mother, Elizabeth, shortly after Abigail's death. After all, it was the custom, since he had an infant daughter and needed someone to run the household. Jemima's demeanor changed as she told of her mother's death a year ago. She had been in poor health for several years and died giving birth to a stillborn son. Jemima and her sisters were still grieving the loss of their mother.

In an attempt to lighten the mood, Elizabeth shared some unusual details about their home. Although Mary Ann hadn't seen any homes as grand as this, she was aware that it was unique in appearance. Elizabeth explained that her father had built it in the style he recalled from their island manor house in Jamaica with sleeping quarters on the lower level and that their house slaves also slept in a room on the lower floor.

Mary Ann was curious and asked about the two other slaves she had seen.

Elizabeth explained that Molly and Isham's children, Winnie, now fifteen years old and Henry, who was twelve, were both born here at the plantation, and according to Maryland law, were thus, like their parents, the legal property of her father. She was quick to add, that there were many other children on the plantation, all born there to slave parents.

Mary Ann shook her head in dismay as she tried to sort through the information she had just received. It was more than she could absorb at the moment, and once again, despite the bond she felt with Elizabeth, she feared for her own future and that of her son. She asked if she might go find William. Elizabeth, sensing her discomfort, arose and accompanied her into the hall and to the back of the house where Molly was tending to her chores. Molly was singing a strange song, which sounded nothing like anything Mary Ann had ever heard. Molly spoke in a sort of broken, but mostly understandable English, but the words to the song were strange, a lingering reminder of her earlier life in Jamaica.

As always, William was happy to see his mother and ran to her eagerly. Elizabeth suggested that Henry, who was sitting watching his mother work, take Mary Ann on a tour of the house and answer any questions she might have. With that, Elizabeth smiled at William and cradled him in her arms. Henry grinned and seemed genuinely pleased that he had been accorded the honor of being a guide.

They walked to the far end of the long hallway and Henry opened the door. A strong blast of cold air and swirling snow greeted them, but Henry appeared not to notice the cold. Henry's speech was much like his mother's with the same lilting rhythm but easier to understand. He pointed to several of the outbuildings that were scattered near the house and explained their purpose. In close proximity to the main house was the cooking house where the food was prepared, and next to that were two additional buildings used for food storage and for laundry. Beyond these were several other outbuildings, which included the meat barn, milk barn, the stable, and farther yet were the five tobacco barns. He seemed proud of his position working in the house and explained that most boys his age would have been sent to the fields to work.

Mary Ann was curious about how many slaves there might be. Henry laughed and pointed to a row of seven small structures to the right of the main house that housed the slaves who worked the tobacco fields. Henry explained that each building housed six or seven people, including men, women and children, who all worked on the plantation. Most worked in the fields, but some, who had the skill, worked as carpenters or, in the case of women, handled the tasks of cooking, cleaning and laundry. He was quick to point to another building located to the left of the house, which housed the white indentured servants who worked the fields as well. He explained that there were several other tobacco fields on other lands owned by the family, including the plantations Privilege, and Scudamore's Lot, which were both located on the south side of Back River. Each had its own set of slave quarters and outbuildings. He noted with pride that his father, Isham, was the overseer of this plantation, as well as the other lands owned by Massa Hayes. Mary Ann shook her head, bewildered by the enormous wealth of this family into whose midst she found herself.

Her thoughts were fleeting as Henry continued with the tour. Henry knew a lot about the operation of the plantation, and about tobacco, and thoroughly enjoyed sharing his knowledge. He pointed in the distance where a few acres of land had been cultivated and were now divided into small beds that were covered with straw. He explained that under the protective straw were planted the tiny tobacco seeds that as seedlings would be planted in the fields. He also pointed out that lettuce seed was always planted along with the tobacco seeds and that mustard seeds were planted around the border of each of the beds. In his most grownup and matter of fact voice he explained that the lettuce and mustard seeds would distract flies and worms from eating the young seedlings. It was all very interesting, but Mary Ann was shivering from the cold and she suggested that it would be best to close the door.

They stepped back into the hallway, but just as they were about to close the door, they noticed a woman trudging through the snow around the back corner of the house. She was clutching a bundle held tightly to her breast, and was struggling to make her way through the snow which was now several inches deep. Upon seeing them, the woman called out to them, but Henry shook his head and started to close the door. Mary Ann was surprised and aghast that he seemed bent on ignoring the woman. She said, with as much authority she could muster, "Henry, you must let the poor woman in."

"No, Misses. We no let the woman in. Massa John beat me if we do dat."

"Of course he will not, Henry! Mr. Hayes is a kind man and I'm certain he would not deny Christian charity to the poor woman." Clearly, she was trying very hard to exert a confidence, which she did not feel in this case.

She turned back and opened the door wider and motioned to the woman to enter. As she did, she could see that the bundle she carried was an infant.

"Massa John not like dis, not one bit. Dat de woman who say Massa John de baby dada, but Massa John say no talk to woman. So we close de door." And Henry, against her best efforts, managed to close the door.

Mary Ann pushed Henry aside and again opened the door. The woman screamed at Mary Ann and her face was contorted in anger. All of a sudden she realized that she had made a blunder and one from which she did not know how to extricate herself. She couldn't bring herself to leave the poor woman and her baby out in the cold, but did not have the authority to bring her into the home where she was, herself, a guest at best, but possibly a future servant. Suddenly, from behind her, another hand was on the door pulling it open and beckoning to the woman to enter.

It was the last person Mary Ann expected to see. There was Avarilla, taking the woman by the arm and drawing her into the hallway. She didn't say a word, but took the child from the woman and nodded for them all to follow her to the warmth of the hearth in back room. Avarilla motioned the woman to a chair by the fire, told Henry to fetch a blanket and handed the infant back to the mother.

The woman cuddled the infant in her arms and suddenly seemed at a loss for words. She had expected to be turned away but was determined that she would see John Hayes. Avarilla was as usual, both dour and unwelcoming, and also self-assured and in total control of the situation.

"You are, I believe, Dorothy Richards?" she asked.

"That's right," the woman countered defiantly.

"I understand that you claim John Hayes is the father of this child, and that you expect some sort of acknowledgement to that effect?"

"Yes, I do, and rightly so." She was still defiant but her face now betrayed a bit of confusion as to how to proceed. "Where is he? I demand to see him!"

Mary Ann suspected that the word demand was ill advised, but decided to keep her opinions to herself.

Avarilla studied the woman for a moment. She was not a young woman, and probably older than Avarilla. Dorothy Richards was not the first woman to tempt John Hayes, and Avarilla was aware that her father was a man of strong sexual urges and needed little or no tempting. With a sigh of irritation, Avarilla calmly announced that John Hayes was not at home and that even if he were at home, he would not, under any circumstances, see her or talk to her. She advised the woman that it would be foolhardy to take her case to court because no one would dare accuse a vestryman of the church of such behavior, especially with someone of such lowly status.

Again, the woman's eyes narrowed, her nostrils flared and her face flushed, but before she could speak again, Avarilla continued, "That is not to say that there might not be a more reasonable solution to the situation that would satisfy your needs."

Now the poor woman looked completely confused, and didn't know whether to rephrase her demands or wait to see what was about to be offered.

"I am in charge of this household!" Avarilla announced.

Mary Ann would discover that this was a phrase that Avarilla repeated often.

Avarilla continued, in a stern manner, that she, as the eldest daughter in the house, would deal with all such matters. Avarilla towered over Dorothy Richards as she continued:

"You must know, that no matter how unfounded the charge, it is unfair to damage the reputation of a fine, respected gentleman of this parish."

The woman's response was a disgusted "Humph," followed by a frown and deep wrinkling of her brow.

Avarilla did not wait, but pulled from her pocket a small pouch. She shook it gently in her right hand and the sounds of coins jingling against each other could be heard.

The woman made a grab for it, but Avarilla quickly pulled her hand away and with a shake of her head, held up her left hand as though to stop the woman's reach.

"There are sufficient funds in this pouch to see you and your child safely through the year, but beyond that, you are left to your own devices. As a condition for receiving this money, you will make no claims against my father or in any way slander his reputation in the parish. Furthermore you will swear to a written statement that John Hayes is not the father of your child."

The woman sat back in her chair and appeared to consider her possibilities. She bit at the corner of her lip and began to fidget on the chair. On the one hand, this had actually been easier than she expected. But on the other hand, she was worried lest she settle too quickly when there might be a better deal to be had. In the end, she decided that a sure thing was better than nothing at all and nodded her consent and again reached for the pouch.

"Not so fast," Avarilla said as she turned, and pulled from her pocket a piece of paper on which, according to Avarilla, was already written the required statement. She instructed Henry to run to the morning room and bring ink and a quill.

Mary Ann thought it unusual that Avarilla could have anticipated the woman's appearance and had prepared the document in advance. She was curious and took the opportunity to glance at the paper as it lay on the table. She was surprised to see that it appeared to be a list of some sort. Elizabeth, noting Mary Ann's interest in the paper, smiled and shook her head. Taking Mary Ann by the arm, she gently drew her to a far corner of the room. There, she whispered to Mary Ann that it was not a statement exonerating John Hayes of misconduct, but rather an inventory listing of available food supplies for the family. With a smile, Elizabeth shrugged and explained that Avarilla was very skilled at handling situations such as this. Mary Ann couldn't help but wonder how many situations there might have been.

Both Hayes and his daughters had assumed that Mary Ann could neither read nor write. It was true, that she had a very limited education, but Philip had taught her to read the Bible. Mary Ann, for some reason, chose to maintain her silence on the matter.

Henry returned quickly, and Avarilla dipped the quill in the ink, pointed to a space at the bottom of the paper and, with a scowl at Dorothy Richards, instructed her to sign.

"I don't know what it says and I can't write my name," confessed the woman.

"That's perfectly fine, just make your mark where I have pointed."

"What kind of mark?" queried the woman.

"An X will be fine," and Avarilla drew and X in the air with her finger.

The transaction was completed quickly. Molly handed the woman her child, now wrapped in a warm blanket, and Avarilla gave her the pouch with the money and ushered her to the door with the admonition that she was never again to make accusations against John Hayes.

The deal had been brokered in less than ten minutes and the woman was out of the house and out of their lives. Molly smiled at Avarilla, who with a satisfied smile of her own suggested that it would be best if the day's activities remained a secret to the rest of the household. With a great sense of relief, Mary Ann nodded in agreement as they walked down the hall to rejoin Jemima and to continue their sewing.

Before entering the room, Elizabeth stopped for a moment, and put her arm around Mary Ann's shoulder, and with a smile, welcomed her into their household, and extended an unexpected offer.

"If you would like, I would love to be of assistance to you with the education of your son."

Mary Ann was, once again, grateful for the interest Elizabeth showed for her and her son. But Elizabeth's next disclosure was even more surprising. She advised that Mary Ann not judge her sister too harshly. She confided that their father had often chastised Avarilla for being unmarriageable, a trait that he attributed to a litany of faults. First he bemoaned her lack of beauty, which, according to Hayes was only exacerbated by her unfortunate limp, which she had carried with her since birth, and further compounded by her brooding disposition. He had, on more than one occasion when "in his cups," complained to friends and neighbors in her presence, that he was saddled with the lifelong financial responsibility for his eldest daughter. He lamented the fact that there were no suitors, at all, much less any gentlemen of position and wealth, who might add to his own fortunes.

Elizabeth concluded that her sister had accepted her fate and had chosen to make the best of it. Accordingly, it seemed, she was stubbornly determined to take advantage of the few God-given traits she possessed; namely her intelligence and determination. Elizabeth explained how Avarilla had schooled herself in a variety of subjects, including literature, law, medicine, and mathematics, which were normally the provenance of men. Elizabeth shrugged her shoulders, smiled at Mary Ann, and added that Avarilla cherished her role as the female head of the household, and, after all, she was very good at it.

Elizabeth, once again, assured Mary Ann that Avarilla's harsh demeanor should not frighten her. It was, as everyone acknowledged, just her nature.

Elizabeth had calmed her fears, but Mary Ann remained apprehensive as she entered the room to continue the day's activities, a routine that would, over time, calm her anxieties and allow her to enjoy her good fortune.

CHAPTER 2
Unexpected Misfortune

*N*ear the end of April, the fields around the house were bustling with activity as the slaves and indentured servants began to carry the tobacco seedlings to the fields where each seedling was planted by hand. It was a labor intensive, back breaking task carried out after heavy rains that left the soil muddy, a condition which Henry explained was the best for planting the seedlings.

As for Mary Ann and William, they were still safe, warm and well-fed guests of the household. As he had promised, John Hayes posted a bond on Mary Ann's behalf and saw to it that she was named executrix of her husband's estate. He also posted the necessary bond with the court and was appointed legal guardian of young William. He seemed quite fond of the boy. Mary Ann wondered if her son seemed somehow a substitute for the son he lost upon the death of his former wife. Whatever the reason, his affection for her son was welcomed.

Gradually, Elizabeth had assumed the role as tutor for both Mary Ann and William. Little by little, she was becoming more comfortable and was surprised when Avarilla even helped to explain to her the various court documents concerning Phillip's estate.

Hayes contacted two neighbors, John Hillen and William Biddison, and asked them to inventory Phillip's personal property. The men listed all items and reported their value to be eleven pounds, ten shillings, and six pence, in addition they found records indicating that 3200 pounds of tobacco were owed to him by neighbors for work he had done.

As Hayes had insisted, Mary Ann petitioned the court for some measure of support from her husband's estate. In response to her plea the court ordered that she be allowed a bed, a gun, laborer's tools, and such household equipment as would be necessary for subsistence. Compared to the wealth surrounding her in the Hayes household, it wasn't much. But to Mary Ann it was enormous, for it gave her confidence in her own ability, although, what the future might hold for her was still a mystery.

The uncertain weather of early spring eventually gave way and by late May, sunshine and warmth prevailed and yielded a burst of color as the trees in the orchard filled the air with the scent of apple blossoms. Mary Ann and her son settled comfortably into the daily routine of the household, and a true bond of friendship developed between Mary Ann and the two younger Hayes women.

Elizabeth talked privately, but enthusiastically about her fondness for John Lenox and her hopes that he might soon ask her father for her hand. She worked diligently every day on the panels for what she hoped would be her bridal bed.

Mary Ann tried hard to learn the many skills displayed by the Hayes women. This included instruction in needlework, as well as the many tasks and skills necessary to manage a large home. One of those skills was planting and maintenance of the flower and herb garden, which Avarilla guarded and cared for with fervent zeal. Although reluctant to do so, she eventually began to share her knowledge of plants with Mary Ann, and the two devoted at least an hour every morning to the small garden near the back of the house. William loved this outdoor time with his mother and Avarilla, who now insisted that he call her

Aunt Avarilla. William tried diligently to pronounce her given name, but to him it was too difficult and always came out as Rilla. Ultimately, Avarilla decided that she liked it that way and she was forever known to William as Aunt Rilla.

Mary Ann embraced with gratitude the routine nature of their days. There was no apparent concern about any of the daily requirements to feed and clothe the family that had dominated her earlier life. For in the Hayes household, there were no such worries and she was made to feel welcome, especially by Hayes's younger daughters and even Avarilla seemed to love young William as much as she.

Summer passed uneventfully, and Mary Ann enjoyed this respite from fear and uncertainty. Young William was especially happy. His color was good, he was filled with boundless energy and never ending questions, and loved the attention heaped upon him by the women of the household. John Hayes' affection for William was apparent as he often let the boy accompany him on small trips to his other plantations.

Throughout the summer, the slaves were constantly in the fields tending to the tobacco. Henry was always available to explain to Mary Ann the complexities of raising good tobacco. He was especially proud of the way his father, Isham managed the process. Since tobacco is not harvested until all the leaves are mature, constant tending was necessary to remove lower leaves that matured first, so that the entire plant would be ready for harvest at the same time. And despite the planting of lettuce and mustard seeds, worms always appeared and fed upon the tender plants. Isham, like most tobacco farmers in the area, herded the turkeys that abounded on the plantation into the field to help rid the plants of the worms. Although Henry delighted in these descriptions, Mary Ann shuddered at the thought, let alone the sight, of the voracious worms being devoured by the equally voracious turkeys. William was thoroughly spellbound by these events, and Mary Ann, reluctantly allowed Henry to take William to the fields to observe the process. For his part, John Hayes smiled his approval and noted that it was always a good thing for a boy to learn the specifics about tobacco farming at an early age.

By late August, the plants were ready for harvest. Again, Henry was eager to share all that he knew about the process. He pointed out that the long, broad, deep green leaves were beginning to crinkle. In truth, it was an amazing site to witness, as the slaves bent over the plants, cut them off at the base of the stalk with a knife, then cut a slit up the middle of the stalk and laid the plants in the sun for several hours to wilt. Early the next day, those plants were gathered and placed on "tobacco sticks" and hung in the special outbuildings used to cure the tobacco. As for the tobacco, the process was not yet completed as the harvested plants required several weeks to turn brown and leathery. At this point the cured leaves were stripped from the stalk, and the thick vein that runs down the middle of each leaf was stripped off and the leaves were then tied into bundles of eight to ten leaves.

These bundles, Henry pointed out, were called "hands" of tobacco. The final step was to pack them into hogshead barrels to be hauled to the nearest warehouse where they would be examined by inspectors appointed by the government. All this was necessary before the tobacco could be shipped to England. These inspectors held a great deal of power, for if a hogshead was found to contain bad tobacco, it had to be burned. Additionally, the proprietary government of Maryland demanded fifteen pounds of tobacco for every inhabitant, male or female, except for children younger than twelve years of age. So, clearly Henry pointed out, it was important to produce the best tobacco possible.

Mary Ann liked Henry, and was happy that he was so involved in the process, and so eager to share every scrap of information available to him but, she quickly determined, she knew far more about the cultivation of tobacco than she cared to know. Furthermore, she could think of no conceivable occasion when any of this could possibly be of importance to her or her son in any way. But, as she would come to realize, only time reveals what providence has in store.

Once the inspectors cleared the tobacco, it was loaded on ships and accounts were settled. John Hayes was jubilant with his success. The tobacco crop was not only deemed to be excellent, but also sizeable, and the price it brought was even better than hoped for. Everyone at Mount Hayes was excited about the bountiful harvest. As for John Hayes, he was happier than Mary Ann had ever seen him.

In late November, at the urging of his daughters, John Hayes was considering hosting a holiday event to celebrate his good fortune as well as that of his fellow plantation owners and parish residents. Even Avarilla seemed receptive to the idea, for she enjoyed exhibiting her skills in managing such affairs. However, within a week's time of beginning their plans, the routine of their carefree days was interrupted by an unexpected turn of events. Jemima was unwell.

The girl had developed a persistent cough and fever that dragged on for several weeks leaving her quite pale and weak. The sickness had so drained her of any strength that she was often in bed and they all missed her distinctive laugh and playful nature. To Mary Ann it was an ominous sign and she was reminded of the similarities to her husband's illness. She felt as helpless now as she had felt then. But Avarilla seemed confident that her younger sister would soon be well again.

Another of Avarilla's responsibilities in the home was care of the sick. Her herb garden not only provided fragrantly pungent additions to their daily meals, but also the source of her many medicinal concoctions. She prided herself on the many dried herbs that she kept for such occasions, and she seemed undaunted by any and all circumstances. But, as time passed, none of her remedies had produced any improvement in Jemima's health, and she grew weaker by the day.

In desperation, Avarilla suggested to her father that they should call in a doctor. This was something that they were all reluctant to do, for frequently the treatments were worse than the disease and all too often those treatments, at best, only prolonged the ailment, but at worst, actually killed the patient.

But the decision was made and Avarilla called to Henry to take their horse, Old Ben, and ride to the home of Dr. Payne. As he heard the order, Henry's eyes opened wide and he started to back away toward the door. He too had heard horror stories about the treatments doctors used and was clearly afraid of them, especially one whose name seemed to fit his occupation. But Avarilla scolded him and told him that Miss Jemima was very ill and that he must go immediately.

Henry went first to the parlor kitchen to seek protection from his mother against whatever evil might await him at the doctor's house. Molly had brought with her from her early years in Jamaica a belief in Obeah, a type of voodoo used for protection and healing. Any use of witchcraft or any power used to gain control of another's welfare was strictly forbidden by Maryland law. The family was aware of Molly's reliance on various chants, potions and talismans to protect herself and her family, but they had warned that if her belief in magic were to be discovered by neighbors, she would surely be tried as a witch. But when Henry's welfare was at stake, Molly's natural instinct was to do whatever she could to protect her son.

Molly shared Henry's fear and dislike for doctors and quickly took Henry by the arm and went downstairs to her room. There she retrieved from the back of a cupboard a small bundle wrapped in a scarlet cloth. When she opened the cloth, it revealed a dried chicken foot with several feathers tied to it with another strip of the red cloth. She wrapped it again into a packet, put it in Henry's hand, and made him repeat some strange sounding words that he didn't understand. She told him to put the bundle in the pocket of his shirt, but not to show it to anyone. Molly warned him to hold onto the talisman during the entire time he was with the doctor. With that, she assured him that he would be protected, if he did as he was told. Henry felt a little better, but was still wary as he went to the barn for the horse.

Henry was a good rider and needed no saddle for Old Ben and normally he would have enjoyed the opportunity to ride the horse, but today, despite the urgency he had heard in Mistress Avarilla's voice, he rode the five miles to the doctor's house at a slow, leisurely pace. In the back of his mind lingered the hope that the doctor might not be home.

The house of Dr. Payne was much smaller than the one at the Hayes's Plantation, and not nearly as well kept. All kinds of wild bushes and vines crowded the long, winding path leading up to the door. It was so narrow that Henry had to get off Old Ben and make his way to the door on foot. From inside he could hear sounds of someone moaning and just as Henry was about to turn and run, the door burst open and a young boy came running out of the house carrying a basin, which appeared to be filled with blood.

Henry could see through the open door that the doctor was leaning over the body of an elderly man and was holding another basin under the man's arm to catch the blood flowing from it. Henry couldn't help himself, but let out a cry of alarm and removing the scarlet wrapped bundle from his pocket, started waving it crying, "No, no, devil man," while backing away from the door.

As it happened, the boy returning with the emptied basin stopped his progress, and the two collided in a heap on the narrow path. The boy, Thomas, was a young apprentice to Dr. Payne and only a few years older than Henry. He was indignant to have been toppled to the ground, especially by a slave, and began yelling at Henry.

In his fall, Henry had dropped the precious bundle and out fell the chicken foot with the feather talisman attached.

This time it was Thomas who was fearful. "What is that thing...where did you get that? Dr. Payne, look, this is the work of a witch. What do we do?"

Henry grabbed it, quickly wrapped it in its scarlet cloth and stuffed it back into his pocket. It was difficult to tell which of the two boys was the most frightened.

Although Dr. Payne's treatments were pretty much limited to bloodletting, which he was performing at the moment, he did not believe in magic or voodoo or other such things.

"It's not witchcraft, you fool...it's a chicken foot! Now get over here and hold this basin for me."

Thomas reluctantly did as he was told, but clearly was not convinced by the doctor's admonition.

Dr. Payne was well aware that when a slave was sent to the doctor's house it meant that he had been sent to bring help. He wiped his hands on a blood-covered cloth, picked up the lancet he had used to cut the man's arm, put on his coat and walked toward Henry. Before closing the door behind him, Dr. Payne instructed Thomas to wait until the basin was half full and then bandage the man's arm and then look after him until he returned.

Dr. Payne walked to the barn and as soon as he had saddled and mounted his horse, the two began to travel back to the Hayes plantation. Payne was in his mid-sixties with a stooped posture, a perpetual frown, and clothes that looked and smelled as though they needed a good washing. Henry suspected that a bath wouldn't have hurt the doctor either.

"Who's in need of my help, boy?"

"Miss Jemima, she be sick, she be bad sick...we hurry."

All of a sudden Henry was in a rush to get home and away from the presence of Dr. Payne. In Henry's view, the doctor's treatments looked suspiciously like voodoo. He was relieved when he arrived at the house and jumped off his horse and waited for the doctor to dismount so that he could tend to both horses. Avarilla had been anxiously awaiting the arrival of the doctor and opened the door as the doctor came up the front steps.

Avarilla led the doctor to the stairs at the back of the house and down to a room on the lower, cooler, level where Jemima, her body drenched from fever, was lying in bed. John Hayes, Elizabeth and Mary Ann followed behind, but waited outside the door to the room. As could have been expected, the doctor examined Jemima briefly and then diagnosed her condition as the ague and announced that the only cure was bloodletting. He asked for a basin to collect the blood.

Avarilla called to Molly with instructions and Molly hurried to do as she had been told, but her face clearly showed the fear and revulsion she felt as Dr. Payne removed the lancet from his coat pocket and proceeded to cut a deep slice in Jemima's arm. Jemima cried out in pain and the entire group assembled outside the door felt her anguish. The procedure seemed to go on forever. After what seemed like an eternity, the doctor asked for a cloth to bandage the arm. Avarilla had anticipated this and was ready with several clean linen cloths for the purpose. Jemima seemed to be sleeping, but she was so very pale, they feared the worst. Dr. Payne assured them that his treatment would be effective. He told them to let her rest for a few hours and then to feed her some warm broth. He picked up his coat and left the house without a look back. Molly, watching him as he got on his horse, shook her head in disapproval and in a low and rhythmic tone began to chant as her body rocked slowly in time to the cadence of her chant.

Jemima's condition did not improve. When she finally awoke, still feverish, pale and so weak from the bloodletting, she could not stand and had no appetite. Avarilla, Elizabeth, and Mary Ann took turns sitting with her and in applying wet towels to her head, and Molly secretly prepared a magic amulet, which she placed under her pillow. Avarilla found the amulet when she changed the pillow under her sister's head, and although she did not believe in its magic, she was touched by Molly's concern and left it where it was. But despite their efforts, Jemima's condition continued to decline.

John Hayes was visibly distraught over his youngest daughter's condition. Two days later, he sent Henry to fetch Dr. Payne once again. As Henry started for the door, Avarilla pulled him aside and told him that he should also bring Reverend Tibbs. Elizabeth frowned and gave her sister a quizzical look and asked why she would send for Tibbs. It wasn't that Elizabeth didn't understand the seriousness of Jemima's condition, but rather that she, like the other members of the parish did not hold William Tibbs in high regard. Avarilla acknowledged her sister's appraisal and agreed with her, but the fact remained that Jemima's illness might well be fatal.

Their worst fears were realized later that day when Jemima could not be awakened. With both Dr. Payne and Reverend Tibbs sitting by her bed, along with the entire household assembled around her, young Jemima Hayes died on Tuesday, December 24, just three days before her sixteenth birthday. There would be no joy at Mount Hayes this Christmas.

~ 39 ~

Although death was a far too frequent occurrence in all families, especially among newborns and the elderly, it always came as a shock when the victim seemed so young and vibrant and on the brink of entering adulthood. Jemima's death produced an oppressive sadness among family as well as house servants and slaves. Her vibrant personality and lilting laughter still echoed in the minds of them all. John Hayes, in particular, sequestered himself in his room, and had it not been for the ministrations of Avarilla and Isham, affairs at the plantation would have come to a screeching halt.

It was Avarilla, along with Molly who washed Jemima's body and wrapped it in a linen shroud. Avarilla brought dried rosemary, bay leaves, and thyme from her garden to sprinkle over the body. A large board was placed on an elevated platform, both draped in dark wool, in the large front room. Jemima's body was placed on the platform and the windows of the room were thrown open.

Avarilla planned the food that Molly was to prepare for the funeral feast and Henry was sent to all members of St. Paul's Parish Church to alert them to the day of the funeral and to invite their attendance. Reverend Tibbs and Dr. Payne were to be among the guests. Throughout this period of grief, it was Avarilla who assumed the burden of supervision of the plantation and arrangements regarding the funeral. In her mind, it was clear that these things were her responsibility, and one that she cherished. She might not ever marry, but she would, one day be mistress of the Hayes estate.

On Thursday, December 26, two days after Jemima's death, neighbors joined the family to offer prayers for the departed. It was a mournful day and the dark skies and snow that began to fall only served to make the day seem even more dismal. Black ribbons were given to each guest to wear as a sign of mourning.

Once again, Mary Ann felt uneasy among so many people whom she had only seen at church during her marriage to Phillip. These were all the wealthy landowners who sat in family pews at the front of the church. They had never spoken to her or acknowledged her existence, since she and Philip had always stood at the back of the church along with the others who, like her and her husband, could not afford the price of a pew. Since her arrival at Mount Hayes, she had remained home on the Sabbath, while William, as ward of John Hayes accompanied the family to services at St. Paul's Parish. She spent her time in the room on the upper floor, which had been furnished for her and William. There, she spent her time reading from the Bible, but mostly she was preoccupied with her own fears and prayers. It seemed quite clear to Mary Ann that the family had not yet decided just exactly what her place was to be within the household.

She felt awkward, and wondered what the opinions of the guests might be. Adding to her discomfort was the arrival of John Hayes's eldest daughter, Jane Stansbury, whom Mary Ann had not met before. Mary Ann was, as usual, wearing clothing that had belonged to Jane and was fearful of her reaction. But her concerns on that account proved to be unfounded, for Jane, dressed in beautiful and elaborate silk, was as pleasant and kind as, Elizabeth.

Among the guests were two who immediately caught Mary Ann's attention. The first was the charming and handsome John Lenox. Elizabeth, despite her grief, was clearly delighted to see the young man. She took Mary Ann by the hand and introduced her to the man she hoped to marry. Mary Ann could immediately understand why

Elizabeth was so fond of him. He was gracious, and kind, much like Elizabeth herself. Mary Ann felt it would be a good match. The other person of interest was neighbor Thomas Harris, who was still mourning the death of his wife, Rachel, who had died the previous month shortly after the birth of their ninth child, a daughter Sarah. Mary Ann felt pity for this widower with seven of his nine children still living at home. Once again she was reminded of the grief she still felt for the loss of her husband. She was, momentarily lost in her own thoughts, and unaware that she was staring at the widower, when he approached her and introduced himself. He was older than she, but not nearly as old as Hayes. He was also handsome. She was suddenly embarrassed by the fact that the thought had even entered her mind, and turned away, self-conscious that others might have read her thoughts. She made a hasty retreat to offer her help to Molly.

She tried to busy herself by helping to replenish the refreshments on the tables. The feast itself was not elaborate, but like most such events consisted of rum punch and a variety of small cakes, which the guests seemed to enjoy. Apparently, Molly's skills as a cook were well known and appreciated by their neighbors. As Mary Ann did what she could to help, she was keenly aware that Thomas Harris followed her with his eyes. She wasn't quite certain what to make of it all, but she was flattered, but uncomfortable. She reminded herself that the guests were there to pay their respects to the family upon the death of Hayes's daughter, Jemima, and felt ashamed that she had allowed herself to indulge in such thoughts.

As was the custom, the assembled friends, one by one, made their way to the front parlor where Jemima's body lay. Despite the concerned ministrations of his daughters,

John Hayes could not enter the room where his youngest child lay without collapsing from grief. Avarilla and Elizabeth were fearful for their father for they had never seen him so despondent, not even at the death of their mother. He tried his best to keep his composure as he acknowledged the concerns of the assembled mourners. When the last guest had departed, he accepted Avarilla's suggestion that he should lie down to rest, and leaned on her as she helped him to his room.

Mary Ann felt compassion for Hayes and remembered the overwhelming sense of loss she had felt at the death of her husband, Phillip. She also was mindful of the kindness he had continued to extend to her and her son. She wished to offer comfort to him as he had to her and she spent many hours sitting quietly with him in his darkened room. She brought bowls of broth to him, but quickly learned that those were declined in favor of a bottle of ale or rum. It seemed to calm him and normally soothed him into a deep sleep for hours.

By Sunday, the sixth day after his daughter's death, John Hayes left his darkened room, and joined the family at St. Paul's for Sunday service.

Jemima had died on a Tuesday and the funeral feast was held two days later on Thursday. As was the custom, the burial would be held several days hence when Bartholomew Hedge, the carpenter, completed and delivered the coffin. The following Tuesday, Hedge brought an oak coffin for which Avarilla arranged for him to be paid 200 pounds of tobacco for his work.

At 1:00 that afternoon, friends gathered at the Hayes home and followed the coffin as it was carried a distance of about a mile to the gravesite through nearly six inches of snow. A wooden fence enclosed the graveyard in which evergreens had been planted among a few graves clustered together on a small rise in the center of the enclosure. A far greater number of graves were scattered around the perimeter of the graveyard. Mary Ann later learned that the family graves held the location of honor in the center on the small knoll, while the graves of multiple slaves and servants were those around the outer edges.

John Hayes was unsteady on his feet as he moved along with the others to the gravesite. Despite Avarilla's attempt to take his arm and steady his movements, he rebuffed these attempts by his eldest daughter. Instead, through the tears, which streamed down his face, he reached toward Mary Ann, and clung to her arm for steadiness. The hurt and then anger, on Avarilla's face, spoke volumes regarding what the future held between the eldest daughter with her father and the woman whom she now viewed as an interloper. Mary Ann was fully aware that her relationship with Avarilla was destined to be an adversarial one. But, there was nothing to be done about it now.

Finally, over the course of the next few weeks, John Hayes gradually came to accept his loss and attempted to return to a semblance of his former self. He began to spend more time with Mary Ann. He often asked her to accompany him on trips to homes of neighbors and even gave her a tour of the plantation grounds. On occasion he would even ask her to read to him after the evening meal.

Avarilla was clearly unhappy with this turn of events.

Perhaps, suddenly aware of his own mortality, John Hayes seemed more than willing to allow Isham and Avarilla to continue to run the affairs of the plantation.

CHAPTER 3

"In the moment of decision, destiny is shaped."

Anthony Robbins

*A*n early spring brightened everyone's spirits and the tobacco chores continued as before along with high hopes for another year of a successful crop.

John Hayes, as he had done in earlier days, began to spend a great deal of time at the local tavern, and surprisingly, Avarilla did not seem to disapprove. This despite the fact that her father routinely came home late at night, disheveled, and drunk to the point that he often needed help to get home.

On one of those nights, Avarilla, with an unexpected smile, took Mary Ann by the arm and in a soft voice, announced that John Hayes had found other interests outside of Mount Hayes. Her next comment seemed almost sinister as she whispered in Mary Ann's ear: "You needn't think that you will ever be mistress of Mount Hayes. That position is mine and mine alone, and you would be wise to remember that."

Mary Ann was stunned. It was true that she had never figured out exactly why John Hayes had been so kind to her and her son, but she had no romantic interest in the man at all, nor had she ever envisioned herself as replacing Avarilla.

It is probable that Avarilla's prediction might have proven to be accurate had it not been for protestations of the elders of St. Paul's Parish. These admonitions were delivered, in person, by Reverend Tibbs and several respected men of the congregation, who informed Hayes that even his position as vestryman was in jeopardy. They made it clear that the disapproval of the congregation was unanimous and that Hayes must mend his vile ways or face the consequences. They also reminded him that his daughters' prospects for a good marriage were at risk by his behavior.

His reputation and position in the community were of extreme importance to Hayes. It was through the influence of his uncle, and his fortunate marriages that he had accumulated his wealth. It was also true that if his reputation were to be destroyed, that in all likelihood so would be his wealth. And, if his daughter Elizabeth were unable to find a good match, he would be stuck with two unmarriageable daughters. Hayes took note.

Everyone in the Hayes household was relieved to see the dramatic change in his behavior. He began to take renewed interest in the affairs of the plantation. He curbed his drinking; at least he did not frequent the local taverns every night. Reverend Tibbs and the congregation noted the change with satisfaction, as did his family, and when John Lenox arrived in late July to ask for the hand of Elizabeth in marriage, John Hayes was ecstatic. Things were indeed looking up. There was a growing sense of normalcy in the household.

But on Saturday, August 9, after dinner he asked Mary Ann to walk with him to lay some flowers on the graves of his first two wives and that of his daughter, Jemima. She was touched and was happy to accompany him. Avarilla started to join them, but Elizabeth pleaded that she needed some help with an inventory of food in the pantry. Reluctantly, Avarilla stayed to help. Hayes in a rare moment gave a smile and a quiet nod of approval to Elizabeth as she proceeded into the house with Avarilla.

It was a slow leisurely stroll for it was much too hot, even at 7:00 in the evening, for too much exertion. At the gravesite, Hayes placed a bouquet of flowers from Avarilla's garden on each of the graves, and at each, he knelt and spoke quietly. Mary Ann backed away slightly for she wasn't certain whether he was praying or talking quietly to his departed family. When he had finished, he stood up, walked toward her and looked directly in her eyes.

"Mary Ann, my dear, you have already become an important part of this family and have provided great comfort during these trying times. My daughters think of you as a sister and we all love little William. I hope you won't think it too forward of me, but you do need someone to look after you, and I..., I think,... I know I am the best equipped to do that."

Mary Ann wasn't certain exactly what was on his mind, but suspected he was about to propose marriage. Before she had time to think the issue through, the deed was done.

"Mary Ann, I propose that we marry, and," he quickly added, "I'll tell you why."

"It is in the best interest of you and your son, because a woman, especially one with a young child, cannot survive on her own."

He was ramping up his rate of speech as he spoke, and the old John Hayes, the one that was self-assured, pompous, and determined to take control of the situation emerged as he had on the first day when he had led her away from her husband's grave at the churchyard.

"Your husband's estate has been satisfactorily taken care of through my assistance and you and William have lived under my guardianship for the past seventeen months."

With that, and with a self-confident tilt of his head and a small bow, he took her hand and asked, "Madam, will you be my wife?

So...., she thought to herself, *that's why Avarilla had seemed so angry.* She had either known or at least suspected what her father was about to do. Mary Ann surmised that Elizabeth must also have suspected as much and subtly conveyed her approved. She pondered a moment, realizing that John Hayes was more like a father than a husband, but also realized that what he said was true. And she remembered her own silent promise to never be afraid of relying on her intelligence and determination for the benefit and survival of herself and her son. And just that quickly she made her decision.

"Yes, Mr. Hayes, I will."

"Good, We'll post the banns tomorrow." And with that he suddenly seemed younger, he practically beamed with pleasure and had a spry spring to his step as they made their way back towards Mount Hayes. Mary Ann was surprised by events of the past year and a half and also surprised that she and William were to be secure beyond her wildest dreams. She would now be Mistress of Mount Hayes, although she had her doubts that she was up to the task, but was equally confident that Elizabeth would assist her now as she had in the past. How Avarilla would respond to the news was quite another matter. Their relationship had been strained, to say the least, but she feared that now, it would turn vindictive. Although all of these thoughts flooded her mind, she was also aware that John Hayes must truly care for her. Unlike his previous wives who brought into the marriage extensive land holdings that enhanced his finances and status, she brought no such assets. Hayes's neighbors were well aware of his propensity for such choices and often referred to his plantation as "Hayes Ambition." This, of course, they did not say in his presence. She and William were about to embark on a new beginning. What would this new future hold?

Early the next morning, Elizabeth came to Mary Ann's room with an invitation to accompany the family to Sunday services. She carried with her one of her own cloaks and handed it to Mary Ann. Elizabeth helped to dress William, who now stood quite erect and who no longer resisted the stays which he wore under his shirt. Avarilla had explained to him that every person of good breeding, men, women, and children wore them their entire lives. It was what proper people did.

The trip to St. Paul's Church was somewhat of an ordeal since it was located south of Back River. Fortunately, John Borman, who, after serving his seven years of indenture to John Hayes, was hired by Hayes to operate a ferry on the north bank of Back River. It was a lucrative, and fortuitous venture since it provided ready transport for the Hayes household as well as for his neighbors. It was so successful that after only a year of operation, Hayes applied for and received authorization to open an ordinary to provide food and lodging for those in need of it.

On this particular occasion, Mary Ann, along with the rest of the household traveled in style in their carriage. When they reached the other side of the river, Henry was waiting with yet another carriage. This one, however, was somewhat crude, and could best be described as a cart. There were three benches that served as seats for the travelers. There were supports along the side that held in place an oilcloth covering, which had been constructed from homespun to which several coatings of boiled linseed oil had been applied to make it somewhat waterproof.

It was a very bumpy ride over equally bumpy roads, and the travelers were jarred and jolted the entire trip. Mary Ann began to wonder if walking the two miles might have been a better option. When they finally arrived at the church, Henry quickly brought a small wooden box, which worked as a step as the family climbed down. It was Henry's job to tend to the horses during the ceremony.

It was with a certain amount of trepidation that Mary Ann, holding William's hand, joined the Hayes family as they made their way to a pew in the front of the church. John Hayes stood aside to allow Elizabeth and Avarilla to file into the row first. Then, giving William a gentle push told him to sit by Avarilla. Mary Ann was surprised as he took her by the arm and guided her to sit by his side during the service. She was conscious of quizzical stares and whispered conversations going on around them. She felt embarrassed and uneasy.

Reverend Tibbs began the service with the expected ritual and order of scripture as prescribed by *The Book of Common Prayer*, and at the appropriate time read to the congregation the first of three required readings of the required announcement. Over the course of three months the banns would be published.

"I publish the banns of marriage between John Hayes of Saint Paul's Parish and Mary Ann Johnson, widow of Philip Johnson of this parish. If any of you know cause of just impediment why these persons should not be joined together in Holy Matrimony, ye are to declare it. This is the first time of asking."

Mary Ann actually held her breath in fear that Avarilla might officially declare her objections. She recalled quite clearly how resolute Avarilla could be when she put her mind to it. But, thankfully, her fears were unfounded and Reverend Tibbs proceeded with the service, which, as usual, was very long. Young William had fallen asleep on his mother's shoulder within the first hour, and Mary Ann was hopeful that he would remain asleep. This was not to be the case, however, and eventually he awoke and began to squirm. It was Avarilla's stern glare, a finger brandished under his nose in admonition, and a vigorous shaking of her head, which quieted the youngster into silent submission. Normally Mary Ann would have found her behavior annoying, for William was not much more than a baby, but today, she was relieved to not attract any additional unwanted attention to herself and her son.

When the service finally concluded, friends and neighbors clustered around with congratulatory good wishes. Everyone seemed genuinely happy for the couple. All except Avarilla, who immediately moved away from the group with the ever present, scowl upon her face.

John Hayes was in a particularly jubilant mood as Henry brought the carriage and prepared to help them aboard. Avarilla immediately stepped up and sat down in the carriage and looked expectantly at her father to join her. But he hesitated, and suggested that since the day was pleasant and the ground was dry, that perhaps Mary Ann might prefer a leisurely walk to the river. Both Elizabeth and Mary Ann were delighted with the suggestion and Hayes, lifting William to Avarilla, suggested that she take the child in the carriage and have something to eat at the

Ordinary while waiting. Clearly, Avarilla was unhappy, but did not know how to extricate herself from this unwanted situation. Henry smiled and flicked the whip across the flank of the horses as the carriage bounced even more vigorously across the uneven ground. Both Henry and William seemed to think it was great fun. Avarilla was not amused.

During their walk, Hayes was eager to share with Mary Ann his plans for the wedding. He had already made a mental list of the guests he planned to invite and could not restrain his urge to share the news that several bolts of fabric, including silk and brocade had arrived from England. With a somewhat sheepish sideward glance, he confided that, in anticipation of her acceptance of his proposal, he had placed the order several months earlier. He hoped that among them, both she and Elizabeth might find appealing fabrics from which their dresses for the wedding might be sewn. His eldest daughter, Jane, had offered the services of Mattie, one of her slaves who was an accomplished seamstress, to oversee the process. Elizabeth practically squealed with delight and gave her father an affectionate hug and kiss on the cheek. As usual, Mary Ann was overwhelmed and unsure of herself, but she was sincerely grateful. She, with an appreciative smile, took his hand, thanked him for his kindness and generosity, and assured him that she too was looking forward to their future.

CHAPTER 4
Matrimonial Preparations

*M*ount Hayes was a beehive of activity following the announcement that there would be two weddings. The first would be the marriage of Elizabeth to John Lenox the fourth week of October. That would be followed a month and one half later by the wedding of Mary Ann to John Hayes. Since the tobacco harvest was in, Isham agreed that he could spare as many slaves as were needed to assist with the preparations. Those men who were most skilled in carpentry and the best cooks and seamstresses, including those from other properties belonging to Hayes would be assigned to work on the events. Hayes fully expected that Avarilla would oversee most of the details, but insisted that both Elizabeth and Mary Ann should feel free to see that their own wishes were carried out. He assumed that Avarilla would be thrilled, but both Elizabeth and Mary Ann had their doubts about her response.

As they expected, Avarilla had a long list of objections. Her primary opposition had to do with the amount of work, not to mention money, required to carry out two weddings in such a short time. She insisted that it made far more sense to hold a double wedding. Both women understood her concerns, but both were equally hesitant. Double weddings were considered to be unlucky. The common superstition held that since a wedding was a joyful occasion, that the combination of two weddings on the same day would produce so much joy that it would be too big a temptation for the devil to ignore. Evil and wickedness were bound to prevail.

Molly was especially upset by the mere thought of inviting the devil into the house, and poor Henry was prepared for the worst. He retrieved the scarlet cloth with the feathered chicken foot from the cabinet where it had lain hidden since the last visit from Dr. Payne. He put it in the pocket of his shirt and carried it with him as a precaution.

Finally, John Hayes put his foot down, literally. He stormed into the room where his daughters and future wife were attending to their morning sewing, stood facing Avarilla, hands on hips, a scowl on his face matching that of his eldest daughter, stomped his right foot and announced:

"There will not be a double wedding! Elizabeth will marry John Lenox on Monday, October 20, three months to the day after the reading of their banns, as dictated by law. As the father of the bride, and the master of this house this is my will and thus it shall be!"

Then, with a nod to Avarilla, and a caustic smile, he asked, "Is that quite clear, Avarilla?"

The room was deathly quiet. Everyone, including Avarilla, stared wide-eyed at Hayes. They had seen him take charge of many situations, but not of this sort. Since the death of his wife Elizabeth, he had left household decisions to his eldest daughter. It was clear to everyone that things were going to be different.

Avarilla, visibly shaken, her jaw set in defiance, seemed unsure of just how to proceed. Finally, with a shrug of her shoulders, and a lowered head, she mumbled, "Whatever you wish."

"That's fine then," Hayes said, with a nod of his head. Then he walked to Elizabeth, took her by the hand and led her to the door, where he turned to once again look directly at Avarilla.

"I nearly forgot. If it meets with Mary Ann's approval, we will marry on January 6th. Twelfth Night, it seems to me, is the perfect time for a wedding."

He noted everyone's surprise, but was quick to add, "I realize that it will be beyond the required three months, but, as Avarilla has pointed out, there are so many preparations to be made, it is important to allow adequate time for the necessary planning."

"We will have a wonderful Christmas, followed by an equally wonderful wedding." Hayes gave a genuine smile to Mary Ann, who was nodding in agreement.

With that, it was settled. The servants were relieved to hear the news. Henry returned his protective talisman to its hiding place.

Later that afternoon, John Hayes summoned Isham and Henry to accompany him to Baltimore to bring the silken bounty back to Mount Hayes. Elizabeth and Mary Ann were giddy with excitement as they shared ideas about fabrics and dress patterns. Avarilla announced that she was going to her room to rest.

When the men returned with the much-anticipated fabrics, the women of the household, including Molly and her daughter Winny, couldn't wait to unwrap the treasured bolts of cloth. There were two bolts of everyday fabric: one of soft wool in a pale grey, and another of linsey-woolsey in dark blue. There were also five bolts of more elaborate, formal silk. Mary Ann had never seen such beautiful fabrics. There were bolts of silver, pink, ivory, pale blue, and gold, the pale blue immediately caught Mary Ann's eye, but she tried hard not to exhibit her preference. After all, Elizabeth was Hayes's daughter and her wedding was to be the first. It was only fitting that she should have first choice in the matter. Fortunately, Elizabeth's attention was immediately drawn to the beautiful silver colored silk with brocaded border of silver threads. She instructed Molly to help her unroll a portion of the bolt so that she might hold it up to her bodice. With a beaming smile, she asked, "What do you think?"

Everyone agreed that it was beautiful and a perfect choice. Elizabeth, ever mindful that there were two weddings to plan, looked at Mary Ann, and with a pained look, apologized for expressing her choice without consulting her. Mary Ann was quick to embrace Elizabeth and assure her that the silver was a perfect choice and added quickly that her own preference was for the blue. Again, both women laughed in delight. It was a wondrous, joyful moment. A moment not shared with Avarilla, who remained in her room throughout the day, only reappearing at the evening meal, during which she appeared to be lost in her own thoughts.

Avarilla was uncharacteristically quiet for the next few weeks. She no longer seemed involved in her usual household routine, and had little to say in the way of casual conversation to anyone. She offered no further objections to the proposed wedding plans, nor did she show any apparent interest in the preparations. It appeared she had accepted her limited role in decision-making regarding the upcoming nuptials. But as Mary Ann was well aware, appearances could be deceiving.

There was so much work to be done, but fortunately there were plenty of willing hands to help. Just one week after Hayes's declaration, his daughter, Jane arrived with her seamstress, Mattie. Accompanying Jane was Samuel Page, one of the finest tailors in Baltimore. Their carriage was also carrying a collection of fine wool and heavily brocaded silk. Jane was quick to explain that the tailor was there to take measurements of her father and the fabrics were to be fashioned into a coat, waistcoat and breeches in the latest style. She felt strongly that it was important that her father be well dressed for the occasion. Seeing young William still wearing a dress, which was typical attire for boys his age, Jane suggested that since he would be five by the time of the wedding, it might be the perfect occasion for him to graduate to breeches, like a young gentleman.

Everyone seemed to think it was a wonderful idea. Everyone except Mary Ann, who was hesitant to see her baby boy dressed as a miniature adult. Hayes saw the hesitation in her demeanor, but quickly assured her that this was the appropriate thing to do. She agreed to the plan, but in her heart, she wanted William to remain her little boy.

Avarilla continued to distance herself from the bustle of activity surrounding the additions to the wardrobe of various family members. Mary Ann felt bad for her, and she blamed herself for the rejection that Avarilla was experiencing. She approached Elizabeth with her concerns and, as she suspected, Elizabeth felt equally concerned about her sister. Together they approached Hayes and expressed their worries. Hayes was amenable to any ideas they suggested to bring Avarilla out of her apparent depression. Elizabeth and Mary Ann both agreed that since there were three bolts of cloth that had not yet been touched, Avarilla should have a new gown for the festivities as well. Hayes was only too willing to permit whatever actions might restore harmony to the household.

At first Avarilla insisted that she did not need, nor did she wish to have a new gown, since she was far too busy to be bothered with such nonsense. The "too busy" part was somewhat confusing since she had basically refrained from all of her normal duties, leaving them to the skilled efforts of Molly. But Elizabeth was determined and taking her sister by the hand insisted that she at least look at the fabrics. Elizabeth noted that the event would bring all of their neighbors to join in the festivities and that there were several widowers to be in attendance. With a reassuring smile, she reminded Avarilla that nothing catches a man's attention better than a beautiful woman dressed in bewitching finery. It seemed a strange approach to Mary Ann, for she had assumed that Avarilla, had resigned herself to her fate as a woman doomed to spinsterhood. Further, it had not occurred to her that this woman with the limp and dour disposition might still harbor hopes of finding a husband. It was a revelation when Avarilla gave an understanding nod and hastened her pace toward the sewing room.

There were three bolts of the silk remaining. These included the pink, the ivory and the pale gold. Avarilla, who had avoided the room like the plague, and therefore had no idea of the choices made by the two brides to be, immediately moved to the gold cloth and her face betrayed her words when she announced, "I suppose, if I must, this would be adequate."

Both Mary Ann and Elizabeth were delighted with this new change of events. Surely this would make things far more enjoyable for everyone. Elizabeth immediately motioned to Mattie and instructed her to take her sister's measurements and to help her decide upon a pattern. Avarilla continued to pretend that she was being coerced in to this new turn of events, but it was clear to all that she was pleased.

It was shortly after this that John Hayes made an unexpected visit to the room. He seemed quite happy with the progress and asked what decisions had been made regarding the various bolts of cloth. Seeing that there were three bolts left, the pink, and ivory silk and the two bolts of everyday wool, he smiled at Mary Ann and announced, "You have been wearing Jane's dresses for quite long enough. See to it that the remaining fabric, is used for yourself."

Mary Ann was dumb struck. She was surprised and happy to have dresses from the less formal fabric. It would be a unique experience to have garments made just for her. But, she wondered, what on earth would she ever do with two such elegant, formal gowns in addition to the one for her wedding? Hayes smiled at her apparent bewilderment and reminded her that there would surely be several balls and parties given by their neighbors and they would attend them all. He fully intended that his neighbors would see his prosperity in the beauty of his new wife. This was a life that Mary Ann could never have imagined in her wildest dreams. It all seemed too good to be true.

The month of September seemed to fly by. Sewing preparations had been moved to the lower floor since the number of slaves assigned to the various tasks of cutting, sewing and fitting had grown to more than a dozen. The skirt of Elizabeth's dress would be open in the front to reveal a petticoat in matching fabric beneath. When the gown was finished, Elizabeth was surprised to learn that Winny had quilted the matching petticoat. The quilting was done in a beautiful leaf and flower design, and expertly crafted. Winny's status as a seamstress was suddenly elevated, and the young girl smiled proudly as the women complimented her work. Avarilla admitted that it was quite pretty, but expressed her disappointment that Winny had been neglecting her household duties in order to produce the petticoat.

Then it was time for the unveiling of the finished gown. Everyone gasped as Elizabeth tried on the gown, which billowed out with graceful fullness thanks to the new petticoat. Elizabeth was a truly beautiful bride. Even Avarilla smiled in appreciation of her sister's beauty.

On Friday, October 17, three days before Elizabeth's wedding, the women went down to the room where the dresses were in the final stage of completion. Avarilla's gown was finished and all nodded their approval. It fit Avarilla to perfection and the graceful flow of the gown seemed to hide the ever-present limp. Or, perhaps, Avarilla was making a special effort to move more gracefully across the floor. Whatever the cause, it was a decided improvement, but for some reason, Avarilla seemed disappointed. She acknowledged that the silk was beautiful, but was disappointed that it looked plain in comparison to Elizabeth's gown. Everyone was quick to reassure her that the gown was perfect as it was. Winny offered to take the dress to Avarilla's room, and Avarilla nodded her permission.

At dinner later that evening, the conversation was animated with talk of the wedding and the grand feast Molly was preparing. It was a happy scene as even the women partook of a small serving of potent hard cider, while Hayes consumed more than his usual amount of rum. It was clear to all that he was intoxicated. Nonetheless, it was one of the happiest occasions Mary Ann could remember. But once again, their mood would be dampened by an unexpected tragedy.

Shortly after leaving the table, Mary Ann went to retrieve William who was being entertained by Henry and Molly. She climbed the stairs and turned down the hall. As she arrived at the door of her room, she was startled by a cry from Avarilla's room down the hall. She, along with the rest of the household, rushed to see what was wrong. Avarilla was standing in the center of her room staring at her beautiful golden gown with an expression of bewilderment. In response to everyone's questions she held the gown out for all to see. There was a triangular piece missing from the bodice. It appeared to have been torn from the dress. Everyone was speechless. What had happened? Who could have done such a thing? It was a mystery with no apparent solution.

John Hayes was furious. He immediately summoned Isham to bring into the back room of the house, all those slaves, men and women, who had been working inside the house during the day. He called to Molly, Henry and Winny and began to question them about anything they might have seen. All proclaimed their innocence and denied any knowledge of how this crime had happened. He demanded an immediate search of the house. Isham and Molly immediately left the room to carry out his wishes. It was less than ten minutes when Molly re-entered the room. She was carrying the missing fabric that had been ripped from Avarilla's gown. Molly was pale with fright as she handed the torn fragment to Hayes.

"Where did you find this?" he demanded.

Molly began to sob uncontrollably and began shaking her head slowly from side to side.

"Stop this wailing immediately and tell me where you found this." Hayes demanded.

"Massa, please, please......" Her response was halted with even greater sobs and pleas.

"Nonsense, tell me now, or by all that is holy I will whip you where you stand!" Hayes screamed at the terrified slave, his face red with anger and the veins on his forehead pulsating with his fury.

With that, Hayes slapped her across the face with the back of his hand, causing Molly to fall to the floor. Isham, having returned upon hearing the commotion hurried toward his wife. But before he could reach her, Hayes moved to the fireplace and from the small case on the mantel removed a pistol and pointed it directly at Isham.

"You take one more step, and I will shoot you both," Hayes threatened.

Mary Ann was frightened, and little William's eyes were wide as saucers as he whimpered and clung to his mother's skirt. She had never seen anyone this angry before, let alone threaten to kill someone. This was a side of John Hayes that she had never seen before.

Molly struggled to her feet and held up her hand toward Isham to not interfere.

"I tore de dress, Massa."

"Why on God's earth would you do that? Haven't I always treated you well? You have always been a part of this family. How could you do such a thing? And why?"

Molly was still sobbing and shaking her head, finally managing to whisper, "I be sorry Massa, no do noting bad. Da tred it be loos. I try to fix, but it tear. I be sorry."

Even Mary Ann knew that her explanation was implausible. She had seen the care with which the dresses had been sewn and there was no way that type of tear could have occurred accidentally due to a tug on a loose thread.

Hayes was now so angry that he was shaking with rage. He ordered Isham to fetch a whip. Isham started to shake his head no, but Hayes again raised the pistol and pulled the trigger and the bullet sped past Isham's right ear.

"I am an expert marksman. My next bullet will take your life, now fetch that whip."

"Isham turned to go, but before he could exit the room, Winny, who was now sobbing uncontrollably, came towards Hayes and meekly said, "*Duppy* man do it."

Molly rushed to her daughter, but Winny said, "*Devil Duppy* man tear dress."

Elizabeth went to Winny and in as calm a voice as she could manage assured her that there were no devil ghosts in the house.

Elizabeth put her arm around the sobbing girl as she spoke: "Winny, just tell us what happened." She had spent quite a lot of time teaching Winny to read and in trying to convince her that there was no black magic or voodoo evil in the house.

After a few more moments Winny calmed herself and began again. "I no tear dress of Mistress Avarilla. I find the piece of cloth. I be frightened. I don't know what to do. I hide it because I be afraid. Must be Duppy man! Ghost do bad thing."

"Nonsense," shouted Hayes. "You are guilty, and now that you are caught, you continue to lie. Where did you find it?"

Winny, in desperation, held out her hands to Isham and pleaded, "Please Da Da, I no lie. I find in sewing room when I go clean." And the tears and sobs erupted again.

The entire room was now a madhouse of confusion. Everyone had an opinion, yet no one really understood what had happened or why. Hayes insisted that the girl had to be punished. It was unthinkable to have untrustworthy slaves living in the house. Hayes was adamant that harsh punishment was the only course of action.

Surprisingly, Avarilla stepped forward and, with a calm voice, gave her own deductions regarding the incident.

"Winny is young, it is only normal that she would admire the dress. She no doubt, wanted to try it on and, in her carelessness, tore the bodice. Not knowing what to do, and fearing harsh punishment, she hid it. It was a moment of weakness and the child succumbed to the devil's temptation. Thank goodness it was only my dress that was damaged and not one of the wedding gowns. The Christian thing to do is to forgive her. Of course, I do believe some sort of punishment is necessary. My recommendation would be that she not be permitted anywhere near the wedding celebration.

There was stunned silence in the room. This was a new side of Avarilla to which they were not accustomed. But, before that thought could register itself, Avarilla asserted the expected side of her nature. She moved toward Winny, who shrank back fearing that the worst might not be over. With her sternest of expressions and severest tone she cautioned the young girl.

"Be assured that if you ever dare do anything so hateful and destructive again, you will suffer the whip from my own hand without mercy! Do you understand?"

Winny nodded vigorously and began to back away, as Avarilla turned her back to speak to Hayes.

"And besides, I'm certain Mattie can do something creative to mend it in time for the wedding, perhaps some beautiful embroidery would do the trick."

Everyone was dumbstruck. Avarilla was the last person in the world they would have expected to be not only forgiving, but also, well, optimistic. It was a revelation.

Almost as quickly as it had begun, the crisis was averted, tempers calmed, and although Isham, Molly, and Winny were still frightened, they were relieved, but utterly confused.

Henry who had stood in the hallway peeking around the door, immediately headed for his room. If ever he needed protection from evil, it was now. He retrieved the scarlet cloth from its hiding place, found a long cord and tied it around the neck of the bundle and then placed it around his neck under his shirt. He made a silent vow to always keep the talisman around his neck. A duppy man was something to be feared, especially if he was lurking in the house with a sharp weapon. He looked around his room with fearful trepidation and clutched the fabric of his shirt to make certain that his protective magic was still with him. He made his way down the hall toward the voices of his parents who were talking with Winny.

Despite repeated assurances from Elizabeth that she would not be whipped for the incident, Winny steadfastly denied having done the deed. She continued to insist that she had found the piece of fabric when she was folding left over silks in the sewing room, and being frightened, had put it back where she found it. Molly and Isham tried their best to comfort her, but were at a loss to understand what had transpired.

Molly was convinced that her daughter was telling the truth, but could think of no possible answer to the mystery except an evil plan carried out through the use of black magic by someone who wished misfortune upon the household. She went to work immediately to summon all her knowledge of protective potions and spells. Isham, Winny and Henry sat quietly against the wall as Molly began swaying back and forth slowly while chanting the ancient words she had learned as a child in Jamaica. For the moment, there was nothing else they could do, except stay together in their room. It was a restless, sleepless night for the household.

Early the next morning, Mattie was summoned to begin the repair on Avarilla's dress. When she arrived, Avarilla took her upstairs where the gown was lying on the bed. Alongside it was another dress, also of gold silk, but in a slightly darker shade. The second dress appeared to be quite old and showed signs of wear, with many stains and small tears in the skirt. Avarilla explained to Mattie that the dress had belonged to her mother, but had been stored away in a trunk since her mother's death. Avarilla pointed to the stomacher, or triangular panel that filled the center portion of the dress. As was the custom at the time, it had been highly decorated with embroidery and beadwork of small jewels and a small bow of black velvet adorned the top edge.

"I think the stomacher would do quite nicely as a repair for my dress. I know it is a shade darker, but with the embroidery I think it will be quite suitable. What do you think Mattie?"

Mattie nodded and smiled in agreement. It certainly would provide ample fabric to cover the torn area of the new garment and, actually simplified the task of repairing it. She also noted that it was fortunate that the stomacher covered the missing area so perfectly.

As expected, Mattie performed the transforming miracle within a couple of hours. The repaired dress, now resplendent with the new intricate details, was certain to be the most beautiful of all the dresses. Avarilla was pleased.

The following Monday, invited guests comprised of the entire congregation of St. Paul's Parish, arrived at Mount Hayes for the wedding ceremony. Reverend Tibbs wore the customary white robe with a red stole hanging around his neck and down the front of his shoulders. The service began mid-morning as was required for such an occasion whether held in church or in the home. Several of the field slaves were assigned to handle the horses and carriages of the guests. The connecting doors between the two large rooms immediately to the right of the front door were thrown open to accommodate the many guests, all of whom were dressed in their finest attire. When the guests had all been greeted, they found seats, where available, although many had to stand. Reverend Tibbs began the service by inviting the family members of the couple who were to be married to join him at the front of the room. He instructed the couple to stand together, hand in hand with the man standing to the right and the woman on the left.

As Elizabeth and her betrothed moved toward the front of the room they were met with the smiling faces and admiring glances of their friends. Reverend Tibbs began by reading the prescribed service from *The Anglican Book of Common Prayer:*

Dearly beloved, we are gathered together here in the sight of God, and in the face of this congregation, to join together this Man and this Woman in holy Matrimony.

Mary Ann knew the rest by heart and, although happy for Elizabeth, she felt a sudden chill, and feared she might begin to cry, as memories of her own wedding to Phillip rushed from the recesses of her mind in a moment of almost unbearable sadness.

She was lost in those memories throughout most of the ceremony. It was only near the end that she mentally rejoined the event. It was that part of the service where wives were reminded of their proper role in marriage. Reverend Tibbs quoted Saint Peter's instruction saying, *"Ye wives, be in subjection to your own husbands."* As she recalled many saintly men held the same opinion.

Immediately following the ceremony, guests crowded around the couple to offer their congratulations and good wishes. Meanwhile the doors between the adjoining rooms across the hall had also been thrown open and William Barney, a skilled fiddle player began to play in the next room as people moved next door to enjoy the music.

There was much to be done to prepare the room for dining. Long tables were moved into the two rooms on the right side of the hallway where the ceremony had been held. The benches were moved to the sides of the cloth-covered tables upon which the finest china was used for the table settings. The center portion of each table was quickly laden with large bowls and trays of steaming food brought from the outside kitchens by women slaves wearing their new white aprons. There were large platters heaped with venison, turkey, mutton, oysters, blue crab, and a pot of steaming mussels, as well as bowls of pudding, tarts and vegetables. The slaves were happy to be present at this great feast and knew that they would be permitted to enjoy whatever food was left over. All except for Winny, she had been ordered to remain in the kitchen the entire day.

It was expected that an abundance of alcohol would be served throughout the day. Many of the guests, particularly the men, felt that alcohol was to be imbibed for a variety of reasons. It could cure the sick, strengthen the weak, and generally make the world a better place. At events such as this, they toasted, and drank from dawn to dark. John Hayes had spared no expense and he was happy that his daughter had just married well and had a fine future ahead of her. He was also happy about his upcoming wedding to Mary Ann. He felt he was a lucky man, indeed, and he planned to celebrate his good fortune with generous portions of rum.

When everything was ready for the meal, Hayes invited them to return to the room across the hall and began the meal with a blessing by Reverend Tibbs and the first of many toasts, followed by a large, delicious meal prepared to perfection.

When the feast was concluded the guests again moved across the hall where the fiddler had again begun to play. Around the perimeter of the room were small tables surrounded by chairs. Occupying some were men who began to play the card game whist. Other tables were available for those awaiting a partner to dance a reel or the minuet, or by those who just preferred to watch.

MaryAnn was quite surprised when John Hayes took Elizabeth by the hand and led her to the dance floor in the next room. She was also surprised to see that John Hayes was surprisingly light on his feet and was an excellent dancer. Elizabeth, as Mary Ann would have predicted, moved around the room as though she were floating. At the end of the minuet, John Lenox bowed to his new bride and father in law and offered his hand to Elizabeth. They, along with several other young couples lined up to dance another minuet. Hayes approached Mary Ann, but with an embarrassed shake of her head and a shrug of her shoulders told him that she did not know these dances. She asked if perhaps he might teach them to her before their marriage. She had danced with Phillip before, but only country-dances that seemed raucous and undisciplined by comparison. The entire scene seemed magical to her. She had never seen so many elegant gowns but she felt equally elegant, in the brand new pink gown with white lace at the bodice and sleeves. She was saving the pale blue for her wedding.

After a few hours of dancing, the servants brought in a small table upon which rested the two wedding cakes. The bride and groom were served first, followed by portions set before each of the married guests. The cake was a rich spice cake filled with dried raisins, currants, citron and nuts and a generous amount of alcohol. The second cake, which would be served to the unmarried guests, was exactly the same type as the first, but hidden within was a nutmeg seed. The belief was that the person who received a serving, which contained the nutmeg, would be the next to be married. The lucky recipient on this occasion was Avarilla Hayes. Probably, the only other person in the room who was happier with this fortunate turn of events was her father. Perhaps the fates were indeed smiling upon him.

As for Avarilla, she beamed with pleasure, and did her best to take a limp free stroll across the room to say hello to the widower, Thomas Harris. Mary Ann noted that he was as handsome as she had remembered and was surprised when he excused himself from Avarilla's presence and walked to the table where she and Hayes were sitting. He congratulated them on their upcoming wedding and wished them a very happy future. With that, he took the hand of his fifteen-year-old daughter, Rachel, who was sitting with some young friends at a nearby table, and joined the dancers on the floor. Avarilla appeared first surprised, then crestfallen, by this apparent rebuff of her overtures to the handsome widower. Finally, regaining her composure, her head held high, and the familiar stern expression on her face, she hurried out of the room with her usual pronounced limp. Mary Ann felt sorry for her, but suspected it would be pointless to try to talk to her when she was in one of her moods. It was fortunate that the other guests were so engrossed in their merry-making that they seemed to have not noticed Avarilla's discomfort.

The celebration lasted long into the morning hours and many of the guests had to be helped into their carriages by the slaves who had accompanied them. Mary Ann suspected, that despite the uneven and bumpy roadway, most would sleep through the entire journey back to their plantations, and would likely suffer the next day for their excesses.

It took over a week for the house to be put back in order. The cleanup was time consuming, as expected. An abundance of alcohol and a lack of self-control had resulted in clumsy spills and broken dishes. Fortunately, nearly all of the alcohol was served in pewter, but it was necessary to make sure it was cleaned properly after use.

At church the following Sunday, Hayes received high praise for the magnificent celebration they had all enjoyed. It seemed to him that his status in the community had risen considerably in the eyes of his neighbors. They could see that he was prosperous and knew how to host a sumptuous party. He graciously accepted the many accolades, and elaborated on how much he had enjoyed seeing so many of his old friends. He cleverly mentioned how he was looking forward to Christmas and the opportunity to join his neighbors in their holiday celebrations. He announced to all that they should be prepared for the next celebration at Mount Hayes, to be held on Twelfth Night when he would marry Mary Ann, the widowed mother of his ward, William Johnson. His friends and neighbors congratulated him again on his good fortune, and realized that Hayes was expecting a *quid pro quo* for his hospitality.

Since the women's dresses were complete, it was time to devote attention to Hayes's wardrobe as well. Henry was sent to summon the tailor, Samuel Page, for the final fittings. Page brought with him two shirts of fine linen to be paired with a cravat of white lace trimmed silk. There was a pair of silk stockings, two pairs of satin breeches, one in black and the second in light tan, a waistcoat of heavy brocaded tan satin, and two coats. The first coat was black from fine wool with gold buttons, and the second was burgundy brocade with silver buttons. Hayes planned to wear the black for his wedding. The final item, time permitting, would be a cloak for severe weather. It would be of heavy wool, decorated with gold filigree and buttons appropriate for a man of his station.

There were also similar items for young William. Page had made a pair of brown wool breeches for everyday wear, and a second pair of pale tan satin for special occasions. He would also have a coat of red velvet and a waistcoat of tan brocaded satin, and of course a white shirt, but no cravat.

Mary Ann had reservations about putting a child this young into garments of such elegant fabric, but she had to admit that she was pleased with how handsome her little boy looked in the new garments. This change in attire meant, of course, that he had entered a new stage in his life and would no longer be considered a baby.

Hayes had not forgotten Mary Ann's desire to learn the formal steps of the dances she had seen at Elizabeth's wedding. He surprised her in early November with the announcement that he had hired a tutor for young William who also happened to be a skilled dance master. He was to arrive the week before Thanksgiving to begin schooling for William and dance instruction for mother and son. Mary Ann couldn't believe how much her life had changed in such a short while. She could never have imagined that she would live in a fine house, with servants to do the work, and opportunities for her son that would never have been possible were it not for the kindness of John Hayes. The man could be so kind and generous, but she had witnessed the rage and violence that could erupt at a moment's notice. It was this dark side of his nature that was troubling.

CHAPTER 5
Murderous Intentions

As promised, the tutor and dance master, Nicholas Buckley of Philadelphia arrived Monday, November 12. After being shown to his room on the upper floor, he asked to see the room where he was to conduct the lessons. They accompanied him to the library. He was not satisfied with the arrangement of the furniture, which was covered with the various sewing endeavors that occupied much of the women's time. Avarilla, with Mary Ann's help, began to move their projects into one corner of the room and instructed Henry to get help and to move the furniture into the desired configuration. Henry called his sister Winny, and the two did as they were told.

As soon as they had finished the task, they left the room and immediately went to find Molly. Both Winny and Henry had huge grins on their faces as they described the new tutor.

Henry couldn't wait to tell his mother about Master Buckley, which was the way he expected to be addressed. Henry did an imitation of the man as he stepped around the room, flicking his handkerchief in disdain at everything in sight. Both Isham and Molly laughed as Henry enacted the man's animated style of constantly moving his hands in a weak, limp wristed manner as he spoke.

Winny nodded in agreement and concluded that the man held himself in a very high opinion. They all agreed that they hoped they wouldn't have to spend too much time in his presence.

It was the first time that there had been a formal teacher in the household and daughters Jane and Elizabeth along with their husbands had been invited to meet the new tutor. Jane was hoping that, if they found the new tutor to be acceptable, her two oldest sons, eight-year-old John and five-year-old Thomas, might benefit from instruction by the tutor as well.

At dinner that evening, Nicholas Buckley was invited to join the family at their table. At first it appeared that he intended to sit at the head of the table, but Hayes was a man clearly in control of his household. As they entered the room, Hayes put his hand on the man's arm and in his most authoritative voice stated, "Buckley, you will wait for me to take my place at the head of the table. Mary Ann, my betrothed, will sit at the other end of the table. My daughter, Jane will sit on my right, my daughter Elizabeth will sit on my left and their husbands shall sit beside their wives. Avarilla will sit to the right of John Lenox. Young William will join us at the table for the first time and Buckley you will sit opposite your pupil and see to his deportment."

Nicholas Buckley was clearly not happy with the arrangement and stated that he was not accustomed to being treated as a servant.

"Servants do not eat at the table with us, but you are in my employ and you will sit where you are told and when you are told."

Hayes continued, "Now, Mr. Buckley, if you would be so kind as to give the blessing."

Nicholas Buckley was, for the first time in his life, unsure of just what to say and clearly expected to be treated as an equal. Hayes made it just as clear, that he determined the rules in his household and Buckley had better learn to accept that.

"Of course," he muttered and began what would be his nightly reciting of the blessing from the *Book of Common*

Prayer: "Bless O Lord this food to our use and us to thy loving service; and keep us ever mindful of the needs of others. Amen."

Following the choral response of "Amen," Hayes sat down and motioned for the others to sit as well.

At first there was an uneasy silence around the table. This was uncharted territory for them all. It was the first instance since Mary Ann's arrival in the household that Hayes had insisted upon prayer before the meal, or that he had been rigid regarding where his family sat. He, of course, always sat at the head of the table, but his daughters normally sat where they pleased, and this was the first time that she had been seated in the place of honor as a family member. William's acceptance at the table was equally unexpected. But quickly enough, conversation resumed and the evening was pleasant. The women chatted about Elizabeth's wedding and the plans for the next.

William was more than a little uncomfortable. He was wearing his new breeches and was frightened lest he spill food on them. He got a disapproving frown and shake of the head from his Aunt Rilla when he made slurping noises while eating his soup. At which point, Hayes commanded Buckley to see that the boy learned proper table manners. "That is as important a part of your job as the learning of his letters and how to read, and of course," he added, "lessons in dance."

Near the end of the meal, Jane broached the subject of bringing her sons to join William in his lessons. Everyone thought this was a grand idea and Hayes suggested that his grandsons should spend their weekdays at Mount Hayes and return home for their weekends. Mary Ann was delighted by this turn of events for it would be wonderful for William to have the opportunity to spend time with children, especially boys near his own age. Hayes was quick to add that Buckley would be paid for the additional students. It was quite clear from the expression on Buckley's face, that he feared he might have committed himself to a less than desirable position. Unfortunately, it had been the only one offered to him and he would have to make the best of it.

Early the next morning, immediately after the morning meal, Jane and her husband brought their sons, John and Thomas to Mount Hayes. As Mary Ann was accompanying William to the parlor for morning instructions, she was delighted to see Jane and her two boys standing at the doorway to the morning room. They entered the room together.

Nicholas Buckley was seated at a table in front of one of the large windows and three empty chairs had been drawn up around the table. Buckley motioned to the boys to sit. It soon became obvious that the chairs were too low for William and Thomas, since they could hardly see the top of the table. John being three years older could manage nicely. Jane immediately went to one of the chests, which were filled with various fabrics and yarns. She selected two pieces of soft wool, and folded each in half, then again, and again until it provided adequate height to elevate the seat for each of the two boys. Once this was accomplished, Buckley, with a flick of his wrist made a dismissive signal that Mary Ann and Jane were to leave the room.

"The young masters do not require the hovering concerns of their mothers. They are here to learn, and learn they shall."

Both William and Thomas appeared frightened, and even eight-year-old John appeared uneasy with this new development. Mary Ann was more than a little reluctant to leave them alone with the strange man, but Jane smiled and suggested that this was exactly the sort of thing the boys needed. Hesitatingly, she gave William a kiss, told him to do as his tutor told him, and the two women left the room.

Mary Ann and Jane went to join Avarilla and Hayes in the parlor kitchen. The time passed slowly for Mary Ann and after what seemed like an eternity, she heard Buckley's voice as his door opened, and gave parting instructions.

"You must practice the letters I have shown you. I expect you to have mastered these few by the time we meet again tomorrow morning for your lessons."

Mary Ann assumed that this would be the extent of the day's work with the schoolmaster, but soon realized that there was a lot more to come.

"I shall expect to see you back in my room after our dinner. We will then begin instruction in the dance. I understand, Master William, that your mother will need instruction as well."

The boys then walked down the hall to the parlor kitchen where the family was awaiting their mid-day meal. As usual dinner was the biggest meal of the day, while supper would be a much lighter fare. When Hayes entered the room and took his place at the head of the table, everyone stood and with a nod of his head toward Buckley, the tutor gave the blessing. Hayes was pleased with how smoothly things seemed to be going. Since Elizabeth and her husband had spent the night, and Jane and her husband were there, he suggested that they all might enjoy observing the dancing lessons. Although Buckley had not anticipated so large a group, he was nonetheless delighted to have the opportunity to exhibit his expertise in the complexities of dance. It would be his time to shine.

The boys were especially hungry and tried to adhere to the constant corrections being made regarding their table manners. They quickly learned that there were lots of rules, and Buckley was kept busy enforcing them throughout the meal. They were not to speak unless spoken to. They were not to eat too fast, but not so slowly that others had to wait for them. They were not to lean their elbow on the table. They were not to make any noise with their tongue, mouth, lips or breath when eating or drinking. William decided that eating at the table with the adults was not going to be as enjoyable as it had been with Molly.

A short while after finishing their meal, William Barney, the fiddle player arrived and the entire family returned to the library to observe the dancing lesson.

Here, Buckley was clearly in his element. He had ordered Henry to bring a sufficient number of chairs for the adults. William, John and Thomas were expected to stand, as did Buckley. He addressed the assembled group beginning with a low, elegant bow, and began with a well-rehearsed lecture, which he read from the introduction to his eighty-three page engraved book regarding the importance of dance.

Every gentleman or lady who is desirous of performing dances in a genteel, free, and easy manner, must by necessity be first duly qualified in a minuet. The minuet is a beautiful dance so well calculated and adapted as to give room for every person to display all the beauties and graces of the body, which becomes a genteel carriage. As this dance is the groundwork of all other dancing, I think it my duty to recommend you have knowledge of it.

And with that, he took a position in the center of the room, and instructed the boys to stand facing him. The lesson began with a bow, since the dance always began and ended with a dignified and graceful bow to ones partner. Both William and Thomas tried their best but their attempts were anything but graceful. Buckley found fault with their posture, the awkwardness of their arms, the duration of the bow, and the unsteadiness of their feet. It was not an auspicious beginning. Even John was criticized repeatedly.

Eventually, Buckley instructed the fiddler to begin to play, and after asking for a volunteer to join him on the floor, Elizabeth complied.

As they danced, Buckley explained the dance. Mary Ann felt overwhelmed, for although he obviously felt that his explanations were simple, to her they only confused her more.

As he led Elizabeth in the intricacies of the minuet he described their movements, "The minuet is comprised of a basic, but complex step, unlike other dances composed of a string of different steps. A couple move with four steps to six beats and move together on a symmetrical track using the entire dance space. This is followed by parallel passes across the floor and one and two hand turns."

"Of course," he explained, "the most important thing is to make it look effortless and graceful."

Buckley and Elizabeth repeated the steps and the explanation and, naturally, they performed it expertly. Mary Ann had her doubts that either she or the boys would ever be able to master the minuet before the wedding. The next few weeks, she decided, were going to be a challenge.

With the beginning of December, a sense of urgency overtook the household. There were so many preparations, including the slaughter of pigs. Since December was normally a chilly month, it was the perfect time. Once again, Henry enjoyed explaining the process to Mary Ann. It was a time consuming task, although not particularly labor intensive, and women did much of the work necessary during the curing process.

After the pigs were slaughtered, the fresh cuts of meat were packed in wooden tubs of course salt for nearly two weeks to allow the salt to draw most of the water from the flesh. The second step was to hang the salted meats in the smokehouse. The smoke house at Mount Hayes was located next to the kitchen, and like most such structures was a wooden shed, without windows or a flue. A fire pit in the center of the structure must be allowed to smolder for one to two weeks. The result is dried, long-lasting, smoke-flavored meat that ages in the same smokehouse for two years before it is eaten. Consequently, the hams, bacon, jowls and fatback that they now enjoyed had been smoked earlier.

Clearly, there was a lot of work necessary to maintain such a large plantation. Hayes was lucky to have Molly and Isham and their children to see that things ran smoothly. It was unfortunate that the lingering memory of the incident with Avarilla's dress was ever present in the back of Mary Ann's mind. As the date neared for her own wedding approached, she was apprehensive that some new evil might be thrust upon them. She had never believed that Winny was the culprit, but was at a loss to understand who could have been to blame. She was ashamed of her suspicion that Avarilla, herself, might have done the deed to warrant the addition of the highly decorated stomacher to the gown. The changes had indeed, made the dress more elegant.

Her three silk gowns now hung in a wardrobe in her room and it had become a compulsion to check daily to make sure that they were still undamaged. She planned to wear the ivory gown for Christmas and Winny had fashioned a long red brocaded satin sash to wear around her waist. She was excited to wear it, but was still doubtful that she would be ready to dance the minuet with Hayes, but was determined to be skilled enough by their wedding to dance the first dance with her new husband.

Hayes had, apparently, been aware of Mary Ann's worry about the garments, and unbeknownst to her, had hired Dominicus Stang, a well-respected local blacksmith to produce a padlock for the wardrobe in her room. Stang arrived near the end of the first week in December and installed the lock. She was pleased and surprised that Hayes had recognized her fears, or perhaps he harbored worries of his own.

William and the other boys were progressing, slowly but surely with their lessons, but dance was still proving to be difficult. As for Mary Ann, she loved the dance lessons, but feared she would never match the grace and poise of Elizabeth.

There had been several invitations to Christmas parties, and one to a ball to be given by Jane and her husband Thomas Stansbury. Hayes accepted all invitations and the household was bustling with their own plans for the holiday season.

Avarilla was in an unusually good mood when she announced her plans to decorate Mount Hayes for the holidays. She sent Henry to gather boughs of pine and spruce, and any plants that still had berries as well as sprigs of holly, and bay leaves. Molly reminded her son to bring in as much mistletoe as he could find.

Molly was pleased that there was quite a bundle that she arranged into large clusters tied with red bows. These she hung throughout the house. It was a widely held belief that the plant helped to ward off evil spirits and promised the fertility of a coming spring. She was still fearful that the dreaded evil ghost might reappear and bring mischief to the household.

Avarilla was amused by Molly's fears, but acknowledged that the mistletoe added a festive touch. She arranged some of the greenery into wreaths, which were hung as decoration. Everyone seemed lighthearted and enthusiastic about the upcoming events.

Mary Ann and Phillip had never really celebrated Christmas. They went to church, of course, but as for decorating their cottage, it had not occurred to them. They were so preoccupied with daily chores and the ever-present concern to have sufficient food for survival. But those days were just a distant memory and Mary Ann was grateful that her son would have a better life than she could have imagined.

There were many preparations in the Hayes household. Avarilla explained that it was the custom to provide rum to the slaves, and often, extra food and to permit them to hold whatever celebrations they might want on their own. These often included singing and dancing in the slave quarters. Avarilla explained that it was far better to provide food and rum in abundance to keep the slaves happy on the plantation and discourage the thought of running away.

In addition to their normal fare, there was also mincemeat pies, cakes, special jellies and brandied peaches prepared by Molly and her helpers as well as rum punch, wine and brandy and the usual Christmas staple, Wassail, a hot mulled cider.

After their evening meal, everyone decided to retire early, for they would have a long and exciting day tomorrow to attend the ball given at Stansbury's Inheritance, the residence of Jane and her husband. Hayes asked Mary Ann to join him in the front parlor by the fireplace while he enjoyed his usual flagon of rum before bed. Mary Ann was happy to do so and Avarilla volunteered to get William into bed.

After tending to William, Avarilla went to her room. Certainly, she thought, she had proven her skill in running the household. Surely her father could acknowledge the extraordinary efforts she had taken to make Mount Hayes cheerful and inviting. But as usual, her efforts were ignored. Her father was determined to marry again. She realized that it was what was expected of him for a husband was necessary for a women to survive. Why then, did he seem so callous and unaware of his own daughter's welfare? She concluded that she had only one option. She would have to take matters into her own hands.

With a deep sigh of resignation, she resolutely opened one of the trunks in the far corner of her room. From it she retrieved a small box carefully hidden in the bottom. She opened the box and selected six tiny black berries. She wrapped the berries in a handkerchief and carried it with her to the serving area at the back of the house. From the storage pantry she selected a beautifully decorated porcelain cup and saucer and placed two of the berries into a small mortar and with the accompanying pestle ground the berries into a paste like substance. Next she put the ground berries into the cup. She retrieved a bottle of mead made from fermented honey. She poured the liquor over the smashed berries, and considered calling Winny to deliver the cup, but decided that it was best to trust no one with the task.

Avarilla placed the cup on a tray and made her way toward the sound of animated conversation and laughter emanating from the parlor.

Mary Ann and Hayes were enjoying a pleasant time in admiring the beauty of the house decked in its holiday greenery, and in discussing the degree of success the boys were having with their studies. Buckley had made it a point to commend young William as the most dedicated and promising of his three young pupils. Mary Ann was so pleased with her son, and felt a modest degree of success with her dance progress. As usual, Hayes consumed several cups of rum and it was clear that he was becoming intoxicated.

When Avarilla arrived at the doorway to the parlor, she forced a smile as she approached Mary Ann. She offered the cup of mead to her, saying: "I want you to know how pleased I am about the upcoming wedding. My first concern is for the happiness of my father, and clearly, you are responsible. I want to welcome you into our family and hope that you and my father will have many happy years together."

Mary Ann smiled and accepted the cup of warm liquid. But the overture was both curious and unexpected. Was this truly a sign of good will from Avarilla? She suspected that it was not, but could not imagine what her motivation might be. Nonetheless she was happy that this strange turn of events did not curb the happiness that she felt. She thanked Avarilla and nodded her appreciation. She expected Avarilla to leave, but instead, she hesitated.

Avarilla continued with a smile, "I hope it is not too hot. Why don't you try a sip and see if it meets with your satisfaction?"

Mary Ann smiled in return and lifted the cup but immediately withdrew the cup from her lips, for it was indeed quite hot. She laughed, and explained to Avarilla that she would wait a bit until the liquid had cooled slightly. Avarilla seemed disappointed, but nodded and turned and headed out the door.

Hayes was delighted to have his betrothed share a drink with him and he lifted his cup and proposed a toast to their future happiness. Hayes had already poured himself a generous portion into a cup and proceeded to down it in one gulp.

Mary Ann, like most women, normally drank only on very special occasions. She supposed this was just such an occasion and tasted the Mead. It was both too sweet and too strong for her taste and she shuddered as the liquid burned its way down her throat. Hayes laughed, seeing her discomfort, and extended his hand toward her. She was only too happy to give it to him and they both laughed as he downed the liquid from the cup as he had done with the rum.

Mary Ann was not only tired, but also realized that Hayes had best go to bed while he was still able to negotiate the stairs. They both stood and Hayes stumbled a bit and grabbed the back of a chair to regain his balance. She moved to assist him but after only a few steps he grabbed his chest and seemed to be having difficulty breathing, Mary Ann called for Molly and Isham who both came running just in time to see Hayes fall to the floor. He was writhing on the floor in pain when suddenly he began to vomit. Molly hurried to fetch a basin while Isham helped to support Hayes's body which was now drenched in sweat. After what seemed like hours, but was probably no longer than fifteen or twenty minutes, Hayes fell into a deep sleep, or an alcoholic induced stupor. It was difficult to tell which.

The commotion caused by these events had aroused the rest of the sleeping household. Winny and Henry hurried to help with the cleanup and Avarilla, stood transfixed in the doorway. Her face was ashen and she too, looked as though she might faint. In a frightened voice she asked, "What happened?"

Mary Ann went to her side and explained that Hayes had consumed quite a bit of rum and had, in fact, also finished her cup of mead as well.

Avarilla was shaking and her face was pale. Mary Ann had never seen her so upset. She insisted that Isham and Molly get her father to bed immediately and followed them to his room where she remained by his side. Mary Ann was puzzled by her response. They had all seen John Hayes drink to excess on several occasions. True, the labored breathing was problematic, but after vomiting, he seemed to be better. Once she saw that Hayes was safely in bed, and that Avarilla had appointed herself as his nurse, she decided to go to bed herself.

Molly returned to the parlor to collect the cups and noticed, with surprise, that rather than the usual cups used by Hayes for his evening rum, there was also a delicate and fragile china cup, such as would have been used by a lady. She lifted the cup to her nose and noticed an unusual odor. She recognized the smell of mead, but there was something else. At the bottom of the cup was a slight paste like residue. Molly swiped her finger across the bottom and lifted it to her lips. Her eyes were wide with fear when she recognized the substance as the deadly nightshade. *Was the devil at work in the house again?* She closed her eyes and began to chant and sway gently with the rhythm of the chant.

When Molly returned to her room, she shared with Isham and her children, the frightening discovery she had made. As in the earlier instance, they all assumed that some minion of the devil was once again threatening the inhabitants of Mount Hayes. Molly feared that the house was cursed.

Early the next morning, Molly was frightened of what awful fate might befall the household next. She, Winny and Henry made the trip to the cooking house and began loading the trays with the morning meal for the family. She was apprehensive as she awaited the arrival of each of the family members. What other evil had infected the house?

Mary Ann's first concern was for her son. But William was awakened easily and seemed eager to begin his day in the company of his new friends, John and Thomas. When they had finished dressing, Mary Ann delivered William into Molly's care and went to Hayes's bedroom to check on his condition. Avarilla was still by his bed with a look of fearful apprehension.

"Did you have a peaceful night's sleep?" she asked.

Avarilla nodded and said that he had awakened several times early in the night, complaining of a terrible headache, dizziness, and a loss of sensation in the fingers of his right hand.

"But," she continued, "he seemed much improved this morning."

Mary Ann was relieved and assumed all these things were the byproduct of over indulgence in alcohol. She assured Avarilla that her father would be fine. When Hayes said he didn't feel well enough to come down to eat, Avarilla immediately offered to bring up a tray of food for him.

Mary Ann suggested that Henry or Winny could bring up the tray, but Avarilla shook her head, insisting that she would tend to her father's needs herself. That was not unusual, for Avarilla was the acknowledged expert on all types of treatments and cures.

Mary Ann left the room and joined Buckley and the boys in the parlor kitchen.

Molly served the meal, but it was clear to Mary Ann that she was not herself. She constantly glanced around the room with trepidation, as though expecting some disaster to befall them. Mary Ann attempted to calm her fears and assured Molly that Hayes would be just fine. Molly shook her head and came close to Mary Ann to whisper in her ear, that the devil ghost had tried to hurt Massa Hayes.

Molly was so frightened that her hands were shaking. Mary Ann took her by the arms and walked with her into the adjoining room and attempted to calm her. But Molly could not be calmed. She still continued to whisper that the devil ghost had tried to kill Hayes.

"What on earth are you talking about?" Mary Ann asked. "Mister Hayes just had too much rum and is now suffering the expected consequences."

"No, no Mistress Mary, devil put poison in Massa Hayes's cup."

"That's nonsense, Molly," Mary Ann protested. "How could anyone poison Mister Hayes?"

Molly hastened to explain. "When I pick up de cups from Parlor, the pretty one with flowers, it be poisoned with nightshade. I see, I smell, I taste. For true, it be poison."

Mary Ann was stunned by the sudden realization that Molly was right, in part at least. Avarilla had brought the cup to her, and had insisted that she taste it. Had she drunk the cup of mead, she would, in all probability be dead! It was a chilling thought. Avarilla would have had no way of knowing that Mary Ann had not consumed the contents, or that Hayes had drained the entire cup. She also realized that had Hayes not been so intoxicated from his earlier drinking, he would probably not have vomited, thus expelling the poison, or most of it from his system. They had been spared the vilest of evils by mere chance.

Mary Ann felt compelled to ask Molly who had poured the mead into the china cup. Molly shook her head and said that she did not know.

Mary Ann suddenly realized the danger that she was in. It was Avarilla who had prepared and brought the cup to the parlor, specifically for her. Avarilla was prepared to commit murder to prevent her father from marrying again.

She wasn't certain what steps to take next. She couldn't tell Hayes about Avarilla's plan, and she certainly couldn't confide in Hayes's daughters or with Molly. It was a secret that she could share with no one. Once again, she felt an overwhelming fear. It was a fear for her own life as well as for the welfare of her son. Suddenly, she had lost her appetite.

John Hayes did not recover as quickly as would be expected from a night of excessive drinking, but this did not seem to alarm anyone else. He eventually got up, around mid-day, but still had no appetite and experienced dizziness and shortness of breath. It was decided that it was best that he not attend the ball. Mary Ann no longer had any interest in celebrating and decided to remain at home as well. Avarilla announced her intentions to attend as a representative of the household.

"After all," she insisted, "it will be rude, if no one from Mount Hayes attends." After thinking it over for a minute, she announced that she would spend the night with the Stansburys.

Mary Ann agreed heartily, and was glad that Avarilla would be out of the house for that night. She had a lot to think about.

CHAPTER 6
Apoplexy

John Hayes's recovery was slow, but it was clear that he was beginning to regain his stamina slowly but surely, and he insisted that he and Mary Ann proceed with their wedding on January 6, just as they had planned. Mary Ann agreed, but suggested that they have a modest ceremony, with only family members in attendance. He was hesitant to change his elaborate plans, but agreed that a large event might well be more than he could handle. He expressed regret that Mary Ann would not have the opportunity to perform the minuet with him as she had hoped. She thanked him, but quickly added that his health was more important than a dance. Secretly, she was relieved for the idea of exhibiting her lack of grace in front of the entire community was more than a little unnerving.

The week of Christmas passed with a subdued atmosphere at Mount Hayes. Both the Lenox and Stansbury families came to escort Mary Ann and Avarilla to St. Paul's Parish for Sunday service as well as on Christmas. Reverend Tibbs offered up prayers for Hayes's speedy recovery and hoped that he might soon join his family at service.

The bounty of baked delicacies was plentiful, but the days were spent quietly. As usual Mary Ann joined Avarilla every morning in the library. Avarilla occupied her time engrossed in a book, while Mary Ann continued with a small sewing project she had begun. She was working on a small black wool square destined to serve as a cover for a small stool. She was doing her best to carry out the instruction she had received from Elizabeth in crewel embroidery. It was a slow, tedious process, but she welcomed it since it freed her mind from the constant worry that something awful might happen again. Neither woman attempted to engage the other in conversation. The atmosphere was quiet and peaceful, yet Mary Ann was tense

On Sunday, December 28, Thomas Stansbury, on behalf of the Hayes family, reported that the wedding of his father-in-law, John Hayes would be held as planned at Mount Hayes, but regretted that his uncertain health prevented the huge celebration originally planned. Reverend Tibbs asked the congregation to continue their prayers for the ailing Hayes.

As the date for the wedding neared, Hayes seemed to regain a good portion of his stamina and resumed his normal routine within the household. All alcohol had been removed to the storage house outside, and although he complained a bit, he acknowledged that for the time being, it was probably for the best.

With each day, Mary Ann became more and more fearful. She pretended a fondness for Avarilla, which she did not feel. She was certain that if Avarilla were to suspect that her scheme had been discovered, neither Mary Ann nor her son would be safe.

At eleven o'clock on Tuesday, January 6, just as planned, Revered Tibbs addressed the assembled members of the family of John Hayes and began the wedding service.

At its conclusion, Molly and her helpers began to arrange the table in preparation for the wedding feast. After eating, they retired to the room across the hall, where Mary Ann was surprised to find William Barney and his fiddle. As he struck up the first notes of a minuet, Hayes arose, bowed to his new wife, and escorted her onto the floor. He motioned to his daughters and their husbands to join him, and nodded to Barney to play the music from the beginning of the piece. She curtsied to his bow and they began to dance. Mary Ann was glad that there were only family members in the room and that they all seemed absorbed in the dance. She was thankful that she did not feel on display in the least, and her husband led here through the intricate steps with ease.

As the music ended, Master Buckley entered the room with his three young pupils. With a slight push forward by Buckley, William, resplendent in his silk brocaded vest and bright red velvet jacket, straightened his shoulders, held his head high and strode across the floor, stopping in front of his mother. With perhaps the lowest, and grandest bow ever observed from one so young, he extended his hand to Mary Ann and asked her to join him. Mary Ann's eyes filled with tears. She was so proud of her son and so hopeful for his future.

At the instruction of Master Buckley, the other two boys were told to carry out their instructions. John approached his Aunt Elizabeth and Thomas walked to his mother, and the two brothers executed a bow of their own. After which, Buckley's three young pupils held their ladies hands as they led them onto the floor to perform another minuet. It was not nearly as graceful, nor as perfectly executed as Master Buckley had hoped, but their efforts produced a hearty round of applause from the family and the household slaves who had peeked in at the door to observe the event. Mary Ann couldn't remember a happier time.

Unfortunately, even with such a small number in their party, the tankards of ale and rum were brought out for the enjoyment of the men. It would not have been a proper celebration without it. As was most often the case, all imbibed to excess, including Hayes. Late in the evening, he excused himself, walked across the hall to the parlor where he sank into his chair by the fire. Within a few minutes he was asleep.

Hayes's departure from the festivities signaled that it was time for everyone to return home. It had been a wonderful, but tiring day and Jane and Elizabeth were happy to get home. They said their goodbyes and congratulations to Mary Ann and went into the parlor to say goodbye to their father. Elizabeth bent to kiss her father on the cheek. She was surprised when he did not awaken. She spoke to him and shook him gently by the shoulder. When he finally opened his eyes, he tried to speak, but was unable. Tears formed in his eyes as he tried without success, to lift his right arm to embrace his daughter. John Lenox took Elizabeth by the arm and shaking his head, concluded that John Hayes was suffering from apoplexy. Avarilla was once again, pale and shaking, quickly nodded her affirmation that her father was suffering a stroke. She looked around for Henry and ordered him to bring Doctor Payne at once.

No one moved. No one seemed capable of moving. Hayes's eyes were wide with fear, and confusion. He did not understand what was happening to him.

Avarilla was the only person who seemed prepared for such an emergency. She glanced around, and seeing that Henry was still standing in the doorway as if frozen, ordered him to do as he was told. Henry turned to go and as he did, Isham told the boy to bring two horses and they would go together to fetch Dr. Payne. It was some consolation, but they were both clearly frightened by this unexpected turn of events.

Avarilla ordered Molly to fill the bed warmer with hot coals and place it between the blankets of her father's bed. She then asked Lenox and Stansbury to carry their paralyzed father-in-law to his room. The men lifted Hayes into a small wooden chair and carried him to the back of the house, up the stairs and into the bedroom. They waited a few moments to rest, and to allow Molly to remove the bed warmer and turn down the covers. It was with some difficulty that they managed to get Hayes settled in the bed, for he was unable to assist and his body was limp and heavy.

They were both relieved and frightened when Hayes immediately drifted into what they hoped was a restful sleep. They were concerned that he might never recover from this newest ordeal.

It seemed like hours before Henry and Isham returned with Dr. Payne. When the doctor drew the lancet from his pocket, none were surprised. Molly had brought a basin and Avarilla was prepared with linen bandages to be applied once the procedure was complete.

As the doctor cut the incision, they all braced themselves for the expected cry of pain from the patient, but Hayes did not awaken. He was alive, but his breathing was shallow and labored.

Dr. Payne left immediately after completing the procedure, but promised that he would return early the next morning to check on his patient.

Elizabeth and John announced that they would spend the night and take turns sitting with Hayes, but Thomas Stansbury explained that he and his wife should return home with sons John and Thomas. Mary Ann knew that the couple had left their youngest child, Daniel, at home under the care of Mattie, but was surprised by the announcement that Jane was expecting another child and was not feeling well.

Elizabeth sent Henry to bring around the carriage and accompanied them to the door with assurances that Hayes would get the best of care.

Throughout it all, Mary Ann had been numb. It had been only a little over two and one half years since Phillip had died, and she had felt both hopeless and helpless. Then, through a series of unexpected and fortunate events, she had been welcomed into the household of Mount Hayes. Her future had seemed secure, but once again, she feared that misfortune and misery awaited her and her son.

Mary Ann refused to leave the bedside of her husband. She clasped her hands in prayer for the strength to withstand this latest misfortune. Although William had been taken to bed several hours earlier, she sent Molly to awaken him and bring him to her. Elizabeth and Avarilla both protested that it was best to let the child sleep, but Mary Ann needed his presence. He was the most important person in the world to her and she needed to hold him, and to assure herself that he was safe. Molly nodded her head in silent understanding and immediately brought William to his mother. He was tired from the day's excitement and quickly fell asleep in his mother's arms. She rocked him slowly, finding comfort in the repetitive motion.

The three women, Avarilla, Elizabeth and Mary Ann sat with Hayes throughout the night. He did not awaken, but his breathing eventually became less labored.

At daybreak, Molly entered the room with a tray of cups and a silver teapot from which she poured a cup for each of the women. She asked Mary Ann's permission to help William to dress and then take him to the parlor kitchen for breakfast. Mary Ann nodded her agreement.

As the women began to talk among themselves, Hayes stirred in the bed. Avarilla was the first to go to the bedside. She took her father's hand and her despair was evident to all. She asked her father how he was feeling and he smiled, a rather odd smile since the right side of his face seemed to be drooping. As Elizabeth and Mary Ann moved to the opposite side of the bed, Hayes, seeing his new bride, lifted his left hand slightly and Mary Ann took it gladly. They all gave a sigh of relief, for these were truly positive signs that the damage from the stroke might not be as disastrous as first feared. But of course, they all realized that it was too soon to tell with any certainty.

As he had promised, Dr. Payne arrived around eight o'clock that morning. He seemed both surprised and pleased that Hayes recognized him but was still not able to speak. He pronounced that the bloodletting had worked, but considering Hayes's condition, he felt it best to be conservative in his approach. He announced that he would limit the bloodletting to every other day, unless the patient took a turn for the worse. Everyone in the room was relieved with the news.

Molly entered with a cup of warm broth and she and Avarilla with the help of Dr. Payne, pulled the patient into a semi-sitting position resting against an assortment of pillows. Avarilla took the cup from Molly and sat down on the bed beside her father. Hayes at first smiled, then shook his head slightly and raised his left hand and pointed a finger at Mary Ann. She sat down on the left side of the bed, took the bowl from Avarilla, and held the cup to her husband's lips. He attempted to take a small sip, but neither his mouth nor his lips would respond in a normal fashion and a small amount of the broth dribbled down his chin. Mary Ann wiped the broth away with a handkerchief, smiled at Hayes and told him not to worry. She asked Molly to bring her a spoon. When Molly returned, she continued with the feeding of her husband. Again, the results were better than they had expected, and although the process was painstakingly slow, he eventually consumed the contents of the cup and smiled his crooked smile in appreciation.

Avarilla's furrowed brow revealed her level of hurt and disappointment. She excused herself, went to the kitchen parlor, retrieved a bowl of porridge and took it to her room. She opened one of her books of Shakespeare and began to read *Othello*, another of her favorites. She felt comfort in the lyrical rhythm of the prose, and allowed her imagination to transport her into that earlier time. She felt a kinship for Ophelia and sympathized with her dilemma regarding whether or not to remain loyal to her father, or to follow her own desires.

After nearly an hour of reading, she put down the book; she was more depressed than she had been when she began. With a shake of her head, she resigned herself to the situation at hand. She returned to her father's room to join Mary Ann and Elizabeth who were still sitting with Hayes.

Over the course of the next few months there were a great many changes at Mount Hayes. John Hayes gradually improved, but it was doubtful that he would ever be the same. Nicholas Buckley was dismissed from employment since it was inconvenient to have the daily commotion from the dance instructions. And, as for William's education, Avarilla offered to serve as his tutor.

"I found an old hornbook in one of my mother's chests. Elizabeth, Jemima and I all used it to learn our letters, vowels and consonants and the Lord's Prayer. She explained, "I believe it will be very useful to William with his studies."

If only Elizabeth were here, Mary Ann thought. She was always comfortable to have Elizabeth spend time with her son. But regarding Avarilla, Mary Ann was fearful, but she felt she had no choice but to accept her offer. Avarilla was far more capable than she to assist with the child's schooling.

In mid March, Isham asked for permission to speak with Hayes about the tobacco crop. His concern was that there had been so much cold and unexpected snow in March that it had been difficult to get the tobacco seedlings planted and they were not growing as well as he had hoped. Hayes had neither the energy nor the inclination to be worried about the tobacco crop at the time and told Isham to do whatever he thought was best.

Isham, with a quiet, "Yes, Massa," departed the room without any clear resolution to his problem. He decided to just wait and see what the weather brought.

By April, the droopiness of Hayes's eye and mouth had improved somewhat, but were still obvious. He could not walk, even with a cane, but he could assist others in transferring him from the bed to the chair. He took his early morning meal and his supper in his room accompanied by Mary Ann and young William. At midday he consented to the indignity of being carried to dinner with the assistance of Isham and Henry. He would remain downstairs for a few hours, until he became tired, at which time he would be carried back up to his room in mid afternoon.

He napped frequently, but seemed to enjoy listening to Avarilla read to him from one of her favorite works of Shakespeare. During these readings he nodded off frequently, and on occasion requested that she read from one of the comedies, rather than always from one of the tragedies, which he found to be rather depressing. His particular favorites were *All's Well That Ends Well*, or *Merry Wives of Windsor*, or *Twelfth Night*. Avarilla would nod in agreement and smile, but the ones that she brought to his room were always her favorites, *Julius Caesar*, *Hamlet*, *Macbeth*, or the occasional *Anthony and Cleopatra*.

Mary Ann often sat in the room and listened to Avarilla's reading. She agreed with Hayes, that there seemed to be quite a lot of death and dying in Avarilla's selections.

The first three weeks of April were surprisingly hot and dry after the freezing weather they had experienced in March. This unexpected drought caused severe problems in transferring the tobacco seedlings to the fields. Water would have to be carried to the fields by hand to keep the young plants healthy. Isham had the worry of overseeing not only the lands at Mount Hayes, but also the fields located some distance away. He needed more hands here to save the crop. He once again, asked for permission to see Hayes. Avarilla accompanied him to Hayes's room where, as usual, Mary Ann was sitting with her husband. Also in the room was Dr. Payne who routinely called once a week to check on his patient's progress.

Isham explained his concerns to Hayes, who became visibly upset, shaking his head back and forth to the point that not only did Mary Ann and Avarilla fear that he might suffer a relapse, but Dr. Payne became quite alarmed as well.

Finally, in an attempt to calm his patient, Dr. Payne offered a suggestion.

"Mister Hayes, have you ever considered selling off some of your land, either here or on one of your other plantations? This great responsibility caused by so much land to manage, seems to be causing you unnecessary distress."

"Besides," the doctor added, "it seems to me that would free up more slaves to do the required extra work, and would also bring in some financial reserves."

Hayes seemed to consider it for a moment, and then addressed Isham, "Let me consider the doctor's suggestions. In the meantime, do the best you can with the labor available."

Isham shrugged, said, "Thank you Massa," although he didn't really understand what there was to be thankful for.

Dr. Payne picked up his bag, instructed Hayes to try to remain calm, and assured him that he would be back to check on him the following week.

Hayes closed his eyes and both women assumed that he had fallen asleep again, but within a few minutes he opened his eyes and instructed Avarilla to send for Henry.

Although she had no idea what her father had in mind she did as he asked. She left the room and returned a few minutes later with Henry following behind.

Hayes instructed Henry to come closer. His eyesight had been somewhat affected by the stroke. When Henry stood by the side of his bed, Hayes told him to ride to the plantation of Thomas Harris, and to ask him to come to Mount Hayes.

"Tell him I wish to discuss a land transaction." And, he continued, "Be sure to ask when we should expect him."

~ 103 ~

"Yes Massa," replied Henry and turned to leave the room.

"Wait a minute." Hayes instructed, "When he gives you a day and time that he will come, then go to John Lenox and ask that he be here when Harris arrives. Now do as I say, immediately!"

"I ride fast Massa Hayes."

"Make sure you do. I fear I may not have a lot of time left."

Both Mary Ann and Avarilla were concerned by this announcement and were quick to ask if he was feeling worse.

"Nonsense, I'm feeling fine, but you know how the boy dawdles unless you build a fire under him," Hayes added with his crooked smile and a twinkle in his eye.

Mary Ann was relieved, but Avarilla seemed concerned when she asked, "What sort of land transaction do you have in mind?"

Hayes's retort was sharp and stern as he responded, "That's no concern of yours, daughter. Now why don't you leave us alone for a while?"

Avarilla was crestfallen. Surely, she told herself, her father had completely lost his senses. He was certainly in no condition to make foolhardy decisions regarding his land holdings.

When Mary Ann asked her if there was something wrong, Avarilla, mimicking her father, turned to Mary Ann and, with a sneer, informed her, "That's no concern of yours, either!"

With that she stormed out of the room with one foot making a distinctly louder stomp than the other.

The trip to the Harris plantation was a pleasant diversion for Henry and the day was fine, although unusually hot for mid April. But as usual, despite Hayes's warning, he allowed Old Ben to trot along at a leisurely pace. He was glad he didn't have to work in the fields, because with the dry weather, the field hands had to carry buckets of water all day in their attempts to save the tobacco plants. The slave cabins were as hot as ovens, even in the evenings. He was happy that his room on the lower level of Mount Hayes was much cooler.

Upon arriving at the Harris plantation, Henry was hesitant as to what he should do. He was not expected, and hoped no one would be upset with him. He rode around to the back of the house and walked up to the door. He knocked softly, and waited a few minutes. When no one answered, he knocked again, more loudly. The door was thrown open by an elderly black woman who glared at him suspiciously.

"Well don't just stand there. What do you want?"

"Massa Hayes send me. I give message to Massa Thomas. Please," he was quick to add.

"Wait here," was the curt response followed by a quick slamming of the door.

Henry was feeling anything but welcome. He was starting to be sorry he had made the trip, which all of a sudden didn't seem pleasant at all.

Two girls, who appeared to be about the same age as Henry, opened the door. The taller of the two smiled and asked the inevitable question, "Who are you and what do you want?"

"I be Henry, I be from Mount Hayes, and Massa Hayes send me to give message to Massa Thomas."

The taller girl, smiled again, opened the door wider, and with a broad, inviting sweep of her hand said, "Please come in. My father is in the library. Come with me."

Henry followed obediently. He had seen Harris before, but had never spoken to him. Harris nodded, and smiled and acknowledged that he had seen Henry at the Hayes Plantation.

"How is Mister Hayes? I understand that he has been quite ill."

"Yes, Massa. He be bad before, but now better, but he no walk."

"Well, what is this message that you have for me? I think you had best tell me, don't you think?"

Henry nodded his head in quick agreement and quickly recited the message. "Massa Hayes want you come to talk about land."

Harris had often made overtures to Hayes regarding the possibility of buying some land, and was pleased that Hayes now seemed receptive to the idea.

"I will be delighted to discuss such a matter with your master. Tell him that I shall call on him tomorrow afternoon, if that is agreeable."

Henry was pleased that things were going so well, and he started talking as he backed out of the room. "Thank you Massa Harris. I tell Massa Hayes you come tomorrow."

And with that, Henry hastened to the back door and the safety of Old Ben's back. He hoped his next chore would go as well. He knew Mistress Elizabeth, and hoped she would welcome him kindly. He was reassured by the fact that her husband's plantation was called Kindness, but was only vaguely aware of its location. He headed toward the general area and hoped he would come across someone who could tell him the precise location.

It was hot when Henry left Mount Hayes around noon, and now, the day was getting even hotter. He decided to stop at a small stream to water his horse and to cool off briefly in the shade provided by a large sycamore tree. He dismounted Old Ben and sat down to rest. It was but a short time before he stretched out in the cool grass and quickly fell asleep. When he awakened from his nap, it was even hotter and he still was not certain of the best route to the Lenox home. He mounted his horse and the two ambled along following the meander of the stream when he saw a group of field slaves carrying shovels over their shoulders. He stopped to ask if they knew the direction to the Lenox plantation. An older man, who appeared to be in charge of the group, grinned a toothless grin and pointed toward the west, explaining that the plantation was about three miles in that direction. Henry thanked the man, but was unhappy to leave the shaded area along the creek to ride directly into the sun. Nonetheless, he did as he was told and eventually arrived at Kindness by late afternoon.

Henry was fortunate that he encountered John Lenox riding toward him as he approached the house. Lenox recognized him and Henry dismounted and explained the purpose of his errand.

Lenox, like his wife, Elizabeth, was a pleasant and congenial man who smiled at Henry, agreed to come to Mount Hayes the following afternoon and told Henry to go to the house and see Mistress Elizabeth. He assured Henry that she would be happy to see that he had some cold water and something to eat before heading back home.

Henry was only too glad to get out of the heat and he was rather hungry. His only concern was that he be able to return to Mount Hayes before dark.

As he feared, it was already dusk when he finally returned. Molly told him that he must immediately go to Massa Hayes and report on the task he had been given.

With a solemn shake of her head she warned him to expect the worst, "Massa Hayes be mad. Why you gone so long?"

Henry merely shook his head as he hurried upstairs. A scolding from Massa Hayes would be bad enough, but he didn't want one from his mother as well.

When he entered the room, he found Mistress Mary Ann sitting by her husband's side. She motioned to Henry to approach the bed, but put her finger to her lips to warn him to be quiet. Hayes was fast asleep. Henry tiptoed to Mary Ann and reported on the results of his errand. Mary Ann thanked him and told him that she would give the details to Hayes when he awoke. Henry was relieved that he would not have to face an angry Massa Hayes. He was hopeful that Hayes might forget by the morning that he had been gone such a long time.

Mary Ann was sitting with Hayes when he awoke the next morning and with a smile she assured him that Henry's task had been carried out successfully and that both Thomas Harris and John Lenox had agreed to visit him that afternoon.

Hayes smiled and nodded his approval. Apparently, as Henry had hoped, there would be no unpleasantness regarding his tardy return.

After her father's unexpected admonition the previous day, Avarilla had decided to stay out of his presence for a while. She was still bewildered, hurt, and angry by her father's apparent decision to exclude her from any business affairs of the plantation. With each passing day, she became more and more worried about her own future.

CHAPTER 7
Mistress of Mount Hayes

Both Harris and Lenox arrived shortly after dinner and were met at the front door by Molly, who then ushered them into the parlor. A warm fire was burning in the fireplace and Hayes was sitting in a chair nearby, and Mary Ann was standing by his side. She greeted both men and motioned to two additional chairs that had been drawn up near Hayes. Hayes seemed remarkably alert, although he usually was ready for a nap about this time.

Once the men were seated, Hayes began to speak.

"Thank you gentlemen, for agreeing to meet with me on such short notice. There are two matters, which I must discuss with you, and I am hopeful that you will agree to assist me."

The two men quickly nodded, and Lenox added, "Of course, father Hayes," in recognition of their new family relationship.

Harris added, "I am at your service, sir."

Hayes seemed pleased and proceeded to explain the reason for the meeting.

"I have decided to sell a portion of Mount Hayes and, as we have discussed on several occasions, I am aware that you, Mister Harris, have an interest in extending your own holdings. Is that still the case?"

"Absolutely," was the immediate response from Harris.

"Good, good," said Hayes with his crooked smile.

"And as for you, Lenox, I need a witness to my next proposal, that being the appointment of my wife Mary Ann as power of attorney to handle the details of the proposed sale."

Lenox nodded and smiled in agreement.

Hayes next request was for Lenox to draw up the necessary paper regarding the power of attorney. He pointed to a desk near the front window and explained, "You will find paper, a quill and ink on the desk. I would like to complete this as quickly as possible."

Lenox sat down at the desk, picked up the quill and dipped it in the inkwell, and then turned to Hayes expectantly.

Hayes seemed to be quite lucid, and in a clear but somewhat weak voice he began to dictate: "I, John Hayes, of Mount Hayes, St. Paul's Parish, Baltimore County, Maryland, on this"... he hesitated with a frown, and turning to Mary Ann, asked what the date was.

Lenox immediately answered for her, stating that it was the twenty-fifth day of April, 1719.

Hayes nodded a thank you in acknowledgement, and began again. "I, John Hayes of Mount Hayes, St. Paul's Parish, Baltimore County, Maryland, on this," here he paused, having once again forgotten the date.

Lenox repeated the date and added it to the document.

"Yes, Yes," Hayes continued, I John Hayes, of Mount Hayes, St. Paul's Parish, Baltimore County, Maryland on this.".

At this point Lenox, fearful that the process might consume the entire day, suggested that he would, with Hayes's permission complete the document and then read it for Hayes's approval.

Both Mary Ann and Harris smiled and nodded with relief.

After only a few more seconds, Lenox laid down the pen, turned to face Hayes and began to read.

I John Hayes, of Mount Hayes, St. Paul's Parish, Baltimore County, Maryland on this the twenty-fifth day of April, 1719, and being of sound mind, hereby appoint my beloved wife, Mary Ann power of attorney to carry out my wishes regarding the sale and transfer of specified lands.

"Thank you, Lenox. That is exactly as I wished it to be."

"Sir, it will be necessary for you to sign the document," Lenox continued.

Lenox and Harris carried Hayes's chair to the desk. Hayes was right handed, and despite the fact that he had regained partial use of his left hand, it seemed unlikely that he would be able to commit his signature to the document. Hayes was frustrated by the fact that he could hardly hold the pen, let alone control it. He was getting increasingly agitated. Lenox suggested that a mark would be sufficient and Hayes finally managed to affix an X to the paper. Lenox next explained that the signature of two witnesses would serve the purpose of validating his signature as being valid and true.

Hayes nodded and asked, "Lenox, if you and Harris would be so kind as to be my witnesses, I would be in your debt."

Both men readily agreed, and signed and dated the document.

With the first half of the business completed, Hayes called for Molly to bring a flagon of rum and three cups. Hayes seemed happier than he had in days. Mary Ann hoped it was a good omen, but was apprehensive lest Hayes over imbibe once again.

Molly quickly returned with the rum and poured three cups of the liquid. She was more generous with the servings for Lenox and Harris. When she handed the cup to

Hayes, he looked at her with disapproval, and demanded that she fill his to the rim as she had done with the others. This, she did, but with a degree of nervousness.

Hayes hoisted his cup with his left hand and proposed a toast to this new undertaking.

Hayes was still having difficulties with his coordination, but brushed Mary Ann's hand away when she tried to assist.

"I'm not dead yet, Madam. I am quite capable of toasting my friends by myself."

With a look of determination, he again did his best to bring the cup to his mouth, managing to spill the greater portion of its contents down the front of his vest.

"Damnation!" He screamed. The anger had returned again, and, as before, his face became red and his hand shook even more vigorously than before.

Mary Ann, kissed him on the forehead, and smiled to him, trying to calm him. Neither Lenox nor Harris had any idea regarding what to do next. Speaking with a confidence that she surely did not feel, Mary Ann suggested that they reserve the actual negotiations regarding the sale of the property for a future date.

"I will discuss with my husband his wishes regarding the location, acreage and price and, at your convenience, we can meet at a future date to discuss the details."

My goodness, thought Mary Ann to herself, *perhaps I can be mistress of Mount Hayes.*

Mary Ann's calm voice and decisive manner seemed to have calmed Hayes. He nodded in agreement, and the two men bowed, shook his hand and followed Mary Ann to the front door.

John Lenox took Mary Ann's hand, and smiling, noted that he quite understood why Elizabeth was so fond of her and that clearly; she was a good wife to his father-in-law.

Harris took his leave by nodding his agreement with Lenox's opinion and told her he was looking forward to their next meeting to discuss the sale of land.

Mary Ann took the opportunity to ask, "What specific land is of interest to you, Mr. Harris?"

"There are several areas into which I would like to expand. I will make a list, along with the desired acreage and have it delivered to you so that you might discuss it with your husband before our next meeting."

With that, he bowed slightly, turned and walked down the steps towards Henry who was holding the reins of the horses of both men.

Mary Ann returned to the parlor to find that Hayes had drifted off to sleep. He seemed to be resting comfortably, so she decided not to disturb him. Molly was coming down the hall toward her, and she quietly asked her to remove the flagon and cups. There was no point in tempting the man. She noted that the spilled ale had saturated a good portion of his vest. It was probably ruined, but she would leave it to Molly to do whatever she could to clean it.

Mary Ann walked to the room across the hall and picked up the crewel project on which she had been working. She collected the various colored skeins of yarn she needed, and returned to the parlor. Hayes slept for nearly two hours before finally awakening. He seemed rested, and in a pleasant mood. He did not mention the meeting held earlier, and when asked if he would like to return to his room, he shook his head no and announced that he believed he might take supper in the parlor kitchen.

Mary Ann was happy that a sense of calmness had returned. Perhaps things were going to be better and her future more secure. She called to Henry to fetch his father. She hummed a tune as the two men carried her husband into the parlor kitchen.

Molly brought William to join them and Hayes seemed genuinely happy as he quizzed her son on his letters. For the moment, Mary Ann felt that her life was once again, more normal. Not long after, Avarilla entered the room. She was startled to see her father downstairs at that time of day, but said nothing. She walked to her place at the table. There was an awkward silence that seemed to last forever.

Finally, Avarilla asked her father, "Are you going to give the blessing, Father?"

Her father's response was brief and to the point. "No, why?"

With that, he called for Molly to put some food on the table.

Mary Ann worried that his mood might change in an instant if another unfortunate accident occurred as he attempted to feed himself. As it happened, Molly brought in a platter of chicken. Hayes indicated that he wanted a leg of chicken. Molly obliged and then served Hayes a piece of bread. When offered soup, he shook his head vehemently. Chicken and bread he could handle by himself.

It turned out to be a pleasant meal. Avarilla remained quiet but ate a hearty meal as well.

After supper, Isham and Henry picked up Hayes's chair and carried him to his room. Avarilla followed them, and once her father was safely back in his bed, she asked if he would like her to read to him.

Hayes thought about it for a moment, and then, pursing his lips and tilting his head to one side, and nodding his head added: "But for heaven's sake, bring something pleasant for a change. Read me a comedy, or don't read to me at all."

He gave a self-satisfied chuckle and smiled at Mary Ann who had taken a chair by his bedside.

Avarilla shrugged in submission and left the room to retrieve a book more to her father's liking.

"Tomorrow my dear, we shall make some decisions regarding how to proceed with the plans to sell some of this land. I am pleased that you are willing to help me with this."

Mary Ann was surprised, and relieved. She had feared that he might have forgotten the meeting and might even have changed his mind about his willingness to sell some of his land. This was another positive sign that he might regain more of his capabilities with time.

CHAPTER 8
Last Will and Testament

*M*ary Ann was reluctant to bring up the topic of the sale of land. Hayes's emotional state was often erratic, vacillating between unexpected bouts of depression, which were just as likely to be replaced by either unusual cheerfulness or, spells of uncontrollable rage. It was an unsettling state of affairs.

Fortunately, it was Hayes himself, who broached the subject of the sale of lands. He appeared to have given the matter a great deal of thought and four days after the visit from Lenox and Harris, he called Avarilla to join him and Mary Ann in his room. Avarilla was thrilled that her father now invited her company and she hurried to his room. She was smiling when she entered. As usual, Mary Ann was sitting by Hayes's bedside, but even this did not diminish Avarilla's delight with what she perceived to be a change in her father's attitude toward her.

She immediately took a chair on the right side of the bed and waited for her father to speak. He seemed to be in one of his good moods, and both she and Mary Ann were curious as to the reason for the summons.

He began by explaining the purpose of the meeting.

"Although my health has improved considerably, I am well aware that I am not a young man, and none of us knows what destiny awaits us. I feel I would be remiss, if I did not put my affairs in order. Therefore, I wish to finalize some decisions regarding disposition of my lands and property after my death."

Mary Ann was immediately concerned about his health, and asked, "Should I send for the doctor?"

Hayes smiled, touched her hand, and assured her that he was feeling quite well, but thought it only prudent to take care of such an important issue while he was able to do so.

Avarilla nodded and smiled her approval, assuming that she was once again in her father's good graces and thus invited to take part in the decision making process.

Hayes continued, "I would like for you to invite Thomas Harris and John Lenox to complete the transaction regarding the sale of lands. I think day after tomorrow would be fine, providing they are both available. Additionally, I would like for Elizabeth, Jane and her husband, and of course, you, Avarilla and Mary Ann to be present. I will also require the presence of John Hillen and Steven Body as witnesses. I have decided that it is time for me to write my will. I want you all to be present."

Avarilla was nearly giddy. She jumped to her feet, kissed her father on his forehead, and grasping his right hand, asked, "What would you like me to do father? How can I be of assistance?"

Hayes's mood changed in an instant. He still had no use of his right hand, but with his left, he lifted the useless right hand from her grip.

"Stop fussing over me! You needn't think that this fawning behavior is going to influence my opinion or judgment. Now leave me alone. I want to speak to my wife."

Hayes turned his head and gazed at his wife, and seemed to calm a bit. Mary Ann was always distressed by her husband's sudden shifts in temperament, even when his displeasure was focused on others. But as for Avarilla, her face was flushed with anger and her eyes flashed with dagger like intent. Mary Ann had seen her anger before, but never with this intensity.

Avarilla turned abruptly, and without a word, left the room.

Hayes continued, as though nothing had happened. "Now, my dear, I understand that Harris is interested in buying a good portion of Mount Hayes since it adjoins his lands. He seems a good and respectable man, and I am willing to honor his request."

Hayes was far from finished with his plans. He continued, "Regarding my will, my concern is for the welfare of my descendants. I propose to leave Scudamore's Lot to Thomas Stansbury, husband of my eldest daughter, Jane. This is the land that her mother inherited after the death of her husband. I wish for my daughter Elizabeth to have fifty acres of Privilege and my personal estate, which of course, means moneys due to me from the county."

Hayes paused, and seemed to be tiring quickly, but was determined to complete his instructions.

"You have been by my side every moment since our wedding. You are a good and kind woman and I care deeply for you and for your son. Although you will not be mentioned in my will, I have decided that you must have your dower, or one third share of my land secured before my death. Therefore, I propose to sell 370 acres of Mount Hayes that borders the lands of Thomas Harris. Your one third dower share shall include the 150 acres upon which sits my house and all outbuildings but only the household slaves."

With that, he relaxed upon his pillow, his energy spent, and closed his eyes. Mary Ann was confused. He had specifically asked Avarilla to come to his room, but apparently, had forgotten to include her in the provisions of his will. Hayes seemed to be fast asleep and she dreaded waking him lest he be angry. She vowed to bring up the topic of the will and Avarilla's inheritance when he was rested, but she feared what his response might be.

Three days later, on Tuesday, April 28, shortly after noon, the specified guests arrived. Lenox had suggested that they bring along John Beale, Clerk of Courts for Baltimore County. It was the responsibility of the Clerk to record all land transactions and to interview a wife regarding the exception of her dower rights. Since Hayes was in no condition to travel, Beale agreed to accompany them to Mount Hayes.

The invited guests, including Avarilla, were shown to Hayes's room where he was sitting up in bed. It was a relief to everyone that he appeared to be in good spirits. Clerk Beale drew up the formal document that authorized the transfer of the property. The document was lengthy, full of what appeared to be a number of redundant phrases describing the metes and bounds that delineated the boundaries of the land to be sold. When he had finished, he read the deed transfer to the group, and when Hayes stated his satisfaction with its contents, Beale took Mary Ann into another room to make certain that she was not coerced into agreement by the influence of others. He explained that the document excluded 150 acres, which included the house, certain named slaves and outbuildings, which were to be her dower share upon the death of her husband. When Mary Ann acknowledged that she understood and approved of the conditions, they returned to Hayes's room with the others and the required signatures were affixed.

It seemed to take a very long time, but the majority of that time had been devoted to the clerk's transcribing of the required legal standards. Once Hayes, Mary Ann and the witnesses had signed, the process was complete. The next order of business was the recording of the last will and testament of John Hayes.

Although the law did not require the presence of a Clerk of Courts for the writing of a will, Hayes asked that Beale remain. The clerk had no other option since he had been brought to the house by carriage with John Lenox and had no other transport back to Baltimore.

Beale was asked to explain the basics of preparing the final document. He noted that the Will, itself, pertained to only land and its structures, the Testament referred to the estate, or movable goods and property. Everyone nodded that they understood.

Hayes began to dictate the terms, but it soon became clear that he was getting tired. He seemed to rush to complete the document, perhaps fearing that he might not be able to finish. The result was that after enumerating his desires regarding his bequest to his eldest daughter, he stopped dictating and announced that he was finished. Jane went to her father's side, and assuring him that she was grateful for his generosity to her, but feared that he had forgotten his intent to also bequeath property to Elizabeth as well. Despite being exhausted, Hayes nodded in agreement and continued.

April 28, 1719

In the name of God amen. The last will and testament of John Hayes being very week of body but of perfect memory blessed be to God for it . First I give and bequeath my Soul to Almighty God that gave it of my body to be buried in decent form and endeavor.

~ 123 ~

Item. I give and bequeath unto my son Thomas Stansbury and his heirs forever all my lands known as Scudamore's Lot which I now dispose of.

Item. I give and bequeath all my horses and cattle and hogs and all other utensils in the endeavor to him the above named Thomas Stansbury and this I do institute and ordain as my last will and testament revoking all other will be my made.

Signed and sealed in presence of....

With later apprehension forgetting of my daughter Elizabeth Lenox and desirous that she should have fifty acres of Privilege, one young horse as aforementioned off what demand I have upon the county, that is forty shillings in money and four hundred pounds of tobacco which is the whole with the above conclusion as witness my hand and seal the day and year above written.

John Hayes
His Mark

Stephen Body
John Hillen

The document had been signed and witnessed, and it was now official. Avarilla could no longer contain her frustration.

"Father, I do not understand. What is to become of me? Have I not cared for you since the death of my mother? Have I not managed all affairs of Mount Hayes that would be the provenance of the mistress of the household? How am I to survive?"

She was near to hysteria as she began to sob and to pace back and forth across the floor in front of her father's bed. It was a sad sight. Whenever she was upset, her limp became even more pronounced than usual, she clutched at her chest as she became more and more distraught. Jane, Elizabeth and Mary Ann all rushed to her side as she slumped to the floor, seemingly overcome with despair. To Avarilla, it seemed obvious that her father had abandoned her, and apparently disowned her. She would have no future at all.

Elizabeth knelt by her side and put her arms around her older sister. She patted her hair and attempted to calm her and assured her that she would always have a home with her at Kindness. This was no comfort to Avarilla who had her heart set on being mistress of Mount Hayes. Once the realization fully hit her that this would never be, her tears stopped as suddenly as they had begun. She did not rise, she did not speak, and suddenly her face was devoid of any emotion as she stared with a blank expression across the room. Her spirit had been crushed by this unexpected betrayal by her father.

Throughout the episode, Hayes had seemed unmoved and detached. When she finally became quiet, he spoke to her, as though explaining something to a very young child.

"Avarilla, as I have told you many times, you have no prospects for a husband. Perhaps things would be different if you were to smile on occasion, and rid your countenance of that infernal scowl, or at least pretend that you like people. Perhaps they would like you in return. Perhaps you could attract a husband and give me grandchildren to someday inherit from my estate. But the fact is that you are strong-willed, overbearing, and difficult to be around. But, for some unfathomable reason, your sister Elizabeth loves you and cares for you. He quickly added that Mary Ann cared for her as well. My instructions are for Mary Ann to welcome you into Mount Hayes after my death. If she should die before me, it is my wish that Elizabeth shall take you into her home. That's all that can be done."

It had been a long tirade and Hayes seemed exhausted from the effort. "I wish to rest now," he said as he closed his eyes. There was nothing for the assembled family members to do but to leave him to his nap.

Avarilla left the room without looking at anyone or saying a word. There was an unhappy silence that enveloped them as they made their way down the stairs and to the door. It was an awkward and unpleasant conclusion to their day.

The land transaction was successfully completed and the deed transfer was duly recorded in the Provincial Court of Baltimore County, while the Last Will and Testament was duly entered into the records of the Prerogative Court of Baltimore County.

Mary Ann was grateful for the kindness of Thomas Harris. He had made several trips to Mount Hayes after the land transaction. During his trips he always called upon Hayes to inquire about the state of his health and always joined him in a cup or two of ale.

On one of those occasions near the end of May, he broached the subject of the continuing education of young William. He had heard that Buckley, the former tutor, had been dismissed shortly after Hayes's illness. He suggested that Hayes might agree to send his ward, William, to join his sons at his plantation, Harris's Delight, to continue his studies. He explained that his sons, James and Richard were close in age to William, and assured Hayes that the tutor had agreed to take on an additional student without additional charge. He suggested that either Henry or one of his slaves could bring William to his estate, which was located a short distance from Mount Hayes.

Hayes considered the matter for a few moments, and concluded that if William's mother agreed, they would welcome the opportunity to continue the boy's education.

With that, Hayes called to Henry to fetch Mistress Mary Ann from the library.

Henry hastened down stairs and hesitantly interrupted Mary Ann who was doing her best to help her son with his lessons. Elizabeth was sorely missed, for she had always been willing to help, and after the departure of Buckley, William missed the companionship he had enjoyed with the Stansbury boys.

Henry entered the room and waited to be acknowledged by Mary Ann before speaking.

"What is it Henry," she asked.

"Massa Hayes he want you come now."

Mary Ann was always worried when she was unexpectedly called to her husband's room. She never knew what situation awaited her.

"Is Mister Hayes ill?

"No Mistress. Massa no be sick. Massa Harris be dere too, and he want to speak to you."

Mary Ann's heart skipped a beat, and she felt her face flush. She told William to continue with his attempts to master the writing of his letters, and hurried up the stairs to her husband's room.

Henry ran ahead and opened the door for her. She hesitated, brushed back her hair with her hands, and straightened the folds of her dress. The thought flashed

~ 127 ~

through her mind that she probably looked disheveled, and wished she had taken the time to attend to her appearance before rushing to the room. But here she was, with Henry waiting for her to enter. Once again, as on earlier occasions when she encountered Thomas Harris, she felt flustered.

Harris rose from his chair as she entered and walked toward her extending his hand. He bowed slightly and lifted her hand to his lips. She understood that he was merely being polite and gentlemanly but she wished he hadn't done it. She was embarrassed and didn't know exactly what to do next. She withdrew her hand, nodded to Harris, uttered a brief, "Good Morning, Mr. Harris," and hurried to her husband's bedside.

Hayes immediately explained Harris's suggestion and added his own approval of the offer. Again, Mary Ann was hesitant regarding anything involving her son. Did Hayes expect William to stay at the Harris estate permanently?

Harris saw the concern on her face and immediately hastened to suggest that one of the slaves might be permitted to bring her son every morning and return him later in the day.

"Of course, our tutor would not be offering instruction on Sundays," he was quick to add. Therefore, William would have those days to spend at Mount Hayes."

Mary Ann was well aware that she did not have the skills to give her son a proper education, and she wanted William to have a better life than she could ever have provided for him on her own. A decision had to be made quickly; she forced a smile and nodded her agreement.

"Splendid," both Hayes and Harris announced in unison, and then laughed at the coincidental nature of their responses.

"If it meets with your approval, I propose that Mistress Hayes bring William to my home tomorrow, or at her convenience, to introduce the boy to the tutor and make whatever arrangements might be necessary."

Hayes enthusiastically agreed that it sounded like a good idea and looking at Mary Ann asked, "What do you think, my dear? Is tomorrow convenient for you?"

To Mary Ann, it appeared that life moved at a strange pace. There were long periods of relative stability and calmness that too often were interrupted by unexpected events requiring life-changing decisions on a moment's notice. She rarely felt that she had any control over her own life or that of her son. It made her feel uneasy.

Nonetheless, she smiled and responded, "I am most grateful for the offer and tomorrow will be quite convenient. William and I shall see you tomorrow afternoon."

"Now, if you will excuse me, I must tend to my son." She again, smiled, and turned toward the door.

Harris touched her arm and announced his own intentions of leaving. "If you don't mind, I must leave as well. I have duties of my own awaiting my attention at home."

Approaching Hayes's bed, he shook his hand and walked to the door and held it open for her to pass.

They walked side by side down the hallway to the stairs and descended without a word. It was an awkward silence. When they reached the door at the end of the hallway, Harris turned to Mary Ann and again took her hand and kissed it. He looked into her eyes and in a gentle voice assured her, "I promise you, that I shall look after your son as though he were my own. He will be educated as well as I can provide."

She didn't know what to say, but fortunately, Harris turned abruptly, strode out the door and down the steps. She watched as he mounted his horse and rode away. She reminded herself that she had a husband who had offered refuge to her and her son when she was most desperate. Again, she felt ashamed that she harbored such secret feelings for the handsome neighbor. She took a deep breath, closed the door and decided to check on her husband before returning to William.

Hayes was still awake, smiling and nodding to her as he boasted, "My dear, things are working out nicely. Don't you agree?"

She was momentarily speechless. Hayes's unexpected assessment was exactly what she was thinking; however, she suspected, her reasons were quite different from his.

Again, she nodded her agreement, returned to his bedside and asked if she could bring him anything.

His immediate response was, "No, my dear. I believe I'm a little tired. I'll just rest for a while. Why don't you see to your son?"

Mary Ann kissed him on the cheek, straightened the covers around him and returned to the library and William's lessons.

The two were busily occupied when Molly entered the room to tell her that Massa Hayes had asked to be brought down to the parlor kitchen for dinner.

Mary Ann hurriedly straightened the parchment on the desk, started to put the hornbook in the drawer, but William objected. Like all hornbooks, the one he had received from Aunt Rilla had a handle with a hole through which a rope was fastened. He wanted to hang it around his neck and wear it to dinner. It was clear to Mary Ann that her son was proud of the fact that he was a student and wanted to show off this symbol of his status. Mary Ann smiled and agreed that he might wear it but suggested that it might be less awkward if it were tied to his belt. William agreed, but clearly thought it was much more impressive if worn around his neck. Once the book had been secured to his belt, they hurried down the hall to dinner.

Despite her attempts to ignore any current activity in the household, Avarilla couldn't help smiling when she saw the hornbook. She even initiated a conversation with William regarding his progress. William was eager to recite all that he had learned and the adults all congratulated him on his progress. That small event had lightened the usual solemn atmosphere of mealtime and the reprieve was a welcome change to all.

The month of May, like the previous month, was unusually hot and dry. In fact, during the entire Baltimore summer, they were plagued by one of the worst droughts to be endured by coastal Maryland. Despite the sale of 370 acres to Harris, and Isham's best efforts, it had been impossible to keep the entire tobacco crop sufficiently watered. Isham had done his best to preserve about half of the expected crop, but even the quality of that half seemed questionable. He feared that Massa Hayes would be furious, and hoped he would not face the whip if that were the case.

Molly had been fearful since the terrible incident last December that some dreadful evil inhabited Mount Hayes. And, now with the disturbing news regarding the crop, she was convinced. Mary Ann tried her best to reason with her. She pointed out that the drought had afflicted everyone around them, not just Mount Hayes. But Molly was not to be calmed. She devoted every spare moment of her waking hours to prayer, incantations, and protective talismans. She feared the end might be near for them all. She had, unfortunately, succeeded in convincing both Molly and Henry that they were all at risk from whatever evil resided among them.

Henry was given the task of taking William to the Harris estate daily for his lessons. Henry welcomed any opportunity to get away from Mount Hayes and its demons.

He normally would mount Old Ben and place William in front of him on the horse. William loved these trips to the Harris estate, as much as he enjoyed the lessons themselves. Benjamin Craddock was the tutor at the Harris household. He was a middle aged man, quite thin of physique, and amazingly animated. He had a pair of spectacles, which he held up to his eyes whenever he needed to see things clearly. In other words, he held the lenses to his eyes during their entire lesson. He was quite stern with the boys and permitted no lax attention during lesson time, and perpetually corrected their posture. William felt fortunate that his Aunt Rilla had drilled into him the importance of a straight back and squared shoulders. It was a lesson he had learned well, and for which he was now grateful. School Master Craddock demanded strict obedience to his rules, and infractions were immediately corrected by prompt and vigorous application of the switch to the young offender. This was an unpleasantness that young William avoided at all costs. His male classmates, Thomas and James, on the other hand, were far more lax in their attention to posture and suffered accordingly.

Eighteen-year-old Rachel, the eldest of the Harris girls, tutored her younger sisters in the skills she had learned from their mother. Her pupils included thirteen-year-old Jemima, and ten-year-old twins, Rebecca and Ruth. The youngest, four-year-old Sarah, was under the care of a kind and middle-aged slave named Bess.

When William returned to Mount Hayes after his daily lessons, he was so exhausted by the intensity and demands of School Master Craddock that he often had a difficult time staying awake during supper. It was on Sundays, when he was free to attend church with his family and then to have the remainder of the day at Mount Hayes, that he would share the events of the previous week with his mother. He constantly chattered about his lessons and his progress, but he also was obviously happy to be around so many children so near to his own age. Mary Ann was both relieved and happy that the experience was so rewarding for her son.

As for the other residents of Mount Hayes, hours seemed to drag on into weeks and before they realized it, the summer was over. As expected the tobacco crop was a dismal failure. The price paid for barrels of quality tobacco was high and the demand was great. Unfortunately the crop yield was low for Hayes and his neighbors. Worse yet, was the news that only a small number of Mt. Hayes barrels were deemed good enough for export. Mary Ann realized how fortunate they were that Hayes had agreed to sell a portion of his lands. Dr. Payne had been right, the sale had provided much needed financial resources to see them through the winter.

The plantation would limp along over the course of the next three years. It seemed to be just as difficult to recover from the failure of the tobacco crop as it was for Hayes to recover from his stroke.

Hayes experienced good days and bad days, all accompanied by varying stages of emotional upheavals. Mary Ann was glad that her son was spending the majority of his time at Harris's Delight rather than here where the entire household seemed steeped in gloom.

Each morning when Mary Ann went to check on her husband's condition, she was always fearful when she opened the door. It had become customary for one of the slaves to sit with him at night. A few of the cooks and laundresses took turns keeping watch over the ailing Hayes. Everyone was aware that it was only a matter of time.

Avarilla was particularly anxious. Her demeanor had remained unchanged since the episode surrounding her father's will. She felt rejected by her father, resented Mary Ann, and saw no hope for her future. She would be the victim of the whims and generosity of others. She had grown so accustomed to taking charge of the day to day running of Mount Hayes, that she was at a loss as to how to occupy her days. She mostly stayed in her room with her books and sought some solution to her dilemma. Those that came to her mind were now too horrible to contemplate.

The grind of the daily routine would continue for a little over three more years. Everyday seemed to be just a little more hopeless than the day before. Even Jane and

Elizabeth who had, early on after their father's stroke, made it a point to visit at least once a week, gradually lengthened the time between their visits to, at best, once every two or three months. Even then, the visits seemed strained and uncomfortable for everyone appeared to be at a loss for words. There were no happy thoughts to entertain them.

Hayes's mental state had also begun to deteriorate. His memory was especially bad and he often lost track of time. Nonetheless, he was aware that his daughters rarely came to see him. He missed William, but did get to see him every evening and on Sundays, but repeatedly asked that Jane bring his grandchildren to visit. Jane now had four boys. Her third son, Dixon, had been born just a few months after Hayes's stroke, and her second son, Edmund, was a little more than two. Hayes had not seen either of them.

When he asked about Elizabeth, he was told that she was expecting a child, but no one dared to tell him when the child, a boy, was stillborn.

Avarilla had swallowed her pride, and returned to read to her father in the late afternoon. These were usually short visits, because he often fell asleep after only a few minutes. Perhaps his sleepiness could be attributed in part, to the monotone voice in which Avarilla delivered her reading.

They all did the best they could, but everyone was fully aware that whatever their efforts, they would not produce an improvement in Hayes's health.

On Friday, December 4, 1722, Molly awakened Mary Ann just before dawn. There were tears streaming down her cheeks as she summoned her to Hayes's bedroom. In her husband's room Mary Ann found the cook who had sat with Hayes during the night. She too was crying and shaking her head. She explained that Hayes had opened his eyes and called out Mary Ann's name. She told him that she would fetch Mistress right away. But before she had finished the words, John Hayes closed his eyes, and departed this world.

CHAPTER 9
Confession

*E*veryone in the household had realized for some time that Hayes's condition would never improve, and that over the past several months he had slowly become weaker and less alert. For the last two weeks he had refused any solid food and accepted only water or broth, and those in small amounts. The finality of his expected death lay like a heavy burden upon them all. Certainly, life at Mount Hayes had not been cheerful for the past three years, but it had been routine. It was perhaps best described as boring, but it was nonetheless predictable. Suddenly Mary Ann's life was once again filled with dread and uncertainty. The dwelling and the 150 acres upon which it stood now belonged to her. But, she also had an obligation to accept Avarilla's presence in her home.

As the assembled members of the household stood in silence around the body of John Hayes, a shroud of sadness and desperation seemed to envelop them all. Molly was swaying gently lost in her prayers. Both Winny and Henry stood with their heads bowed, as did their father.

Mary Ann felt guilty that she could not shed a tear, but instead, was thankful that her husband's dreadful suffering had come to an end. Avarilla moved to her father's bedside and dropped to her knees, sobbing uncontrollably. She grasped her father's hand and in a soft whisper, begged for his forgiveness.

"I did not mean to harm you. I would never intentionally cause you pain and suffering. I brought this terrible affliction upon you because of my jealousy. Please forgive me."

Her face was contorted from grief and dismay as she turned to Mary Ann, still on her knees and continued her plea.

"May God forgive me for the evil that I have done. I was afraid that if my father married you, I would be thrown out of the house, and be forgotten. The drink was meant for you, not for him. And now father is dead. He has disowned me and I am thrown upon your mercy for my existence. I am doomed."

Mary Ann didn't know what to say to the distraught woman who had hated her enough to try to kill her. She just stood there as Molly and her family stared in puzzled dismay.

Finally, Mary Ann walked to Avarilla, helped her to rise to her feet, and responded to her confession.

"I have known for some time that you attempted to poison me. As a result I have been apprehensive about what you might try next. I have worried for my own safety as well as that of my son. I had no idea to what depths your hatred might provoke you." Mary Ann paused and looked around the room.

"You have asked God to forgive you, yet you have not asked that of me. Perhaps you think it would not be granted, and truly, I'm not certain that I can. There have been many occasions since that awful night when you offered the poisoned cup to me, when your attitude and behavior toward me have made me fearful for my life."

"Are you telling me that you have changed? Or are you simply upset that you were unsuccessful in your first attempt and haven't had the courage to try again?" she asked.

Avarilla's face was suddenly ashen as she stood with her mouth open, but without making a sound. She had never before witnessed Mary Ann being openly disapproving of her behavior. In the depths of her soul, she already knew that everyone around her had abandoned her and that she had lost everything of importance for her existence.

Avarilla turned slowly and walked to the door and down the hall to her room. She sat in the silence of her room and tried to foresee what her future might be. It seemed hopeless. She looked at the chest across the room. It was the chest that held the small box with the deadly nightshade berries. She stared at it for several minutes, then finally turned her attention to the books on the table in front of her, picked up her copy of *Hamlet*, and opened it to the page marked with the silk ribbon.

Mary Ann turned her attention to the task at hand, and sent Henry to notify Reverend Tibbs and to alert their neighbors of her husband's passing. Molly and Isham attended to washing and dressing of Hayes's body and in preparing the funeral bier, draped in black upon which the body would be placed in the parlor.

Molly was completely competent to attend to the necessary food and other details, but Mary Ann was feeling somewhat guilty about her confrontation with Avarilla. After all, the woman had just lost her father and clearly, was guilt ridden. Mary Ann felt pity for her and went to her room and knocked on the door. Avarilla did not answer. Mary Ann knocked a second time and announced her presence, "Avarilla, it's Mary Ann. I'd like to speak with you please."

The identifiable uneven footfall of a limp approached the door and opened it.

"What do you want?" she asked.

Mary Ann paused a moment before speaking. She hadn't planned what she was going to say, and was momentarily at a loss as to how to begin. Finally she spoke.

"Avarilla, I am aware of how much you loved your father, and how harsh his treatment was of you, but you must keep in mind that his failing health affected him both physically, mentally and emotionally. I know your father wanted you to be cared for, and you must know that I will honor his request. You will have a home here at Mount Hayes as long as it is in my power."

Avarilla had not expected this conciliatory tone from Mary Ann, and was hesitant to say something that might jeopardize the precarious nature of their relationship. But the woman just could not suppress her bitterness.

Her response was a softly muttered, but sarcastic, "You are too kind."

The woman could be so exasperating that Mary Ann was tempted to leave her to wallow in her own self pity. But then she remembered Elizabeth's cautioning her that it was just Avarilla's nature and that she was very competent in running the household.

Mary Ann sighed and began again.

"I thought you might be willing to assist with the planning of your father's funeral. You are more experienced in planning things and I would appreciate your help."

Avarilla tried her best to mask her pleasure at this change of events, but as usual, her comment was a curt, "Whatever pleases you."

Mary Ann's first thought was that it would please her if no one were to be poisoned at the funeral, but she decided to hold her tongue. She was hopeful that things would get better.

Avarilla immediately threw herself into supervision of the preparations. She advised the cooks that neighbors would be arriving on Wednesday, December 5, for the funeral, ordered Winny to get busy preparing the black ribbons for the mourners, and started preparing the list of pies and cakes to be baked.

In its own way, the necessity for quick action helped the household to keep busy and to occupy their minds as an escape from the unpleasant atmosphere.

As was the custom, Bartholomew Hedge had been notified and delivered the coffin on Saturday, December 8. The entire parish again arrived to join the procession that followed the coffin to the family grave plot. It was strangely reminiscent of that dreary, snowy day five years earlier when they had buried young Jemima. The weather was somewhat better on this occasion than it had been then. The ground was frozen, and it was cold, but the sun was shining in a cloudless sky.

On the walk back to Mount Hayes with eight-year-old William by her side, she was reminded of how she had felt that cold day in March when she and William had sat alone by Phillip's grave, and now, she had just come from the burial of her second husband.

She was amazed at the many changes they had experienced. She reminded herself that she now had a home, an elaborate one, with beautiful furnishings, slaves to attend to the chores and a son who was getting an excellent education. She was fortunate, and she should be grateful, she chided herself.

But although she was grateful to Hayes and loved him like a father, she did not feel the great loss she had felt at Phillip's death.

Her thoughts were interrupted by the sound of William calling to Thomas Harris and his children as he ran towards them. The Harris family had been a godsend for William and for her. At the Harris estate, he had become more outgoing, at ease around children his own age and around adults as well. He was the light of her life and she was very proud of him.

Harris approached her, extended his hand, took hers in his own and offered his condolences. He and his children accompanied them back to Mount Hayes and Mary Ann invited them into the house for some refreshments. They happily accepted and the children immediately headed for the parlor kitchen and warmed themselves by the fire. Mary Ann called to Molly to see that there was plenty of food for their guests.

Mary Ann invited Harris into the front parlor and they sat by the fire. Despite the sunshine, they were both chilled from their walk back from the gravesite.

Mary Ann was eager to express her gratitude to Harris for the attention he had given to William with his schooling. Harris laughed and added, "It has been my pleasure. After all, your son is quite the scholar and has been a good influence on James and Richard. He's a great favorite with the twins too."

Mary Ann's bright smile indicated the pleasure his remarks gave her. After all, every mother likes to hear compliments about their children. But Harris wasn't finished speaking. He arose from his chair and sat near her.

He sat there for a moment, just looking into her eyes, without speaking. The silence began to be uncomfortable and Mary Ann looked away and stood up, announcing that she would have Molly bring them some warm cider, or rum if he preferred.

"No, not at the moment, thank you. Harris replied, Please come sit by me for a bit."

Mary Ann did as he asked, but felt her face flush, and was suddenly very uncomfortable. After all, she had just buried her husband. She feared that he might take her hand, and self-consciously clasped her hands together in her lap.

Harris seemed to sense her discomfort and leaned back in his chair and smiled. "I realize that this is a somewhat awkward moment, considering the occasion, but," he was quick to add, "I believe you already know that I have feelings for you. You are a very beautiful woman, but more than that, you are a warm and caring person and a wonderful mother. As you no doubt know, my wife, Rachel died four years ago giving birth to our youngest child, Sarah. Custom dictates that I should have taken a wife before now, but I have been enchanted by you since the first moment I saw you."

Mary Ann looked at the floor, turned her head to glance at the fire, and fidgeted with the handkerchief in her hands. This seemed so inappropriate, yet, she remembered an old saying, *"When a widower comes to a funeral with flowers, more than likely they are for the new widow, and not the deceased."* Since there were more men than women in Baltimore, and an unmarried woman with a child needed the support of a husband, it was the expected thing to do.

Nonetheless, she was uncomfortable, despite the fact that she too had immediately felt an attraction to this handsome neighbor. It was also true that he had eight children still living at home without a mother.

She still had no idea how to respond, but she smiled at Harris and he returned her smile and was just reaching for her hand when Winny came through the door with cake and drinks. Mary Ann was relieved by the diversion, but she was also truly happy for the first time in three years. She had a lot to think about.

They quietly sipped their warm cider and slowly ate the delicious spice cake they had been served. There were a few moments of uncomfortable silence, but Harris leaned toward her and suggested that it might be a welcome diversion for her to visit his home.

He quickly noted, "I realize that you will have many matters that will need your attention. I was hoping that, perhaps in a couple of weeks, you might accept my invitation to come with William and spend the day while he is involved with his studies. I would be honored if you would accept my invitation."

His smile was infectious, and she found it impossible to say no.

"I think that would be quite enjoyable, Mister Harris, I will look forward to it."

Harris smiled even more broadly, and took her hand and covered it with his other hand. He lowered his eyes, cocked his head to one side, and asked, "Since we are such good friends, do you think you could call me Thomas?"

She laughed and assured him, "Yes, Thomas, I will."

"Good, good! he exclaimed. How about the week before Christmas. That Friday is, I believe, the twenty-first of December. The house will be decorated for the holidays and my hope is that you will find it pleasant."

"I'm sure I will. It is most thoughtful of you. I look forward to it," she assured him.

"As will I, Mary Ann. I hope you won't mind if I address you so," he asked, as he took her hand.

"Not at all, Thomas."

He picked up his hat and cloak from the chair where he had tossed them, and put them on as he started toward the door.

When they arrived at the front door, he once again took her hand and kissed it, saying, "Good day Mary Ann, I look forward to our next meeting."

Before she realized what she was saying, the words were out of her mouth, "As do I, Thomas."

For some unexpected reason, Mary Ann was not as preoccupied with the usual tasks required to settle an estate. She decided that she could just wait until her next meeting with Thomas. Thoughts of him always brought a smile to her lips and a wistfulness she could not explain. She was looking forward to spending the day with him at his home.

Avarilla, on the other hand, was the epitome of gloom. Her shoulders were drooped and she moved with a slowness that suggested the hopelessness she felt. She remembered her father's request and Mary Ann's assurance that she would do as he asked. But she was well aware of the lingering animosity between them. She was afraid to ask her about her intentions for fear she might force her out of the house immediately

Her other concern was in regard to Elizabeth. Although she had promised to care for her, Avarilla was confused by her younger sister's recent behavior. Elizabeth had seemed uncharacteristically distant during their father's lingering decline. Even at the funeral and burial, Elizabeth extended little more than a greeting and farewell. It was unsettling. Had Mary Ann told Elizabeth about the cup of poisoned mead? Had she managed to turn her younger sister against her?

Avarilla had become so anxious about her future that she had no appetite and the fit of her clothing revealed how thin and frail she had become. For the time being, there was nothing she could do but wait and hope for the best.

Had Avarilla shared her worries about Elizabeth with Mary Ann, she might have taken some comfort in knowing that she too had been concerned about Elizabeth. Fearing that she might be ill, Mary Ann had approached Elizabeth a few weeks earlier after church one Sunday. Elizabeth softly confided that she had suffered a miscarriage the month before.

Tears filled Elizabeth's eyes as she confessed her distress that God had now twice denied her a child. She feared that she would never have a child of her own. She had been unable to lift herself from the terrible depression she felt. Those feelings had only been intensified by the death of her father, and now, her usual outgoing personality had been replaced by one of quiet, sad reserve. She avoided social gatherings whenever she could and preferred the solitude of her room.

Avarilla spent most of her days in her room as well, absorbed in her books or brooding about her future. When Molly asked if she would like her to cut and bring in holly and mistletoe and other greenery to decorate the house for the Christmas season, Avarilla's reply was, "Ask your mistress, Mary Ann, she makes the decisions for the household now."

Molly was surprised, for Avarilla had always taken pleasure in supervising all activities in the house. It was unsettling to have such uncertainty, but Molly went to find Mary Ann for instructions. She found her in the library humming softly and admiring the embroidered fabric that she had just finished. Molly smiled as well and nodded her approval of the nearly complete project.

Molly remembered her purpose in coming to Mary Ann and asked if she would like to have greenery brought in. Mary Ann nodded with enthusiasm.

"That's a wonderful idea, Molly! I'm sure Avarilla will be pleased and will help us decide on how best to display them."

Molly gave a half-hearted nod in agreement, but she was not optimistic about the outcome.

Molly and her two children collected the greenery and displayed it on the large table in the parlor kitchen. Mary Ann was pleased with the assortment and sent Henry to ask Avarilla to join them.

Avarilla entered the room with her usual brooding scowl. Mary Ann pointed to the assortment of plants and berries on the table and asked, "Tell me Avarilla, what would be your recommendations as to how best to use these?"

Despite her best efforts to act uninterested, old habits die hard, and Avarilla immediately began to gather a cluster of pine branches and on top she added a holly branch loaded with bright red berries. She quickly became absorbed in the task and ordered Henry to the lower level sewing room and bring up a pair of scissors and whatever red fabric he could find. Henry quickly returned with an armload of various fabric remnants. Among them was a fairly large piece of red velvet left over from the bolt used to make William's first coat.

Avarilla was at once apprehensive and with a look of annoyance picked up the velvet, handed it back to Henry, and ordered him to return it to the sewing room.

"Well, we obviously cannot use this. It is far too fine, and, besides it belongs to young Master William. We wouldn't want to do anything that would upset his mother, now would we?"

Mary Ann could not suppress a smile of amusement. She shook her head slightly, took the red velvet from Henry's arms, and cut a fairly wide, very long strip from the bolt. Smiling, she handed it to Avarilla.

"Don't be foolish, Avarilla. This will make a beautiful bow to adorn the greenery. Don't you think?" She asked.

Avarilla seemed disappointed that Mary Ann was being gracious. Grudgingly she began to tie the fabric around the base of the greenery and finished it with an elegant bow. But, when the task was completed, she was quite pleased with her handiwork. The red velvet was beautiful.

It wasn't long before Molly and Winny joined them as they created various assortments, including the mistletoe that would be hung in the doorway of all of the rooms.

The two weeks before her scheduled visit to Harris's Delight were pleasant and uneventful, but Mary Ann was concerned when she awoke early on the Wednesday two days before her planned visit to the Harris estate, she was concerned that it had begun to snow. She bundled William up, wrapped with a blanket around his shoulders, and supplied one for Henry as well for their trip to the Harris's. William was delighted with the snow, but Mary Ann was always concerned for her child's welfare. It became dark so early in the winter, and she feared that if the snow continued at its current rate of accumulation, the return trip that evening might be difficult. She instructed Henry to ask if William might spend the night.

"Now Henry, you must ask Master Harris politely. Ask him if he would allow William to spend the night. And, she quickly added, bring me his response."

Henry smiled, hoping that he would not have to return late that night to bring William home.

"Yes, Mistress. I take good care of Master William." And with that, he gave Old Ben a quick kick with his heel, and they headed out in what had become a blizzard.

Henry liked Massa Harris. He liked everything about Harris's Delight. Bess was as good a cook as his mother, and everyone in the household was always nice to him. On this particular morning, Bess opened the door and ushered them to the fire, taking care to shake the snow from the two blankets before bringing them into the house.

Harris walked into the room and greeted them with a smile, and told them how glad he was to see them on such a snowy day. Henry was glad that he didn't have to search for Harris and immediately told him of his Mistress's request that William spend the night.

Harris beamed a wide smile, "Of course. That is an excellent idea. From the looks of it, we are in for quite a bit of snow. Tell your mistress that I propose that William remain here tomorrow night as well. Also tell her that I shall send either a carriage or a sleigh, whichever is required to bring her here day after tomorrow for her visit."

Harris then turned to Bess and asked that she give both boys something warm to eat and drink.

"William, when you have finished, please come to the library for your lessons with Master Craddock. Henry, don't forget to give my message to Mistress Mary Ann."

CHAPTER 10

"The course of true love never did run smooth."

William Shakespeare
A Midsummer Night's Dream

*W*ednesday and Thursday seemed to creep by as Mary Ann eagerly awaited her visit to the Harris estate. By late Thursday night, the snow had stopped, and on Friday morning, the sun shone bright and clear. The icicles on the trees and the crystal flakes of snow glittered in the sun like so many diamonds. Mary Ann smiled as she dressed in a soft gray wool gown. Today would be a good day.

Molly hurried to her room to announce that Massa Thomas had arrived with a sleigh. Mary Ann felt giddy with delight. He had made the trip himself, to escort her. Although she had been to the Harris plantation once before, to meet the new schoolmaster, she had been so concerned about her son and the new change to their routine, that she had hardly noticed her surroundings at all. She hurried down the stairs to meet Thomas.

His smile, as always, was infectious, and she returned it with joy. He took her hand, kissed it, helped her on with her cloak, and held her arm as they walked down the snow-laden steps. It was a rather precarious venture, and Mary Ann slipped and would have fallen had it now been for Thomas who grasped her around the waist. She felt her pulse quicken as he held her close for a moment before continuing down the steps into the waiting sleigh.

Henry was holding the reins of a beautiful black horse. Around the horse's neck a number of small bells were attached to the harness. As they were about to climb into the sleigh, Molly beckoned to Henry from the front door.

She was holding two parcels covered in heavy wool. They contained bricks that Molly had heated. Thomas waved and thanked her and placed the warm parcels on the floor of the sleigh to keep their feet warm for the trip back to Harris's Delight. Mary Ann thought the estate had been aptly named. She smiled and when Thomas offered her his arm, she moved closer to him and put her arm through his.

He flicked the reins and the horse responded quickly with a smooth gait as the bells chimed in rhythm with the horse's hooves.

Their arrival was greeted by the boisterous laughter of eight children as they bounded down the stairs, which fortunately, had been cleared of the treacherous snow. School Master Craddock, had released them, albeit briefly, to greet Harris and his guest. It was a warm welcome, and Mary Ann felt a happiness that she had not known for a long time. Nothing, she thought, equals the pleasure of the company of so many happy, healthy children.

Thomas helped her climb down from the sleigh and again held her arm as they walked up the steps, which like those at Mount Hayes narrowed as they neared the door. The children were chattering away and seemed sincerely glad to see her. William was smiling broadly, and not waiting for Harris to make introductions, loudly announced to all, that she was his mother. He quickly added,

"Isn't she pretty?"

Mary Ann was embarrassed, but Thomas only smiled and added, "Yes, indeed, William. Your mother is very beautiful and kind as well."

Bess met them at the door and shooed the children down the hall to the schoolroom, midst protests from them all.

Harris hastened to assure them, "You will have plenty of time to visit with Mistress Hayes later. You must tend to your lessons now."

Mary Ann and Thomas entered the front room where a fire was blazing brightly. As they seated themselves by the fire, Mary Ann noted that the room was, in many ways, much like the parlor at Mount Hayes, but with several more upholstered chairs. Some were covered in crewel embroidery. Thomas noticed her interest in the chairs and explained that his wife, Rachel had done the embroidery. There were also two larger seating pieces drawn up on either side of the fireplace. These sofas were meant to accommodate two people at a time. Realizing that the household included eight children, it became clear that the family spent quite a bit of time together. The walls on either side of the fireplace held shelves, all crowded with books. Over the mantel, hung a painted portrait. Mary Ann had never seen anything like it. The woman in the painting was seated, and with her were four children. The tallest was a handsome boy of about ten or eleven years old, a younger boy who appeared to be about four and a girl whom Mary Ann guessed to be about six. The woman was holding a baby of only a few months.

"That's my wife Rachel with our oldest son Thomas, and our daughter Rachel, son James and the infant is Jemima."

Mary Ann was enchanted. She had never seen such a thing.

Thomas explained, "The artist was a German painter. Rachel insisted that the painting had to include all of our children at the time. As you well know, young children don't stand still very long. It took several months working with one child at a time. Rachel was insistent, and I am certainly happy to have the painting now. But at the time, I was impatient to get the man and his paints out of the house."

Mary Ann could see the sadness in his eyes as he stared at the portrait. Clearly he still missed his wife as much as she missed Phillip.

"Your wife was very beautiful. I understand how great a loss you feel, it is much the same as that which I have felt," Mary Ann offered as she touched his hand.

In an attempt to lighten the mood, Harris took her arm and led her to the doorway.

"There's much more to see. Come, let me show you the rest of the house."

They toured the entire house, which had a somewhat different organization of rooms than that of Mount Hayes. The house was constructed in the shape of a large letter H, with two wings extending on both sides from the center portion of the house. There were four large arched structures, each supporting two chimneys. Thomas explained that the large entry room had been the scene of many happy balls and parties in earlier years. On both sides of this room were four more very large rooms that served much the same purpose as those at Mount Hayes. There was a formal parlor, a library, a parlor kitchen and a storage pantry and three large bedrooms, which included the master bedroom and one for the boys and another for the girls. A small number of house slaves lived on the lower level.

Many Ann found it charming, and more importantly, it seemed a happy home.

They enjoyed a delicious meal of venison, turkey, boiled vegetables and dumplings and a variety of sweets.

It was a large and hearty meal, and after finishing, Thomas suggested that he take her on a tour of the grounds. He confided that unless he got into the bracing cold air, he might well fall asleep from the amount of food he had consumed.

Mary Ann laughed and agreed. Thomas called for the horse and sleigh to be brought around to the front and asked Bess to reheat the bricks and prepare the bundle.

The children were disappointed that they were not to be included in this outing, but knew better than to object when ordered back to their studies by Master Craddock.

Harris's land holdings were far more extensive than Mary Ann had realized. They were gone for several hours and both were feeling quite chilled, when Mary Ann asked: "Would you mind if we go back now? It's very cold."

Harris apologized and headed the horse back to the house. When they arrived at the front door, he hesitated for a moment, and took her hand. "I hope very much that you like it here. I wanted you to see the estate, but I fear there is still more that we did not cover. I wonder, if you could ever see yourself as mistress of Harris's Delight?"

If that was supposed to be a proposal, it was a very unusual one, and one to which she did not know how to respond. She sat confused and silent.

Harris aware of her hesitation to answer, added, "Of course, I realize this is not an appropriate time to speak of such things."

He jumped down from the sleigh and helped her to step down and, as before, took her arm as they walked up the stairs. As soon as they entered, he called to Bess, and instructed her to bring some hot tea into the parlor. He added, "Also inform School Master Craddock that young William and his mother will be departing within the hour to return to Mount Hayes."

They drank their tea in relative silence by the fire. Mary Ann was confused: Harris suddenly seemed withdrawn. When they had finished with their tea and had warmed themselves, he sent for Dan, a middle-aged slave with a wide and nearly toothless grin, and told him to hitch up the horse and bring around the sleigh. When Dan had readied the sleigh, Harris accompanied Mary Ann and William to the front door. He patted William on the head and told him that there would be no further lessons until after the Christmas holidays. He took Mary Ann's hand and kissed it, but did not look into her eyes as he had done before.

The ride home was far different than the very pleasant one she had enjoyed earlier. William was sleepy, and immediately laid his head on her lap and fell asleep. She didn't understand how she could have offended him.

On Sunday, the snow began again and added to the several inches left from the previous snowfall. This time there were strong winds and the new snow produced large snowdrifts. William had a cold and a constant cough and she decided that they would not make the trip to church. It was a lonely Sunday.

The snow continued until mid-day December 24. She was heartbroken that her parting with Thomas had been so abrupt. Each day she waited expectantly for some word from him. She had hoped that he might visit on Christmas, or perhaps send for her and her son to join his family for the festivities. As it was, it was a sad, lonely day.

She told herself that she was just being silly. She was no longer a child. She should know better than to have such strong feelings for a man that she barely knew. She chastised herself for thinking that Thomas had been planning to propose. What a fool she was.

She tried her best to stay busy with her sewing and attention to household matters, to which Avarilla seemed disinterested. She tried her best to entertain her son and to enjoy this unexpected time with him. The unforeseen stopping of the lessons suddenly made her fearful that Thomas might have sent her son away for good. Had he decided that he was no longer interested in either her or her son? She was at a loss to understand. He seemed such an honest and honorable man. As the days following Christmas, and the New Year dragged by, she again resigned herself to a lonely, nearly solitary existence at Mount Hayes. Normally, Twelfth Night was a day for celebration of Epiphany, but it had also been the night, one year ago, when her husband had drunk the poisoned drink. She was beginning to think that Molly might be right. The house was a place where evil dwelt.

Avarilla spent nearly all of her time in her room, absorbed in her books, William was bored, and Mary Ann was miserable. That evening, she and the household went to bed early. It was dark by five thirty in the evening, and there seemed nothing better to do to pass the time. Her sleep was not a sound one, as she tossed and turned and tried to understand why Thomas had suddenly lost interest in her.

Early the next morning, Molly came to her door and told her that Massa Thomas was waiting in the parlor, and said he was eager to see her. Her heart leapt in her throat, but after a moment's consideration, she was confused. Was she to be a momentary diversion, only to be tossed aside and then be drawn back to him on a passing impulse?

~ 157 ~

She dressed slowly, trying to decide just how to greet the handsome neighbor. She acknowledged to herself that she was attracted to him, but his abrupt dismissal of her and her son at his estate was puzzling. Once again, upon thinking about it, she decided to hold her tongue. She would not exhibit anger, nor take offense at his recent rejection of her. She remembered that she was now mistress of Mount Hayes, and as such, she must be a gracious hostess. She opened the door to her room and slowly descended the stairs.

She was surprised to see that Thomas had not waited in the parlor, but was standing at the foot of the stairs. He was smiling up at her and had a small package wrapped in parchment in his hand. He took her hand in his, and as he had done many times before, kissed it, and looked deep into her eyes. As usual on such occasions, she felt flushed, and uncertain as to what she should do.

"Shall we go to the parlor?" she asked as she moved toward the front of the house.

"Of course," he responded.

A fire was already burning in the fireplace and the room seemed warm and cozy. The sun was shining, and the weather had warmed to the point that the icicles hanging from the eves were starting to melt and made a soft, drip, drip, sound as they hit the sills.

Thomas did not immediately sit, but placed the small package on a table and took both of her hands in his. He began with an apology.

"Mary Ann, my dearest, I offer my humble apologies to you for the impertinence of my question to you when last we met. It was inconsiderate, and thoughtless of me to make such a proposal to you at a time when you surely were bombarded by the memory of so many unfortunate events. I had completely forgotten that Hayes had first been taken ill around this same time of December of last year, and that your marriage had been on Twelfth Night. Worst of all, he died only a little over a month ago. I hope you will forgive me for that time, and for this as well."

Once again, Mary Ann was speechless.

Thomas continued, "This is still probably entirely the wrong time to intrude upon you, but I have been so worried that you might have mistaken my actions. I could wait no longer to see you again."

Mary Ann sat down, fearing that, had she not, she might have fallen. She felt light-headed, and so happy that she began to cry.

"Oh, my word, I have done it again!" Thomas exclaimed. "I am truly sorry. I will leave at once."

Mary Ann quickly got to her feet, touched his arm, and begged, "No, please do not leave. I have missed you so."

She took a deep breath, sat down, and began again. "I was afraid that I had angered you somehow, and that you were abandoning me and my son."

Thomas knelt by her side, and again took her hands in his, saying, "Nothing could be farther than the truth. I have intended for some time to ask you to marry me, but feared it was too soon after all you have suffered."

She wiped a tear from her cheek, smiled at him, and suggested softly, "If there is something you would like to ask me, Thomas, now is the time."

He laughed and nodded his head in understanding, saying, "I guess I'm not very accomplished at this am I? "Mary Ann, will you do me the honor of being my wife?"

She laughed through even more tears, and threw her arms around his neck, realizing, as Avarilla entered the room, that it was a most inappropriate thing to do.

Avarilla turned abruptly and with an expression of disgust, muttering something under her breath. Neither of them could hear what she said, but neither of them cared.

Suddenly realizing that Mary Ann had not officially responded to his proposal, he asked, "Well, mistress, may I have an answer?"

Mary Ann was suddenly very quiet, and she paused briefly before answering.

"I do indeed want to become your wife, Thomas, but I feel there are things we must discuss.

"Things, what things?" he asked with concern in his voice.

"Avarilla, for one. Hayes asked and I promised that Avarilla would have a home at Mount Hayes as long as it was in my power to provide it for her."

Thomas, his face suddenly showing concern, asked, "What would you like to do?"

"What I would like to do is to never see her again, but clearly I must honor my commitment."

Thomas was silent for a moment, apparently deep in thought, but finally spoke.

"As I'm sure you understand, once we are married Mount Hayes belongs, by law, to me."

Seeing the frown on Mary Ann's face he continued. "Wait, let me finish. My hope is that you, William, and I and my children will live at my home. What would you think about leaving Avarilla at Mount Hayes? She could live out the rest of her life there, and I will be glad to permit the house slaves to remain there with her. I will continue to farm the land and will see to it that she has sufficient funds to maintain her and the house."

Mary Ann was stunned, but excited by the offer. "Oh Thomas, would you really be willing to do that?"

"For you, my dear, of course." With that he wrapped her in his arms in a warm embrace and the two kissed for the first time and neither were in the least concerned if Avarilla walked into the room again.

"Now then, it's settled. May I have my answer now?"

Once again Mary Ann paused. "That is a most generous offer, but," she paused again.

"But what? Confound it woman, just tell me your concerns!"

Mary Ann was hesitant to continue, but there had been so many upheavals in her life as well as in those of her son, she felt compelled to pursue yet another point. "It's William, I want to know that his future will be secure."

Harris, relieved, smiled once again, and proposed an additional solution. "My dear, as I told you before, Mount Hayes becomes mine only because of Maryland law regarding property rights of married women. I promise you, that when William becomes of age, he shall have Mount Hayes as his home. I also promise to treat him as my own. This is my pledge to you."

Mary Ann was overcome with a mixture of joy, love, and unending gratitude to this man who had come to the rescue of her and her son. She smiled, and gave Thomas an answer to his question.

"Yes, Thomas, I accept your proposal and am honored to be your wife."

It was decided that the banns of marriage would be read for the first time the following Sunday, January 19. They strolled hand in hand to the back of the house where William was eating breakfast. He immediately jumped to his feet when he saw Thomas, and ran and hugged him around the legs. Thomas lifted the boy in his arms and

~ 161 ~

said, "Young man, your mother and I have news to tell you, but finish your breakfast first."

William, once again, forgetting some of the many rules he had been taught regarding table etiquette, finished his porridge as quickly as he could. Then, he immediately demanded, "Tell me."

Mary Ann and Thomas both laughed at the child's inquisitiveness, and each holding one of his hands, walked back to the formal parlor.

William was so excited that Mary Ann feared he might be anticipating a present, but he would not be calmed until he heard the news.

Thomas hesitated a bit, cleared his throat, and began, "Well, my boy, I hope it will meet with your approval that your mother and I plan to marry."

William began to jump up and down, threw his arms around his mother's neck and kissed her cheek, and turned to Thomas, and announced, "I know, I know, they told me, but I was afraid it wasn't true, "he shouted.

"Who told you William?" Thomas inquired.

"Everybody, Thomas, Jr., James, Rachel, and Jemima, everybody?"

Mary Ann was curious, "How did they know?"

"I may have mentioned it," Thomas whispered.

The next three months seemed to fly by. There were so many plans to be made, so many decisions in combining two households. They had both approached Avarilla with their plans to marry, and she was, as expected very upset. But upon learning that she would remain at Mount Hayes, with a staff and funds, it was as though some magic hand had erased all her fears and despair. But as was her nature, she was unable to express any true feelings of gratitude. She assumed it was no more than what she was entitled.

Thomas and Mary Ann were married on Saturday, March 14, 1724, in St Paul's Parrish Church. They had discussed the possibility of having the wedding at home as had been Thomas's wedding to Rachel, and Mary Ann's earlier two weddings. Ultimately they jointly decided that it would perhaps bring better fortune to be married in the church. Reverend William Tibbs performed the ceremony.

Their marriage was a happy one with a home filled with the laughter of their children. They gave elaborate parties and balls attended by their many neighbors and were honored with many invitations in return.

They rarely saw Avarilla, except on those few occasions when she went to church. They had noticed that she had developed a lingering cough and that she looked sickly. Mary Ann suspected that she might have contracted consumption. She and Thomas made a couple of trips to check on her and the condition of the house, but they were never made to feel welcome, despite their generosity to her.

William was another story. Avarilla always seemed delighted to see him and would have Molly prepare something special on his behalf. But William was growing up and the bond that had developed between him and the Harris family was a strong one, and over time he made fewer and fewer trips to Mt. Hayes. This was in part due to the strong affection he felt for his youngest stepsister, Sarah who was four years younger than he. Over time, the two fell in love and both Thomas and Mary Ann were pleased when the couple married in St. Paul's Church in March 1732.

The celebration two days after the wedding was held at Harris's Delight and everyone from the surrounding area was invited. This included Hayes's daughters: Jane and her husband Thomas Stansbury, Elizabeth, who was recently widowed, and Avarilla, who declined the invitation.

Shortly after the wedding, Thomas and Mary Ann revealed to the newlyweds that Mount Hayes was to be theirs as a wedding present. William was overwhelmed and delighted and insisted that Sarah must see their new home immediately.

Sarah, unlike her sisters, loved horses and was quite a good rider. The two rode the few miles to Mount Hayes. William raced up the stairway to the entrance and was greeted by Molly, who now moved slowly due to the aggravations of age and rheumatism. But she smiled broadly and welcomed the couple into the home. William immediately asked where he could find Avarilla.

"She be in de flower garden, Massa William, law, she be glad to see you and Mistress."

William and Sarah proceeded to the back and to the garden where he had spent so many happy hours with his mother and his Aunt Rilla.

He was shocked at how pale she looked, but she immediately came toward them with her arms outstretched. "William, it makes me so happy to see you. Let's go inside for some refreshments."

"First, Aunt Rilla, I am pleased to introduce to you the new mistress of Mount Hayes, My wife, Sarah."

"What? Avarilla stammered, I don't understand."

"We have been given Mount Hayes as a wedding present. Isn't it wonderful?" he asked.

Avarilla suddenly looked as though she might faint, and William rushed to support her. "Let's get you inside, Aunt Rilla, you don't look well."

As another bout of uncontrollable coughing overtook and shook her frail body, she responded. "Yes, I think that it is best if I go to my room. I'm very tired."

William and Sarah did as the woman had requested and helped her to her room and called to Molly to attend to her. Avarilla looked at the young couple, and with a dismissive flick of her hand toward the door, announced, "I think it best if you go now."

William was stunned. Avarilla had always seemed fond of him and glad to have him around. The greeting embarrassed him, and he was upset that Avarilla had not welcomed his new bride. He turned to Sarah and suggested that they would come again later when Avarilla was feeling better.

When they returned home, he told his mother about his meeting with Avarilla. He explained that he had only wanted to introduce his bride, the new mistress of Mount Hayes, to his aunt. As soon as Mary Ann heard the words she immediately knew why Avarilla had acted as she did. She decided that in a day or two, she and Thomas would accompany William and Sarah to Mount Hayes to reassure Avarilla that she would always have a home there.

Three days later Henry arrived from Mount Hayes with an urgent plea that Massa Harris and Mistress Mary Ann must return to Mount Hayes with him. They were alarmed by the fear in Henry's voice. What had Avarilla done now, they wondered?

William and Sarah joined Thomas and Mary Ann on the trip to Mount Hayes. They traveled by carriage with Henry following along behind on a horse. When they arrived, both Isham and Molly were waiting at the door. They walked up to Avarilla's room. Winny was waiting outside the door, her eyes wide with fear.

"Winny, what has happened?" Mary Ann asked.

Winny did not answer but stepped aside as she opened the door. Avarilla was slumped over a table where she had been sitting. Thomas immediately went to her side and placed his fingers on her throat to search for a pulse. He shook his head slowly. Avarilla was dead.

Mary Ann walked to the desk where she found one of Avarilla's favorite books, *Hamlet* open on the table. To the right of the book was a delicately decorated cup and saucer. The cup was empty save for a small paste like residue on the bottom. Alongside it was a small black empty box.

Mary Ann turned to look at Molly, who was rocking slowly and chanting.

"What happened Molly?," she asked.

"Don't know Mistress. Mistress Avarilla, she no eat, she no talk, she jus cough. Then, she added softly, she be sad."

Mary Ann stepped closer to the table and looked more carefully at the open book. A black silk ribbon marked the page. Mary Ann had not noticed before that there was also a scrap of parchment on which were written a series of numbers: 3-1-56.

It took a moment before she noticed that Avarilla had been reading from Act three, Scene one. She was saddened, but not necessarily surprised to read from the beginning of line 56:

> *To be, or not to be, that is the question.*
> *Whether 'tis nobler in the mind to suffer*

The slings and arrows of outrageous fortune,
Or to take arms against a sea of troubles,
And by opposing, end them?
To die; to sleep;
No more; and by a sleep to say we end.
The heart-ache and the thousand natural shocks
That flesh is heir to, 'tis a consummation
Devoutly to be wish'd. To die, to sleep.

Mary Ann paused for a long moment and picked up the scrap of parchment and put it in her pocket. She closed the copy of *Hamlet*, and silently said her goodbye to the woman who had caused her so much pain.

She turned to look at Molly, and the two women exchanged a brief moment of unspoken understanding.

"Send for the doctor and for Reverend Tibbs, Molly," Thomas instructed, and to William and Sarah, "I suggest that you postpone moving into Mount Hayes for a while."

There was little speculation, if any, regarding the cause of Avarilla's death. She had been sick for quite a long time, had grown quite frail and most certainly her death had been the result of consumption. And the matter was closed.

Avarilla was buried in the Hayes graveyard next to her parents.

Part Two
Sarah the Survivor

Mt. Hayes Plantation
North Side of Back River
Baltimore County, Maryland, 1732

CHAPTER 11
The Melancholy Bride

Sarah carefully folded the dress, and although the day on which she had worn it had been one of the happiest days of her young life, she couldn't shake the shock and sadness of the scene that they had found at Mount Hayes earlier that morning.

She ran her hand over the folds of the satin dress, wishing that her mother were there to offer comfort and counsel. There had been other occasions during her life when she had lamented the fact that she had never known her mother. Despite the fact that she had been loved, protected, and coddled by both her father and her older siblings throughout her life, she felt cheated and guilty that her mother had died giving birth to her. She had worn this dress, which her mother had worn on the day that she married her father. She had hoped that by wearing it, she would somehow feel her mother's presence at her own wedding. During the ceremony, her mind had perhaps, played a cruel trick, allowing her to believe that her mother was truly with her. But now, after the events of the past day and a half, she was ashamed of the fear that gripped her, and worried that fate was, at last, punishing her.

She tried her best to shake off these morbid thoughts as she carefully placed the dress in the old chest where it had lain for the forty years since her mother's wedding. As she closed the lid, the door to the room opened and her husband, William came to kneel by her side. He held her in his arms as the unwanted tears began to stream down her cheeks. The look on his face clearly revealed that he was suffering as much as she. She looked up into his eyes, and whispered a soft, "I'm sorry."

Her words conveyed a depth of feeling and anguish that they both shared. The discovery of the body of Avarilla, slumped over the desk in her room at Mount Hayes would be permanently etched in the minds of the young couple. They were both painfully aware that Avarilla's death, although through no premeditated action or plan of their own, lay in some measure upon them. They sat on the floor for what seemed like hours, holding each other, willing the pain to subside. Finally, a knock on the door interrupted their silent grieving.

William, with a sigh, and a kiss for his young bride, acknowledged the knock.

"Come in."

Mary Ann hesitated as she entered the room. She had known and understood that the incident at Mount Hayes had deeply upset the couple. Her son, William, had loved his Aunt Rilla, and had felt that she loved him as well. He had assumed that she would love his bride and be happy to have them at Mount Hayes. He had no way of knowing that the words he had used to present his bride would have resulted in such dire consequences.

He had introduced Sarah as the new mistress of Mount Hayes. Initially, when Avarilla's demeanor abruptly changed from happiness to distress, he assumed that it was merely due to her age and physical ailments.

Mary Ann, however, knew immediately what the effect of his words must have been. Avarilla had always assumed that she was the true and rightful mistress of the Hayes estate and that this illusion was forever wiped away by William's pronouncement. When they were summoned back to Mount Hayes earlier that morning, Mary Ann was fearful of what they might find. Those fears were realized when she found the open page from *Hamlet*, marked with a ribbon. Lying beside it was the scrap of paper indicating the damning passage. Mary Ann had closed the book and put the paper into her pocket, hoping that William and Sarah would never know that Avarilla had chosen to take her own life, rather than to accept yet another of life's cruel misfortunes. Although she had been careful in her attempts to conceal her actions, the deception was not lost upon the young couple. Yet, neither would ever openly acknowledge it.

Mary Ann struggled to find just the right words to give comfort, yet none came to mind. Finally, she resorted to the time honored method of dealing with such a loss. She directed her thoughts and comments to the details for the funeral arrangements. She asked for their help in delegating the necessary tasks and the three sat down together around a small table as Mary Ann handed a sheet of paper and pen to Sarah. These were duties which neither William nor Sarah had ever been called upon to handle, but the responsibility forced them to devote their attention to something other than their grief. They began to assemble a list of guests, made decisions about the refreshments to be served, and decided upon the time and date for friends to come by to offer prayers and condolences to the family. Arrangements had to be made to have a coffin built, and finally, preparations for the funeral itself.

The planning consumed a little more than an hour, and all three felt drained by the process. Nonetheless, the time and attention devoted to the details and obligations required, had produced a degree of calmness and an acceptance that life, as always, must go on.

Over the course of the week they were kept busy with the preparations. The funeral followed the usual pattern practiced by the members of the Anglican Church, and Avarilla was laid to rest in the family plot a short distance from Mt. Hayes. On the day of the burial, the early morning had been bright and clear, but by mid-afternoon as the mourners made their way, walking behind the casket toward the cemetery, there was a sudden chill in the air as the sun was hidden by menacing dark clouds that moved swiftly overhead. Sarah felt the chill and shivered as she clutched her husband's arm and haltingly continued forward.

She felt as though a heavy burden had been suddenly draped around her shoulders and she began to sob softly. William held her more closely and was touched by his young wife's sorrow and compassion for the woman to whom they would soon say their final good-by. He felt certain that Sarah would recover her composure once the service was concluded. He could not foresee what life would hold for them once they moved into their new home at Mount Hayes.

It was several months after the funeral before Sarah and William completed the plans and necessary repairs at Mount Hayes. The home had been a showcase for years under the watchful eye of its former owner, John Hayes and the efficient management of two of his slaves, Isham, the overseer, and his wife, Molly who managed the household. But, after the death of Hayes and the eventual re-marriage of his widow, Mary Ann, followed by the unexpected death of Isham from a tragic fall, things began to deteriorate slowly.

While Hayes's daughter Avarilla was alive, she was a strict taskmaster, but with age, both she and Molly often fell behind. Additionally, Molly's daughter Winny had fallen in love with Sam, a handsome slave from a neighboring estate, and the two had runaway and left the area to avoid capture and punishment. Molly did her best to attend to matters, but she missed her husband, and her daughter. She was filled with pride in her youngest, son, Henry, who had grown into a fine young man, but he too was gone. He had been given the luxury of an education by Mary Ann and had gone with her upon her marriage to Thomas Harris to serve as overseer of the Harris plantation. Molly missed them all desperately, but with the death of Avarilla, it was more than she could bear. She slowly slipped deeper and deeper into a morose depression as she immersed herself into the small comfort offered by her beliefs in her Jamaican traditions, practices and incantations of Obeah.

She had lost interest in her appearance and her clothing was soiled and torn. Her hair, no longer covered by the usual bandana, was unkempt. She spent the majority of her time in her darkened room, rocking and chanting softly as she manipulated a variety of exotic items into magical amulets and potions. It was a dismal, and unsettling sight to behold.

Mary Ann loved her son and his bride and wished nothing but happiness for the young couple. She suggested to her husband that it might be a comfort for Molly to have her son near her. She knew how much William cared for Henry for they had grown up together. Thomas, realizing that Henry would be a productive and welcome addition at the estate, readily gave Henry to the couple as a wedding gift. Both Mary Ann and Thomas knew that Henry was quite capable as overseer for the couple's new home at Mount Hayes. Both also hoped that the Henry's presence might lift Molly from her doldrums.

William was grateful for the offer, but hesitated to accept. He looked upon Henry as a friend, rather than a slave. He discussed his hesitancy with Sarah and she immediately understood. One of the traits she found most appealing in her husband, was his gentle, caring nature and loyalty to those whom he held dear.

They discussed the matter at length. Finally, after several days of agonizing over the proffered gift, they agreed on a course of action. They would accept this generous gift, but only under the condition that they would grant Henry his freedom. He approached his mother with their decision first. As usual, Mary Ann was proud of her son's compassion. She encouraged him to present his proposal to Thomas.

Later, after the evening meal, William and Sarah, hand in hand, found Thomas sitting by the fire reading from his Bible. As they entered the room, Thomas looked up and immediately detected a degree of hesitancy and apprehension in their demeanor. He put aside his Bible, leaned back in his chair and motioned to the young newlyweds to sit down. There was a brief, rather uncomfortable silence as William and Sarah looked at each other, hesitant as to how to begin. The gift had been a most generous offer, for educated and well-trained slaves were worth quite a bit of money.

Thomas, with a slight sigh of exasperation, leaned forward in his chair, held out his open hands and inquired:

"Well, what is it? You both look as if you're about to face the executioner? Just tell me what's on your minds."

Sarah began, haltingly, in an attempt to pave the way for what her husband was about to ask, mumbled in a weak voice, "Well, father, you know how much we love you and how grateful we are for all the generosity you have shown to us."

Thomas interrupted, shaking his head.

"For goodness sake, you two. Talk to me."

With that, William cleared his throat and reiterated Sarah's comments and added that they would like to discuss the generous gift of the slave, Henry as a wedding present.

"Sir, I don't want to appear ungrateful, for indeed I am in your debt in so many ways. The last thing in the world that I want to do is to incur your disfavor. But, truth be told, I cannot in good conscience accept Henry to serve in my household as a slave. I hope you can understand that we grew up together and, as he was a few years older than me, he was both a tutor in the tobacco fields as well as a trusted friend."

Thomas gave another deep sigh and leaned back in his chair. After a few moments consideration, he asked, "So what exactly are you saying...are you are refusing the gift?"

Sarah and William both shook their heads vigorously and Sarah got up from her chair and knelt by her father's chair.

"No father, not really. William...well we both, have a request. Granted, it is a big one, but one that would give us both enormous pleasure. Tell him William."

With that, William, in a calm, but determined voice explained.

~ 177 ~

"Sir, we would like very much to have Henry as an overseer at Mount Hayes, but as a free man."

There, he said it. He took a deep breath and awaited the verdict.

Thomas smiled at the naiveté of the young couple.

"You do realize, of course, that once the manumission papers are signed and recorded in the courts, Henry will be a free man and may do as he pleases. There will be no guarantee that he will choose to remain. He may take off for parts unknown and you will never see him again."

William nodded in understanding.

"Yes sir, I have considered that possibility. However, it is my fervent hope and expectation that Henry values our friendship as much as I, and will chose to stay. Plus, I sincerely doubt that he would leave his mother in her current state."

Thomas smiled, pleased with the couple. They were good honest souls, with a Christian heart of charity. He was proud of them, nodded and added that if they were certain of their decision, he had no objection. He suggested that they have the papers of manumission drawn up, signed and filed with the court as soon as possible.

Sarah hugged her father and kissed him on the cheek. William rose and extended his hand to his father-in-law.

As if by magic, Mary Ann and Bess appeared at the doorway with a tray of Bess's sweet cakes and a flask of hard cider to celebrate the event. Both were wearing big smiles of approval and it was clear that they had been listening outside the door.

By the end of the week the necessary papers had been signed and filed with the court and from that day forward, Henry was a free man. He joyfully accepted the position as overseer of Mt. Hayes. He was surprised and overcome with emotion as he accepted the documents that guaranteed his freedom. He was quite aware that he had the legal right to leave, but he was overjoyed at this new opportunity. Additionally, he was offered a generous salary, which would allow him to provide for himself and for the care of his mother, Molly.

Molly's spirits improved greatly with the arrival of her only son at Mt. Hayes. Henry, however, found himself beset by a dilemma.

The task of overseeing the vast acreage at Mt. Hayes, brought to Henry the sudden realization of the nature of the duties required of him. Not only were workers needed to do the field work, but also to handle the household duties, which his mother was clearly no longer able to manage. Those workers would be, as they always had been, mostly black slaves with a small number of white, indentured servants. He couldn't help feeling twinges of guilt and sadness that these men and women would probably never enjoy the type of freedom he had been given. It had been one thing to oversee the work of slaves while he was also a slave. Now he feared that he would face resentment from those whose fate he now controlled. He hoped he would be up to the task and said a silent prayer that this recent and unexpected gift of freedom would be the beginning of a new and better life for him and his mother.

As for Sarah and William, they settled into their new home and slowly adapted to the routine. It was different and a bit frightening to the young couple, and although the wedding itself had seemed to them the beginning of their new life together, it suddenly seemed quite real to be in their own home without parental advice or supervision. They were pleased, however, that Bess was going to accompany them to their new home. Not only could she help supervise the household help, but she was also an accomplished cook and a trusted mother figure to Sarah.

During the first few weeks at their new home, Sarah experienced a wide range of emotions. At times she was fearful that she would not be able to manage the household on her own, but then at other times, she smiled in quiet delight that the decisions she made for their home were hers. Of course, she always consulted with William, but he was so agreeable and so pleased with any changes she suggested, that her self-confidence grew. Life was good, and she and William gradually settled into a comforting routine. Each evening, after their meal, they would retire to the parlor where they enjoyed the comforts of a blazing fire and a chance to talk over the events of the day.

William shared with her his concerns that their tobacco would not be of the highest quality. He had been busy talking with neighboring planters about his concerns. For the most part, they concurred and pointed out that they had discovered that their field yielded top quality tobacco for only about three years. After that, the crops tended not to thrive and their tobacco was often deemed of too poor a quality to be profitable. They had learned that the only option left open to them was to buy more and more land for their tobacco and resort to other, less profitable crops such as corn, for their worn out fields. William was considering whether or not they had the financial resources to purchase more lands of their own. It was a risky proposition.

Despite their concerns over the ever-important tobacco yield, their attention was diverted by the warmer days of summer and by Sarah's realization that she was pregnant. She was filled with joy. She and William were going to be parents. Their evenings then became focused on their plans for the baby. Sarah was eager to tell their parents the news, but most of all, she wanted to share her news with Bess.

Early on a bright sunny morning in June, Sarah lingered in the kitchen while Bess finished cleaning the table from the morning meal. When Bess finished her task, Sarah asked her to sit at the table with her for a moment. She had been eager to tell Bess the good news, but now she suddenly felt flushed and nervously twisted the handkerchief in her hand. Bess sat patiently at the table, waiting for her young mistress to speak. Finally, Sarah hesitatingly began.

"Bess, there's some news that I want to share with you."

With those words out of her mouth, she suddenly started to fidget in her chair, and continued to twist the handkerchief, and appeared to struggle for words.

Bess had seen that look on the face of expectant mothers many times, and smiled, and touching Sarah's hand, eased her nervousness.

"Lord, child, you're 'bout to have a young'un. I sure hope you're gonna 'low me to help take care of the child, just like I done with you."

Sarah, jumping from her chair, threw her arms around Bess. She was bewildered and surprised that tears were streaming down her cheeks as they were from Bess as well. It was one of the happiest moments of her life, perhaps even more than when she told William. He had, of course, been thrilled, as was she. But he could not know the amount of fear and trepidation she felt regarding this new welcome, but terrifying event. Bess was the voice of calm, confident assurance that she so desperately needed. If Bess was with her, Sarah knew that all would be well.

It was a pleasant and uneventful pregnancy. There was no morning sickness and she felt wonderful. Both she and William were thrilled that they were about to become parents. Although the weight gain and the rather dramatic change in her figure were to be expected, the reality was a little more extreme than she had anticipated. Bess did her best with needle and thread to try to keep her wardrobe in pace with the event, but it was a challenge. And, despite William's constant assurances that she was beautiful, she didn't feel that way. It was not until she felt the unmistakable kick of the expected baby, that she fully realized that she was about to have a child. Suddenly, all concerns about her figure vanished in the excitement of the awaited birth.

Before long, the tobacco crop had been harvested, cured and packed in the hogshead barrels to be delivered to the wharf for inspection. The crop was better than they had hoped and they had even more reason to celebrate. Soon the winter holidays were upon them and William wanted to have an elaborate party to celebrate with friends and neighbors their double good fortune. Sarah, on the other hand, was reluctant, and would have preferred to wait until after the birth to celebrate. There was that ever-present fear that something might go wrong and she preferred to spend the days with family. Besides, she felt uncomfortable and a little awkward and knew that guests would be dressed in their finest for the festivities, while she would be clothed in an old gown that no longer fit. Bess had done her best to alter Sarah's clothes to accommodate her growing girth, but despite all efforts, her body stretched the limits of any seamstress. She was happy to be pregnant, but by her ninth month, she was more than ready to welcome their child. Why couldn't William wait a few weeks? But William was insistent, and she agreed.

On Saturday, December 1, they sent Henry to Harris's Delight with a written invitation for their family and a few neighboring friends, to a dinner and a holiday celebration on the following Saturday, December 8. Their invitation, of course, indicated that they would welcome their guests to spend the night and to attend services at Saint Paul's Church the next day.

Although Sarah was looking forward to the arrival of her family, the list of guests brought to mind the losses the family had suffered over the past few years. She missed her brothers, Richard and James, who had both drowned three years ago. Now only Thomas, the oldest of her three brothers survived. But, even the excitement of having him and his wife Sally caused Sarah to be fearful that her sister-in-law might be somehow despondent when she learned the news that Sarah was so excited to share.

Thomas had married Sally Offutt seven years ago. Sadly, they had no surviving children. A son, Thomas, born 17 December of 1726, and a daughter, Mary, born in July 1728, both died of malaria in August of 1728. Although Thomas and his wife had also fallen victim to the disease, they had survived, but neither had enjoyed good health since their illness. This was especially true of Sally, who though pregnant twice since, had lost both early in the pregnancy. Sarah hoped that they would come to the celebration, but feared that her sister-in-law might be pained by the news of her own pregnancy.

Despite these reservations, she was happy at the prospect of enjoying the company of her three sisters. She prayed that they would enjoy their brief stay at Mt. Hayes, and share in her joy about the expected child. Nonetheless, she couldn't help a certain amount of apprehension.

Twenty nine year old Rachel, was still unmarried and, truth be told, her prospects for marriage seemed rather slim. She was a warm and loving sister, but was quite particular where potential suitors were involved. As far as anyone could tell, she was doomed to be a spinster. She had a lengthy list of rules for any possible suitor, and had succeeded in chasing away every likely one in sight.

Twin sisters, Rebecca and Ruth, both received attention from several young men and Rebecca seemed quite fond of James Perry. The family fully expected an engagement announcement at any time.

Sarah was eager to have her entire family together for her very first efforts at hosting a gala family event, and she was eager to see the expression on the faces of their guests. She was confident they would both be thrilled with the news of the forthcoming birth.

She and Bess, along with Henry's assistance, did their best to make Mt. Hayes shine again as it had in earlier days. Garlands of holly, mountain laurel and mistletoe were tied together and hung throughout the house, and many hours were spent planning the food to be served.

By that next Saturday, Sarah was as excited about the celebration as William. They were giddy with delight as they awaited their first guests. Mt. Hayes seemed to have returned to its glory days. The decorations were beautiful, and the scent of the pines and bay leaves, along with the aroma of baked pies and cakes, filled the house. William constantly complimented Sarah on her appearance, and even though she was pretty sure he was exaggerating, she was nonetheless glowing.

The first of their guests to arrive were Thomas and Mary Ann who were generous in their praise of the appearance of the house. Sarah felt a burst of pride and for the first time felt like the true mistress of Mt. Hayes. It was a wonderful feeling.

Next to arrive were Thomas and Sally. They came with arms laden with a cake and several jars of preserves that their cook, Nan had prepared. Sarah was relieved that the couple both expressed their good wishes and joy for the expected child. Sarah smiled and hugged them both with a sense of relief.

Her sisters, Rachel, Rebecca and Ruth arrived together. James Perry, escorted them into the hallway. He was trying his best to present himself in a self-assured manner, but it was quite clear that he felt uneasy. Sarah welcomed them all into their home and complimented the girls on their appearance, and couldn't help laughing when they tried to return the compliments. Suddenly she was no longer embarrassed by her appearance, but felt quite blessed.

William had invited musicians to entertain and there was dancing, eating and good spirits all around.

Early the next morning the family, with the exception of Sarah, loaded into their sleighs for the trip to the church. It had snowed late in the night and the temperature seemed to be dropping steadily. It was agreed by all, that it would be best for Sarah to remain warm and comfortable at home.

Sarah was happy to spend the next day resting. Bess, Molly and Henry prepared a meal and the three good friends sat down to eat together.

The next ten days seemed to fly by. There were so many preparations to make for the new baby and there seemed to be a never-ending parade of neighbors stopping by with good wishes. The young couple appreciated the good will, but Sarah tired easily and both wished for a little peace and quiet.

Finally, late in the evening of Monday, December 17, Sarah went into labor. William was a wreck, but fortunately, Bess and Molly were prepared. Molly's role was primarily devoted to chanting and preparing special talisman's to protect the new child. Finally, early in the morning of Tuesday, December 18, Sarah and William welcomed their first child, a boy. His given name was William, after his father, but they decided to call him Will to avoid confusion. Sarah felt it was the most joyous moment of her life.

CHAPTER 12
The Porcelain Cup

*T*here had been snow on the ground for over a week, but the sunny days made small trips pleasant despite the crisp chill in the air. Mary Ann and Thomas were eager to see their new grandson, but just as they were preparing to leave the house, snow began to fall. It was accumulating on the existing snow at a rapid rate. Despite Mary Ann's objections, Thomas decided it would be prudent to wait until the weather improved.

The snow continued throughout the remainder of the day and well into the night. When she looked out the window the next morning, Mary Ann was reminded of her first visit to Mt. Hayes when she had been so frightened and uncertain of what her future might hold. This visit promised to be one of unbounded joy, if only the weather would clear.

The next three days seemed like an eternity, for the sun did not return until Saturday, December 22. Although it was evident that the trip would still be difficult, both Thomas and Mary Ann could wait no longer. They loaded the sleigh with presents for William and Sarah and, of course, for the new baby, brought enough personal items to permit an extended stay, wrapped themselves in heavy blankets, and headed for Mt. Hayes. This promised to be a most wonderful Christmas.

Bess and Henry met them at the door and as they approached the stairs, William came bounding down the steps with the biggest grin that his mother had ever seen on his face.

"It's a boy, a perfect, handsome little boy!" He proclaimed as he hugged his mother and accepted congratulations from the couple.

"Come see for yourself. He's got Sarah's eyes."

Bess nodded in vigorous agreement, but added, "But law sakes Massa William, he looks a lot like you too."

William was overcome with pride and gave Bess an appreciative hug as well.

As they entered the bedchamber, Sarah put her finger to her lips to signal the need for quiet. Baby Will was fast asleep, finally. She was happy to see her family, but was in need of sleep. Mary Ann suggested that Sarah should get some rest and that they leave baby Will in the care of Bess. Everyone agreed, except for Sarah, who insisted upon accompanying the group as they moved into the adjoining room to chat.

Thomas instructed Henry to bring in the gifts and other items from the sleigh. William asked Molly to bring some refreshments and as she was leaving the room, suggested that hot rum sounded particularly good. There was already a fire blazing in the fireplace of this room as well as in the room where the baby was sleeping soundly. They drew their chairs closer to the welcome fire to warm themselves. Everyone seemed to be talking at once. There were so many questions, so many ideas about what the future might hold for young Will. They were having such a good time. Sarah was particularly happy to have their family with them to share in their first Christmas in their new home. Everything was perfect.

Shortly, Molly arrived with a tray of cakes and beverages. Following close behind her was a young girl whom Mary Ann had never seen before. She was quite pretty, and much taller than either Mary Ann or Sarah. She appeared to be about fifteen or sixteen years of age. She was carrying another tray which held small plates and cups.

William noticed the quizzical expression on his mother's face and answered her unspoken question.

"I don't believe you've seen Hannah before. She was orphaned four years ago when her mother, Dorothy Richards, died.

At that moment, Molly seemed to lose her balance and nearly dropped the tray of refreshments she was carrying.

She uttered a soft "Pardon, Mistress, I'll be more careful," and cast a troubled glance at Mary Ann.

William gave Molly a gentle pat on the back to reassure her and continued with his introduction of Hannah.

"Reverend Tibbs arranged for Avarilla to serve as guardian for Hannah. She has proven herself to be quite talented and skilled in a variety of areas both in the house and outside. Apparently, Aunt Rilla even taught her how to manage the herb garden."

Mary Ann thought the name Dorothy Richards sounded vaguely familiar, but couldn't remember if she had ever met the woman. For the moment, that was unimportant and she smiled at the girl. She was surprised that although Hannah nodded politely, her face betrayed no emotion. She did not appear sullen, but nor did she appear happy. Mary Ann was somewhat surprised that the girl seemed to mask her feelings so successfully. But, she felt momentarily ashamed that she was judging the girl when she knew nothing of the hardships she may have suffered.

"Put the tray there, Hannah and be careful," instructed Molly.

Hannah did as instructed and then backed away stopping near the door where she continued to stand quietly.

William rose to his feet, picked up two mugs and poured generous portions of the warm rum from a large metal flagon. Molly selected a pewter cup from the tray, filled it with hot tea and handed it to Mary Ann. She then picked up a beautifully decorated porcelain cup and saucer, filled it with tea, and brought it to Sarah.

Mary Ann uttered a commanding, "No."

She jumped to her feet and knocked the cup of steaming liquid from Sarah's hand. The cup and its contents fell to the floor scattering shards of the broken cup and its contents over the surface.

There was a stunned silence as everyone stared at Mary Ann and the broken cup. They could not imagine why she had reacted in such a reckless manner. It was so unlike her.

Sarah looked as though she was about to cry and William rushed to her side. Some of the liquid had spilled on her gown and he helped her into the adjoining room to change.

Mary Ann, now pale and beginning to tremble, remained standing as if transfixed by some unknown horror. Thomas was immediately concerned for his wife. He had never known her to behave in so rash a manner. Tears began to trickle down her cheeks. He moved quickly to his wife's side and held her in his arms. He didn't know what to say. Her behavior seemed to defy any rational explanation. After a few moments, Mary Ann seemed to calm herself. She stared down at Molly who was in a rush to clean up the pieces of the broken cup and to mop up the puddle of liquid on the floor. Hannah had not moved but remained standing by the door, but her face betrayed a heightened sense of awareness as though she might bolt from the scene at any minute.

Mary Ann's tone of voice was stern and demanding as she spoke to Molly, "Why did you bring that cup? Why on God's earth would you serve that cup to Sarah?" She demanded.

Molly crouched on the floor and began to rock slowly as she too began to wail in loud uncontrollable sobs.

William came running from the next room and he and Thomas stared at the two women in bewilderment. What had been one of the happiest days of their lives had suddenly become a disaster. What was worse, neither of them had any idea what had caused Mary Ann's unexpected actions.

The entire group suffered a few moments of uncomfortable misery until Mary Ann finally seemed to calm herself. She wiped away her tears, moved toward Molly, who shrank back fearing the worst. Mary Ann stooped to the floor and began to help clean up the distressing mess she had created. She put her arm around Molly, but reiterated her original question:

"Why did you offer that particular cup to Sarah?"

Molly, steadily trying to move away from Mary Ann, shook her head, shrugged her shoulders, and offered her explanation.

"It was happy day, special day and I think a pretty cup would make Mistress Sarah happy."

Mary Ann did not fully accept her explanation. How could she not remember that it was this very "special" cup that had contained the poisoned drink? The drink that Avarilla had prepared in an attempt to poison her. Surely she remembered that it was this same cup that Avarilla had used to bring about her own suicide.

Finally, she decided that perhaps there was no sinister plot. Maybe Molly had forgotten. She was getting old and rather frail. After all, she had always been a faithful and loyal servant. Besides, the hated reminder of past evil was finally gone from her life forever. Its pieces lay shattered on the floor at her feet. She took a deep breath, helped Molly to her feet and suggested that she go to her room and rest. She assured her that all was forgiven and Molly eagerly, turned and hastened out the door followed by Hannah.

Mary Ann smiled at her husband and son, offered a brief apology and immediately went to Sarah to console her, and to offer her help in calming the newborn who had been startled awake by the commotion in the other room. She suggested that Sarah climb into bed and get some rest. Bess was holding the baby, but Mary Ann insisted that she would tend to the child until he went back to sleep. She cuddled her grandson in her arms and recalled how happy she had been the first time she had held her own son in her arms. When the child had calmed down, she placed him in his cradle, sat down beside it, and rocked it gently as the child drifted off to a peaceful sleep once again.

In the adjoining room the two men stared at each other in silent confusion for several minutes. Both felt helpless to make any sort of appropriate action to deal with what they had observed. Their unspoken but shared hope was that this was the end of whatever past event had produced such bizarre behavior from a woman known for her composure in the face of dire events.

It had been an exhausting day and although only mid afternoon, both couples decided it was time for a nap before the evening meal. Their shared hope was that the rest of their visit would be less exhausting. After all, it would be Christmas in only three days.

Later that day, after a nice rest, they gathered in the common room for supper. It was a quiet, polite atmosphere with an almost palpable sense of "walking on eggs," lest some careless remark or action provoke another dramatic outburst. Both Thomas and William kept a close watch on Mary Ann, albeit out of the corner of their eyes. Their concern and discomfort was not lost on Mary Ann, who tried her best to concentrate their discussions around the new baby and Christmas events.

After the meal the family adjourned to the parlor and little Will was, as expected, the center of attention. He was a good baby. He smiled and made cooing noises when his mother cuddled him. Despite the earlier event, in all, it was a most pleasant evening.

When Sarah left to take her newborn upstairs to bed, Mary Ann confessed to being quite tired as well and climbed the stairs beside Sarah. She gave little Will a kiss on the forehead, hugged Sarah and apologized again for her earlier outburst. Sarah smiled, and said that the earlier event was already forgotten. She assured Mary Ann that she was delighted to have her in her home.

After Sarah had entered her bedchamber and closed the door, Mary Ann quietly tiptoed back down the stairs. There was no sign of Molly or Hannah and Bess was upstairs with Sarah. She went into the pantry and began to search the shelves. She thought perhaps there were other cups identical to the one she had broken. If so, she was determined to destroy them as well. She searched each of the shelves carefully and although there were a few porcelain cups, none matched the distinctive decorative style of the one she had broken. She felt relieved and quietly returned to the upper floor and prepared for bed.

It was not long after that, Thomas joined her. He was still concerned and confused about his wife's outburst. He hesitatingly sat on the edge of the bed, took her hand in his and kissed her. He sat there for a few minutes, searching for just the right words to broach the subject of the earlier incident. Mary Ann was well aware that he had a right to know the reason for her ill-mannered behavior.

"I am so sorry. I can't begin to tell you how much I regret my outburst. I know how much I upset Sarah. Well clearly, I upset everyone. But, there are some things I need to tell you. We've never talked about the night that John suffered his attack."

"No, we have not, and there's no good reason why we need to talk about it now." Thomas interrupted.

"Oh but there is," Mary Ann continued, "it's important that you understand."

"Avarilla and I never had a comfortable relationship. Although she seemed to truly care for William, she always viewed me as an interloper, someone who was there to destroy her relationship with her father. I believe she hated me."

Thomas quickly interrupted, "I'm sure you are mistaken. Avarilla, as we are all aware, had a rather unpleasant demeanor with everyone."

"Perhaps so, but her actions speak of motives that go far beyond demeanor. She tried to poison me on the night of my wedding to John Hayes."

Thomas stared at her in disbelief. "Surely you are mistaken."

"No, Thomas, I am not. That fateful night Avarilla, not Molly, brought refreshments to John and me. It was a cup of warm mead served in that same porcelain cup. But, I do not like the taste of mead and John knew this and took the cup from my hand and drank it...you know the rest."

Thomas found it hard to believe that Avarilla had done such a vile thing, and asked, "But how can you be so certain that it was Avarilla who put the poison in the cup?"

"Because she confessed at the foot of her father's death bed and asked his forgiveness," she explained.

Thomas was stunned by the revelation. His brow was furrowed with pain and confusion. *What could Avarilla have hoped to gain by poisoning Mary Ann?*

Mary Ann knew exactly what he was thinking and responded.

"Avarilla had always felt she was entitled to be the mistress of Mt. Hayes and she saw my marriage to her father as an obstacle. Clearly her plan did not anticipate that her father would drink from the cup."

There was still more that her husband needed to know and she continued.

"You remember the morning that we were called to Mt. Hayes, and we found Avarilla's body? She did not die from consumption as everyone believed. She had committed suicide by drinking the same poisonous drink from the same porcelain cup she had once offered to me."

Thomas shook his head in disbelief. It was incomprehensible to him how anyone could be that evil. He pulled Mary Ann to him and held her tightly for several minutes. He understood the fear that had prompted her actions and realized that she was only trying to protect Sarah.

Finally, with a sigh, she lifted her head from his shoulder and confided that she was relieved that the episode was over and realized that the cup had presented no real danger to Sarah, and that she had over-reacted.

Thomas smiled, kissed her and nodded in agreement that the cup had not been a threat to his daughter. There was no evil to be feared. Mary Ann hoped that was the case.

CHAPTER 13
First encounter

Mt. Hayes
October, 1737

Both Sarah and William doted on young Will, but Sarah in particular, found it increasingly demanding on her time to care for her very active, inquisitive four year old as well as their fifteen month old daughter, Ruth. Ruth was a pretty little girl who looked a lot like her mother. She had blond curly hair, blue eyes and a sweet disposition, but she had recently learned to walk and climb. Sarah found that despite the watchful eye of Bess, the two children were a handful. And then of course, the fact that she was expecting their third child in about two months only contributed to her fatigue.

These considerations certainly were a factor in their decision to discuss the matter of Will's education. Although most formal instruction normally did not begin until around the age of six, young Will was clearly bright with a keen inquisitive nature and an aptitude for learning which is unusual for someone so young. He had already learned to read from the Bible and from the *Book of Common Prayer*. It was not long before William and Sarah decided that their son could benefit from instruction by a qualified tutor.

William had experienced education at the hands of two very different tutors during his youth. The first was Nicholas Buckley, tutor and dance master. William remembered him as a pompous and rigidly stern taskmaster who tolerated no independent thinking on the part of his young pupils. He also remembered how happy he had been when his stepfather, John Hayes, had dismissed Buckley. However, he now realized that Buckley's dismissal had more to do with Hayes' worsening health than it did with the tutor's skill...or lack thereof. It had been a welcome change when Sarah's father had suggested that he be allowed to come to the Harris plantation to be tutored along with his children.

Sarah had been taught a few basics, such as reading, and some rudimentary math by their tutor, Benjamin Craddock, but the bulk of her training had come from instruction from older sisters in those skills deemed necessary to run a household.

William, on the other hand had benefitted greatly by the more relaxed yet thorough education he had received from Craddock. Craddock had permitted him to pursue a variety of topics that he found appealing. As a result, William had received a well-rounded education.

As a child, William had assumed his tutor to be an old man, but in looking back, he realized that he had probably been no older than early thirties. He discussed with Sarah, and her father, their thoughts regarding Craddock as a tutor for young Will. They were in agreement that the man would probably be in his mid sixties by now, and if still alive and in the area, would be an excellent choice to tutor young Will. Inquiries were made in nearby parishes, and fortunately, Benjamin Craddock was located and happened to be seeking new employment.

Arrangements were made for Craddock to come to Mt. Hayes for an interview on Monday, October 31, 1737. William was curious to see his former tutor, and hoped that he would not feel awkward in discussing employment with the man. He remembered him as a lively, enthusiastic, well dressed man with a ready smile, but firm where matters of education were concerned. His scheduled appointment was for 2:00 in the afternoon. Craddock arrived on horseback about twenty minutes early and apologized explaining that he had misjudged the distance and had allotted more time than required.

Bess had met the man at the door but William, sitting in the front parlor, came as soon as he heard voices in the hallway. He was more than a little surprised by the man's appearance. His clothing showed the signs of hard wear and William feared that he had fallen upon hard times.

Benjamin Craddock smiled that infamous smile that William remembered from his childhood and walked toward him with his hand extended. William feared that he had made a mistake and over estimated the man's teaching skills. Good tutors were always in demand among the gentry and he was puzzled by the man's appearance. Craddock had been and still was a good judge of people. He was immediately aware that his somewhat disheveled appearance had been a shock to his former student.

He held out his hand to William, smiled and in way of explanation, shook his head and acknowledged that he had been without employment for nearly two years and had to resort to whatever small jobs he could find.

"It is so good to see you Master William, I was delighted to hear from you. I'm sure you must have many questions regarding my current situation. I fear that my misfortune has been of my own making."

"Let's have a seat in the parlor and we can talk," William suggested.

As soon as they were seated and William had requested that Bess bring them some refreshments.

Craddock began, "A few years before I became your tutor, I made the acquaintance of a German immigrant who was attempting to establish a printing shop in Baltimore. His father, like mine, had been a teacher. We became friends and occasionally enjoyed a draft of beer together and talked about our plans for the future. He eventually became discouraged with his attempts to support himself in Maryland and moved to New York. He wrote to me once he arrived in New York, but I had no further contact with him for quite some time. I would guess more than a dozen years passed without a word. So you can imagine my surprise when I received a letter from him telling me that he had managed to establish himself in New York City and was printing a newspaper there. He went on to say that he was enjoying a good measure of success and asked if I would consider moving to New York to tutor his son, Nicholas, who had just turned six years of age. That was in the summer of 1733. As it was, I had just finished a job and was looking for employment. New York sounded promising and exciting. I packed up my belongings and went to New York to accept his offer."

William was immediately interested. Travel had always been something that had fascinated him and he was eager to learn more.

Craddock shook his head slowly and continued, "It was the worst decision of my life. My friend was a well-educated and enthusiastic journalist. When he found a story that intrigued him, he followed it. Repercussions be damned."

By now William was intrigued and encouraged his old friend to continue.

"Well, the story Zenger published involved the Governor of New York, William Cosby."

"Wait!" William interrupted, "You don't mean John Peter Zenger who published *The New York Weekly Journal*, do you?"

"One and the same, and if you are familiar with the story, you know that Zenger strongly criticized the governor in his articles and as a result, he was arrested on Governor Cosby's orders in 1734."

William nodded in consent. "Yes, I remember hearing about the trial."

"Well," Craddock continued, "Zenger was charged with libel and Governor Cosby issued a proclamation calling the articles in the paper 'scandalous, false and seditious'. The result was that Zenger was sent to prison where he languished for over eight months before a trial date was set. Zenger's wife Anna managed to keep the presses running and continued to plead her husband's cause. Well, the case roused public interest well outside New York. This was fortunate for Zenger, because Andrew Hamilton, a well known Philadelphia lawyer, traveled to New York to defend him. Hamilton's strategy was to argue that a truthful statement, even if defamatory, could not be charged as libel. Well...to make a long story short, Governor Cosby had created a lot of enemies during his tenure as Governor. The eventual jury decision was that Zenger was found not guilty."

"Well, I should think that could only have been good news for you. Wasn't it?" William asked.

"No it wasn't. The Governor's reach was long and unforgiving. And, despite Zenger's acquittal, his finances were completely exhausted and he could no longer afford to keep me employed. My efforts to find other employment in New York, were, as you can imagine, hindered among the well to do families who could afford a tutor. I finally gave up and returned to Maryland. I'm sure you must realize that favorable word of mouth recommendations are a prerequisite for gainful employment in my field. I suspect, that had you not known me as your tutor, you would never have considered me as a teacher for your son. After all, I was branded, along with Zenger, as a troublemaker and traitor to the authority of the British government. Although I am in sore need of employment, I would quite understand if you feel that I am unworthy to be entrusted with the education of your son."

William was touched by the man's story and felt empathy for his situation. He smiled at Craddock, moved to where he was seated and put his hand on his shoulder. But the man's appearance was disturbing and before making a final decision he wanted to discuss the matter with Sarah.

William smiled and as he was walking to the door commented on Craddock's implied question.

"I'm sure you understand that I would like you to meet my wife, Sarah and our son, Will, before we come to a final decision."

With that, William walked out the door to ask his wife and son to join them. Bess was standing just outside the door, pretending to be busy sweeping the floor, but William was fully aware that she had been listening at the door.

"Bess, would you please ask Mistress Sarah and Will to join me in the parlor?"

Bess nodded in obedience, but then muttered her objections as she walked upstairs.

"That sure is one raggedy looking man! He smell bad too! Don't know why Massa William bring that sort of trash into this house. Muddy up my floors with them dirty shoes!"

William smiled, but mentally acknowledged that Bess might have a point, but permitted her to continue upstairs to get Sarah and Will.

Sarah had been excited to see the former tutor. She remembered well how much her brothers and her husband had liked him. Will was bouncing up and down urging his mother to hurry so that he could meet him.

Craddock rose when the three entered the room and gave a slight bow as he smiled to the beautiful young woman whom he remembered only as a child.

"It is with great pleasure that I have this opportunity to see you again, Mistress Sarah. And this, I assume, is young master Will?"

Will walked toward him, gave a well-rehearsed bow, held out his hand and greeted the tutor saying: "I am very pleased to meet you sir. Are you really going to be my tutor?"

Craddock smiled and confided, "I sincerely hope so."

With that William and Sarah excused themselves. Once they were out of hearing, William gave a brief summary of what he had been told by Craddock. Both parents held a soft spot in their hearts for the man whom they had respected so much so many years before. It was heartbreaking to see him in his current situation. They both felt sorry for the man, but despite her fond memories of the past, Sarah had some reservations.

Craddock was not the man she remembered from her childhood. Clearly he was in need of employment, but she wasn't certain that she would feel comfortable with him in the house. It was only after William assured her that Craddock, despite his appearance, was the man for the job that she relented.

One of the traits that she so admired in her husband was his compassion for others. Despite her own doubts about the man, she respected her husband's wishes and with a silent nod of her head, Sarah agreed.

When they returned to the parlor they found young Will sitting next to Craddock reading from the Bible. Craddock immediately rose to his feet and acknowledged his approval.

"This is quite a clever young lad. He is certainly advanced for his age."

William and Sarah smiled and indicated that they would like him to become Will's tutor. Craddock thanked them profusely and promised that their son would be in good hands.

Shortly thereafter, Bess entered the room with a tray of small cakes and a pitcher of rum.

Craddock smiled in appreciation noting, "Ah yes, you know young man, spirits are not only good for the soul, but can cure the sick, strengthen the weak and enliven the aged."

And with that, he accepted a serving of the anticipated concoction and lifted his mug and offered a toast to their new venture.

Sarah smiled, but in her heart, she feared they might have made a mistake in hiring the man. But, it was one of those life decisions whose merit would be revealed only through the passage of time.

William asked Craddock when he could begin.

He replied, "Immediately, if that meets with your approval."

"But surely you must need a few days to handle your affairs and to collect whatever clothing and books necessary?" William inquired.

"No sir, I have no matters that require my attention, and I have brought with me a bundle of clothing that will meet my needs. It is in a roll behind my saddle. I'll fetch it."

Sarah was aghast and fearful that whatever items were contained within the bundle would be in no better condition than what he was wearing. She held up her hand to stop Craddock's movement toward the door and called to Bess to send someone to bring the tutor's meager possessions into the house.

William again shook Craddock's hand and motioned toward the stairs, "Let me show you to your room."

Sarah gave her husband a quizzical look for she had assumed that due to Craddock's unkempt appearance he would be given a room on the lower level with the household servants.

"What room do you have in mind?" she asked.

"Why, the bedchamber at the far end of the second floor, to the right of the stairs, of course," was his reply.

She shook her head and her face expressed the same concern as the tone of her voice, "But William, that room has been closed for the last four years. It was your Aunt Rilla's room, the very room where she died. Don't you think that would be..." She paused for a moment, searching for the right words, "well... disrespectful and just wrong?"

"Calm yourself, darling," he replied as he pulled her close to him and kissed her. "Surely you are not superstitious?"

"I'm not superstitious, merely cautious," she insisted.

"Don't be foolish, I'm sure Master Craddock doesn't object. Do you, sir?"

Craddock immediately assured them that he harbored no such fears and was grateful for whatever accommodations they made available to him.

With that the three walked up the stairs and turned to the right at the hallway.

"Will you please show Master Craddock to his new quarters? I must check on the children." And with that Sarah turned and hurried back down the hallway to their room at the other end of the hall.

Sarah felt fatigued and frustrated. Hiring a tutor was supposed to make life easier, not more difficult. She went over in her mind a growing list of objections she had regarding the new tutor and was eager to share her concerns with Bess.

Bess was, as she expected, in the room with the children. She was holding Ruth on her lap when Sarah entered. Bess was still grumbling about Craddock's appearance and shared her criticisms about the man with Sarah. Sarah nodded her head in agreement and was relieved that someone else shared her reservations about the man. But the fact of the matter was, he was hired and would be living in the room down the hall. Sarah asked Bess if she had any suggestions on how to handle the situation.

"Well," Bess began, "he shore e'nuf could use a bath and some better clothes...and clean his self up!" she hurried to add.

Sarah nodded her head in agreement, but could not think of an expedient solution. She knew that both her father and husband were considerably taller than Craddock and that their clothes would not fit without extensive alteration. She thought a few moments longer and finally remembered that there had been several trunks of clothing removed from John Hayes' room after his death. She wondered if those might fit the new tutor.

She mentally chided herself for what she deemed to be a callous disregard for the departed, especially since she had objected to Craddock's occupying the bedroom in which a death had occurred. Now, here she was considering asking the man to wear the clothing of a man whose death, not unlike Avarilla's, was attributed to evil intent. It was a conundrum. But, she reasoned, Craddock had not known Hayes and it would be foolish to waste perfectly good clothing. Often such items would have been distributed to house slaves. She finally concluded that since she just moments before practically invited the devil into their home, the damage was already done. With that, she shrugged her shoulders and gave Bess instructions.

"Bess, would you check in the storage room in the lower level. If you look in the trunks that contain Mr. Hayes clothing, you may be able to find some more appropriate clothing for our new guest."

Bess nodded and agreed that most anything would be an improvement. She called for Hannah to bring the necessary bed linens and a basin of hot water and some towels to the bedchamber at the end of the hall. She then made her way down the two flights of stairs to the lower floor and began her search for the trunks of clothing. With every step, she shook her head in disgust for their new guest. When she finally found the trunks she began to rummage through them to find clothes that might be serviceable.

She had not known John Hayes, but could tell by the size of the clothing in the trunks that he had been about the same height as Craddock, but clearly of much greater girth. She finally selected a pair of men's breeches, leggings, a shirt, cravat and a coat. But, although they had been locked in a trunk since Hayes's death, and would not be a perfect fit, they were nonetheless, far better than the man's current attire. She shook out the dust as best she could and pressed the cravat.

When she had finished, she carried the clothes up the stairs to Craddock's room. She knocked several times before the man finally answered. She could see on the table by the bed, a flagon of what she supposed was rum. It was evident that he had been imbibing heavily for his speech seemed slurred. Bess scowled at the man, shoved the clothing into his hands and told him to get himself cleaned up. She turned immediately, and still mumbling her disapproval, hurried back down the stairs to attend to the preparation of the evening supper.

The family assembled later that evening in the kitchen parlor. Henry always joined them for meals and William asked if he would mind calling the new tutor to join them.

"He's in Avarilla's old room," he added.

Henry's reaction was even more surprised and fearful than Sarah's had been. He hesitated a moment, opened his mouth as if to speak, but thought better of it and turned and headed up the stairs. He decided that he would knock on the door and alert the man to come downstairs but he was not about to enter the room. In Henry's mind and in that of his mother, Molly, that room held nothing but evil.

Henry knocked on the door and called out, "Master Craddock, sir, the family would like you to join them for supper in the kitchen parlor."

There was no answer and finally, with great trepidation, Henry opened the door. There, lying face down at the foot of the bed, was Craddock. Henry was convinced that whatever evil had caused Miss Avarilla's death had reared its ugly head again. Assuming that the man must surely be dead, he backed away in fear and hurried down the stairs to alert the family.

His eyes were wide and he looked as though he might faint at any moment.

Molly rushed to her son's side and asked, "What's wrong, Henry?"

Henry stood there shaking his head and pointed toward the stairs. William immediately jumped to his feet and bolted up the stairs to the open door at the end of the room.

Sarah remained wide-eyed and shaken and lifted her son to her lap and held Will tightly. She feared the worst.

There was a deathly silence as those at the table seemed frozen in place, afraid to move lest some unforeseen evil might envelope them all.

From upstairs, they could hear scuffling noises as though there might be a struggle going on. Finally, Bess could stand the suspense no longer. She lifted her skirts, ran to the stairway and climbed to the second floor as quickly as she could.

When she arrived at the door, she found William attempting to drag the listless Craddock to the bed. Seeing Bess at the doorway, William called out to Bess.

"Come give me a hand, Bess. Help me get him onto the bed."

Although Bess was not a superstitious person, she hesitated a moment and asked, "What's wrong with him?"

"He's drunk. Now give me a hand."

Shaking her head and mumbling a litany of "I told you so's!" she helped William hoist the man onto the bed.

"We'll just have to let him sleep it off."

As they walked to the doorway, William continued, "And Bess, make sure that all spirits are locked away in the pantry tonight."

Bess nodded vigorously and with a disgusted "Humph!" followed William as he returned to the rest of the family who awaited them with fearful anticipation.

William had regained his composure and didn't want to alarm his wife and poor Molly who had already begun to rock and softly chant, seemingly lost in her own world.

"Everything is fine, my dear. Well, not exactly fine, but certainly nothing to be afraid of. There are no evil spirits at work here, just the inevitable results of too much drink. The man had stumbled and then apparently fainted. He's in bed now."

He smiled at everyone, hugged his wife and son, and suggested, "Will, would you please give the blessing?"

Will was surprised for this was the first time he had ever been awarded the honor, but he beamed with pride as he recited from the *Book of Common Prayer*, "Bless O Lord this food to our use and us to thy loving service; and keep us ever mindful of the needs of others. Amen."

Will smiled with pride as he enjoyed the approving glances from those surrounding him at the table. Things seemed to have returned to normal, which was a blessing unto itself.

Their supper, as usual, was light and consisted of leftovers from their noon time meal. They dined on terrapin stew, biscuits, jam, and cider.

Young Will was still confused and wondered why Master Craddock had not joined them for dinner.

When he enquired, his mother quickly explained, "Master Craddock was exhausted from his journey here and is merely resting. I'm sure he will be quite rested in time for your morning instruction."

She hoped the smile that she gave to her son exuded more confidence than she felt. But again, only time would tell.

Early the next morning William dressed quickly and hurried down the hall to Craddock's room. He was hoping to find the man in a better condition than what he had encountered the evening before. He knocked on the door and opened it. Craddock, still wearing the same disheveled clothing as the day before, was sitting at the small desk near the window.

"Good morning," William began, "how are you feeling this morning?"

Craddock ran his hand through his hair, frowned and shook his head in a bewildered way.

"Actually, I feel rather strange," he began. "After you showed me to this room yesterday, I sat down at this desk and began to make preparations for today's lesson. I had been working here for several hours, I know it was quite dark outside for I had lit several candles. I heard a knock at the door and said, 'Come in'. I glanced briefly at the door and saw a woman standing there holding a cup of what I believed to be hot rum. I told her to put it on the table by the fireplace. I turned back to my work and heard her walk to the table and then back out the door. I worked a few minutes longer and sat by the fire and drank what turned out to be hot mead. Shortly thereafter I began to feel unwell and stood up to lie down a bit before supper. As soon as I stood up, I felt very dizzy and unsteady on my feet. I really don't remember anything more until morning. Clearly I must have managed to get to the bed for I awoke this morning lying fully clothed in the bed."

William felt both annoyed and amused that the man had concocted such an elaborate story in a pitiful attempt to cover up his intoxicated state the night before.

"Well, I hope you are feeling better this morning."

He was interested to see just how intricate the man would be with his ruse, and asked, "Who brought you the cup of mead?"

"I really couldn't say. I barely glanced at the woman, and when I woke up the cup was gone. All I can tell you is that her footsteps indicated a distinctive limp."

William was concerned. Surely the man was just trying to minimize any potential criticism regarding his alcohol consumption. But his story about the woman walking with a limp was worrisome for none of the servants in the house had a limp. At any rate, he decided not to share Craddock's story with Sarah. She was already anxious about the man's capabilities. It was possible, he supposed, that Bess or Henry might have revealed to Craddock some details about the room's former inhabitant, perhaps even more plausible that the man's imagination had just been fueled by liquor.

He turned toward the door and suggested that Craddock come down and join the family for their morning meal.

When Sarah brought Will downstairs, William put his arm around her waist and kissed his son. He could see from the concerned expression on her face that she was apprehensive about their choice of a tutor.

"Craddock seems fine this morning. I'm sure that he was excited that he had new employment and indulged himself a bit too much in celebration. I hear him coming down the stairs now. I've already talked with the man and I'm sure this will not be a common event. There's no need to discuss it further."

They enjoyed their usual meal of porridge and their conversation centered upon Craddock's plans for Will's education.

Through the diligent efforts of Bess and Molly, necessary alterations were made on the clothing offered to Craddock. Although once he was cleaned up and well fed on a regular basis, not only did his appearance improve, but also his level of confidence. Sarah had no complaints about his teaching approach, for Will was making excellent progress, but the issue of his drinking to excess, was a constant concern.

On most evenings after supper during his first month at Mount Hayes Craddock would make a trip to the pantry. Bess noticed and informed Sarah that she had seen him bring a large basket to the pantry where he would then fill several flagons with rum from the barrel. She noted that all of the flagons were empty by the next morning.

Sarah and William discussed the situation and both agreed that his appearance, most mornings, indicated that he was still feeling the effects of his excesses. William promised Sarah that he would talk to Craddock. Sarah nodded in agreement but secretly doubted that her husband would be as forceful as needed.

When William first confronted the tutor with his concerns about his drinking habits, Craddock sought sympathy, explaining that he had not been feeling well and only drank for health reasons. But when William in a firm tone, explained that based on an accounting of the amount he consumed each night, he had far exceeded any reasonable explanations based on health concerns, he became at first defensive and finally, defiant.

"After all," he explained, "I am an educated man, a man respected for his skills as a teacher, and despite the fact that you and Sarah are my employers, I am entitled to be shown more respect regarding when and how much alcohol I am permitted to consume. Isn't my pupil progressing well under my tutelage? Furthermore, does a man allow his wife to make decisions usually reserved for her husband, who is after all, the head of the household?"

William began to waiver in his resolve. Young Will was indeed doing quite well with his studies, and clearly loved his tutor. Additionally, he reasoned with himself, a man should have the right to make decisions for himself, and Craddock was right. Their conversation ended with Craddock's promise that he would do his best to reduce his alcohol consumption as much as his health would allow.

But for her part, Sarah was adamant. The man was an employee. He was hired to minister to the education of their oldest child and had shown disrespect to the family by allowing himself to succumb to the evils of alcohol. It was an issue that provoked several heated disagreements between the young couple and roused emotions never before encountered between the two.

Eventually, William began to fear that Sarah's anxiety regarding Craddock's excessive drinking was harmful to her health and to their unborn child. He confronted the tutor with his concern for Sarah's health and informed him of his decision to lock away all alcoholic spirits in the house and that everyone must respect his decision to prohibit any and all consumption of liquor of any kind until after the birth of their expected child.

Craddock fumed in silence, but there was nothing he could do about William's decree if he wanted to keep his job.

The beginning of the season of Advent marked a time of spiritual reflection and expectation for the coming of Christ. For the members of St. Paul's Anglican Church the daily and Sunday readings from the *Book of Common Prayer* focused on two biblical messengers of the coming of the Messiah, i.e., the prophet Isaiah and the accounts of John the Baptist as the predecessor of Christ.

It was a season of self-examination and often involved consuming only one full meal during the day. Despite Sarah's determination to observe all of the religious rituals during this period, William reminded her that fasting was only a recommendation and not a requirement. He felt that both Sarah and their unborn child needed substantial nourishment for the health of both. It was a time of hope and expectation as holiday festivities commenced.

It wasn't long before William began to feel sorry for Craddock. Besides, he reasoned, the tutor had paid his penance and should be permitted to enjoy the festivities along with all of their guests. He wasn't looking forward to the conversation he was about to have with Sarah, for he knew her feelings about the situation.

It was mid afternoon on Thursday, December 15, and Sarah was lying down resting in preparation for the festivities they had planned for their guests over the coming weekend. William walked into the room and suddenly lost his nerve. He turned and was about to leave when Sarah spoke.

"What is it my darling? I'm sorry to be so lazy today, but I am just so tired."

William smiled and started to leave the room again, "I'm sorry, I didn't mean to disturb you. We'll talk later."

Sarah sat up in bed, looked at him with a quizzical expression, and responded with what sounded to William much like a command.

"Don't be foolish, Dear, I can tell from the expression on your face that this is something of importance to you. Tell me."

Well, William thought, *there it was*. There was no hiding his feelings from her and in fact, sometimes he suspected that she could read his thoughts.

"No, it's nothing that can't wait until you are rested."

Sarah, tilted her head, stood up, put her hands on her hips and continued, "Tell me now."

William walked slowly back to the bed, put his arm around Sarah's waist and sat down beside her and began, "It concerns the tutor. The man has sincerely been doing his best. He now looks quite presentable and Will seems to be very fond of him. Will is making quite a bit of progress with his numbers. I think the man has earned a certain level of trust from us...don't you agree?" he was quick to add.

"Just what changes did you have in mind?" was her first question, although she had a pretty good idea what his answer would be.

"Well, my Darling, I was thinking that the man should be permitted to enjoy a glass or two of rum or hard cider at upcoming holiday celebrations. It seems demeaning to restrict him so, especially when everyone around him will be enjoying our hospitality."

Sarah sighed, shrugged her shoulders and feeling too exhausted to object answered, "Whatever you think is best."

With that she returned to the bed and tried to get some rest before the evening's festivities. They would be hosting a number of guests from surrounding plantations as well as family members. She always enjoyed these events but hoped that she would have the stamina to do what was expected of her as hostess.

The first to arrive were her father and stepmother. Mary Ann kissed Sarah, told her she looked beautiful and kneeled to the ground as Will ran toward her. She picked him up, kissed him and expressed her surprise at how much he had grown. He was eager to tell them about his lessons and recited a poem he had memorized for the occasion. Bess soon arrived with little Ruth toddling alongside. She too ran to her grandparents who lavished kisses on her as well.

Their other guests arrived about a half hour later at around 7:00 that evening. The weather had been clear for the past several weeks and the temperature was unusually mild. Sarah was no longer as self-conscious by her appearance as she had been during her first pregnancy. She had given up wearing stays several months earlier because they were just too uncomfortable. Nonetheless, she always envied her fashionably dressed guests. For the current party, she was dressed in a beautiful long brocade waistcoat, which fastened in the front. She wore a silk scarf around her shoulders, which covered most of her stomach.

The guests all arrived with best wishes for the expected child and congratulated Sarah and William on the beauty of their home.

Mt. Hayes was magnificently dressed in pine and holly boughs with cluster of holly berries and red velvet bows. Candles were lighted in all of the windows and on the mantels of the fireplaces.

Musicians were seated at the far end of the large parlor and were playing as the guests entered the room. On one side of the room a table had been prepared for the punch bowl that was brimming with Apple Toddy. It was, without a doubt, the most popular drink in Maryland at the time.

The toddy took quite some time to prepare and age. Bess had begun her preparations for it near the middle of November. The drink consisted of a combination of roasted apples, skin, seeds and all, mashed up together, a generous amount of apple brandy and sugar, sealed tight in a stone jar until ready for consumption.

After the guests had socialized, danced and were ready for a rest, they moved into the adjoining hall where there were many tables that had been prepared for the evening. The tables were laden with a great variety of foods, many of which were provided by the bounty of the Chesapeake Bay. There was turtle soup, oysters, crab and codfish as well as roast beef, venison, smoked ham and turkey. Additionally, Bess and Molly had prepared a wide variety of cakes, puddings, fruits and pies. More large punch bowls were available to quench the thirst of the revelers.

After their banquet, they returned to the parlor where the musicians once again began to entertain the guests. Most were too uncomfortable from having stuffed themselves with the delicious food and too much toddy to dance any more but some of the men sat at tables and began to play cards while other sat and enjoyed the fellowship of good friends.

Shortly after midnight, most of the guests began to collect their coats and to thank their host and hostess before leaving. Of course, Mary Ann and Thomas would be spending the night and a room had already been prepared for them. After Sarah had satisfied herself that those who intended to leave had left, she chatted briefly with those who remained before excusing herself.

Mary Ann confessed that she was a bit tired as well and the two women walked toward the stairs together. Sarah put her arm through Mary Ann's and confided to her about her concerns regarding the tutor. They both turned to look for the man. There he was. He had moved a chair near to the punchbowl and by his appearance, had been enjoying a bountiful amount for several hours.

In exasperation she exclaimed, "Oh dear, look at Craddock!"

Mary Ann was shocked to see that the man was having a difficult time staying seated on the chair. He looked as though he might slide to the floor at any moment.

Sarah walked to where her husband was talking with a group of friends. She tapped him on the shoulder, smiled, wished him a good evening and looked toward the punchbowl. William followed her gaze, kissed her on the cheek, and whispered that he would take care of the situation.

Sarah turned and joined Mary Ann as they walked to the stairs. She paused to look back and saw her husband with his hand on Craddock's shoulder just as he was about to pour himself another drink. William helped him to his feet as best he could for the man was so unsteady that he could not have navigated the length of the room without assistance.

She shared a knowing glance with William and proceeded up the stairs ahead of the two men. Surely, she thought, William will now see how foolish it is to allow Craddock to remain. She sighed deeply and made a mental note that her husband would probably be unwilling to dismiss the man during the Christmas season.

"I understand how you must feel," Mary Ann sympathized and put her arm around Sarah's shoulders. "I'm afraid my son will not want to dismiss him at least, not until after twelfth night."

Sarah nodded in acknowledgment that sometimes William's forgiving nature could be exasperating.

The revelers slept later than usual the next morning. It had been a wonderful party and William and Thomas were planning to participate in a foxhunt at a neighboring plantation later that day.

Both Sarah and Mary Ann were happy to have a leisurely day to spend with the children. After a late breakfast, they went to the day room where Sarah wanted to share with Mary Ann some of the handiwork she had been working on.

Mary Ann was lavish with her praise, both for the success of the evening's party, but also for the good manners of the two young children. They were still sitting by the fire chatting when William and Thomas entered the room to take their leave for the foxhunt.

Sarah was concerned that Craddock had not joined them for breakfast and that no one had seen him yet. She asked William if he had seen the tutor and when he indicated that he had not, she tilted her head, raised her eyebrows and waited for her husband to take the hint.

"I guess I had better go check on him," was his hesitant reply.

Mary Ann, having seen the man's appearance the night before and having been informed about the earlier episode, added her own advice to her son.

"Yes, I think that would be a very good idea…I'll come with you, William," Mary Ann added.

William was apprehensive as he approached the door to Craddock's room. He opened the door only to find that his fears were answered.

Lying on the floor was Craddock. The floor under his head had a small puddle of blood. Mary Ann let out a gasp as William rushed to the man and knelt by his side. He discovered that Craddock, although injured was breathing. He was quick to reassure his mother that the man was alive. He needed help to get Craddock to the bed and called out for Henry to come to the room.

Mary Ann had suddenly turned quite pale and seemed breathless. She was staring at the rocker beside the fireplace. Although neither of them had touched it, it rocked slowly, as though someone had just gotten up from its seat. William soon realized the source of his mother's fears, but was quick to reassure her that one of them must have accidentally bumped the rocker when they rushed to Craddock's side.

But Mary Ann only shook her head slowly as she pointed to a scrap of paper under Craddock's outstretched hand. The paper was blank with the exception of the three numbers written on its surface. The numbers, 3-1-56, filled Mary Ann with horror.

William was at a loss as to what to do. Fortunately, Henry arrived at the door. In a stern voice, William ordered his childhood friend to help him examine Craddock to discover the extent of his wound. Hesitatingly, Henry, eyes wide with fear, approached the body lying on the floor.

First they rolled him over on his back. They could see a large gash on Craddock's forehead. William looked up and saw a bloodstain on the edge of the fireplace mantel. He tried to reassure Henry that the man, probably in a drunken stupor, once again, had tripped and hit his head on the mantel.

Henry reluctantly nodded his head in agreement and gladly followed William's instructions to fetch Bess to bring a basin of water and clean towels. Henry turned and hastened out of the room relieved to be away from whatever evil dwelt there.

Mary Ann waited for Bess to arrive with the necessary items and helped them move Craddock's unresponsive body to the bed.

Bess began her incessant mumbling about the evils of demon rum and the apparent worthlessness of the man she was attempting to revive.

Eventually, Craddock began to move his head from side to side and gave a soft moan.

"What happened, who pushed me?" he asked.

William, in an attempt to calm the man, explained in the calmest voice he could muster, "You must have tripped and hit your head on the mantel. I'm sure you're going to be fine."

Craddock was attempting to rub the wound on his forehead while Bess did her best to push his hand away.

"Keep them hands off your head. I'm tryin my best to clean up this mess."

Craddock did as instructed, but continued to insist that someone had shoved him as he stood up from the rocker.

For the moment, Mary Ann had a question of her own.

"Where did you get that paper?" Mary Ann demanded.

"What paper are you talking about?" he asked shaking his head and looking bewildered.

"This one," she said as she held it up to his face so that he might see.

Craddock was becoming quite agitated as he continued to deny any knowledge of the paper and kept insisting that someone had pushed him into the sharp edge of the mantel.

Mary Ann felt she was on a precipice. She didn't know what to believe or what to fear. All she knew was that the paper in Craddock's hand held the same three numbers she had found on Avarilla's desk the day they found her body. The numbers were those that marked the passage from the book she had been reading. It was the passage in which Hamlet was contemplating his own suicide. She suddenly felt quite sick to her stomach. Was this some sort of cruel joke?

She took a deep breath, took her son's hand in hers and assured him that she was quite all right.

"But, there are some things you should know. We'll talk later. It's best if Sarah not be worried with these matters now."

With that, she put the slip of paper in her pocket, turned and walked back down the stairs to where Sarah was waiting.

~ 223 ~

Sarah was fearful that Craddock had, once again, drunk himself into oblivion. She was going to have to insist that William dismiss him immediately. It had been a long night, and now a worrisome beginning to a new day. Added to that was her realization that she had begun to feel the first signs of labor.

She smiled at Mary Ann, and said, "Please send Bess to my room, it seems that our new baby is getting impatient."

Mary Ann was immediately concerned and for the moment the earlier incident was pushed to the back recesses of her mind. Her immediate thoughts were for the well being of Sarah and the new baby.

As it often happens, the early contractions were limited to only a few hours. After a brief rest and assurances from William and Mary Ann that Craddock would be gone immediately after Epiphany, everyone relaxed.

The news cheered Sarah and she felt that a huge weight had been lifted from her shoulders. The man was not going to be with them much longer.

Despite the fact that the contractions had stopped and Sarah assured them that she was feeling fine, Mary Ann insisted that she would not leave until the birth of her new grandchild.

Both William and Sarah insisted they would send word when the baby was born, but Mary Ann was adamant that she and Thomas were not leaving until after the much-anticipated event. Sarah's silent prayers had been answered. She hugged them both in grateful appreciation.

Two weeks later, on Thursday, December 29, Sarah gave birth to a handsome baby boy. The couple had already decided upon names for the child. A girl would be named Sarah, and if a boy, they would name him Philip, in honor of William's father.

As Mary Ann held her new grandson, her eyes were filled with tears. They were tears of pride, of happiness, and a certain amount of sadness as she was reminded of the untimely death of her son's father.

Will and Ruth were both excited to have a new baby brother and were eager to hold him and to rock his cradle, albeit somewhat more vigorously than necessary. Fortunately, Bess was always present and capable of controlling any excessive behaviors around the baby.

As for William, he spent quite a bit of time going over in his mind the words he would use to terminate Craddock's employment. He was filled with uncertainty. Should he offer the man a recommendation or would that be unfair to whoever might choose to hire him. It now seemed a certainty that left to his own devices, Craddock could not control his excessive drinking. As fate would have it, Craddock had been doing some deep thinking of his own.

On Thursday evening, January 5, the day before Twelfth Night, Craddock asked William if he could spare a moment for a private discussion.

"Of course," William answered, "let's go to the front parlor."

In a move that surprised them both, William then asked Bess to bring them both a cup of rum. William feared that both of them would probably need a drink to get through what was about to be an unpleasant talk.

The fire had been lit, but Thomas busied himself for a few minutes stirring the embers and added another log to the fire. Finally, Bess arrived with the rum and William sat down opposite Craddock.

"Master William, I want you to know how grateful I am that you were kind enough to offer me employment in my time of need. I realize that my behavior regarding my alcohol consumption has been of great concern to you and to Mistress Sarah. For that, I sincerely apologize."

William was surprised, and his natural instinct was to try to ease Craddock's discomfort.

"No, no, I'm sure the situation has been uncomfortable for you as well," he replied.

Craddock seemed impatient to say what he had to say without interruption. He shook his head and held up his hand as if to hush whatever William might say next.

"Master William, I am embarrassed to confess that I have been fearful for my life since I first arrived here."

"Fearful?" William was astonished by the man's audacity. No one in the family, or in the household for that matter, had ever threatened the man in any way, except to insist that he curb his drinking. What was he thinking?

"Sir, as I said I am embarrassed by my own weaknesses, fears, or superstitions, if you wish. But, ever since my first night here at Mt. Hayes, I have fallen victim to whatever evil presence abides in that bedchamber."

"Victim?" William asked, "In what way have you been victimized other than by your own excesses?"

Craddock began to fidget nervously in his chair. This was not going as he had hoped. He began again.

"Sir, if you would permit me to explain. I mentioned to you that first morning when you found me on the floor that I had felt ill after drinking the hot mead and that I remembered hearing footsteps and seeing a female figure."

"Yes, yes," William interrupted, annoyed by the man's rambling explanation.

"Well, Sir," Craddock continued, "every night, I have been awakened by the sound of footsteps seemingly walking across my room. More than once, I have felt as though someone was pushing me. Once, when opening the shutters, I felt hands on my back trying to push me out the window. I was sorely in need of employment and afraid that if I were to tell you of my concerns, you might dismiss me on the spot. In order to sleep through these nightly disturbances, I resorted to alcohol, which was the only way I could sleep without being awakened by those dreaded sound of footsteps. I know I have disappointed you and for that I am truly sorry. But, the fact of the matter is, I must leave this place immediately, if I am to preserve my own sanity."

William sat in stunned silence. He didn't know what to say. It had been his intent to dismiss Craddock, and should have felt relief that Craddock had made the move himself. But instead, he felt unnerved by their conversation. He couldn't decide if this was a case where Craddock's drinking produced his hallucinatory experiences, or were the strange experiences he described the cause of his drunkenness?

Craddock saw the concerned expression on William's face and hastened to assure him that he held no ill feelings toward William or Sarah and that as much as he regretted it, he would have to resign from his current employment at Mt. Hayes.

With that, Craddock rose from his chair, shook William's hand and announced that he would be leaving as soon as he collected his few belongings.

Less than an hour later, Craddock returned from his room upstairs. He was wearing the same tattered clothing he had worn the day he had arrived. He carried a small bundle that contained his books.

"Please extend my thanks and apologies to Mistress Sarah and to you too, Sir. With your permission I shall take my leave and saddle my horse."

"Wait, William insisted, I don't know what to say, but be assured that you have been a good tutor for Will. He will miss you greatly."

William offered the man his hand, called to Bess to have someone saddle Craddock's horse, and said his last "Goodbye" to Benjamin Craddock.

CHAPTER 14

"When one door closes, another opens."

Alexander Graham Bell

St. Paul's Parish
January 1738

Sarah had been concerned that her husband would weaken and at the last minute be unable, or unwilling to dismiss Craddock from his position as tutor to Will. She had spent the morning in the room with the children and had expected William to join her there. When she told Bess to ask him to come to the nursery, Bess rolled her eyes, shook her head slowly from side to side.

"Master William and that tutor are in the parlor and they both look mighty serious," was her reply.

Sarah found the news comforting. William had finally summoned the courage to deal with the unpleasant task.

Several minutes later, she heard footsteps coming up the stairs and continue down the hall. Bess quietly opened the door a mere crack to peek down the hall. She turned to Sarah with the news that Craddock had gone to his room. They could hear Craddock moving about and some opening and closing of trunks. Both women smiled in mutual understanding that William had accomplished his intent.

A short time later, they again heard footsteps as Craddock left the bedchamber and walked down the stairs of Mt. Hayes for the last time. Sarah gave a sigh of relief.

When William finally entered the room, she rushed to him, gave him an affectionate hug and kissed him.

"I know how difficult that must have been for you. You had such fond memories of the man from your childhood. But, I know you realize there was no other option. The man had to go."

William smiled, returned Sarah's hug, walked to his children and gave them each a kiss on the head. He was at a loss as to how to explain the situation to his wife. He did not want to deceive her, although he knew she would readily accept a small lie that confirmed her interpretation of Craddock's departure. But more importantly, he didn't want to frighten her by telling her the truth and the details of Craddock's revelation. The man clearly seemed convinced that he had been the victim of some awful evil that dwelt in the room down the hall. He weighed his options and decided upon a compromise solution.

"Sarah, my dear, you will be delighted to know that Benjamin Craddock is no longer in our employment. He has packed his things and left for good."

She rushed to his side once again, and he took her in his arms.

"Oh William, I know how much you dreaded it, but it had to be done. I'm so proud of you my darling. It feels as though an enormous weight has been lifted from my shoulders. I was fearful of what sort of mischief or downright evil the man might have undertaken in one of his drunken stupors. I am relieved that he is gone."

William's conscience would not permit him to misrepresent his actions. He began, hesitatingly, to relate his encounter with Craddock.

"Actually, I didn't have to tell him to go. He had already made up his mind to leave on his own volition."

"What do you mean?" Sarah murmured.

"Apparently, he was embarrassed by his own behavior and by the excessiveness of his drinking, and voluntarily ended his employment to avoid any unpleasantness."

William silently congratulated himself on the version of events he had just related to Sarah. He had not told an outright lie. He had, however, lied by omission, but he felt justified in sparing his wife from the troublesome details Craddock had revealed.

"You know my dear, I don't know your feelings on the matter, but I think the sooner we forget about Craddock and the worries he has brought, the better off we will be. I suggest, for the time being at least, we lock the door to that bedchamber and leave it that way. What do you think?"

Sarah smiled, hugged her husband, and nodded in enthusiastic agreement.

"I think that is a wonderful idea!"

For the moment at least, the issue of Craddock's dismissal was closed. But, Sarah reminded him, they would have to find a replacement for she was certain that Will would be crushed to know the tutor was gone.

William nodded in agreement, but the idea of bringing another stranger into their home was not appealing in the least. He had been so consumed with how best to handle the unpleasant task of dismissing Craddock that he had thought of little else. However, upon thinking about Craddock's disclosure of the unusual events he claimed to have experienced, he recalled a small detail he had forgotten.

It was the morning after the party. He and Mary Ann had gone to Craddock's room and found him unconscious on the floor with a large gash on his forehead. Mary Ann had been startled by a slip of paper under the tutor's hand. He remembered that she had put the paper in her pocket, but did not explain its significance. She had cautioned him not to worry Sarah about the incident, but had confided that there were things they needed to discuss.

William decided that now was the time to have that discussion with his mother.

As it turned out, the visit with Mary Ann only added to the mystery. She explained the meaning of the numbers pertaining to the passage from Hamlet that she had found on Avarilla's desk. Neither could find any possible explanation for its appearance at the time of Craddock's injury.

Near the end of January, the weather had cleared, the snow that had covered the ground for several weeks had melted and Sarah and William decided it was time to baptize little Philip.

On Sunday, January 22 the family made their way to St. Paul's Parish. There was the usual amount of excitement about the baptism and also curiosity to see the new clergy, the Reverend Benedict Bourdillon. He had just arrived at St. Paul's two weeks earlier and reports of those who had braved the inclement weather to attend services had very kind words regarding the new rector. This had not been the case with his predecessor, Reverend William Tibbs, who had served St. Paul's Parish for a little over thirty years. During that time, he had embarrassed himself and the parish by habitual drunkenness and a variety of other complaints including charging money for administering communion to the sick. Everyone seemed to agree that it was time for a change and hope for the best.

Unlike Tibbs, who had remained single throughout his life, Bourdillon was married with a family. He was born in France, but had been educated in England at Cambridge University. He had a warm, engaging personality and clearly was well educated. The parishioners of St. Paul's welcomed him with open arms.

It was a well-known fact that a clergyman, especially one with a family, found it difficult to manage his expenses on the meager income he received. Bourdillon, like many others of his profession, found that they could better support themselves and their family by providing tutoring to promising youths in their parish. Due to the scattered nature of the large plantations, it was often easier to allow pupils to be lodged during the week with the clergyman and his family. As it happened, Bourdillon had brought with him his personal library, which was very extensive. Additionally, his wife, Johanna, was an exceptional cook. William was eager to meet the man. Perhaps this might be a good solution for young Will. He was cautious not to reveal those thoughts to Sarah. He would wait to see her reaction to their new spiritual leader.

The church was crowded on this particular morning and Sarah enjoyed the opportunity to chat with many old friends whom she had missed during the cold snowy days of the past month. She was intrigued by the comments of those who had already witnessed the services held and the sermons delivered by Reverend Bourdillon. The consensus was seemingly unanimous. St. Paul's Parish now had a leader whom they could trust and admire. Several friends announced that they were considering sending their sons to the Reverend for tutoring.

William smiled and uttered a silent prayer of thanks that Sarah was so impressed with the man that she broached the subject of sending Will to Bourdillon for tutoring.

"William, I know this might seem a rather abrupt decision, but Will really does need a good tutor and there are several of our friends who have already decided to seek out Bourdillon as a tutor for their sons. And I really think it would be so good for Will to have the opportunity to share the company of other boys his age...plus we wouldn't have to house another stranger in our home. What do you think?"

William did his best to hide his own enthusiasm for the idea and paused, seemingly to consider his wife's proposal before answering.

"Well, my dear, if you think this would be best for our son, of course we will consider the matter."

With that, he placed his arm around her waist and guided her toward their waiting carriage. As they entered the carriage, he softly sighed in relief. It seemed an unpleasant episode from the recent past was about to be resolved in a most promising manner.

"What would you think of my bringing Will early this next week for an interview with Bourdillon and make inquiries regarding his fees and to see if he would be willing to accept our son as his pupil?"

"Oh yes, William. I'm so glad that you agree. I think it will be a wonderful opportunity for Will."

And with that, Sarah snuggled against her husband and rested her head on his shoulder, and reminded herself of her good fortune in having a husband as kind, loving and wise as her William.

As he had promised, William made arrangements to bring young Will for an interview with Reverend Bourdillon on the following Wednesday. William had hoped that Will would be thrilled to have a new tutor, but his son's reaction was a bit troubling. Will had sincerely liked his old tutor and was a little intimidated at the thought of meeting the parish pastor. Craddock had been such a good tutor and he had enjoyed their classroom time so much. There was no way of knowing what his new instructor would be like.

For Will, it was a scary situation. He was slow in getting dressed, dawdled over breakfast and did everything in his power to delay the meeting. Sarah, realizing her son's discomfort, did her best to comfort him.

"I know how sad you are that Master Craddock has left. He was such a wonderful teacher and I know how much you miss him."

Will nodded in silent agreement, but his eyes were filled with tears.

"Oh my dear sweet boy." Sarah wrapped her arms around her son and tried again to reassure him.

"Master Craddock is tutoring other children who will benefit from his skills just as you have. But you are older now and ready for more advanced instruction. Reverend Bourdillon studied in England at one of the finest universities and besides, he has children of his own. You will have other boys near your own age that will study along with you. Don't you think that might be pleasant?"

Will looked at his mother, and not wanting to disappoint her, sighed deeply and nodded reluctantly.

Sarah smiled and kissed her son on the forehead.

"Besides," she continued, "no firm decision has been made yet. Let's wait until our meeting today and see how things go."

Will knew how much his parents loved him and trusted that they would always do what was best for him. He put on his jacket, smiled at his mother, took her hand and headed for the door.

Sarah wiped away tears of her own as she walked with her son downstairs to join William waiting with the carriage. She suddenly realized just how much she would miss her son while he was away from home. He seemed so small, and so young. She said a silent prayer that they were making a good decision. But again, only time would tell.

When they arrived at the clergy house in mid afternoon, Bourdillon and his wife, Johanna, met them at the door. The pastor was of medium height and build with a shock of black curly hair and piercing eyes that seemed to change color dependent upon the intensity of his mood. He had a ready smile, and a pleasant manner as he welcomed his guests. His wife offered them a heartfelt welcome. As for her appearance, she was a bit more round than she was tall.

The clergy house was a one story, frame structure located a few hundred yards south of St. Paul's church. The church sat on a small rise that offered a panoramic view of the countryside. The location suggested that the spot had been chosen so as to watch over the parish and its residents.

After introductions had been made all around, Johanna tapped young Will on the shoulder and suggested that he might like to sample some fresh cakes that she had been baking. Will was a bit tentative and looked to his parents for direction, but almost immediately, upon hearing the sound of children's voices coming from the other room, took Johanna's extended hand and moved toward the kitchen. As they walked out of the room, Johanna turned back to explain that her sons Theodore and Thomas were already enjoying some of the cakes.

The interview, if that's what it was, progressed smoothly, although it was difficult to tell exactly who was doing the interviewing. It soon became clear that Reverend Bourdillon had very definite requirements of those whom he agreed to tutor. It was evident to both William and Sarah that they really didn't have any idea about how to evaluate the potential expertness of a candidate for tutor. The session was basically dominated by Bourdillon's questions about young Will. Was he studious? Was he polite? Did he accept direction and criticism without complaint?

By the end of the session, William and Sarah found themselves practically begging the pastor to accept their son as his pupil.

Before giving his consent, Bourdillon announced that it would be necessary to interview the boy in private.

William and Sarah nodded their agreement and watched as the man strode to the kitchen and instructed Will to follow him into his study.

Will, with a degree of hesitancy, wiped the crumbs from his face and, eyes wide with apprehension, followed the pastor into the adjoining room.

Both William and Sarah felt overwhelmed by the procedure for they had not felt in control of the situation. The man's mere presence invoked a sense of submission to his will. They stared at each other and shared an unspoken moment of helplessness.

Before they had a chance to communicate their thoughts with each other, Johanna emerged from the kitchen with a large plate of cakes and cups of hot cider. Her presence, much like that of her husband, seemed to fill the room, although in her case it seemed warm and affectionate, almost motherly rather than domineering.

Sarah smiled and accepted the offered food as did William. Both were thankful for the opportunity to concentrate on the cakes and thus avoid speaking.

Johanna chattered on about her sons and how much she loved St. Paul's and its parishioners. She was so pleased that everyone had welcomed them so warmly. From this, she diverged her conversation into a variety of subjects, which she discussed in a most animated fashion. Sarah felt fortunate that the woman was apparently quite content to carry on the conversation all by herself.

After what seemed an eternity, but in reality was probably no more than a quarter of an hour, the door to the study opened and Bourdillon and Will walked out together hand in hand. Will was practically beaming and couldn't wait to tell his parents about all the many fields of study he could explore. He was clearly eager to be a pupil of the Reverend Bourdillon.

Sarah and William held their breaths waiting to see what the pastor's reaction to Will might be. They were pleased beyond words when Bourdillon paid high praise to their son.

"Young master Will is clearly a bright young man. He has been fortunate to have already received a quite satisfactory basic education from his previous tutor. I am pleased to offer him a place in my home as my pupil."

The young parents smiled, nodded their appreciation and didn't know quite what to do next. There had been no discussion about fees or about living accommodations and if there would be an additional charge for room and board. And, from all appearances, Bourdillon seemed to think that their decision had been made for them and that they should be grateful to him for agreeing to tutor their son.

Sarah silently acknowledged to herself that there was no end to the number of challenges parenting brought with it. She looked at William expectantly. He smiled at her, nodded his head, and turned his attention toward the clergyman.

"Sir, we are so delighted that you approve of the progress our son has made at such a young age. It appears that this might, indeed, be a wonderful opportunity to provide him with an exceptional education."

He paused for a moment, determining in his mind how best to proceed.

"I'm sure you must be aware that there are certain matters that we must consider. We have two younger children and a large household to maintain under the constraints presented by the quantity and quality of our yearly tobacco yield. For that reason, there are financial matters which would need to be determined."

With that, William allowed himself a quiet sigh of relief that he had finally addressed the issue. They both waited expectantly for the pastor's response.

Bourdillon appeared to consider his response carefully before speaking. Finally, he cleared his throat, rose to his feet, hands clasped behind his back and began to slowly pace from one side of the room to the other.

"I understand your concerns, and I fully appreciate the unpredictability of weather and crop returns, but I'm sure you realize that this is an enormous commitment on my part. I am offering you the benefit of comfortable accommodations and fine food in my own home as well as the assurance that your son will receive an education equal to that he might receive in the finest school in England."

With that, he stopped pacing and sat down in a chair facing the young parents.

"I was hoping that you would be agreeable to a yearly payment of fifty pounds or the equivalent in tobacco."

He could instantly sense their hesitancy, and truly was looking forward to having a pupil as bright and eager as young Will.

"I understand the unpredictability of a profitable tobacco crop and do not want to place an undue financial burden on you and your family. I myself am keenly aware of the constraints placed on a growing family as I too have young children."

Both men looked at each other with a sense of shared desperation. Finally, William turned to Sarah and suggested that perhaps it would be best if they discussed the matter at home.

Sarah nodded in agreement and they stood in preparation to leave, but the anxiety on their son's face caused them to stop.

"Perhaps...," the word hung in the air as it was uttered by both William and Bourdillon as though from an orchestrated script. Both men stopped in mid sentence and stared at the other before breaking into a shared moment of amused and embarrassed laughter. Clearly, each was eager to reach an agreement. Bourdillon spoke first.

"What if we were to settle on the amount previously suggested, but with the stipulation, that if the tobacco yield is poorer than hoped, we will adjust the payment in accordance with the amount of financial loss experienced by you?"

William did not stop to discuss the matter with Sarah, but immediately extended his hand as a sign of good faith.

He considered it to be a fair, and Christian solution to the problem.

Both men smiled and each felt that he had successfully negotiated an agreeable settlement. The only thing left to do was to settle on a schedule for Will's tutoring. They needed to decide how many days per week he would be at the clergy house and when the lessons should begin.

William suggested that the lessons begin the first full week in March when generally, the weather became milder. Bourdillon readily agreed and further suggested that Will and his other pupils would remain at the clergy house and return home every other weekend rather than at the end of each week's instruction. He pointed out that this would relieve the parents from a weekly trip to pick up their child and return him two days later. Both men agreed, shook hands to confirm the arrangement and reiterated that Will would begin his instruction after church service on Sunday, March 5.

Sarah realized that it was she who had suggested Bourdillon as a tutor in the first place and had understood at the very beginning that it would require Will to spend time at the clergy house. But now that the actual decision had been made, she felt a bit resentful that the two men had taken the decision entirely out of her hands and concluded the arrangements without consulting her. She loved her husband and she understood that men ultimately made the final decisions regarding the family, but the reality hit home leaving an unpleasant sense of resentment. It was not so much resentment against her husband, whom she loved with all her heart, but rather a resentment of the societal rules that left women subservient to men. But no amount of sulking would ever change the reality. She bit her lip, vowed to remain silent on the matter, and smiled as the men discussed the remaining details.

The ride back to Mt. Hayes was anything but peaceful. Will was practically beside himself with excitement. He clearly had been fascinated by Bourdillon and entertained his parents, non-stop, with all of the wonders that would be revealed to him through the intellect of Benedict Bourdillon. It seemed Will was in awe of the man.

Despite William's hasty agreement to the altered contract Bourdillon had suggested, he was painfully aware that he had not consulted Sarah in the final decision. She had seemed to accept the situation without complaint but he feared she had been hurt by his hasty acceptance of the proposed plan. He could think of no good way to broach the subject and decided to postpone any discussion until a later date. At the moment, because of Will's excitement and despite their own concerns, both parents were happy for their son.

It was dusk by the time they arrived home and Bess met them at the door and ushered them into the parlor where a warm fire was blazing and despite the inviting atmosphere, Sarah felt drained by the day's activities. She excused herself and went upstairs to rest before the evening meal.

She climbed the stairs slowly, tired, but also consumed with thoughts of how different it would be with Will gone for weeks at a time. At the top of the stairs, she hesitated to rest a bit. As she glanced down the hall, she was surprised to see a light shining under the door to the locked bedchamber. She was annoyed, but concluded that Bess had probably decided that the room needed to be cleaned. She made a mental note to discuss it with Bess later that evening, and made her way to her own bedchamber for a rest.

As soon as she opened the door to her room, Ruth gave a squeal of delight and ran to her mother. Bess was sitting in a rocker, holding Philip and arose from her seat to hand the child to his mother. Sarah felt rejuvenated by the reception from little Ruth and sat down to rock Philip. She felt a sense of calmness which eased away the concerns that had troubled her on the way home from the clergy house.

Bess turned to leave and explained that she was going to begin preparing supper. As she opened the door and stepped into the hallway, Sarah was reminded of the light she had seen under the door of Avarilla's old room.

"Bess, were you in the far bedroom down the hall earlier today?

"Land sakes no, Miss Sarah," Bess answered vigorously shaking her head from side to side.

"You know Master William locked that door after that nasty ol' tutor left. Nobody been in there since."

Sarah felt certain that she could not have imagined that there was a light. She arose from the chair with Philip and walked to the door. From her room, it was impossible to see the other doorway clearly. She walked down the hall followed by Bess with Ruth tagging along behind tugging at her skirts.

"See there, Miss Sarah, ain't no light coming from that room!"

Sarah shook her head, confused, and tried the handle of the door. Sure enough, it was locked just as it had been the day Craddock had left the house.

She smiled at Bess, shrugged her shoulders and decided it must have been her imagination.

"I guess I was wrong. Go along and fix supper, please. I'm going to rest a bit."

As Sarah walked back to her room, she was still somewhat troubled. She was quite certain it had not been her imagination. There most definitely was a light shining from under the door to the locked room. As soon as she entered her bedchamber, she moved to the table by the bed and opened the drawer in which William had put the key the day Craddock left. The key was there. Exactly where William had left it.

She decided not to mention the incident to William. She feared that he already suspected that she was overly sensitive to everything these days. But as she started to close the drawer, she hesitated. Still holding the key, she closed the drawer and turned to look about the room. Her eyes fixed upon the chest that held the wedding dress that both she and her mother had worn. She opened the chest, carefully lifted a fold from the dress and placed the key within the fold. She smiled to herself, feeling a bit foolish, but also relieved as she closed the chest.

As she rose to her feet and turned she uttered an alarmed cry when she saw Hannah standing quietly inside the door.

"Hannah, you startled me. You didn't knock and I didn't hear the door open."

Hannah did not offer an explanation for her presence in the room, but merely smiled. It was an expression that Sarah had rarely observed on the young girl.

The tone of Sarah's voice clearly indicated her annoyance, when she demanded, "What do you want, Hannah?"

"Bess wants to know if Master William will be eating with us this evening." Hannah asked, her head tilted to one side, hands on hips and with what Sarah perceived as an insubordinate attitude.

"Of course Master William will join us. Why would Bess ask?"

Once again, Hannah smiled that same smile Sarah had seen a few moments earlier and which she now interpreted as being smug and disrespectful.

"I 'spose it's because he rode off on his horse a few moments ago. Flew out of here like the devil himself was chasin' him," was her response.

With that, Sarah had tolerated quite enough insolence from Hannah. She pushed past the girl at her doorway and rushed down the stairs to the kitchen where Bess was busy preparing the meal.

She had practically run down the stairway and was quite out of breath when she demanded "Bess, where has William gone?"

"Land sakes, Miss Sarah, ain't nothing to be worried about. Henry asked Master William to come see some changes he had made in the new tobacco barn and to see if he approved. He'll be back shortly, in time for supper."

Bess, wiped her hands on her apron, gave Sarah an affectionate hug and assured her that everything was fine and that she would send Hannah to call her when it was time to eat.

"No," Sarah practically shouted.

Noticing the startled look on Bess's face, she smiled at the woman she trusted so much, and with a sigh, settled in a chair by the hearth.

"I'll just sit here by the fire and watch you. I feel comfortable around you."

Bess looked at her mistress. She had cared for her since she was a child and immediately was aware of Sarah's distress.

Sarah knew that Bess could read her like a book.

"I'm fine, Bess. Hannah came into my room without knocking and I felt her behavior was disrespectful. I guess I'm just overly tired."

Bess was like a protective mother hen and her feathers were now ruffled and her anger was obvious.

"Don't you worry none, Miss Sarah. I'll give that girl a good talkin' to. I'll see that she's whipped too."

"No, no, Bess. Just talk to her and that will be quite enough."

Sarah was relieved and knew that Bess would take care of the necessary discipline of Hannah. She was glad that William wouldn't have to hear about the event. She didn't want him to think that she was becoming unstable, because he was already worried about her emotional state.

She leaned her head back on the rocker, and eventually, the rhythmic motion of the chair, the warmth from the fireplace and Bess's contented humming as she worked, lulled Sarah into a brief, but much needed sleep.

She was awaked by the gentle touch of Bess's hand on her shoulder as she helped Sarah from the chair and told her that William had returned and that supper was on the table in the parlor kitchen.

Conversation during their meal was focused primarily upon the day's meeting with the Reverend Bourdillon. Although children were expected to not speak until spoken to when at the table with adults, both William and Sarah encouraged Will to share his thoughts regarding his interview with his new tutor. It soon became apparent that the man had already filled their son's head with grand plans and expectations. They were surprised to learn that Bourdillon had already suggested to Will the idea of someday studying in Europe.

William nearly choked on his supper when Will began to excitedly relate all the ambitious plans his new tutor had for him.

William interrupted his son in mid-sentence and suggested that they had heard quite enough about what might or might not happen within the next several years. He suggested instead, that they enjoy their meal and leave conjecture about the future for another time.

Will looked crushed and Sarah felt sorry for her son, but was pleased that her husband felt as she did. He was a little boy about to leave home for extended periods where he would be at the grace and mercy of the new, untested tutor. She hoped their decision to place their trust in Bourdillon would prove to be a good one.

Sarah had been relieved when Bess had offered to handle the situation with Hannah, but was surprised to learn a few days later that Hannah would be spending the next four weeks working and sleeping in the brick outbuilding which housed the laundry. Sarah was well aware that the building had the unpleasant aspect of always feeling either too hot or too cold dependent upon the outside temperature relative to the amount of activity on the inside.

Normally there were four female workers in the laundry building. Hannah would be the fifth. They were of varying ages and all were indentured servants, with the exception, of course, of Hannah. The others had agreed to the indenture in order to acquire transport to the colonies and the time of servitude for each was seven years. Hannah, on the other hand, had been bound to work in return for food and board because she was an orphan. She would have to work at Mt. Hayes until such time as she could find employment elsewhere in order to support herself on her own.

Sarah hoped that this disciplinary action would force Hannah to realize the error of her ways and change her behavior. The girl acted as though she felt entitled to whatever generosity was extended to her. Sarah's fear, however, was that the punishment might only serve to increase Hannah's apparent animosity toward her. She chided herself for always second-guessing every decision whether the decision were her own or someone else's. She made a mental note to try to be more optimistic in the future.

The next few days were quite pleasant and she and Bess began to plan in earnest the items that Will would need for his extended stays with his new tutor. William spent several hours each day reviewing with Will his most recent lessons so that he would feel prepared for his new "adventure." That was the word they routinely used when talking with Will about his upcoming enrollment at the clergy house. Sarah prayed that her son would not be homesick. He was, after all, only five years old. She knew that she would feel lost without him.

Each Sunday during the weeks leading up to the beginning of Will's term with the tutor, the family made the trek to services. On each occasion, the pastor and his family went out of their way to welcome Will and tell him how much they were looking forward to having him in their home. Johanna always gave him a warm hug and Bourdillon's two sons, Thomas and Theodore, were thrilled at the prospect of having a new friend join them in their lessons. After each of their Sunday trips, Sarah felt more and more secure in the decision to take this major step to further their son's education.

Everyone was in a happy mood when they climbed into their carriage to make their way home on February 26 after Sunday service. It was a clear day, but as they neared home, Henry called out to them. William partially arose from his seat beside Sarah and stuck his head out the window to see what Henry was yelling about. He followed the path of Henry's outstretched hand and saw a large cloud of billowing smoke coming from the direction of Mt. Hayes. Henry was using the whip to urge the horses faster. Sarah's face was white with fear. Fire was one of the most dreaded disasters that could befall a family and their dwelling.

When the carriage neared the house, but had not yet stopped, William jumped to the ground and ran toward the back of the house in the direction of the smoke. He turned briefly, to warn Sarah and Will to remain in the carriage. Henry jumped down and followed closely behind William to the rear of the house where they found one of the outbuildings, the one that housed the laundry, already nearly consumed by the flames.

All available hands were trying to put out the fire with buckets of water, but it was clear that their efforts were of no avail. William quickly went to several of the men clustered around the fire to ask what had happened. All looked frightened and none seemed either able or willing to speak.

William turned to look toward the main house and saw Sarah hurrying toward him. She had left the carriage immediately after William but had gone directly to the main house to check on Phillip and Ruth and the other residents of the house. Will had followed closely behind his mother. To her great relief, she found Bess in the front parlor trying to calm young Phillip and little Ruth. Once she had assured herself that her children and the household staff were all safe, she left Will in the care of Bess and hurried outside to join her husband.

"What happened? Is anyone hurt?" were her first questions.

William shrugged his shoulders, shook his head in bewilderment.

"I don't know," was his brief response.

"I don't understand," muttered Sarah, "none of the servants work in the laundry house on Sundays. It is always their day of rest."

At about that time, Henry approached them from the far side of the burning building. He was clearly very upset and tears filled his eyes. He was slowly shaking his head and seemed to be having a hard time catching his breath.

"What is it Henry?" William asked as he put his hand on his old friend's shoulder.

"Was anyone hurt?"

Henry stumbled towards them, and was sobbing convulsively as he slumped to the ground.

"It's Molly," he cried. "My mother is dead!"

Sarah immediately knelt on the ground beside Henry and put her arms around him.

"Oh Henry, I am so sorry. Why was she in there today of all days?"

Henry shrugged his shoulders and shook his head in bewilderment.

"I don't know," was his weak reply.

William walked behind the now smoldering building where he found a body covered by a blanket. With a great sense of unease, he lifted a corner of the blanked. One of the slaves had dragged Molly's body from the inferno and had suffered some serious burns in the process. Others had covered Molly's body, which was burned almost beyond recognition, and were now trying to minister to the injured man who had tried to save her.

"Was anyone else in the building?" William asked the assembled group.

Everyone agreed that there was no one else caught in the fire.

Sarah approached William who immediately arose and ushered her back to the other side of the building.

"You don't want to remember her this way," was his only comment.

Sarah returned to the house.

William and Henry worked alongside the servants for several more hours to be assured that the fire was completely out. When they finally entered the house, they were both covered in soot and their clothes and their hair reeked of smoke.

Bess immediately called down to the lower level where several slaves were huddled in prayer and ordered them to bring water and fresh towels for the two exhausted men who went upstairs to take off their soiled clothing.

After several minutes two young house slaves came up the stairs with basins of hot water. Their eyes were blood shot and they clearly had been crying. Everybody heard the news and everyone was mourning Molly's death.

Almost everyone, for following close behind the others was Hannah. She carried several clean towels and cloths and handed the items to Bess.

Both Sarah and Bess were disturbed to see no sign of grief on Hannah's face, but only that same self-satisfied expression that was so infuriating.

Both Bess and Sarah blurted out the same questions at almost the same instant.

"What are you doing in the main house? Where were you when the fire started?"

Hannah just smiled and before answering, lowered her chin and tilted her head sideways, then looked up in what appeared to be an attempt to appear demure.

"I had come into the main house to borrow a Bible and to say my prayers. It is, after all, the Lord's Day you know."

Sarah wanted to slap her, but was too well mannered, but she was ashamed to admit, was quite happy when Bess administered the blow for her.

Hannah looked stunned. Her eyes flashed and for a moment, Sarah feared that Hannah would attack Bess. But Bess's eyes flashed back in an instant as she stood her ground and her face clearly expressed her response to Hannah's unspoken challenge.

Hannah finally looked down at the floor and slowly began to back away. Bess reached out to stop her retreat, but Sarah touched Bess's arm and shook her head.

"Let her go, Bess. We'll deal with her later."

By the time Bess had fed the children and gotten them into bed, it was getting late and although none of the adults had eaten since early morning, no one had an appetite. They retired early, aware that there was much work to be done and many questions to be answered. The next few days would be challenging.

CHAPTER 15
Avarilla's Revenge

Mt. Hayes
1738

*T*he morning after the fire found the inhabitants of Mount Hayes consumed in a shared state of mourning. No one could explain how the fire could have started or how it had so quickly burned out of control. Nor could they find the reason for Molly's presence there. But the most troubling of all, was the issue of Hannah's possible role in the awful disaster.

News of the fire and of Molly's death traveled quickly. Mary Ann had been shocked when word reached her. She was particularly concerned when Sarah and William shared with her the many unanswered questions regarding the tragedy.

The immediate issue was to attend to the arrangements for the funeral and burial. Generally, the slave community was prohibited from conducting funeral gatherings, although they often did so privately away from the view of their masters. Nonetheless, it was not unusual, especially when house slaves were involved, for the masters of the plantation to play a role and to pay the expenses for a funeral. William and Sarah helped Henry with the arrangements and welcomed family and friends who called to offer condolences.

On Friday, March 3, the day of the funeral, William and Sarah lead the procession that followed the casket as it made its way to the Hayes Cemetery. Henry was surprised and overcome with emotion when the cart bearing the casket did not stop at a spot near the perimeter of the graveyard where slaves were generally buried, but moved on to the mound near the center of the cemetery where members of the family were buried. There, William spoke briefly about the important role Molly had played in the household and how much she would be missed by all of its residents. Following his brief remarks, Reverend Bourdillon delivered a sermon followed by a reading from the *"Anglican Order for the Burial of the Dead"* as it appears in the *English Book of Common Prayer*.

At the end of the service, the field slaves standing at the rear of the gathering, moved outside the fence that enclosed the graveyard and waited silently for the master and his guests to return to the house. Among these were the two surviving daughters of John Hayes, Jane and her husband Thomas Stansbury, and Elizabeth, widow of John Lennox and recent wife of Luke Trotten. They joined Mary Ann and Thomas along with William and Sarah as they walked slowly back to the house that would never again hear the soft, lilting voice of Molly as she sang the melodies and chants reminiscent of her early life in Jamaica.

The group seemed lost in their own thoughts as they silently made their way toward Mt. Hayes. They were suddenly distracted when Hannah literally pushed her way through the small group, then turned and gave one of her many impudent smirks, as she lifted her skirts high enough to show her bare ankles. This was a clear indication that she was not wearing either stockings or a shift. The women in the group as well as most of the men let out a collective gasp. Hannah laughed as she turned and slowly continued to lift her skirt from side to side as she walked toward the house.

The startled group of family members, stopped in their tracks, aghast at the girl's insolence. The first to speak was Elizabeth.

"Who was that?" Elizabeth asked, shaking her head in disgust.

"That's Hannah, she's a house servant," William explained with an exasperated sigh.

"Why? Why on earth would you have her in your house?" was Elizabeth's immediate question.

William offered the only explanation he had for the situation. "Apparently, Avarilla took her in after the girl's mother died."

"Why?" Elizabeth asked again. "She clearly has had no proper upbringing. Her behavior, her demeanor, well, everything about her is insulting. Especially on a day such as today."

Sarah was so relieved to hear Elizabeth's reaction to Hannah, that she nodded her head in enthusiastic agreement.

"Why," Elizabeth insisted again, shaking her head. "Avarilla wasn't exactly known for her tolerance or generosity for that matter. I don't understand why she would bring such a girl into the house."

William was looking for a way to answer Elizabeth's questions but was not having much luck.

"I really don't know. Other than the fact, that according to Henry, Avarilla had known the girl's mother and felt obligated in some way to try to help the girl." William explained with a shrug of his shoulders.

"Who was her mother?" Elizabeth demanded.

"I believe her name was Dorothy Richard's. Isn't that right, Sarah?"

Sarah really didn't want to be drawn into the conversation, which she was enjoying immensely. Clearly, she thought, she was not losing her mind. Others saw the inappropriateness of the girl's behavior.

Before Sarah could respond, Elizabeth turned to Mary Ann with yet another question.

"Mary Ann, wasn't that the name of the woman who brought a child to the door, the day after you arrived...remember? She was demanding to see my father, who she claimed was the father of her child? You must remember...Avarilla intervened and gave her some money to go away." Elizabeth insisted.

Mary Ann's face registered her surprise and she suddenly recalled in great detail, the incident at the back door on that cold and snowy day.

Although both women remembered their only meeting with the mysterious Dorothy Richards, they were at a loss to understand how a relationship might have developed between Avarilla and the girl's mother.

This was all news to William. He turned and saw Henry walking along slowly a few feet behind them. His head was bowed, his hands were in his pockets, and his face was filled with despair. William hesitated to intrude upon Henry's grief, but hoped he might shed some new light on Hannah and her mother's relationship with Avarilla.

"Henry, would you come join us please?" he asked, as he extended his hand toward Henry.

Henry looked up, nodded in agreement, wiped a tear from his cheek and slowly moved toward the group.

"Henry," he began, "what can you tell us about Hannah and her mother and their relationship with Avarilla?"

Henry paused a moment before answering. Finally, he responded. "Molly said Mistress Avarilla felt she had an obligation to the girl."

With that, he looked at the ground and began to slow his pace as though hoping that would be the end to the questions.

"What do you mean, an obligation?" William demanded.

Henry was now in apparent distress, he kept shaking his head from side to side, and in a barely audible voice begged, "Please, don't make me say."

William was getting exasperated with Henry's reluctance to provide information regarding this new mystery.

Finally, Henry took a deep breath, as though it might be his last and began. "Mistress Avarilla said that she had an obligation to her half sister."

There, he had said it, and despite his status as a free man, began to slowly back away, fearful of some awful punishment that might befall him for his disclosure.

It took a few minutes before the group finally realized the true meaning of Henry's revelation.

Elizabeth was the first to speak.

"Dorothy Richards was telling the truth when she accused my father of being the father of her baby." She took a deep breath before continuing.

"That baby was Hannah!"

The group shared a moment of quiet contemplation. There was no outrage. There were no accusations of disrespect directed toward Henry. He breathed a sigh of relief, and related the rest of the story.

"Mistress Avarilla gave money to Hannah's mother on a regular basis and when the woman died, she brought Hannah into the house. She promised her that when she died, Hannah would be the rightful heir and the new mistress of Mt. Hayes."

Everyone stood in quiet, puzzled confusion. Avarilla was not, never had been, nor ever would have been Mistress of Mt. Hayes. She had heard those words from her father's mouth on his deathbed. The woman had clearly lost her mind and had, in the mean time, fostered in the girl the unrealistic expectation that she would someday inherit Mt. Hayes.

Sarah, in some small way, was relieved to hear an explanation of the girl's behavior, although it certainly did not excuse it.

"I do remember that day," Mary Ann confirmed. "Well..., she paused before continuing, "this is certainly an unexpected revelation. Do you think Hannah could have been responsible for some of the unusual events that have occurred?"

The group all appeared to be considering the possibility.

Sarah, who was recently told by William the real reason for Craddock's departure, nodded in agreement as she asked, "Do you think it was Hannah who frightened poor Mr. Craddock? Do you think she actually tried to poison him, or push him out the window? Could she have been that wicked?

Mary Ann was deeply troubled by all of the possibilities raised by Henry's disclosure and a new question presented itself. *Was Hannah also responsible for the fire in the laundry building? And if so, had she deliberately targeted Molly?*

Those questions also arose in the minds of the assembled group. Finally, William turned to Henry and asked the question on everyone's mind.

"Henry, can you think of any reason why Hannah might have wanted to hurt Molly?"

Henry, his head bowed, eyes downcast, cleared his throat, and took a deep breath before speaking. When he looked up, his eyes were once again filled with tears as he spoke.

"It's all my fault," he began.

"Of course it's not your fault," William interrupted. "How could it possibly be? You were with us at church the morning of the fire."

"No, Henry continued, Early that morning Bess needed clean linens for the bedchambers. Hannah was supposed to have brought them, but she was nowhere to be found. I offered to fetch them while Bess tended to the children. As I was walking down the stairs, Molly asked why I wasn't on my way to church with the family. I explained the reason for my errand, and she insisted that I go along to church and that she would go to the laundry building."

Everyone stood puzzled by Henry's explanation. They stood in shocked silence as they tried to understand the implications of Henry's disclosure.

Sarah was the first to speak. She found it hard to get her breath as she haltingly began to share her anguish.

"Oh, Henry! It is I who am to blame. Clearly Hannah was trying to exact revenge upon Bess. But I am the one who didn't have the courage to discipline Hannah myself. Bess undertook the unpleasant task and sent Hannah to work in the laundry building."

Sarah went to Henry and put her arms around him as they both sobbed uncontrollably.

A sad day had suddenly become even worse.

The group stood silently as though fearful to move. Each was searching for some reasonable explanation for such awful evil. The only conclusion, unspoken, but shared, seemed to be that Hannah was the embodiment of the devil himself.

William looked at Sarah and then at his mother. He then suggested that prayer seemed the only reasonable path available to them all. The small group, held hands as they knelt together and prayed for Divine guidance in their efforts to deal with whatever wickedness had taken residence in Mt. Hayes.

As they arose and began walking toward the house in silence, Sarah felt a great sense of relief that they would soon get Hannah out of their lives forever. She hoped William would be as eager as she to attend to her dismissal.

Bess met them at the door and ushered them into the front parlor where she already had steaming cups of hot cider and warm cakes on a table in front of the blazing fire.

Each of the group of mourners was glad to sit and contemplate the events of the past week. It was several moments before anyone spoke.

It was Mary Ann who broke the silence.

"Well, William, you have some serious decisions to make. Clearly Hannah must leave Mt. Hayes immediately, but aside from that, do we have any evidence to show that she intentionally caused the fire and that she intended to cause the death of someone from this house?"

"Of course, she did these horrible things and many others besides!" Sarah exclaimed. In her mind there remained no doubt as to Hannah's guilt.

Elizabeth agreed with Sarah and nodded her head vigorously.

Jane, who had remained silent throughout the walk from the cemetery, interjected her own opinion.

"I understand everyone's feelings and suspicions, and I saw for myself the disrespect and inappropriateness of the girl's behavior. But, I don't see any real proof. There could have been any one of a number of reasons why Molly happened to be in the laundry house and no one knows yet how the fire started. Perhaps Molly saw the fire and attempted to somehow put it out."

Mary Ann realized that Jane, who had married and left Mt. Hayes long before she had arrived there, and surely remembered Henry only as a young boy, and had not witnessed Avarilla's resentment regarding her father's will. Furthermore, it would be difficult for anyone to think that a young girl such as Hannah could have been guilty of so much violence.

Mary Ann saw the disappointment on Sarah's face as Jane continued with her reasons to not rush to judgment against Hannah.

At that moment, Sarah felt panicked by the thought that anyone might come to Hannah's defense. She arose from her seat and excused herself, saying that she would tend to her children and then needed a rest.

Sarah walked to the stairway at the rear of the front hall and made her way up the stairs. Even though it was still mid-day, the sky was overcast and the upper hallway was rather dark. Out of force of habit, Sarah turned to look down the hall at the door to the bedchamber at the far end. It was almost too much to bear when she saw the light coming from under the door. She knew it had to be Hannah, but considering the vile behavior she had exhibited, was afraid to confront her. She went through her own bedchamber to the adjoining nursery where her children were playing. She locked the door to both rooms, picked up Philip and sat in the rocker to contemplate the day's events.

Shortly after Sarah's withdrawal, Elizabeth, Jane and their husbands began making preparations to leave. It had been a stressful day for everyone and there were no easy answers to the many questions the events of the day had provoked.

Thomas arose, planning to leave as well, but Mary Ann insisted that they should stay and spend the night. She felt uncomfortably responsible for much of the trouble that had befallen William and Sarah. Avarilla's hatred had been directed at her, whom she blamed for her father's abandoning her and depriving her of her inheritance. It was doubly unfortunate that Avarilla had managed to instill in Hannah that same hatred and sense of entitlement for her disinheritance.

Mary Ann excused herself to visit her grandchildren and to talk with Sarah. William and Thomas remained seated by the fire, both lost in their own thoughts as to how best to proceed.

As Mary Ann reached the top of the stairs, she saw Hannah leaving the room that had been Avarilla's. Hannah looked at Mary Ann with an expression of defiance as she produced a key from the pocket of her apron, and with a flourish locked the door and then paraded down the hall toward Mary Ann with the same flaunting behavior as before. She stopped in front of Mary Ann, dangled the key in front of her and slipped the key back into her pocket before laughing and moving towards the stairs.

Hannah stopped on the second step of the stairway, paused for a moment, then turned and walked back to confront Mary Ann, but now, her face was contorted with rage as she began to speak.

"You realize, of course, that I am the only blood relative of John Hayes living in this house now. You…you managed to beguile an old man into marrying you and then you turned him against his own flesh and blood. Avarilla knew from the beginning what your scheme was. You turned our father against her. You robbed her of her birthright. It was you who made her life so unbearable that she took her own. You are responsible for her death, and you and the rest of your spawn shall pay the price."

With that, she tossed her head with an audible snort of derision and stomped down the stairs.

Mary Ann stood silent in disbelief. She had never witnessed or endured such a vile threat. The extent of her hatred was both shocking and frightening.

Mary Ann knocked at Sarah's door and called out to her. Sarah quickly opened the door and the two women hugged. Mary Ann shared with Sarah the events of the last few minutes. Both women shook their heads in disbelief.

"She has to go immediately!" Mary Ann blurted out.

"I know," began Sarah, "I certainly agree, but I fear William will be hesitant to just send her away."

"You know how he is," Sarah continued, "it's not yet spring and he will feel obligated to find other employment for her."

Sarah sighed, and returned to the rocking chair. Mary Ann picked up Ruth, and sat on the bed as the two women shared several moments of silence as they tried to consider all options. Both were united in their determination to evict Hannah from the house immediately. They were concerned for their own welfare, but more importantly, for the welfare of the young children who might fall victim to one of Hannah's diabolical schemes. They remained in the room watching Philip and Ruth as they slept peacefully in their beds.

When one of the housemaids knocked on the door to tell them that supper was ready, they picked up the children, unwilling to chance leaving them out of their sight, and went downstairs to the parlor kitchen where William, and Thomas were already seated.

The table was already laden with food for their meal and Bess was preparing to take the children into the kitchen with her, but Sarah shook her head no, and insisted that Bess and the children remain in the parlor kitchen during the meal.

Sarah noted the absence of Henry and was immediately concerned. "Where is Henry?" she asked.

The words were barely out of her mouth when Henry entered the room. He was frowning and was out of breath when he announced that Hannah was nowhere to be found.

"What do you mean," William asked.

"Bess asked me to keep an eye on Hannah and not to let her out of my sight. I have looked everywhere and I can't find her or any of her things. It appears she has left the house for good," Henry explained.

Both Sarah and Mary Ann feared that this might be another of Hannah's ploys and insisted that a search must be conducted and that all servants were to be questioned regarding Hannah's whereabouts.

Thomas and William agreed but did not share the women's sense of urgency and suggested that they at least finish their meal. After all, no one had eaten since early morning.

After they finished eating, Thomas, William and Henry announced that they would conduct a thorough search of the home at which point, Mary Ann interrupted.

"Be sure to search Avarilla's old room, I saw Hannah leaving it earlier. She had the key, locked the room and then dangled it in front of my face before putting it in her pocket."

Sarah's eyes were wide with fear. There was now an urgency to deal with Hannah once and for all.

The men searched the house from top to bottom, paying particular attention to the second floor where the family slept. William searched every inch of Avarilla's former room as well as all of the trunks in the room. In the master bedchamber he carefully searched the drawer in which he had originally kept the key to the room down the hall, but also the trunk that held Sarah's wedding dress. Their search revealed no trace of Hannah or her possessions.

Next, they directed their attention to the many outbuildings, searching each one carefully and questioned all of the slaves and the indentured servants. None had any information about Hannah or her whereabouts. Henry, fearing that someone might have helped Hannah, informed all of the residents of the plantation of their concerns that Hannah had been responsible for the fire that claimed Molly's life. Upon learning this last unimaginable detail, everyone joined in the search of the outlying areas. But, despite many hours of searching and questioning of neighbors, there were no clues as to her whereabouts. After several weeks of searching with no results, everyone concluded that Hannah had run away to avoid punishment.

Both William and Thomas assured the women that Hannah surely had fled in fear for her life, and that was no longer cause for concern. Both Sarah and Mary Ann feared that they were being too optimistic, but prayed that they were right.

CHAPTER 16

A bad penny always turns up.

Old English Proverb

Mt. Hayes
1738

*W*ithout Hannah's destructive behavior and the worry it created, life at Mt. Hayes hummed along pleasantly through the spring and summer months. Despite the unusual amount of rain they had experienced early on, the dry days of autumn proved especially suited for the harvesting, and drying of the tobacco. Once the tobacco had been bundled into hands and loaded into barrels it was ready to be transported to Chesapeake Bay to be loaded onto ships for transport to England. It was one of the busiest and most stressful times of the year for tobacco planters. So much rested on the results of their labor and the quantity and quality of the tobacco they produced.

These were happy days for William and his family for the additional acreage he had purchased had produced tobacco of exceptionally high quality and brought a good price. Perhaps the most pleased of all was Henry. He knew that he had proven his skill as an overseer and was gratified by William's high praise for his efforts. Both men shared a jovial journey from the wharf back to Mt. Hayes and were eager to share their good news with Sarah.

When they arrived home, William jumped down from his horse and quickly made his way inside. Bess was preparing food in the kitchen and was immediately aware that William had good news to report. She gave him a big smile and pointed toward the stairs.

"Mistress Sarah is upstairs with the children. She sho' 'nuf gonna be glad to see ya'll Master William. I can see by your face that you got good news."

William patted her on the shoulder, nodded his head in agreement, and bolted up the stairs with the news of his success. As he opened the door, he could hardly wait to tell Sarah of their good fortune.

"Sarah, you will be delighted to learn, my dear wife, that ours has been one of the most profitable crops of all of our neighbors. It was well worth the chance we took when we bought more new land. We must have a party to celebrate our good fortune, don't you think?"

Sarah laughed at her husband's childlike exuberance over their good fortune. He put his arm around her waist and began to swing her around the floor as he danced and hummed a familiar melody. She felt like a newlywed again. She gently pushed back as she suggested that he might be a little gentler with his lively dancing.

"But you love to dance! And now we have every reason to celebrate our success, don't you agree?"

Sarah took him by the arms and led him to a small wooden bench by the fire.

"I do indeed, agree that we have good reason to celebrate. You have been so busy with the harvest and other tasks in the fields that I didn't want to worry you," she began.

William's face suddenly registered concern.

"What do you mean? He asked. "Is there something wrong? Are you ill?"

"No of course, I'm perfectly fine and there is absolutely nothing wrong. Quite the contrary, in fact, we are going to have another child. I didn't want to say anything until I was certain."

William jumped up, picked her up off her feet and began to swing her around again.

"Stop!" she demanded still laughing, "I'm quite well, but as I said, you need to be a little more gentle."

"Oh, I'm so sorry. Did I hurt you, are you certain you are alright?'

"Of course, I'm fine, and I certainly agree that we have many things to celebrate and much for which we must be thankful."

"When?" was William's next question.

"Mid summer," was Sarah's quiet reply.

"Then, by all means, we must entertain our friends during the upcoming holiday season and share our good news with them all."

"I think we should begin planning right away, don't you?" Sarah asked. "Let's do this, this time, before I get to the point that my formal gowns don't fit."

With that they walked arm in arm down the stairs.

"Let's share the news with Bess and the rest of the household," William suggested.

Sarah smiled, looked into his eyes and confessed that Bess already knew and therefore, it was likely that everyone, at least most if not all of the household staff, already knew as well.

Her suspicion was confirmed when they walked into the kitchen and it was immediately clear from the big smiles on the faces of Bess and Henry that Sarah's hunch was correct.

The holiday season was a truly blessed time for residents of Mt. Hayes. There had been a bountiful harvest, the joy of an expected baby and the friendship and fellowship of family and friends to share in their good fortune, promoted a sense of tranquility and optimism for the future. But perhaps the most comforting thing of all was the calm and peaceful atmosphere at Mt Hayes, which was no longer plagued by frightening and mysterious incidents.

Additionally, Sarah and William were looking forward to having young Will at home from the week before Christmas until after Twelfth Night. Each time they had spoken with Pastor Bourdillon, he had been very enthusiastic regarding Will's progress. He even confided that his only regret was that his own sons did not possess the academic ability of their son. He also continued to mention, albeit casually, that Will would most certainly benefit from the many educational advantages offered by more formal education in England. William and Sarah accepted his congratulations regarding their son, but gave no indication as to whether or not they planned to send him to England for a higher level of instruction. For Sarah, it was difficult enough having him away from home for a week or two at a time. She didn't know how she would be able to be parted from him for such extended periods that would be required if he were to study abroad.

But for the moment, they reveled in the excitement of having their family together for the holiday season. As usual, MaryAnn and Thomas spent the majority of the days before and after Christmas at Mt. Hayes. Everyone was happy to enjoy the festivities, those hosted by them as well as those of their neighbors. All were keenly aware that by early February the chores for a successful tobacco crop would be upon them, and so they enjoyed the luxury of these happy and relaxing days.

As was the case with her earlier pregnancies, this fourth one was also pleasant and worry free, and the prospect of a life without turmoil was a welcome turn of events.

On Sunday, July 29, 1739, Sarah gave birth to another boy, whom they named John. Early the following week, William visited Pastor Bourdillon to make arrangements to have the child baptized on Sunday, August 12.

When the day of the baptism arrived, Mary Ann and Thomas, the proud grandparents, arrived early at Mt. Hayes to accompany William and his family to St. Paul's Parish Church. As usual for that time of year, it was extremely warm, hot, in fact. The church was crowded and despite open doors and windows, there was no breeze at all.

At the end of the service, among the announcements was notification that a burial would be held immediately afterwards. This was unusual in and of itself, for generally only the poor, who had no family burial ground of their own, were buried in the churchyard. Additionally conducting the burial after a Sunday service was not typical. Immediately after the announcement, there was an instant, whispered reaction among the congregation.

Pastor Bourdillon hastened to explain the reason for this unusual circumstance.

"My friends, I hope you will understand the reasons for the urgency and the decision to have the burial here. We will be burying an infant. It is the mother's request that her child, who died just two days ago from scarlet fever, be buried immediately, to avoid any possible danger to members of the community, especially to other children. She is recently widowed and has no family cemetery in which to bury her child. She is seeking a Christian burial and it is our intent to accommodate her request. Indeed, it seems to be the only option available to this grieving mother."

At the conclusion of the announcement he looked toward the back of the church and asked the young mother to stand and receive the condolences and support from the congregation.

The members of the congregation turned as one to look at the women. Mary Ann was both shocked and dismayed when she saw Hannah stand in response to the pastor's request.

Mary Ann turned to look at Sarah who was clutching her own newborn son. There was a look of absolute terror on Sarah's face as she and William gathered their children and quickly made their way to the waiting carriage. Mary Ann and Thomas, as well as the majority of the congregation, also left the church as quickly as they could.

As their carriage slowly made its way through the throng of people hurrying to leave, they could see at the far corner of the churchyard a small grave had already been dug. Walking toward that grave was Hannah, carrying in her arms a blanket wrapped around the body of the child she was about to bury. When she reached the grave, she looked toward the departing churchgoers and her eyes focused on William and his family. Hannah stared directly at them with an unmistakable glare of contempt before stooping to place the bundle into the small wooden casket the church had provided.

Sarah suddenly felt quite sick to her stomach as she clutched her own infant son in her arms. She couldn't understand how such an ominous event could have erupted on the very day they had christened their own child. There were no tears. Her fear and grief were so overwhelming that it was all she could do just to breathe.

In fact, there was no conversation among the group as they made their way back to Mt. Hayes. All suffered in their own way. Sarah especially was consumed with feelings of guilt she had so often felt in the past. She could not understand why she felt that she was in some way cursed. Mary Ann reached out her arms to the new baby and nodded to Sarah as encouragement to release the child into his grandmother's arms. Sarah, as though in a daze handed the baby to her. No one spoke. There were no words that could ease the effects of the timing of Hannah's return, or of the awful scene they had witnessed as they left the church.

When they arrived home, Henry brought a small box and assisted the occupants to step down from the carriage. They moved in silence up the steps of the house. Bess met them at the door and upon seeing them, was immediately fearful, but dared not ask what had happened.

No one spoke as William and Sarah ushered their children upstairs and retired to their bedchamber, as did Mary Ann and Thomas. The adults all seemed lost in their own thoughts.

Young Will looked anxiously at his parents and despite the many questions he wanted to ask, was fearful to break the terrible silence that enveloped them all.

As if in response to some unspoken order, the family retired to their beds until time for the evening meal.

In response to Bess's summons to the kitchen parlor, the family moved downstairs and Bess began to serve the food she had prepared.

In an unexpected, but welcome suggestion, Will asked, "Father, May I say the blessing?"

William smiled at his son and nodded in agreement as tears began to stream down the faces of the adults seated around the table. The sight of this unusual reaction by the adults troubled Ruth who began to cry as she ran to her mother's lap. It was several minutes before a sense of calm was restored and Bess quietly took Ruth, Philip and baby John to the kitchen.

The family retired soon after their supper to their rooms on the second floor, for no one yet felt like talking. It was one of those events, which required passage of time before anyone would feel comfortable discussing possible consequences of the experience.

The next morning Sarah did her best to concentrate on her children and tried to put the events of the previous day out of her mind. As William constantly reminded her, they were all fine and there was absolutely nothing Hannah could ever do to bother them again. Nonetheless, Sarah insisted upon keeping Will home for the following week, in just an abundance of caution. After all, where Hannah was concerned, you could never be too careful.

The family, as well as many others of the congregation of St. Paul's Parish did not attend church services the following Sunday, and it was not until Sunday, August 26, two weeks after the christening, that Sarah and William brought Will with them to church and after the service, left him in the care of Bourdillon to continue his studies.

When they arrived home, they found Bess, sitting on a blanket, entertaining the children under a tree on the east side of the house. It was a large elm and offered shade from the summer sun. John was fast asleep in Bess's arms while Ruth was playing with a corn husk doll and Philip was trying his best to stack a small number of wooden blocks that Henry had made for him. But despite Philip's best efforts, his lack of hand, eye coordination caused the blocks to tumble before reaching the desired height. It was a fact that created a bit of frustration for young Philip. It was an idyllic scene and one that brought a smile to the young parents. It seemed, that after all, the unpleasant event of two weeks earlier was just that and nothing more to be feared.

William and Sarah sat down under the tree with Bess and their children. After Henry had unhitched the horses and safely stored away the carriage he joined the family as they spent a little more than an hour enjoying the peace and tranquility of their family.

The next few weeks, except for the demands of the tobacco fields, were uneventful. On Monday, September 10, Sarah joined William and Henry on the trip to return Will to his tutor. When they arrived at the clergy house, there was a horse tethered to a large tree in the front yard, and they assumed that there was a visitor inside the clergy house. They gave it little thought for they could hear the sound of children's voices coming from the rear of the house. They walked around the corner of the house and found Bourdillon's sons, Theodore and Thomas playing.

As soon as Will saw his friends he ran to join them and excitedly started telling them about all the interesting things he had done at home. William and Sarah walked together back to the front of the house, but before they could knock, Bourdillon's wife, Johannah approached from the path that led from the church to their home. She had just left the church where she had been doing some cleaning. She smiled at the couple, and opened the front door and invited them inside. The door to Bourdillon's library was closed and William assumed that he must be preparing the week's sermon.

"I'll call my husband," Johannah offered.

"No, please don't bother him if he's working, we just came to deliver Will," William explained.

"It will be no bother to him at all," Johannah said as she walked to the library door and knocked before opening it.

"Oh," Johannah muttered, as though surprised to find that he was not alone in the room. A young woman was seated in front of his desk.

"I didn't know you had a guest," she explained.

Bourdillon arose from his seat behind the desk, walked around to the front and indicating with his hand the woman seated there explained, "You remember Hannah Richards don't you my dear? She is the young woman who lost her infant son to scarlet fever a few weeks ago. She is seeking employment and would be quite willing to work for room and board. I was just telling her that I was certain you would welcome some help with the cleaning."

With that, Hannah turned around, curtsied to Johannah and gave her a most charming smile. Johannah was immediately aware of the audible gasp she had heard from Will's parents when they saw the young woman. She turned only to see that the young couple seemed distressed by the woman's presence. In fact, William had put his arm around his wife's waist. Sarah looked as though she had seen a ghost and was quite pale.

As Hannah walked toward the couple with her hand outstretched, Sarah shrank back in fear.

"It's so good to see you both again," she said mockingly. "And how are those beautiful children of yours? In good health, I hope."

The sinister look in Hannah's eyes along with her tone of voice, was too much for Sarah. She turned, and ran out of the house and climbed into the carriage.

"My goodness, exclaimed Hannah, is she alright? She looks as though she had seen a ghost?"

"No, Hannah, my wife is not alright. We had hoped that since you fled Mt. Hayes, after the mysterious fire which caused Molly's death, that we would never see you again."

"Here, here now, "Bourdillon interrupted, "this poor woman has suffered a painful loss of her own. Have you no Christian charity?"

Hannah's eyes blazed with a fury far more extreme than any of them had ever witnessed.

Johannah stepped between her husband and Hannah and in a stern voice, told Hannah to leave her house and never to darken their doorway again.

Bourdillon, shaking his head in disbelief, dropped to a chair as though he had been smitten by an unseen hand.

"My dear wife, this is uncharitable of you. Do you not recall that this poor woman just lost her child. She has had to resort to employment in an inn in Baltimore Town where she is oft beset by unwanted advances from all sorts of crude and disrespectful men."

William walked toward Hannah and paused briefly before asking a question that had been troubling him.

"Tell me, Hannah, what was the name of your husband? Or have you ever had one. I challenge you to present proof of a marriage, and to prove that you have not given birth to an illegitimate child. For if that is the case, you have born false witness in a house of worship. That is blasphemy, is it not Reverend?"

Hannah stood as though transfixed, and seemed to be searching for a response.

Johannah was now even more determined to remove this contemptible woman from her home. She issued a clear warning that she would see that the authorities delivered upon her the prescribed punishment for her sins.

Hannah shrank back, clearly frightened by the woman's threat, for she knew that as punishment she would either be placed in the stocks, or worse yet, she would be whipped in public.

But Johannah was not finished.

"As for your illicit and blasphemous behavior, and whatever other sins you have committed, the Lord will exact punishment upon you."

Benedict Bourdillon appeared dumbstruck. His wife of fifteen years had never before spoken in such an authoritative and decisive manner.

With that, Johannah took hold of Hannah's elbow and with a considerable amount of force, ushered her out the door with a final warning.

"Don't you ever darken our door again. Do you understand?" She demanded. She stood at the door watching as Hannah mounted her horse and raced away from the house. Only then did Johannah close the door, and turn to face her husband.

"I didn't mean to offend you my dear and as you know, I am not one to intervene with any of your decisions. But I fear that you are far too trusting and see only the good in everyone. Sometimes, that trust is unearned. Couldn't you see the fear in the eyes of this young couple? Remember, they are trusting us, not just you, but us, with the care of their oldest son? Clearly this young woman, Hannah, is not someone that we should welcome into our own home. Now, if you will excuse me, I have work waiting in the kitchen."

With that, Johannah straightened her posture, lifted her chin and held her head high as she walked to the side door, which she opened and then called to her sons to come inside. Next she walked into her kitchen and closed the door. The loud rattle of heavy kettles and skillets emanated from within the kitchen.

Bourdillon, looked perplexed, threw up his hands, and shook his head slowly before commenting.

"I have committed a grave error in judgment, for which I shall pray for forgiveness and guidance. And…I will try to make amends with my wife as well. Apparently, we don't need any household help. I shall be careful to remember that in the future."

William felt sorry for the pastor, but couldn't help but smile. He thanked Bourdillon for his excellent tutelage of Will, wished him good health and went outside to make sure that Hannah was nowhere to be found before returning to the carriage where Sarah was waiting.

"You left too soon, my dear," he offered with a smile. "I think it's safe to say that our son is perfectly safe in the Bourdillon household. Mrs. Bourdillon seems quite capable of making sure of that."

"I hope you are right, William, but I don't understand how you can be so positive. Hannah has proven herself to be quite untrustworthy."

William gave Sarah an affectionate hug and called out to Henry.

"Let's go home, Henry," William suggested, and Henry flicked the whip over the horse's back as they began the trip back to Mt. Hayes.

As soon as they arrived home, Sarah immediately ran upstairs to check on her children. They were all sleeping soundly and she gave a sigh of relief. Perhaps she had overreacted, again. After all, what could Hannah Richards possibly do to hurt her or her children now?

It was only later that day, well after dark that Sarah on her way upstairs had paused to look down the upper hallway toward Avarilla's old room. She stared in disbelief when she saw a light coming from under that door. Would this nightmare never end, she thought. She called downstairs to Bess who came immediately.

Bess, saw the look on Sarah's face and looked in the direction she was pointing. There it was. A light was shining from under the door. Bess immediately hurried down the hallway and tried the door. They were both shocked when the door opened with the turn of the handle. Bess turned and stared at Sarah. They both remembered that the last person to leave that room had been Hannah, right after the fire. Mary Ann had told them that she had seen Hannah leave the room and lock the door and then put the key in her pocket. There was no conclusion to be reached other than that Hannah had been in the house again.

As if struck by the same fear at the same moment, the two women rushed down the hall to the nursery. The children were all asleep in their beds, but Sarah was still filled with fear. She went to each of her children to make certain that they were sleeping. She was relieved that they were all quite well and sound asleep. She stopped over the cradle of her youngest, John. He was such a good baby. She was puzzled that he was wrapped in a heavy blanket. It was so very hot in the room. She quickly picked him up and unwrapped the blanket and then laid him down gently in the crib. She sat down beside the crib in the rocker. She had been so relieved that they all seemed fine that it took a few minutes before she gave the blanket another thought.

"Bess, why did you put such a heavy blanket on John?" she asked.

"I didn't put no blanket on that child, I swear Mistress Sarah." Bess insisted. "sides, I never seen that blanket before," she insisted.

Sarah picked up the blanket from the floor where she had dropped it before putting John back in his crib.

She studied it for a moment, before the ghastly reality hit her. She had seen this blanket before. She began to sob as she looked at Bess and explained.

"Hannah's dead child was wrapped in this blanket. I saw it just before the child was placed in the casket at the church. Her baby died of scarlet fever!"

Her words seemed to hang in the air like a dark cloud. She was having a difficult time trying to breathe again. Bess, fearing for Sarah's health, grabbed the blanket ran downstairs to find William, then she planned to burn the blanket.

Bess found William in the front parlor talking with Henry about the crop and the weather. When he saw the expression on Bess's face he immediately rose to his feet and demanded, "What's wrong? Are the children alright? What about Sarah?"

Bess explained as quickly as she could and William hurried to the stairs at the back of the house and climbed them three at a time.

They both knew how deadly scarlet fever could be, but now all they could do was watch their children, try to keep them safe, and pray.

Three days passed without any signs of illness, and everyone in the household hoped for the best. They prayed that Hannah's evil plot had been unsuccessful. The children all seemed healthy and happy. But on the third day, baby John was feverish and his cheeks were flushed. He cried incessantly, and despite their best efforts, the baby died two days later. A day after his death, both Ruth and Philip became ill as well and within a week's time, three of their children had been taken from them by the evil that was Hannah.

Sarah sank into a deep depression. She didn't want to eat, she could not sleep and finally, much to the distress of everyone in the household, walked into Avarilla's room where she sat in the rocking chair in silent mourning.

William was beside himself with worry and he sent Henry to bring Mary Ann and Thomas. He needed all the help he could get. As soon as Henry arrived at the Harris home, they immediately dropped everything and accompanied Henry back to Mt. Hayes. Everyone feared for her health and for her sanity, for that matter. They had tried everything in their power to comfort her and to bring her out of the awful agony she was experiencing. William insisted that he should bring Will home to visit, but Sarah would not permit it. She was so fearful of whatever evil she felt permeated her world.

Sarah's condition did not improve and lasted through the fall harvest and the holiday season. She remained secluded in Avarilla's room and did not leave the room even at meal time. Although Bess carried meals to her daily, she ate barely enough to sustain her life. After a month of her mourning, William brought Will home. Sarah made no objection to his presence and seemed not to remember why he had been away. Even throughout Christmas and Twelfth Night, the halls of Mt. Hayes added to the bleakness of the situation since there were no candles, no boughs of holly and evergreens that normally adorned them. Nor was there the sound of children's laughter and excitement. It felt as though life itself had been drained from the house with the death of the three children.

Mary Ann and Thomas, when he could spare time from the demands of the plantation, spent as much time as possible at Mt. Hayes in attempts to awaken Sarah from her trance-like state. Finally, in early March, once the weather had cleared, Mary Ann sent Henry to bring Sarah's sisters in hopes that they might be able to cheer her.

The arrival of twins, Jemima and Rebecca, provoked no real response from Sarah. She seemed lost in a world of her own, but when her eldest sister, Rachel, the lovable but unmarried spinster, arrived she brought with her a sense of purpose and a plan. Rachel was a take-charge woman. She ordered everyone else out of the room and sat and began to talk with Sarah. Unlike the others who had attempted to coax Sarah from her depression, Rachel was determined and spoke to her in a firm tone. She reminded her that many mother's had lost children to disease, even their brother Thomas and his wife had faced a similar disaster, but moved on with their life. She reminded her that she had an obligation to her husband, to her son Will, and to the rest of the family. There was no clear indication that Sarah had taken her words to heart, but two days later, with the help of Bess, the two women managed to get Sarah cleaned up, and dressed in her finest dress. Sarah made no objection, but allowed the women to take charge. She was not angry, nor did she cry. In fact, she seemed completely devoid of emotion. She seemed to have given up and was merely waiting for whatever destiny fate might have in store for her.

Rachel asked that the family accompany them to Annapolis in neighboring Anne Arundel County. There was a preacher whom she had heard a great deal about. She felt confident that he was just the man to offer comfort and help to her younger sister. Rachel offered no additional information about the man other than that he was from England. Despite their requests for more information, she merely said that they would have to see for themselves. William felt that there was no alternative but to agree to any plan that might offer hope. Once everyone was ready, Sarah, William, Mary Ann and Thomas followed Rachel into the crowded carriage and began their thirty-two mile trip to Annapolis.

CHAPTER 17
The Great Awakening

Annapolis, Maryland
1740

*W*illiam was hopeful, although he had no idea why Rachel was so positive that this preacher that they were traveling to see could possibly help his wife. He was completely unprepared for the experience.

As they neared Annapolis, the great number of people traveling toward the town immediately surprised them. There were carriages as well as wagons filled with people and literally hundreds traveling on foot. Mary Ann was the first to voice her alarm.

"What on earth is going on? She asked. Are these people fleeing from something? I have never witnessed such a mass of people on the road. What do you think it means?"

Rachel only smiled and nodded her head. "They are all on their way to hear the same man I told you about."

"Surely you are mistaken." Thomas interjected. "There are people of all ages, young, old, entire families. There must be a disaster of some sort. Why else would they be in such a hurry?"

"I suspect, it's because they don't want to miss a moment of his sermon," was Rachel's reply.

Directly ahead of them was a side path that moved slightly west of the main road. The entire throng turned onto this smaller path and pushed forward.

"Just follow the crowd, Henry," Rachel called out.

"But this way will lead us away from town," Thomas noted. "I don't see any sign of buildings in this direction, only open fields."

Rachel just sat quietly and enjoyed the perplexed expressions on her fellow passenger's faces.

After they had traveled about a quarter of a mile down the small path, they could see a huge crowd already assembled and could hear a loud, clear voice booming across the landscape. It was necessary for them to get out of the carriage in the midst of hundreds of other vehicles in order to move closer to the sound of that voice.

The man moved about from a small rise under a large oak tree at the far end of the field. His voice was powerful, melodic, and filled with emotion as tears streamed down his face. He moved about as he spoke and his body was animated by his words. He appeared to be overcome with passion. He spoke freely, clearly from the heart and without the benefit of notes or papers of any kind. His audience appeared transfixed by his voice and his presence.

William and Sarah and the others moved through the crowd as best they could. They were still quite a distance from the mound but the man's voice was so powerful that they could hear quite distinctly every word he spoke. William recognized the passage the preacher was citing. It was from the New Testament, Mathew Chapter 11: Verse 28.

"Come unto me, all ye that are weary and heavy laden, and I will give you rest. Who are the weary and heavy laden? When you are obliged to cry out under the burden of your sins, and know not what to do for relief; when this is your case, you are weary of your sins. It does not consist in a

weariness all of a sudden; no, it is the continual burden of your soul, it is your grief and concern that you cannot live without offending God, and sinning against Him; and these sins are so many and so great, that you fear they will not be forgiven. Let me beseech you to come unto Christ, and He will give you rest. You shall find rest unto your souls."

Suddenly, William became aware that Sarah had grasped his hand and was whispering a question?

"Who is this man?"

Their small group looked first at Sarah, then at each other. She was absorbed in the speaker's words and her eyes glistened with tears.

"His name is George Whitefield. He's from England," Rachel whispered.

"He's certainly a powerful speaker," Mary Ann noted, "but he seems so young."

"Yes," acknowledged Rachel, "he's only twenty-six years old but he's already quite famous. He has been conducting revivals such as this all through the colonies. I think he is a wonderful man."

"So do I," murmured Sarah.

William placed his arm around Sarah's shoulders, mouthed a silent "Thank you," to Rachel and smiled for the first time in months, before directing his attention to the evangelist once again.

The man seemed tireless in his crusade and the sermon lasted for nearly an hour longer. Near the end there was a small number who were offended by his remarks when he criticized those ministers whom he described as "Unconverted" and "having Christ in their heads, but not in their hearts." The departure of those critics did not go unnoticed by Whitefield who roared out after them, "The Devil's at your heels!"

It was a moving and powerful scene. By the time Whitefield had finished there were at least two thousand people surrounding the small mound on which he stood. Many rushed forward to speak to the man. Many seemed overcome by emotion and fell to their knees in prayer.

Sarah looked at her family, smiled, hugged her sister Rachel and murmured softly, "I felt that he was speaking directly to me. It was as though a great burden has been lifted from my shoulders. He has given me the path to salvation. This was truly a blessing. Thank you."

They stood silent for a few moments, confused, but thankful for the response from Sarah. William took Sarah's hand and the group began their trek to rejoin Henry who had remained with the carriage. It took quite some time for they had to weave their way among the throng scattered about the vast field of worship. But they felt no urgency and walked at a leisurely pace. Although Sarah was still quite frail, she seemed revitalized by the profound power of the sermon. It was as though she had been awakened from some long and horrific nightmare and finally felt the courage to face the future. When they finally reached their carriage, Sarah paused and turned to face her family.

"I am ashamed of the worry and pain that I have caused you all."

As one, they all shook their heads and hastened to calm her concerns.

William pulled Sarah to him, smiled down at her and assured her that his love for her was constant.

Sarah returned the smile, nodded her appreciation to her assembled family and climbed into the carriage.

By the time Henry had managed to maneuver the carriage into the line departing the scene it was nearly dark.

Thomas, concerned for Sarah's welfare and the fear of being waylaid by thieves, suggested that it might be best if they stayed the night at an inn. William agreed, but looking at the mass of people on the roads, suggested that it might be difficult, if not impossible, to find a room at any of the local inns. Everyone agreed that if they encountered satisfactory lodging on the trip home, they would take advantage of it.

They were fortunate when they arrived at the Norwood Ferry that crossed the Patapsco River. There was a very nice inn run by Edward Norwood and his wife and there were two rooms available.

Mary Ann suggested that the women would share one room and the three men would occupy the other. All agreed, although William regretted that he would not be spending the night with his wife.

It had been a long and tiring day, but everyone felt that the trip and the experience had been well worth it. They sat down around a table to enjoy a late but meager meal of bread, cheese, apple pie and rum prepared by the innkeeper's wife.

As they joined hands around the table, William said grace.

"Merciful Father, pardon our sins and give us thankful hearts for these and all other blessings. Bless this food to our bodies and our bodies to your service. Amen."

Sarah looked at William and once again, uttered a soft "Thank you."

Thomas, like everyone else at the table, felt an enormous sense of relief that the family seemed, finally, to be on the road to normalcy. He suggested that another cup of rum was called for in celebration of the day's events. The men happily agreed to the suggestion, but Sarah was still weakened by the many weeks of seclusion during which she had slept little and eaten less. But despite this she seemed amazingly calm and happy, but very frail and tired. Both Mary Ann and Rachel politely refused the rum asked that they be excused to go straight to bed. Sarah welcomed the prospect of a good night's sleep, and the women jointly arose from the table and went to their room.

Once in their room Sarah sat down on the edge of the bed. For the moment, she appeared lost in her own thoughts. Mary Ann and Rachel both began to undress and prepare for bed, but were concerned for Sarah. She was so very quiet that they feared her recent recovery might be about to regress back into depression and isolation, but they were hesitant to interrupt her silent meditation. After removing their outer garments and dressed only in their shifts, Rachel and Mary Ann began to turn down the blankets of the bed.

Sarah remained seated on the bed, apparently unaware of the actions of the other two women. The two women exchanged worried glances but said nothing. Rachel sat down beside Sarah and Mary Ann moved a chair near the bed. After what seemed like an eternity, but was probably no more than five or six minutes of silence, Sarah took a deep breath and released a long, barely audible sigh. She turned and looked at the two women and opened her mouth as though to speak, but sighed once again and looked down at her hands folded in her lap. She appeared undecided as to how to begin. She reached out and took hold of Rachel's hand and looked first at her sister and then at Mary Ann before finally speaking.

"I don't know exactly how to explain my feelings, she began, but I have a confession to make."

Deep concern registered on the faces of both women. They were fearful of whatever it was that Sarah wished to confide. Mary Ann immediately arose from her chair and moved to kneel in front of Sarah.

"My child, you are one of the kindest, most gentle souls I have ever known. Whatever is troubling you, I'm certain has been no fault of your own," Mary Ann insisted.

"You don't understand. It's this unrelenting feeling of guilt that has always haunted me," Sarah murmured.

"What on earth could you possibly feel guilty about?" Rachel countered. You have always been a good person and I have never known you to intentionally cause harm or mistreat another."

"Oh but I have," Sarah sobbed. "My mother died because of me. My children died because of me and I have feared that my soul was cursed and provoked pain and suffering on those I love most."

Both Mary Ann and Rachel were stunned by her revelation. Kind, sensitive, gentle Sarah had been guilt ridden since childhood by things over which she had no control. They immediately put their arms around her shoulders and attempted to calm her. But Sarah pulled away from them, and with a sincere, and heartfelt smile, shook her head.

"No, please, let me finish. The man who spoke today understood my pain. His words were those that had echoed in my mind for so long, but I didn't see any relief or any way to ease my suffering. But now, he has shown me what I must do. I must seek forgiveness and salvation. I must confess my sins before God. She frowned slightly as she continued. Forgive me, I guess I have been practicing."

The three women, clasped hands and knelt together by the side of the bed. They bowed their heads and Rachel began reciting the Lord's Prayer. Mary Ann and Sarah joined in the prayer, which was followed by their own silent communications and prayers with God. They remained kneeling together until Sarah murmured her own "Amen."

They rose to their feet and Sarah, turned to face them.

"Thank you for your love and support. I am so grateful for your understanding. I think I will be able to rest tonight."

In the room below the three men enjoyed one more cup of rum before they too retired upstairs to their room.

The women awoke after a pleasant night's sleep and went downstairs to join the men who were grumbling about the miserable night they had endured due to the starts and stops of loud snoring. The women smiled in amusement as each of the men blamed the others about their disrupted sleep. The women only smiled in amusement as the accusations flew regarding which of the men had been the biggest offender. It was a pleasant and entertaining distraction.

By mid morning they had enjoyed a hearty breakfast of cornmeal mush and molasses with cider again prepared by the innkeeper's wife. As with the previous night's supper, Sarah's appetite had returned and she now looked rested and not as pale as she had been the day before. They paid the inn-keeper, complimented his wife on her cooking and climbed into their carriage to enjoy a leisurely trip back home.

It was obvious that everyone at Mt. Hayes had heard the sound of the carriage wheels and the horses' hooves as they approached for they were all standing at the top of the stairs that led to the front door. Their faces showed the apprehension they all felt, and they had no idea what to expect. Bess was particularly worried that the trip might have been too tiring for Sarah. The group remained standing at the top of the stairs as the travelers began to step down from the carriage. There was an audible gasp from them as they caught their first glimpse of Sarah. She looked up, smiled and waved to them as Bess hurried to welcome her mistress back home.

"Land sakes Miss Sarah, it's so good to have you back home. It's like a miracle done brought you back to us!"

Sarah gave Bess a big hug and confessed, "You're right Bess. It, indeed, was a miracle."

Bess, grinning from ear to ear accompanied the family up the stairs and into the house and then immediately pointed toward the front parlor.

"I didn't know just when you would be home, but I got terrapin stew and fresh baked cake. I'll have everything ready just as soon as I can. You come sit down and rest. Lord knows it's so good to have you back and feelin' so much better."

They all laughed, listening to Bess as she hurried toward the kitchen and belted out orders to the rest of the household staff.

They enjoyed the opportunity to sit down in the comfortable chairs of the parlor. Traveling by carriage was more comfortable than riding a horse, but any trip of considerable length soon took its toll on the body, especially over rough roads.

They were all eager to share their impressions of the Reverend Whitefield, all that is except Sarah. For her, the experience had produced a profound and life saving change. This was especially obvious when Sarah asked when they could bring Will home for a visit.

"I need to make amends to him. I fear he may think that I do not love him. Can we go later today?" she asked, looking at her husband with pleading eyes.

William was relieved that Sarah, indeed, seemed on the road to recovery, but was fearful that in her weakened condition she might have a relapse of some sort.

"I am eager to see our son as well, my dear, but I think it would be better to get some rest today. But I promise, we will leave first thing tomorrow morning, if you wish."

Sarah smiled and nodded her agreement and laughed as she asked, "Do you think Bess has the food ready yet? I'm starving. Aren't you?"

Everyone stood and agreed as they headed down the hall to the parlor kitchen.

Just as they had planned, the couple left home shortly after breakfast the following morning. William felt that they both had their lives back as they made their way to the clergy house. As for Sarah, she was eager to see her son, but wondered what Reverend Bourdillon's opinion of Whitefield might be. Would he share her admiration and respect for the great orator? Could he be one of those ministers described as having God in their heads, but not in their hearts? As she pondered these questions, she unconsciously wrinkled her brow. It was quickly noted by William.

"Is something wrong?" He asked.

Sarah smiled and shook her head. "No, I was just wondering if Reverend Bourdillon has heard Whitefield speak, and if so, what he might think of the man."

"Don't concern yourself, my dear. You felt the power of the man's words. You know in your heart what his message meant to you. That is all that matters. Let's just concentrate on having Will back with us for a few days."

Sarah smiled and nodded in agreement. "You're right, I know. It would be foolish to base my feelings on anything other than my own experience."

It was only Wednesday and the clergyman, aware of Sarah's long-standing problems after the death of her children, did not expect to see them. When they arrived and knocked at the door, there was no answer. Sudden panic swept through Sarah and her old fears returned.

"What could be the matter? I don't understand why no one is home. Where could they be?"

William consoled her as best he could and walked around to the back of the house where he found the entire Bourdilon family, as well as young Will, busily working in a small garden plot, preparing it for planting.

Sarah had followed close behind and shouted out to her son. "Will!"

They all looked up from their work and Will gave a squeal of delight upon seeing his parents. He ran to his mother's outstretched arms and gave her an enthusiastic hug as she bent to embrace him. His appearance, as well as that of Reverend Bourdillon, his wife and sons suggested that they were all peasants for they were all quite dirty from the task in which they had been absorbed.

Johanna immediately came forward apologizing, and instructed Will and her sons to immediately wash up and change from their work clothes. Bourdillon approached with a broad smile and welcomed the couple.

"Hard work is good for the mind, the body and the soul, don't you agree, sir?"

William laughed, shook the man's hand, and concurred.

"I certainly do. It's good to see that the boy is being prepared for what lies ahead, for his mind as well as his body. Education is a many faceted thing and I'm pleased to see that he is receiving instruction in all areas."

Reverend Bourdillon was pleased with the response, but suggested that they retire to the house where he and his wife would need to attend to their appearance as well.

William and Sarah followed their host into the house and sat in the parlor to await the return of their hosts and their son.

Johannah was the first to return having washed her hands and face and put on a clean apron. She brought in a tray with a small assortment of cakes and a flagon of cider, cups and plates and offered the refreshments to her guests.

Will was in a hurry to see his parents, and especially his mother who seemed more like she had been before the death of his siblings. She was clearly happy to see him. He was greatly relieved, especially when she informed him that he would be returning with them to Mt. Hayes for the next several days.

Will was so excited he could hardly contain himself and kept asking , "Are we leaving now? Can we leave now? I'm ready to go."

Sarah's heart was filled with joy by the reception she received from her son and her reservations about discussing her recent experience with Reverend Whitefield faded away. After all, that discussion could wait until another time. The important thing at the moment was to reassure her son of her love for him.

"I hope you will understand how important it is for me to have Will home with us for a few days. I have missed him so," she confessed.

Bourdillon and Johannah both nodded in understanding. The bond between mother and child was more important than a couple of days of missed lessons.

William, Sarah and Will thanked the Bourdillon's for their understanding and kindness and hurried to their carriage.

It had been such a long time since Sarah, and William for that matter, had felt blessed by good fortune. William had his wife back, Will had his mother back, and Sarah had her life back. The future held a lot of promise. That was her hope.

CHAPTER 18
"The best laid plans oft go awry."

Robert Burns

1742 – 1745

*T*he religious fervor that spread through the colonies like a wave, awakened and propelled a new sense of personal accountability into the lives of those it touched. This included a new consciousness of the importance of a personal relationship with God. It also insinuated a challenge to the British position of unconditional allegiance to the King as head of the church. It emphasized the view that to be truly religious, one had to trust the heart rather than the head. It relied more on feeling than on thinking and believed that biblical revelation was more reliable than human reasoning. It was a new way of thinking.

There was a readily available opportunity for anyone with an interest to hear some of the greatest theologians and speakers of the day. Foremost among these was George Whitefield whom Sarah and her family had heard, and who was often labeled as "peddler of divinity" in the local press. They, like many of their neighbors, would make every effort to hear other such evangelists, including Jonathan Edwards, whose powerful sermon "*Sinners in the hands of an angry God*", was printed and widely circulated among those who could not travel to hear him.

Perhaps, however, ultimately it would be John Wesley, a cleric for the Church of England and his brother Charles who organized small groups that became known as the Wesleyan Movement, that would have the most lasting effect upon Sarah and her family. Despite the great comfort

Sarah and her family experienced by embracing these new concepts, it could not alter the numerous, unrelenting hardships that many couples, like Sarah and William encountered.

Foremost among their concerns was how best to cope with the unpredictability of an annual tobacco crop.

The problem was three fold. First, tobacco quickly depleted the nutrients in the soil and could be grown no more than three seasons in the same field before leaving it fallow for another three years. For those who could afford it, this meant that plantation owners were constantly in search of more land to buy.

Secondly, tobacco grew best in uncultivated soil, thus requiring that the newly acquired land be cleared of trees and brush. This was a slow, time-consuming task, which required a large number of workers, as did the planting, harvesting, and preparing tobacco for shipment.

Third, the necessary work force generally relied heavily on slaves and indentured servants, and acquisition of both required a large outlay of money.

It was a conundrum, which overtime resulted in a market monopoly by the wealthiest of planters. This was the situation facing William and Sarah, and other families like them, struggling to maintain their former lifestyle.

The volatility of tobacco production was a topic that William and Sarah discussed often with their neighbors. All but a very few found themselves faced with similar concerns and growing debts but few ideas as to how best to deal with the situation.

Although both Sarah and William were thrilled with the birth of their son, Thomas, on May 17, 1742, they had many concerns regarding how to provide the same opportunities for him that they had been able to give to their eldest son, Will. Will was now nine years old and in three more years, it would be time to make a final decision regarding his future. It was common for boys by the age of twelve, to be apprenticed to learn a trade, or, if wealth permitted, to be sent to England for further education. They were acutely aware that Reverend Bourdillon had filled Will's head with expectations of being given a formal English education. They also knew that their son was now looking forward to it.

Fortunately for the tobacco planters of Baltimore County, 1742 was a year of optimal weather for tobacco and many hoped that this phenomenon would continue and provide a reversal of fortune for them all. Of course, this was not to be for 1743, true to form, was filled with multiple severe storms throughout late summer into fall, followed by one of the worst snowstorms they had ever experienced in February and March of 1744. This proved to be disastrous for the tobacco crops of both years and thus for the financial future of many planters.

In late September of that year, William and Sarah shared with their parents the news that Sarah was expecting another child. Their conversation eventually brought up the inevitable topic of their financial situation, and how it might impact their children's future. It was a subject to which Mary Ann and Thomas had given much thought.

"I quite understand your concerns," Thomas began, "for we know how much Will has been anticipating traveling to England to study. But the fact of the matter is, that although he is indeed a bright young man, there is no guarantee that he would be accepted into such elite schools. And what would he study? Does he have an interest in the sciences, in law? Does he hope to become a member of the clergy?"

Sarah gasped a startled "Oh", at the introduction of religion into the discussion. "It never occurred to me that Will might want to become an Anglican pastor. I just assumed that he might have wanted to consider...," here she paused as if searching for just the right words, but sighed without finishing her thought.

"Regardless of what the boy's wishes might be, I have always assumed that he would choose to become a tobacco planter like his father and me. And, if that is the case, I don't see how a lengthy and expensive trip abroad to study would help him at all."

William picked up on Thomas's train of thought and added, "And, if he were to complete his education there, he would not return until he reached the age of twenty-one."

Once again, Sarah murmured another shocked "Oh, I really hadn't thought about that. I had assumed that he would be gone only for a year or two, but certainly not for nine years. I've been preoccupied with worries about the dangers of crossing the ocean and all of the horrible misfortunes that might befall him. I just hadn't thought it through."

"As I mentioned before," Thomas continued, "your mother and I have also been concerned about the current turn of events. Assuming, of course, that Will would hope to become a planter, although not necessarily a planter of tobacco, we have thought of a possible solution."

"Your mother and I would like to provide a gift, an enticement if you will, that might alter Will's desire for an English education."

Both Sarah and William were immediately curious and attentive.

"I don't understand, Sir. What do you have in mind," William asked.

"It is something that we had planned to carry out on the occasion of Will's reaching the age of maturity. But I think, it might be prudent to take care of it now, or at least on his birthday this December."

Thomas paused before continuing.

"I intend to deed to Will a gift of 100 acres of a track of land along Herring Creek in Anne Arundel County. Our hope is that it might prove to be a sufficient motivation to keep the boy here."

William and Sarah were both overcome by emotion at the generous gift Will's grandfather had planned. They both felt confident that it would indeed be a powerful motivation to keep Will in Maryland, and for the time being, the couple felt an enormous sense of relief and held out hope that Will would be so happy with his unexpected good fortune that he would be content to remain in Maryland. But as with most things, only time would tell.

As they had planned, Thomas and Mary Ann Harris surprised their grandson Will, with the gift of land on December 18, 1744, on the occasion of his eleventh birthday. At the time, no mention was made regarding the important decision that would have to be made the following year.

Almost exactly one month later, on January 18, 1745, Sarah gave birth to another son whom they named Joseph. It was a happy household as they welcomed their new son and renewed hopes for a prosperous year ahead. But the weather was harsh and hopes for a good crop were dashed once again. It soon became clear to William and Sarah that they faced a serious financial dilemma. Their lives and those of their three sons were about to change dramatically.

As was the custom, Thomas and Mary Ann had made a tradition of spending a good portion of the time leading up to Christmas at Mt. Hayes. This of course, gave them the chance to participate in the celebration of the birthday of their oldest grandson, Will. This year marked his twelfth birthday, an occasion that routinely signified the time when a young boy entered upon the road to manhood. Normally, it was a time of anticipation and excitement, however, Wednesday, December 18, 1745, proved to be different.

Although Will had been told on his previous birthday of the generous gift of land by his grandfather, the actual document, which had already been registered with the courts, had not yet been presented to him. Everyone hoped that the physical evidence of the generous gift would soften the blow of the news he was about to receive.

As though by divine acknowledgement of the ominous event about to take place, the skies suddenly darkened and a large flash of lightning startled them all as the low rumble of thunder announced the beginning of a sudden, unexpected snow storm.

Will and his younger brother Tom both, surprised and then excited, rushed to the window to observe this unusual phenomenon. The adults glanced at each other nervously as they prepared to unleash an unexpected storm of their own. Once the boys had returned to their seats, William and Sarah began to share their news with Will.

Will sat in stunned silence as his father began to layout before him the worst news he had ever heard. He would not...nay, could not sail to England to continue his studies. His face betrayed the intensity of his visceral response to his fate.

For the last six years he had been enthralled by his tutor's expansive praise of the joys of academic life at Cambridge and of the resulting promise of a life of wealth, social position and respect. He had felt not just fortunate, but blessed, and ultimately entitled to the opportunity. Now, this news he had just received from his parents and grandparents felt like a betrayal. Anger filled his heart, but years of training to be obedient constrained his desire to lash out at this unexpected parental tyranny. He was so preoccupied by this new and unexpected deceit that he was unable to speak and was barely aware of the next bit of betrayal about to be forced upon him.

His father and grandfather, keenly aware of the panic in the boy's face, moved closer to him. They sat down on either side of him and each placed a hand upon his shoulder, an action that they hoped would console him. But the effect was anything but comforting and felt to young Will like enormous chains forcing him into submission to this unforeseen decree. He was going to be forced into an apprenticeship. Despite the continued efforts to explain the hardships facing the family, Will felt betrayed. He felt that his life was no longer his and that he was destined to a life of near servitude for at least the next six years.

He did not cry, for his anger strangled any remnants of sadness. He was breathing rapidly now and his face had become a rather alarming shade of red. He appeared to be struggling to find the words to express the unfair cruelty of the moment.

Finally he spoke and the contempt in his young voice was palpable, "Tell me sir, what kind of apprenticeship do you have planned for me?"

His grandfather was the first to speak. "Well, Will, since you are now a landowner, I assumed that you might want to be a planter."

Will stood abruptly, shaking his head in disbelief.

"After taking such careful pains to explain to me the dire nature of being a tobacco planter and how that because of it, you can no longer afford to send me to England to study," Here he paused for breath, "I cannot understand how you would condemn me to such a life."

They had never seen their son exhibit such disrespectful behavior and could not understand his daring to behave in such a manner.

William rose to his feet, his own face now contorted in rage as he faced his ungrateful son.

"You will remember your place young man! Your behavior is unacceptable and will not be tolerated!"

Will responded quickly. "Pastor Bourdillon told me about your...", here he hesitated briefly but then continued, "your new found faith, and your contempt for the established church. That's why you won't let me go to England to study...Isn't it?"

There was a stunned silence in the room, broken only by the cries of baby Joseph and the whimpers of three-year-old Tom. Will sat down, apparently surprised by his own outburst. The scene had shocked the sensibilities of the adults. They all loved Will, and had done everything in their power to provide him with the best education they could afford. Now, suddenly, it appeared that the influence of Pastor Bourdillon had been of greater impact on their son than their love.

Finally, William walked to face his son and cleared his throat before speaking.

"You have broken the hearts of those who have always loved you and cared for you. We are dismayed by your boorish disrespect toward your family. It reveals an ungrateful nature of which we were unaware. I suggest that you retire to your room to contemplate the harm you have done here today. And remain there until such time as you are summoned."

Will, paused a moment, appeared to be about to speak again, but changed his mind, turned and walked out of the room.

Mary Ann, her eyes filled with tears, moved to sit beside Sarah who was sobbing softly. In fact, all of the occupants of the room, adults and children alike, found themselves tearful, miserable and confused.

Bess, who as usual, had been standing just outside the door listening, returned to the kitchen and began filling a tray with cups, a flagon of rum and a container of hot cider. Shaking her head she walked quietly back to the room, knocked, waited for permission to enter, placed the tray on a table, walked to Sarah and offered her hands to take little Joseph from her arms. Sarah nodded in appreciation and handed the child to Bess. She nodded to Tom to take Bess's hand as she took the children upstairs.

Finally, Sarah looked at William and in a soft voice, asked, "How could we have been so blind that we did not realize the impact of that man on the soul of our child?

George Whitehead was right when he said that the clergy had God in their head but not in their heart. He has turned our son against us."

Mary Ann arose from her chair and began pouring a serving of rum for each of the men and hot cider for herself and for Sarah. They sat staring into the blazing fire, each lost in their own thoughts and regrets. Each wondered in their own way, how they would ever survive this awful and unexpected rift in their family.

Sometime later, Bess returned to ask what time she should prepare the evening meal. As one, they shook their heads and indicated that no one had an appetite. They retired to their rooms early that night as the thunder-snowstorm continued throughout the night.

As they prepared for bed that night, each, in their own way, prayed that the morning would bring relief from the raging storm and a solution to their dilemma.

It was a restless, sleepless night at Mt. Hayes, but by morning, the snowstorm that had deposited over a foot of snow, had finally stopped although the sky was still dark and menacing. The day didn't hold a lot of promise.

The household arose at the usual time the next morning, but everyone seemed to move very slowly. They feared that they were no better equipped to deal with Will's unexpected rudeness and surprising outburst than they had been the evening before.

Sarah had forgotten about the powerful storm the day before and was surprised when she looked out the window to see nearly a foot of snow. She stood transfixed at the window, unwilling to contemplate the significance of what she saw. William glanced toward her and was concerned when he saw the look of horror on her face. He rushed to her side. He had seen that look before and was terrified of what it might mean.

"What's wrong, my dear. It's just a big snow. Nothing we haven't seen before. Besides, we have no reason to venture out into it today. We can just enjoy its beauty."

He was looking at Sarah's face and had done no more than glance out the window. Sarah pointed to the snow covered ground outside their window. There, clear as day, were footprints leading from the front door, down the steps and towards the woods. She looked crestfallen and appeared faint.

"He's gone." she whispered as she pointed to the disturbed blanket of snow. "I fear we will never see our son again"

William was as concerned as Sarah, but dared not show it.

"Well, we're certainly going to have another talk with that young man. I'll send Henry out immediately to bring him back home."

The fear in Sarah's eyes prompted him to reassure her that he and Thomas would undertake the search as well.

"Trust me, my darling. We will have him back safe and sound in the house in no time at all."

He hoped his tone of voice sounded more optimistic than his true feelings. There was no way of knowing just how long the boy had been gone. As for his destination, he felt certain that he had gone to seek refuge at the clergy house. Having Thomas and Henry gave him a small degree of comfort. This would not be a pleasant meeting.

In less than thirty minutes the men saddled their horses and began their search for Will. Although warm enough to start to melt the snow, the sky was still overcast and menacing. All three men shared the opinion that Will was on his way to seek comfort from his tutor. It would be a difficult confrontation for none of them liked the idea of confronting Bourdillon.

Although the snow was melting at a fairly good rate, the footprints were still visible enough to follow. As expected, they led to the door of the clergy house. They dismounted, instructed Henry to watch the horses and walked to the front door of the house. Before they could knock, Johanna opened the door and motioned to them to enter. She took their coats and asked that they be seated. She hurried to express her concerns regarding Will's unexpected arrival there in the middle of the night.

"I can't imagine how worried Mistress Sarah must be, and you gentlemen as well. I am so sorry that the boy has given you such worry. He is in the kitchen eating. I will fetch him immediately."

She turned and hastily walked toward the kitchen door. Before reaching it, Bourdillon walked into the room from his library and took hold of his wife's arm and admonished her to leave the boy alone.

"I will handle this," he announced in a firm commanding voice.

Johanna opened her mouth to speak, but thought better of it and sat down in the nearest chair.

Bourdillon, clearly disapproving of his wife's demeanor, pointed to the kitchen and reminded her that there were children who needed her attention.

Johanna arose from her seat, hesitated briefly as though about to speak, but sighed and went into the kitchen.

It quickly became clear to William and Thomas, that Bourdillon intended to take charge of the meeting. He remained standing, towering over the two men and began by chiding them for their poor treatment of Will.

"Your son, is one of the brightest pupils I have had the good fortune to tutor. He has come to expect the opportunities that parents of extreme wealth can and should provide for their sons, particularly their first-born son. I can't imagine how heart breaking it must have been for him to learn that this wonderful opportunity, which had been offered to him and which he had embraced with his whole heart, had been suddenly denied him for the most of egregious of reasons."

He seemed to become more animated as he clasped his hands behind his back and began to stride slowly back and forth across the room as he continued.

"Although God may have blessed you planters with extensive property and unimaginable wealth, you are too greedy to see to the welfare of your children. Meanwhile, a poor servant of the Lord, like myself, must struggle to support my own family while attempting to save the souls of arrogant, selfish men like you who abandon their children in their time of greatest need. "

There was venom in the man's voice and whatever Christian charity might have once dwelt in his heart had long since been replaced by distrust and resentment of his parishioners.

William and Thomas were stunned by the man's lecture and amazed at his audacity. They stared at each other in disbelief. The man was clearly overstepping his authority where parental rights were concerned.

William stood, faced the man squarely and forcing himself to use a civil tone, announced his intent to bring Will home to Mt. Hayes where he belonged. With that, he stepped around the clergyman and started toward to door to the kitchen. He had taken only two steps when he felt Bourdillon's hand grab his arm in a powerful grip.

"The boy has begged me to permit him to stay with me. He does not wish to return to the unpleasant atmosphere that abounds at the plantation. He fears for his safety and it is my duty to offer him sanctuary here where he is embraced in Christian love."

At that moment, the kitchen door opened and Johanna pulled young Will after her. Her face and demeanor were stern and she seemed determined to complete her task. She nearly dragged Will to his father and handed him over to him.

"You belong with your family. It is not the place of any man, clergy or not, to interfere between a father and a son. I cannot allow this Benedict. You have exceeded your authority."

Johanna finished her speech, turned on her heel and retreated to the kitchen. By the time she reached a chair, she felt weak and faint. She had never before talked to her husband that way. She hoped she hadn't gone too far.

Bourdillon was temporarily speechless after his wife's outburst but he soon regained his composure and, chin held high, delivered what would be the final blow to the two men.

"After talking with Will last night and hearing the circumstances of his situation, I have agreed to his request to be apprenticed to me. As you know, it is customary for a boy of twelve to begin necessary instruction either in an advanced school such as those in England, or failing that, to learn a trade, or skill, if you prefer. The purpose of course is to provide him the opportunity to be self-sufficient in adulthood. Granted, as a clergyman, in the Anglican church, he quickly added, he will never enjoy the great wealth of his heartless parents and grandparents, but he can learn to do God's work. We signed the necessary documents just before you arrived."

William and Thomas sat down as though struck by some invisible force. It appeared that Bourdillon, for the moment, as least, held the upper hand.

Thomas arose and made a request. "I'd like to personally hear from my grandson that this is the course he has chosen."

Will hesitatingly walked toward his father and grandfather, but did not say a word.

"Is it true that you have signed a paper of apprenticeship with the clergy?" Thomas asked.

Will nodded his head, but did not look his grandfather directly in the eye. "Yes sir," was his soft reply.

His grandfather shook the boy's hand, bowed slightly. "You must know Will, that your family's love for you is constant. If at any time you need us, you must come to us. Do you understand?"

Will nodded, but before he could speak, Bourdillon interrupted. "Do you understand, Sir, that once a contract of apprenticeship is signed and recorded, any breach of that contract carries severe penalties."

William stepped forward and asked, "Is this what you really want Will? If it is not, you must speak now before the document is recorded with the court."

"Yes, father. It is the only opportunity available to me. I will not be a planter."

William gave his son a hug, despite the fact that Will did his best to push him away.

The two men left with a heavy heart and both worried about the reaction they would surely receive from the boy's mother and grandmother.

Immediately after the departure of the men, Mary Ann joined Sarah in her bedchamber and neither woman budged or spoke a word as they stood their silent vigil awaiting the return of the men.

Bess, along with the rest of the household servants, clustered around other windows at the front of the house. No one spoke, but the silence only intensified their growing concern.

When they first heard the sound of approaching horses, there was a mad rush to the front door. Bess flung open the door and everyone rushed down the steps to embrace the wayward child. While the anxiety of their wait had been intense, the arrival of the three men without Will, was nearly too much to endure.

There was a loud chorus of questions from the distraught household.

"Had they found Will?"

"Was he injured?"

"Was he safe?"

"Where was he?"

Finally, William held up his hand to silence the many questions. He wanted to speak with Sarah alone but realized that everyone shared their concern. He thought it prudent to give everyone an answer to relieve their fears.

He walked to Sarah, whose face was ashen and the fear in her eyes was awful to see. He put his arm around her and immediately assured her and the others that Will was unharmed and was at the house of the clergy. He paused for a moment before adding that Will would be continuing his lessons with his tutor.

With that, he smiled at the assembled group, suggested that everyone return to their chores and ushered his wife up the stairs and to their room where he could explain the most troubling aspects of the circumstances. He suggested that Thomas and Mary Ann join them. After all, he thought, it's best to explain the situation once and for all and then decide how best to deal with it. Although, in his heart, he feared there was nothing that could be done. And, he reasoned, if that were to be the case, they must accept it. After all, they had two young sons at home. They must not neglect them. They must now make plans to insure that they never have to endure such an emotional trauma in the future.

CHAPTER 19

"The heart will break, but broken live on."

Lord Byron

*A*fter sharing the news of Will's decision with the family, William sat down beside Sarah. He put his arm around her and held her hand. Of course the news had been a shock, but all in all it was better than he had feared. Their son was safe and would continue his education under the tutelage of Benjamin Bourdillon. And, despite the brashness of the pastor, he appeared to sincerely care for their son.

"My dear, we must take heart. Will is still close by. We can see him often, and after all, he is only a boy. Surely, in time, he will realize that his family loves him. He most likely will have a change of heart and return to us."

Sarah shook her head and murmured, "I hope so."

But in her heart she feared that they had lost their son forever, for once the contract for apprenticeship was recorded in the court, Will would be bound to the clergy until he reached the age of twenty-one.

Thomas had seemed to be lost in deep thought during William's explanation. His furrowed brow betrayed the depth of his concern as he finally spoke.

"I think we may have jumped to an unfounded conclusion," he began. "I do not think Bourdillon fully understands the legal restrictions that are binding here."

Both Sarah and Mary Ann were immediately alert and hopeful as they waited for Thomas to explain.

"I believe that in cases such as this, especially when the apprenticeship deals with training for a profession, such as law, medicine, or as in this case, the clergy, rather than a craft skill, the requirements are different."

Everyone was immediately attentive and hopeful.

"Please explain," Sarah begged of her father.

"I will need to consult advice from the court on this matter, but I believe that consent of the parent is of more importance than consent of the child."

Sarah was the first to speak. "Then we must make the necessary inquiries and negate this contract immediately!"

William nodded in agreement, but was quick to caution that they must handle the matter with great care.

"After all, my dear, we must consider the impact of our decisions upon our son. It is my hope that once he has time to consider the obligation he would be under for such a long time, that he might be willing, perhaps eager to change his mind."

Sarah hugged her husband, smiled, nodded her head in agreement and was relieved by the sudden renewal of hope.

Thomas immediately arose from his seat, and assured Sarah and Mary Ann that they would deal with the matter immediately.

"William, I think it best if we leave immediately if we are to make it to the Prerogative Court of Baltimore County before they leave for the day," Thomas suggested.

The two men immediately hurried to get their coats and sent Henry to saddle two horses. It would be a cold trip for although the weather had cleared somewhat, it was still bitterly cold.

The two women joined their husbands at the front door with high hopes that this family crisis would soon be resolved. As they men walked down the steps, Thomas turned to caution them that they might have to spend the night in Baltimore City.

"Don't be alarmed if we don't return tonight. It gets dark so early and I feel it would be dangerous to travel in the dark."

Sarah and Mary Ann quickly nodded in agreement and waved to the men as they rode away on their mission.

As it turned out, their husbands did not return and the women spent a long, worrisome night awaiting their return.

Their meeting with the Clerk of the Prerogative Court resolved one problem only to create a new one. Fortunately the contract had not yet been brought to the court, and thus nothing was as of yet, binding. Furthermore, Thomas had been correct in his belief that Will must have the consent of his parents in order to enter into an agreement such as the one proposed by Bourdillon.

The clerk explained in detail that agreements such as this were open to negotiation on a couple of important issues. The two most important included the length of time of the obligation. The second was responsibility for the support of the child. An apprentice to a skilled craftsman would work in exchange for training as well as food, lodging and care. In the case of the professions, most often the parents would have to pay for the child's care.

Although their meeting had concluded rather briefly, the two men decided to spend the night in Baltimore City rather than hurry back home. There was much to be discussed and some very hard decisions to be made.

On the one hand, they could hold firm in their objection to the clergyman's plan and refuse to sign the document. They could force their son to abide by their plans for him. Both William and Thomas were fearful that such a tactic might lead the boy to run away from home again to somewhere beyond their reach.

The second option would be to grant their approval, but negotiate the terms and length of the apprenticeship. But their fear was that Bourdillon's unfounded opinion that they were among the wealthiest of his parishioners would make negotiations with him difficult if not impossible. There was much to consider.

They had taken a room at a small inn located next to the court. They stayed up late into the night trying to come to grips with how best to deal with the situation. Over breakfast the next morning they agreed that it would be most prudent to allow Will to choose the course his life would take. They would do their best to negotiate for a short term of apprenticeship and hope that the clergyman would provide at least a portion of the child's support. But most important of all, they must exert every effort to keep the bond of family strong.

Once they had reached a decision, they paid the innkeeper for their meal, put on their coats and walked out the door to their horses. Once out of town, they rode their horses at a hard gallop. They were preparing to share their views with their wives. They were not looking forward to that discussion.

Strangely enough, despite the fact that Mary Ann and Sarah had no knowledge of the legalities involved, they too had spent long hours pondering the decision at hand and had ultimately reached the same conclusion. "We must allow Will the freedom to choose for himself."

Words were not necessary when William walked up the stairway to the front door of Mt. Hayes. He looked at Sarah, tears welling up in her eyes as she looked at him and nodded in agreement.

"I know," she whispered. "We must let Will choose. If not, we will surely lose him forever."

Later that day William and Sarah rode together to make the final arrangements with Bourdillon. They had seen Will through the window as they approached the front door, but when Johannah answered, there was no one in the room but her.

Johannah could hardly bear to look at the couple. She extended her hand to Sarah and then embraced her while whispering softly the words "I'm so sorry" over and over.

Sarah smiled and conveyed her gratitude to the woman who had been so kind to her son.

The following week, William and Thomas reached an understanding with Bourdillon regarding the funds he would need to continue with Will's education. It was a sizeable amount, but in return Bourdillon agreed to bind the boy only until his eighteenth birthday, which would occur on December 18, 1754.

Once the contract was signed, both parents felt a sense of relief. Will seemed happy and hugged his mother, and in a very grownup way, shook hands with his father and thanked them both.

When they left, all parties were respectful of each other. Sarah and William were determined to treat Bourdillon in a cordial manner and vowed to forgive the clergyman's earlier rude and insulting behavior. It was time to move on with their lives.

Nonetheless, every Sunday for the next six years Sarah and William, health and weather permitting, attended services at St. Paul's Parish. It was the only way they could see their son. Eventually they gave up hope that Will would wish to visit them.

During the first year and one half, Will seemed devoted to his studies and to his duties assisting his master, but gradually over time, his demeanor changed. Sarah was heartbroken that he appeared to be so unhappy. And neither of them could understand why he was so sullen and disrespectful when they spoke with him. It was apparent that he blamed them for his unhappiness with the apprenticeship. But there was nothing to be done at this stage. He was bound by law to serve out the terms of the agreement.

Although life at Mt. Hayes was different without the presence of their oldest child, it was not unpleasant. Both William and Sarah along with Thomas and Mary Ann, were still committed to a more personal relationship with God and attended meetings by the several evangelical speakers who were drawing large crowds and converts to their meetings. It gave them a sense of peace, which helped to sustain them through difficult times.

Their immediate concern was how best to provide for the education of their two young sons, Thomas and Joseph. But the idea of bringing another stranger into their homes as a tutor was not appealing. Fortunately, providence would offer an unexpected solution.

Sarah's older sister, Rachel, always accompanied them to every revival. And it was now the accepted conclusion by everyone, including Rachel, that it was to be her lot in life to remain a spinster. She was in her mid-forties with no foreseeable possibility of having children of her own, but she doted on her two young nephews. It was she who suggested that she would love to help with the boys' education. She even suggested that she could serve as a governess for the boys and would come to live at Mt. Hayes. She was quick to add that food and lodging would be adequate compensation.

Sarah and Thomas were both surprised by Rachel's unexpected proposal. But it was indeed a godsend. Rachel loved the boys and they loved her and it would be pleasant for Sarah to have the companionship of her sister. It was decided. Rachel and a trunk with her clothing arrived at Mt. Hayes one week later.

The boys, especially Tom, loved the fact that his Aunt Rachel shared a lot of activities that he enjoyed as well. She could ride, hunt, fish and didn't hesitate to put on a pair of men's britches when the activity required it. Aunt Rachel was a lot of fun to be around. Of course that didn't mean that she would tolerate bad behavior from the boys. She could be a rigid disciplinarian when the situation required it and held the boys to a high standard in their studies. The household ran smoothly as Rachel was a big help to Sarah in that regard as well.

Although the pain that Sarah and William experienced over the behavior of their eldest son was ever present, their lives moved along smoothly. The boys made steady improvement in their studies under Rachel's supervision. A sense of normalcy had returned to Mt. Hayes.

Sarah was always amazed by the very different personalities of each of her three sons. Will was studious but outgoing and rather slight in build. Tom, on the other hand, was quite tall for his age and although clearly intelligent, preferred outdoor activities and was eager for any new adventure. Joseph, the youngest, although slightly taller than his oldest brother Will, was not as athletic as Tom. He was rather timid and felt uneasy around large groups of people. In the beginning their one common trait was that they expressed love and respect for their parents. Sadly, over time love and respect from Will, began to diminish. Sarah prayed that once Will was freed of his apprenticeship and no longer under the powerful influence of the clergyman he would embrace his family once again.

Wednesday, December 18, 1754, was the eighteenth birthday of William (Will) Johnson, Jr. On that day the conditions of his contract of apprenticeship to Benedict Bourdillon of St. Paul's Parish, were met and he was free to pursue his own interests.

Sarah had planned a large party to commemorate the event and had sent Henry two weeks before to invite friends and family to help celebrate. The preceding Sunday, after the service, Sarah had reminded Will that they were looking forward to honoring him at the party. His response was a brief nod of his head, followed by a brief reply.

"Of course, you can count on me."

Sarah had been disappointed in his lack of enthusiasm, but attributed it to the pressure he might be feeling as he now faced new obligations on his own.

The days before Christmas were always filled with many preparations. Holly, berries, boughs of fir and mistletoe needed to be collected and arranged. Bess and the rest of the household were busily preparing a large bounty of special foods. William had hired musicians for the day and the arrangement of the two large parlors was adjusted to accommodate dancing, chairs for those who preferred to watch and the hall where they would enjoy the banquet It was a busy, but very happy time.

Thomas and Mary Ann arrived two days early to help with the preparations. Rachel found it difficult to keep the boys' attention on their studies, and finally decided that they should have a few days to enjoy the celebration as well.

The day of the party was the most perfect day Sarah could have imagined. The day was bright and sunny, a bit crisp, but no snow, ice or rain to present difficulty for travel.

The party was planned for early evening, but guests began to arrive around three o'clock in the afternoon and Bess made sure that there was plenty of food and her famous Maryland Toddy to keep them occupied and happy.

Sarah was always a gracious hostess, but she seemed to be constantly standing at one of the front widows peering into the distance in anticipation of Will's arrival.

By seven o'clock that evening, all of the invited guests had arrived. All that is, but the guest of honor. Sarah was beside herself with worry.

"Oh Rachel, what do you think could be wrong? He promised he would be here. Could there have been an accident? I'm afraid he might be ill. Should we send Henry to look for him?"

William was standing nearby and was concerned about his son, as well. But now, his concern was focused on his wife. She had held such anticipation for this day. They had both hoped that today would be the day of their long awaited reconciliation with Will.

~ 325 ~

William approached Sarah, put his arm around her waist, kissed her on the cheek and jokingly commented that he hoped no one would mind since he couldn't find any mistletoe at the moment. But his attempt at humor fell on deaf ears, for Sarah was near tears.

"I'll send Henry along to look for Will. I'm sure there must be a good reason why he is detained."

His words expressed a confidence that he did not feel while his anger was difficult to contain.

"I think we should go ahead and invite our guests to dine without further delay. Otherwise, some may be so full of Bess's punch that they won't be awake to enjoy it. I'll go tell Bess that we will eat immediately."

With that, he smiled at Sarah, gave a warm embrace and turned and walked through the hall toward the kitchen.

Bess, as usual, with her keen ears and instinct, was already giving orders to everyone to hurry up and get the food on the tables for their guests.

William gave Henry instructions, but warned him, that in all likelihood, Will's tardiness, or worse yet, absence was planned.

Shortly after that, the guests were all seated, the blessing had been given, and large quantities of steaming hot food were ladled onto the plates.

The guests themselves had no reason to doubt William's brief explanation regarding his son's failure to arrive on time. For their part, the guests had no way of knowing what kind of conflict there might have been between parents and child.

But of course, Rachel, Thomas and Mary Ann shared the same worry and fears as Sarah.

William had instructed the musicians to play softly while the guests enjoyed their banquet and for all intents and purposes, it was a grand and perfect gala event.

In the very midst of their meal, an unkempt, intoxicated young man flung open the front doors and staggered across the room to address the assembled guests. He held in his left hand a crumpled stack of papers, which he tossed on the floor and in his right hand a large flagon from which he took a large gulp before speaking.

The musicians immediately stopped playing and the startled guests turned toward the disturbance.

It was Will. He could barely stand and his speech was slurred as he attempted to address his startled audience.

Sarah sat as though frozen in her chair. Her face ashen and fear in her eyes. Both William and Thomas immediately arose from their chairs and made their way toward Will.

"Son", William began, "let's get you something to eat and cleaned up a bit. It appears you have started celebrating without us." He forced an embarrassed laugh.

"Don't you call me son! You have ruined my life, and for that I will never forgive you!"

William was temporarily taken aback by his son's condemnation. But Thomas, moved quickly to his grandson, seized the flagon from his hand and forcibly pushed him back out the front door, closing the door behind him.

"You are an ungrateful, spiteful man who has broken your parents and grandparents hearts for the last time. I have already given you a large gift of land and that I shall not attempt to take back. But know now, that is the last gift or bequest that you shall ever have from me or from the family. You have been the engineer of your own fate and now you must deal with that...on your own!"

With that, Thomas turned back toward the room and closed the door upon the grandson whom he had loved so dearly, but had now disinherited.

When he reentered the large room where the guests were dining, he took a deep breath, tried to calm himself, and finally forced a smile.

"My apologies to you all for that unfortunate spectacle to which my grandson has subjected you. I'm sure he will be quite embarrassed once he is sober. Now please, the food is getting cold."

Thomas returned to his seat by Mary Ann, grasped her hand, smiled at her, and whispered, "let's just try to get through the evening."

William had returned to his seat as well and quietly attempted to help Sarah to regain her composure.

"I share your pain, my dear, but we must think about our guests."

Even though most of the guests had little or no realization of the magnitude of the guest of honor's actions, the former gaiety of the evening was replaced by an uncomfortable lull in the conversation.

The party ended early.

Once all of the guests had departed, the entire household retired to their rooms for a restless, sleepless night. At breakfast the next morning it felt as though an enormous cloud of despair had descended upon them all.

Tom and Joseph had witnessed the unsettling performance of their older brother. They were both confused and angry. They worshipped Will. In many ways, he had been their idol, but now they could not understand why he had behaved in such an awful manner, but neither dared to ask questions.

The silence was finally broken when Tom, cleared his throat to attract their attention, and offered to say grace. The sound of his voice was like a tolling bell calling them back to the present.

When he had finished, he looked at his parents and grandparents and they were all surprised by the maturity of their twelve-year-old boy.

"I promise to you all, that I shall always love and respect you, and will try my best to make you proud of me."

Nine-year-old Joseph nodded his head vigorously and added in his very soft voice, "Me too."

Both Sarah and William realized that their eldest son had chosen to sever all ties with his family and there was nothing they could do about it. They prayed for him and wished only the best for his future, but that future was beyond their control.

It seemed that there was no end to the disappointments rained upon them by Will's actions. Exactly four weeks after his drunken rant at the party, Pastor Bourdillon gave the first reading of the marriage banns for Will Johnson and Eleanor Jacobs. There was at first a shocked silence followed by a buzz of whispered comments among the parishioners.

No one in the family had any idea that Will had planned to marry or even that he had an interest in any young woman. It was more than a shock to Sarah and William: it was yet another very public denunciation of his family.

On each of the following two Sundays, the banns were read once again and the wedding was held the following Wednesday, January 22, 1755, at the bride's home in neighboring All Hallow's Parish, Anne Arundel County. No messenger carrying an invitation to the wedding came to Mt. Hayes or to Harris' Delight. Each new and unexpected blow ripped open the still bleeding wound of Will's rejection of his family. It weighed heavily on their hearts.

During these trying times, Rachel was a source of great comfort and support. She, perhaps more than anyone else in the family, understood the futility of trying to change things over which you have no influence. She had learned to embrace the life she had rather than bemoan what could never be.

One morning in early March as Rachel was just collecting her books for the boys' morning lessons, she passed by Sarah's bedchamber and saw her sister sitting on the edge of the bed. There were no tears, but Sarah's head was bowed, her shoulders heavy with the weight of her depression. Rachel was pained to see her sister suffer so. She entered the room and moved to the bed and sat down.

"We can pray together that God give us the strength to accept those things over which we have no control,and to be thankful for the many blessings that are bestowed on us. We must take joy in those things. We owe that to ourselves and to those we love and who love us."

Sarah sighed deeply, and nodded her head slowly.

"I know you are right, Rachel, but I miss him so much."

"Of course you do. So do we all. But Will is an adult now. His behavior at the party was…well, I don't know what it was. But it happened, he is gone, and you must focus your attention on the family that is here. You have two wonderful sons with you now. They both love you very much. They need to know how much you love them as well."

With that, Rachel stood up, straightened her skirt, picked up her books and walked toward the door. She stopped there, turned around, cocked her head to one side, hands on hips, and extended her hand toward Sarah.

"Aren't you coming?" she asked. "There's a lot of life left to be lived. Let's go live it!"

She smiled at her sister and waited for her to join her at the door.

Sarah laughed softly and stood up.

"How did you get to be so smart?" she asked laughing.

"I grew into it," Rachel replied.

Change is hard, but inevitable, and slowly but surely life at Mt. Hayes settled into a comfortable and productive routine. But within the period of just two years, their comfortable existence was broken by the announcement of St. Paul's Parish on August 27, 1756, that the baptism of Absalom Johnson, son of Will and Elenor Johnson would be held the following Sunday. This was the only notification received by William and Sarah that they were grandparents. On the day of the baptism, neither the grandparents nor great grandparents were asked to participate in the ceremony. After the service, William and Elenor took great pains to ignore the family. This was yet another crushing heartbreak delivered in a humiliating and very public setting. It was an experience that would be repeated on five more occasions in the next several years with the birth and baptism of each of Will's six children.

As on earlier occasions, it was Mary Ann and Rachel who counseled Sarah and reminded her to focus on the blessings in her life, rather than on the disappointments over which she had no control. Foremost among her concerns was that Tom and Joseph should not suffer because of their elder brother's behavior. It eventually became clear that their prayers for reconciliation between them and their eldest son would not happen.

As for Tom and Joseph, they were fortunate that they understood that their parents loved Will, despite his vile treatment of them. They also knew how much they were loved as well, but they missed their older brother.

CHAPTER 20

"Whoever loved that loved not at first sight?"

Christopher Marlowe

Tom was quite different from his older brother Will. Will had always been studious and preferred spending spare time in reading or almost any indoor activity. He had the demeanor and interests of a scholar, his younger brother Tom, however, preferred to be outdoors.

Tom was several inches taller than his older brother and had a muscular build. He was an excellent rider and could handle any horse with ease. He was also a skilled marksman as well. He, like his father and grandfather, welcomed every opportunity to join their neighbors for a foxhunt. It was not unusual for him to spend most of his free time hunting, fishing and exploring the extensive land holdings around him.

On one of his rides through the countryside he set out with the intention of visiting his older brother. He felt a bit apprehensive about the kind of reception he might receive from Will. Happily, his fears were unwarranted, for as he passed out of a small grove of trees along the banks of Herring Creek he came face to face with his brother Will. Will, like Tom, was on horseback and the two faced each other for several moments of contemplation. Neither seemed willing, or perhaps able to make the first move. It was Tom who finally broke the silence. He smiled broadly at his brother, jumped down from his horse and approached Will with his hand extended.

"I've missed you my brother," he began.

It was just the right move and the right gesture. Will got off his horse and walked toward Tom. He grabbed the extended hand, and simultaneously, they embraced each other. Both were fighting back tears, and the intensity of their emotion was clear.

"I have missed you as well, Tom. I have seen you, but at a distance, at services at St. Paul's, but I didn't realize how much you have grown. I'm certain that I could no longer better you in a physical endeavor. Nor would I care to try," he quickly added.

The two walked to the shade of a nearby tree and sat down together. There was much to talk about, but also a great deal of things that both were reluctant to discuss. Neither dared to address the schism that loomed between Will and his family. For the moment, it was sufficient to simply enjoy their reunion.

Over the course of the next few months they would meet on a regular, pre-arranged basis. Their conversations eventually turned to Will's wife and child, a subject that Will was eager to discuss. But there were still topics that aroused uncomfortable antagonism between the brothers. Foremost among these, was Will's feelings towards his parents and grandparents. It was apparent that no amount of encouragement from Tom, would change Will's rejection of the rest of the family.

Eventually, Tom resigned himself to the knowledge that Will felt justified in his actions, and no amount of cajoling was likely to bring about change in his attitude or his behavior.

It was a sad state of affairs, and one over which young Tom had no control. His visits with his brother gradually occurred with less frequency, and finally stopped altogether. Although greatly saddened by this state of affairs, Tom did not dwell upon those things he couldn't change and found plenty of other activities to occupy his time.

One of his favorite pastimes involved the many animals on the plantation. He seemed to have a way with them and from a very young age had enjoyed helping to take care of the chickens, hogs and horses. There were also many dogs, which were always around, and he could be counted on to find some scraps for them from the kitchen.

On one October morning, Bess called to him to come to the cook house where one of the dogs had just given birth to a litter of puppies in an empty box just behind the door. Tom made it a point to see to it that the pups were not removed from their little sanctuary and that the mother had ample food. He checked on them daily and became attached to the largest of the litter whose coat was a combination of black, white and brown. He enjoyed holding and petting his favorite and before long, the young dog began following Tom wherever he went, including his trips on horseback. They became quite inseparable.

On this particular day in 1757, the family including grandparents, parents and fifteen-year-old Tom left Mt. Hayes early in the morning to attend a much promoted revival in Anne Arundel County to hear the renowned speaker, Jonathan Edwards. Tom enjoyed the opportunity to travel anytime and anywhere, and since this was to be an outdoor sermon attended by hundreds if not thousands of people, he was eager to go. As they climbed into the carriage, Tom asked if he might ride on top with Henry. Sarah and William were both quite aware that the motivating factor was to allow Tom's faithful dog to ride along with him. It was a pleasant journey.

There was a large crowd assembled in the open field to hear the evangelist and people congregated chatting in small groups awaiting the arrival of the anticipated speaker. At the first appearance of Jonathan Edwards the crowd erupted into loud cheers as he made his way through the throng of well wishes who reached out to touch the famous orator. A small platform and podium had been erected and the crowd pushed forward to surround him as he climbed the three steps to the platform.

He began with a prayer that instantly quieted the assemblage as the hushed silence lingered well after the prayer had ended and they waited for him to begin his sermon. The clouds had been ominous all day, but the chance of an impending storm had done little to hinder the efforts of the thousands who wanted to see him and to hear his words.

As was his custom, he took a sheaf of folded papers from the pocket of his coat and carefully opened and spread them on the podium before him. Edwards sermons, unlike the extemporaneous ones they had heard given by George Whitehead, were written and rehearsed beforehand and provided a ready reference if his memory failed him. He had barely begun his sermon when a loud roll of thunder and a sharp bolt of lightning announced the beginning of a heavy rain. Edwards did his best to ignore the pounding rain and ever increasing lightning, but it soon became apparent that this was no small shower. People scattered in all directions trying to reach their horses and carriages.

Due to the enormous size of the crowd, most families had to leave their carriages some distance from the field and were completely drenched when they finally reached their conveyances. The roads, such as they were, were quite muddy and as more and more travelers began to move out of the area huge furrows were left in the mud making it difficult for the carriages to maneuver. When they finally reached their carriage, Henry helped them into their seats and took the reins and flicked them over the horses' backs. It was difficult to move among so many vehicles and so many deep, muddy ruts but Henry did his best. They were shocked when their carriage suddenly shook violently as the horses reared and pulled at their reins until Henry finally regained control.

"What's wrong Henry?" William called out through the window.

"It's the carriage in front of us", Henry replied. "They're stuck in a deep ditch in the mud and it looks like the back wheel of their carriage has broken."

Despite the pouring rain, both Thomas and William jumped down to offer help. There were two men, one well dressed, the other obviously a servant, struggling to move the carriage enough to deal with the broken wheel. Tom soon jumped down to help his father and grandfather. In no time at all, the men were covered in mud from their boots, to their britches and sleeves of their coats. After several unsuccessful tries to release the broken wheel from the mire, William shook his head in defeat as the unrelenting rain continued. It was raining so hard that it was difficult to hear each other. Thomas touched the stranger on the shoulder and pointed to their carriage and motioned the man to follow him.

The man nodded in understanding but pointed to the window of his stranded carriage. A young girl was staring wide-eyed from within. The man mouthed the words, "my daughter". Thomas nodded in understanding, looked down at his muddy clothing and walked back to his carriage and asked Mary Ann to hand him one of the blankets they had brought with them. Mary Ann did as she was asked and

Thomas quickly returned to the disabled carriage and handed the blanket through the window to the girl. She wrapped the blanket around herself and waited for instructions. She looked frightened and unsure, but when Thomas opened the door and told her that he would carry her to the other carriage, she stepped out into his arms. He moved as quickly as he could manage through the treacherous mud and helped the girl into the carriage. Mary Ann and Sarah did their best to reassure her that everything would be fine, but suggested that the best use for her blanket might be to protect the seat for the men.. She readily agreed and they spread the blanket on the opposite seat.

William, Thomas, and the stranger crowded into the carriage. Young Tom and his faithful companion dog, climbed up on the seat beside Henry and they began to extricate themselves from the mire and resumed their trip home.

Once they seemed safely out of the quagmire, the stranger introduced himself. He was Mordecai Hall of Deers Race Plantation here in Anne Arundel County and the girl was his daughter. As soon as everyone realized that the stranger would naturally wish to get to his own home, William called out to Henry to stop for a moment to determine the best route to the Hall plantation. As luck would have it they were but a few miles from the Hall residence and directions were called out to Henry who adjusted his course toward their new destination.

The rest of their brief ride was carried out in silence with the pounding storm providing evidence that the worst was far from over. When they neared the point where a path veered from the more traveled road,

Mordecai Hall called out to Henry the direction of the home.

The day, so far, had been anything but expected. They had not heard the great Jonathan Edwards speak, other than the prayer. They were all soaked to the bone. The ladies gowns had been somewhat protected by their long cloaks, but the men were a wretched looking bunch. When the carriage finally stopped in front of the door to Deer's Race Manor, they looked at each other with a sense of relief and finally of amusement. They were indeed a sorry looking lot.

Mordecai and the other men stepped down from the carriage and a servant came running down the stairs with a step stool to assist the women in getting out of the coach. The rain had let up a little, but they all hurried up the stairs and were ushered into a parlor where a servant was busy laying a fire in the fireplace. Wet cloaks were handed over to waiting servants and the women sat down close to the fire. The men were so covered in mud that they stood forlornly, in the middle of the floor.

"Come with me gentlemen, I'm sure we can find some suitable clothes." Mordecai directed.

With that he motioned toward the door and led the men and young Tom toward the back of the house. Following close behind was his fourteen-year-old daughter. Mordecai instructed the men to have a seat on one of the wooden benches that lined the walls of a small storage room by the kitchen parlor. He gave instructions to have a large tub brought to the room and to fill it with hot water for the men.

With a stern look, he told his daughter to go back and join the women. She immediately stood, but seemed hesitant to leave, but with another stern look and an admonition to go, she left and walked to the front of the house.

Within a few minutes Mordecai returned with an armful of clothes and instructed the men to make use of whatever they wished. He excused himself to go to his own room to avail himself of the same type of facilities there.

Thomas and William agreed to allow young Tom the privilege of bathing first, which he gladly did. He was fortunate that there were clothes that would fit him. When he had finished bathing, he dressed himself in a pair of stockings, a pair of britches, and a fine white shirt. He picked up his pile of muddy clothing and left the room. When he entered the parlor kitchen he was surprised to see the girl from the stranded carriage.

She stood, looked him over from head to toe, nodded approvingly, cleared her throat and acknowledged, "You look quite presentable now."

Tom felt uncomfortable, but gave a slight bow, extended his hand, which was again covered in mud from the soiled clothing he was holding, and introduced himself.

"I'm Thomas Johnson, at your service."

She had extended her hand as well, assuming that he was going to kiss her hand, but was shocked to see the disgustingly muddy hand that he extended, and immediately withdrew hers.

"I'm sorry", he stammered, as he looked at his own dirty hand.

"That's quite alright", she said, as she handed him a dainty handkerchief from her pocket.

"You can just leave the soiled clothing on the bench in the storage room. One of the servants will see that they are washed."

He nodded, turned and opened the door to the storage room just at the moment that his grandfather was standing completely naked preparing to step into the tub of hot water. Tom more or less threw his dirty laundry into the room, mumbling over and over, "I'm sorry, I'm sorry."

Clearly, only the embarrassment of his grandfather and the young lady matched his.

She had turned around and remained standing with her back to Tom until he realized that she was waiting for some sort of signal from him that the worst was over.

"I'm truly sorry, Miss, the door is closed. You can turn around now." Tom stammered.

When she finally turned around she was still blushing, as was Tom. He quickly wiped his dirty hand on the handkerchief, which left it soiled, He folded it and handed it toward her. "Here, thank you."

She looked at him, shook her head in disbelief, rolled her eyes and refused the return of the handkerchief saying, "You keep it."

He looked confused, embarrassed, and carefully put the delicate, lace trimmed soiled cloth in his pocket.

They stood there for a few moments of uncomfortable silence. Finally she spoke.

"You said your name is Thomas?"

"Yes", he acknowledged.

"I think I'll call you Tom," she stated. "Is that alright?"

"Certainly. That's what everybody calls me."

"Well, my name is Welthy."

"Welthy?" Tom repeated. "What kind of name is that?"

"It's my grandmother's name. I'm Welthy Ann Hall. If that's alright with you Mr. Tom." She fumed.

Tom, looked down at the floor for a few moments. This wasn't going well at all.

"It's very nice to meet you Miss Hall. Would it be alright if I call you Ann...no, I mean...may I call you Annie?"

She thought about it for a moment, attempting to look stern and offended, but a smile gradually insinuated itself into her demeanor and suddenly the two were laughing.

Just at that minute Henry came in through the back door with Tom's dog in tow. Henry had done his best to dry the dog, but no amount of human attempts to dry a wet dog work quite as well as when a dog shakes his body vigorously. Which, of course, is what the dog did as soon as he saw Tom.

Tom was happy to see his dog, but immediately worried that he would not be welcome in the house.

Again he found himself apologizing but realized that Annie wasn't listening to him. She was kneeling by the dog, rubbing her hand along his back and the dog seemed to like it.

"Is this your favorite?" She asked.

"Yes, I guess he is?" Tom acknowledged.

"Well, he is a beautiful animal. Is he a good hunting dog?"

Tom was delighted that the young lady seemed to enjoy so many of the same things that he enjoyed.

"He does, but of course he's still young, but I'm sure he'll be a top notch fox hound in no time."

"What do you call him?"

"What do you mean?" Tom asked.

"Is he permitted in your home? Does he sleep at the foot of your bed?"

"Well, yes." Tom admitted.

"Well then the poor animal deserves a name. What do you call him?"

Tom paused again, before finally answering. "I call him Dog," he replied as Annie burst into laughter.

"You're going to have to do better than that, Master Johnson, you must find an appropriate name for your favorite."

"How do I do that?" he asked, perplexed by her instruction.

"Something about him, that is true to his temperament and the kind of dog he is, of course."

At that moment the door to the storage room opened and William and Thomas entered the kitchen. They had been offered clean clothing by their host and felt much better and the unspoken decision to forget the earlier embarrassing open door moment was unanimous.

The group moved down the hall toward the front parlor, with the exception of Dog, who remained in the kitchen with Henry. When they arrived in the parlor, they found Mary Ann and Sarah chatting by the fire with Mordecai and enjoying a cup of hot cider.

The rain had subsided a bit, but the skies were still dark and promised another round of heavy storms. Their host immediately suggested that they spend the night since that was the least he could do to repay their kindness in helping him and his daughter in their hour of need.

Later, they enjoyed a delicious meal prepared by the servants. They had a good night's sleep in warm comfortable beds.

When they awoke the next morning the sky was clear with a few white fluffy clouds and a lot of welcome sunshine. After breakfast and profuse thanks, the families exchanged invitations to visit each other. The idea sounded very appealing to Tom.

On the ride back to Mt. Hayes, Tom and his dog again rode in front with Henry. Tom seemed lost in thought when his daydream was disrupted by the sound of Henry's voice asking him his opinion of the Hall family.

"Well", Tom began, "I thought they were very nice people, yes, very nice indeed."

"I thought you might." Henry replied. "That young lady was very attractive. Don't you think?"

"What?" Tom paused a moment. "Well, yes...I guess you could call her attractive."

"Yes sir, I thought she had real nice brown eyes." Henry continued with a mischievous grin on his face.

"No", Tom said immediately, "her eyes are green, well sometimes they looked blue, but they definitely aren't brown! You must be color blind Henry."

They rode along in silence for a few more miles. Tom still had his arm around his dog's shoulders and he would occasionally stroke the dog's head and neck and in response the dog's tail thumped in resounding appreciation against the seat.

Finally, Tom cocked his head to one side, looked at Henry and revealed the subject of his silent contemplation. "Wag...Yes...I think that's it. I'm going to call him Wag."

Henry looked at him, not comprehending exactly what he was talking about. "Call who Wag?"

"The dog of course. I suppose he should have a name, and I think the name Wag best captures his temperament. What do you think?"

"I think it's an inspired name, Tom. I 'spect Miss Hall will like it too."

With that Henry flicked the reins and smiled that smile that older folks enjoy when a young man is smitten by the charms of a young lady. But the story of Annie and Tom must wait for another time.

Finis

About the Author

Lois J. Lambert, a native of Piketon, Ohio, received her A.B. degree in History from Wilmington College, and her M.A. degree in Anthropology from the University of Cincinnati.

She is a retired teacher and former Coordinator of Education at the Cincinnati Museum of Natural History. After retiring from education, she embarked upon a new career as an author and speaker.

Her first publications included two award winning regimental histories: *91st Ohio Volunteer Infantry*, 2005, and *Heroes of the Western Theater, 33rd Ohio Veteran Volunteer Regiment*, 2008.

Her next efforts were directed toward the role of women during the Civil War and included *Treasured Memories of a Civil War Widow*, 2011, and *Julia and Ulys*, *the Childhood, Courtship and Early Married Life of Julia Dent and Ulysses S. Grant,* 2013.

Legacy's Promise, a departure from her earlier nonfiction works, is her first historical fiction novel and the first book of her *Legacy's Promise Series.* A collection of historical romance inspired by a true story.

Lois is the mother of two children, and the grandmother of four. She and her husband live in Loveland, Ohio, along with, Jubal, the family feline.

Watch for the next book of the Legacy's Promise Series
and check out other great stories at our website:

www.BadgleyPublishingCompany.com